Mercury

ALSO BY AMY JO BURNS

Shiner

Cinderland

Mercury

Amy Jo Burns

CELADON
BOOKS
NEW YORK

MERCURY. Copyright © 2023 by Amy Jo Burns. All rights reserved. Printed in the United States of America. For information, address Celadon Books, a division of Macmillan Publishers, 120 Broadway, New York, NY 10271.

ISBN9781250908568

For my sister and brother

Reader, they've set a place for you at the table.
"You're welcome," the mother says.
—Maurice Kilwein Guevara,
"Late Supper in Northern Appalachia"

Mercury

1.

Waylon Joseph crouched behind Mercury's ballfield bleachers on the south end of town, smoking a cigarette and hiding from his wife.

A day moon hung in the June sky as a crop of boys played a baseball game beneath it. Tiny mitts waved in the air as the ball soared wide. The rest of the park stooped beyond the field—a moldering pond, a slanted gazebo. I-80 beckoned just down the road and past the cedar trees, and yet Way couldn't hear even one truck's sorry bellow as it sped past.

The air around him felt thick, like honey and longing.

Waylon tapped the edge of his Salem with his finger, and ash fluttered to the dirt. *Today,* he told himself. *Today you have to tell her.* He'd said the same thing yesterday. The day before, too. Every day since he'd visited the bank.

Marley appeared between the bleachers' rusted planks—the burnt-orange patina slicing her right through her middle. In her pink coach's ball cap and cutoff jeans, she didn't look a day past eighteen, when Waylon had fallen in love with her. She'd been somebody else's high school sweetheart back then. Now, her auburn hair tangled in the breeze as she hoisted her hand toward the sky, and a field of eight-year-old boys waited for her to speak.

"Look alive," she called toward the outfield.

A crack split the air as the other team's batter hit a pop-up. The center fielder snatched the ball, and the inning ended.

Way leaned his forehead against the bleacher's hot metal. It had taken only two words from Marley's mouth to snap the boys to attention. She had such sway, and she couldn't even see it. In the last eight years, so much of their marriage had become about power—who had it, who gave it away. A slippery, constant leveling of the scales.

Marley cheered and took a nearby toddler from the crowd onto her hip, simple and sunny, as if life were one endless summer afternoon. Even her toes were painted hot pink. Waylon stank in his tar-spattered work clothes and boots. Other fathers, men Waylon went to high school with who had the balls to sit in the stands rather than cower behind them, clapped as Way's son emerged from the dugout. *Good eye, good eye,* they cawed as the ump called two balls in a row, their eyes never leaving the jut of Marley's hip in her shorts, the rise of her legs in the heat.

Vultures, Waylon thought. *Every last one.*

Unaware, Marley popped a fresh stick of spearmint gum into her mouth. She held a hopeful ember in her eye as her son took the batter's box, as if he had every virtue Waylon lacked. And he did, their boy. Theo was freckled and adventurous like Marley, loyal without cause. He swung at bad pitches like his heart had never been broken, rounded the bases as if time would never run out. Just like Waylon had always wanted to be.

The field was still wet from yesterday's rain. Theo tapped a metal bat against his cleats to clear dirt from the spikes, as Waylon used to do when he was young and itching to swing for these same fences. Back then, George Bush Sr. had been president and invaded the Middle East. Now it was 1999, and the president's namesake had just announced his plan to run for office and finish the war his father had started. It was unsettling, how rituals like that passed from father to son.

Theo was now part of a long tradition in the Joseph family of children who had been disappointed by their fathers. Mick Joseph had never attended any of Waylon's baseball games. He was too busy slapping a fresh coat of paint no one wanted on every picket fence in town and belting out the wrong lyrics to "Bad Moon Rising." Now, though, Way wondered whether Mick had been there after all, lurking behind the bleachers like he was. Waylon once vowed Theo's future would be different, with a dad who sang over him and rejoiced.

Funny, how those things never worked out.

A cloud passed over the sun, and a third strike shot past Theo's ready bat and into the catcher's mitt. He ran toward his mother. Marley whispered in his ear, bumped his fist with her own. As Waylon watched them, his heart felt dry and chapped. Theo looked just like Marley when he laughed, even if Way couldn't remember the last time she'd done it.

He drew a hand down the length of his face and imagined the kind of family the two of them made while he was up on the roof. At twenty-six, he and Marley were still young enough to mend what they had torn. As he watched his wife run her palm against Theo's cheek with such tenderness in her fingertips, he almost believed it to be true.

Way, she'd said a long time ago as they lay in bed together on a cold winter night, and he should have listened. *I think you're right to be scared.*

Waylon was about to light a second Salem out of self-pity. Then he heard a stark trilling.

The pay phone behind him shivered through the quiet air, and the entire crowd looked toward it. A curious event: a pay phone ringing, like a snowfall in July. For Waylon, it was an omen. He knew it was his brother Baylor hunting him down, ready to demand he fix whatever their father had done now.

As a war vet and self-appointed mayor of Mercury, Mick Joseph was a living monument in town. Just yesterday, he lurched through the streets in his gray Astro van with a ladder dangling off the top, holding up traffic when he halted to fetch the glasses that had flown off his head and into the road. If it were only that, Waylon wouldn't sweat it. But his father had built so many things in his life that he never bothered to take care of. Houses, marriages, sons. He made people laugh. He also took whatever he wanted. Mick was dapper, and devil-stained, and draining as hell.

Waylon wondered which neighborhood widow he'd horrified this time after penning her the same tired love note and banging on her door at four o'clock in the morning with a sad bouquet of geraniums he'd filched from his own lawn. What bill had he refused to pay—water, or gas? Had he interrupted the Presbyterian preacher again, by standing up in the middle of the sermon to slap his paws against the keys of an upright piano?

Everyone agreed he needed to be caged. No one but his three sons was expected to do it.

Waylon, brutally cursed ever since his mother christened him the "steady" one, knew the task would fall to him. He felt it in the weight of the small golden cross she'd hung around his neck when he was ten and that he hadn't taken off since. Baylor—the tallest and oldest by thirteen months, the watchtower and lookout—had no such trinket from their mother. He knew how to signal trouble but never how to avoid it. And Shay Baby, the youngest at nineteen, was still his daddy's best boy. Much like Theo, Shay held all his father's wishes, and none of his regret.

This left Way to clean up the mess, just the way he had when he was a kid in Mick Joseph's house, and Mick spilled a glass of milk without bothering to sop it up. Waylon hated it now as much as he'd hated it then. Yet Way, safe and sure, still itched to perform his part. He, out of all the brothers, would be the last to give up. The Joseph name still meant something to him, even if he was no longer certain what that something was.

Waylon ignored the pay phone as it jangled on its hook. Someone hit a line drive, the first baseman snagged it for the third out, and Marley's team took the field again. Was it the fourth inning, or the fifth? Way couldn't recall.

Marley turned toward the bleachers, and he ducked his head before she had the chance to spot him. From behind the stands, he could choose her over and over, even though she still thought he'd chosen someone else when it mattered most. Still looked at him with betrayal in her eyes. That was the truth of them: trading hearts and shifting loyalties. Trying to hold on, bare-gripped and barely there.

The pay phone halted its ring, only to begin again.

As a bear might pull himself from winter sleep, so Waylon stood and stretched before sauntering to the pay phone, the scorch of fifty pairs of eyes hot against his back. He picked up the phone mid-ring. For the first time, Baylor's voice on the other end of the line didn't mention their father at all.

Mick Joseph, who hadn't had enough money to attend college so he read through a set of encyclopedias instead, liked to say that a man is proved a fool by what he doesn't know. Yet a crueler outcome, in Waylon's case, was to be proven a fool by what he thought he knew, but didn't.

Way thought his own secrets were the worst in the Joseph family, but he was wrong.

Ten minutes later, Waylon met his older brother where he'd requested—at the entrance to the only Presbyterian church in town. Mercury had other denominations to offer—Methodist, Baptist, Catholic—but this was the only house of worship the Joseph family had devoted themselves to since 1970, when Mick returned from Vietnam. Baylor leaned into the doorframe, his black hair dipping into his eyes, his nails rimmed with tar from the jobsite at the Chinese restaurant two towns over. His skin never burned in the bright sun the way Waylon's did, so he often went shirtless from May to October, musculature on full display, announcing to every woman between twenty-two and forty that he was untarnished and un-attached.

He'd thrown on a T-shirt from his father's business, navy blue with white block letters. JOSEPH & SONS ROOFING was plastered across the front of it. The company's title always unsettled Way because of its un-truth. The "sons" were the ones who showed up for work, and not Mick Joseph as the name promised.

Weak Waylon and *Big Baylor*. That was how Mick referred to his two oldest children when they worked together on a roof. All his life, Waylon had wondered whether it was true.

Baylor never paid those things any attention, just as he didn't mind his boots tracking dirt through the house. He had a crowbar in one hand, a shovel in the other.

"Let's get this over with," Baylor groused as he held the door.

Together they walked into the cool dark of the church stairwell, where the interim pastor sat in his own sweat. He'd been stuck in Mercury since the last pastor had an affair and skipped town four years earlier. The term "interim" sounded like an indictment, as if the church couldn't get anyone to come without the promise that they'd also get to leave. The last time Way had spoken to this man was the worst day of his life, and he didn't care to remember it.

The pastor's name was Lennox, and he looked up at the sound of them.

"I know we should have fixed the roof long ago," he said. "I know."

Lennox led them into the sanctuary, and they passed the carved baptismal font that Mick had built, a woven tapestry of the Apostles' Creed embroidered and hung by Waylon's neighbor. This church had preachers come and go, but it survived because it had the people of Mercury's guts in it. Folks in town scrubbed it, decorated it, patched it, married their sweethearts in it, baptized their children in it. The building stood for a spark of the eternal in an ending world, though Waylon never felt his own mortality more than he did when he sat in these pews.

Lennox explained what had happened.

Earlier that day, the church mothers were teaching summertime Bible lessons in the chapel when cold sludge began to drip from the ceiling. Clumps of plaster fell on the children's laps with a splat. Rainwater had leaked from the steeple above them, casting a deep bruise across the saintly white ceiling of the sanctuary.

"Why is it so ... purple?" Baylor asked, as drops dribbled onto the crushed velvet pews. They'd need to be steam-cleaned before Sunday, the musky stench strained from the air.

"We'll fix it," Waylon promised, without first seeing the leak itself, which he knew his brother would hate. Their father loved making guarantees, too-good-to-be-trues. It was painted on the side of his Astro van:

THERE'S NO LEAK A JOSEPH CAN'T FIX

His boys had been brought up to see this promise through.

"Don't expect a discount," Big Baylor spat, "just because you're a church."

He grabbed the side of his neck and squeezed, which Way knew he only did when he felt anxious, as in—hardly ever. A pale, hook-shaped scar lay just below his ear, the only part of his body that didn't tan. Bay was itching to get up in that attic. Get his hands dirty. Ruin it so he could make it right.

So Waylon got to work.

Inside the sanctuary, the purple wave continued to spread. Outside against the brick facade, Way mounted his steel ladder, with no one to mind the base.

"Be careful, son," Lennox called from the open window.

Once astride the roof, Way scampered up the slick slope to a flat patch just below the steeple that rose into an ornate bell tower. Sure enough, a puddle had formed below a bit of copper flashing that had been stapled to the roof. Way ran his hands through it, pushed the water till it slid down the incline. He could see the water seeping beneath the slim metal toward the steeple joists, felt how the wood beneath it had gone soft. All of it would need to be torn out and replaced.

He scaled down the ladder and peeked his head through the sanctuary window.

"You should have let us fix this ten years ago when we told you it was time," Baylor was lecturing Lennox, even though Lennox hadn't yet lived in Mercury back then. Baylor, whose usual interface with customers was little more than an adenoidal growl. He stood on a ladder of his own and nosed the stain with the curve of his crowbar.

"It's the flashing," Way called. "It leaked."

Baylor smirked.

"See for yourself," Way said.

And just like that, the brothers switched. But this time, Way stood back to look at the vast room before him. As high as this ceiling was, the base of the steeple reached even higher. The answer to his question lay in the space between the ceiling and the roof.

"What's up there?" he asked Lennox, even though he knew Lennox wouldn't know.

He took the crowbar to the back of the sanctuary and opened the tiny door that led to the counting room where the weekly offering was kept. He looked up and found the same purple swirl on the low ceiling, with a hatch. A hatch like that meant an upper room waited beyond it.

The opening had been painted shut years ago. Specks of dried paint hit Waylon's face as he took the crowbar to the edge and pried open the lip. Bay yelled something to him from the other side of the wall that Waylon couldn't hear. He felt a sudden breeze.

Way believed in haunted places, not because he was a Christian, but because he was a roofer. His whole business was revealing stories untold, ones that hid until they began to leak.

A collapsing ladder unfolded before him, and Waylon boosted himself into the crawl space. Then he took his Zippo from the back pocket of his jeans, next to his cigarettes. Flicked it. That's when he saw them—one, then two, then ten bats fled into the sanctuary. Way fell from the hole and landed with a smack on the floor.

"Should I get a BB gun?" Lennox asked, curls of silver hair falling in his eyes.

"No," both Waylon and Baylor said as Bay appeared and pulled Waylon to his feet.

"Easy as shit to get rid of those bats," Baylor lied. "Leave the windows open tonight and they'll do the rest."

But then a leaking burst forth. A burbling stream of dark liquid shot out from the hatch and onto the floor. At this, even Lennox cursed.

"What is that smell?" he asked.

Waylon was accustomed to stenches, but this one he couldn't place. Once again he pulled himself into the upper room and felt around with his hands.

"What's all this fabric?" he asked, yanking a bit of it into the light below. It was damp and stained his hand purple. "The color is bleeding."

"Looks like old choir robes," Lennox answered.

Seating himself on a platform at the edge of the opening, Way reached down a hand that waited for Baylor to toss a flashlight into it. He spread the light through the space until it illuminated a petrified hunk. A rank odor pulsed from it as it lay on top of a heap of choir robes. Whatever it was, it had been in there a long time.

Way began to feel queasy. No other exits existed, as far as he could tell. Beams stretched from the platform all the way to the ladder that led to the bell tower. One misstep, and someone would fall right through the plaster of the sanctuary ceiling. The stink had been roosting there undisturbed since before the attic door had gotten painted over. Waylon handed back the flashlight and wiped his palms on his jeans.

"Call Patrick," Way said of the local rookie cop, who moonlighted with town sanitation because crime in Mercury was scarce. Patrick was Shay Baby's best friend and not even old enough to drink. "A shitload of bats died in here."

As he said it, the hardened chunk of bat carcass slid off the fabric heap in one disgusting piece. Beneath it hid a large object spooled tightly in plastic. Way squinted. Felt his stomach churn. He pulled at the plastic, and the whole thing rolled off the mound of robes toward the hatch and halted at its edge.

"Shit," Waylon said, and tumbled off the ladder.

All three men stared at what lay above them.

At the attic opening, something sinister appeared inside the plastic. The knob of a wrist, the bend of a shriveled hand.

Waylon looked to Baylor, who had shut his eyes. A beat passed before he opened them, and Way caught a flicker of the brother Baylor had been only once, past midnight, splayed out on the carpet of their house with his palms shaking in the dark. Way could still hear the visceral pleas plunging from his mouth—*please, please*—the dial tone of a telephone tossed to the floor. Waylon knew nothing about the truth of this body above him, only the chronic ruin it reminded him of. Baylor coughed, his bloodshot eyes ranging across the sanctuary until they landed on Waylon's and held. What hung in the air between the brothers wasn't what had died at their hands, but what still lived.

Lennox made no move for a phone. Waylon made no move toward the door.

With a sniff, Baylor righted himself and thrust his crowbar over his shoulder. His scar hovered above it like a broken halo.

"See?" he said as he stalked into the hall. "You should have fixed the roof when we said."

Before Waylon found the church stairwell, and then the harsh sun, he found a cool floor to press his head against in an empty bathroom. Then, he threw up all over it.

2.

Shay Joseph missed the news of the leaking chapel because he wasn't where he was supposed to be. Then again, he hardly ever was. If his brothers needed to find him, he reasoned, they knew where not to look. He lazed on the floor of the abandoned apartment in the attic of his father's great house on Hollow Street, fan turning far above him, his favorite piece of beach glass tucked tight in his grip. The gray carpet beneath him had gone matted and flat. His mother's old paperbacks still lined the bookshelf to his right, their bindings so cracked and faded that he couldn't even read the titles. These novels were the only items of hers left in the house, because this was a room no one else ever visited.

The rest of the Victorian that sprawled beneath the attic had always felt like a dollhouse to Shay, with its bright front porch that Mick made him repaint every spring. Shay, the beautiful son, was charged with the window dressings. *Make it look pretty, make it look clean.* They were all marionettes in the house Mick Joseph had built, dangling from his fingers, jumping to life at the flick of his wrist.

Shay hid in the empty apartment when he didn't want to see his brothers. It was more and more frequent these days, this desire to be lost and never found. He was nineteen years old, blond-haired and emerald-eyed, and coming apart at the seams. Not because he'd made more promises than he could keep, like Waylon, or because he wanted to be left alone, like Baylor, but because he felt forgotten, and being forgotten was safer for Shay than being seen.

His mother taught him that.

Beneath him, the front door groaned. Theo's laughter followed two sets of footsteps, then a clang shot through the air as his bat and mitt hit the foyer floor. The sound withered as he headed toward the kitchen at the back of the house. Shay's nephew had come home with Marley, who was Shay's favorite person in the world. He loved his brothers, truly, but sometimes he didn't like them much. They looked at him and saw one thing: a roofer. Or a Joseph, to be more precise, which to them was one and the same.

Marley, though? She was the only person who looked at him and didn't predict his future. Shay wanted so very much to learn how to remain in the present like she did, to tie a rope around a moment and pull it tight. Marley looked at Shay in a way his mother never had, even before she'd lost her mind.

At that, Shay chided himself. The sheets hanging over the old furniture around him tussled in the fan's breeze like phantoms. What a heartless phrase, *lost her mind*, as if it were his mother's fault, as if it hadn't been stolen from her along with everything else.

Shay slipped out of the dark apartment and found Marley downstairs in front of the stove. She had tucked a sack of rolls beneath her arm like a football, the cordless phone caught beneath her ear. When she lifted her arm to press a button, the rolls came loose and toppled out of the bag onto the floor.

"Hell," she said as she bent to retrieve them.

"Language," Theo called out from the living room, where he was trying to balance in a headstand against the wall. "Grandpa wouldn't like it."

"Grandpa," Marley muttered, "can go f—"

She glanced up to find Shay in the corner, and her face broke into a grin. There was Marley, ever hopeful, blossoming like a summer bouquet.

He leaned down to fetch the last of the rolls and asked about the baseball game. Marley took a can of Diet Coke from the fridge.

"You know how they say some years are for rebuilding?" she said, popping the tab.

"Sure."

"Whatever step needs to happen before you can even build the first time—that's where we are."

Shay placed the rolls on the counter. "Well, they say fundamentals are key."

"*Super* key."

He laughed. "I don't miss playing in those Little League games. They're so long."

What Shay meant to say, but didn't, was that his whole boyhood had felt too long, one with too many rules and not enough mercy.

Marley took a slow sip from her can. "Theo looks just like you out there," she said of her son, who had wandered toward them in search of a snack. "Bored."

"Makes sense," Shay answered. "He's the baby of the family now."

"Hey," Theo called out. "I could beat you in a race right now, old man."

"Try it, kid," Shay teased as Theo shimmied himself onto the counter and then jumped onto Shay's back. Shay twirled him in a circle.

"Mom," Theo said as he spun. "When can we eat?"

That was Theo, the youngest of the Josephs: always climbing things, always hungry. Always assured that his needs would be met. Marley was making dinner for six, as she did each weeknight for everyone who lived in the house on Hollow Street. None of the Joseph men, other than Shay, bothered to tell her when they'd appear. Tonight was spaghetti, Shay's favorite.

He moved toward the fridge to mix a salad, Theo hanging from him like a cape.

"They're gonna know, you know," Marley said as she stirred the sauce.

Shay stilled before the open refrigerator door.

"Know what?" he asked.

"That you didn't go up on the roof today," she added.

At that, Shay relaxed. He had a choice then to reach for honesty, but he didn't take it. It happened often in this kitchen where Marley and her doe eyes offered an open invitation. With her, he could lay his burden down, if only for a moment. What Marley couldn't promise, though, was privacy. No one in the great house knew the meaning of the word.

"I don't mean to correct you"—he smiled—"but I haven't been up on the roof all week."

"Your dad will only have odd jobs for you for so long."

Shay grunted. "He thinks I'm his errand boy."

"It's so hard," Marley joked, "being the favorite son."

Shay smiled, even though the truth made him sad. He was beloved because he favored Elise Joseph in appearance, his round face and dimples, the curled cowlick in his light hair. To be the favorite son was to be mistaken for Mick's younger self, mixed with flecks of his wife. Mick didn't know the real Shay at all.

The phone rang; Shay lifted it from its hook. Listened to the voice on the other end of the line.

"A body," Shay repeated. "Who?" He waited, and then hung up.

Marley's pasta had boiled over. She ignored it, even as the water pocked the stovetop. "What is it?"

"It was Patrick." Shay ferried Theo to the couch in the living room before returning to the kitchen. "They found a body up in the church attic."

A ghost drifted between them.

Marley was stunned. Shay stole the question from her lips. "No identity yet."

He bent beneath the sink, grabbing a face mask and a pair of thick gloves. "Looks like I'll be working today after all."

He made light of it, but Shay felt sick. This was why he had no hint of remorse for lately roofing only when he chose. He was the baby, the ham, the family prize. He could make even Baylor laugh, and no one ever asked for anything more. As he was the youngest by eight years, everyone in the family still thought of him as a child. The Josephs expected so little of him when he had so much to give. Shay knew how to kid because he knew how sadness could fall swiftly, like a hatchet to the heart. But the shadow side of it—that phone call in the night, that begging like it's a last wish, that cleaning of Waylon's puke because of what his sensitive body couldn't stand—this was where Shay took the wheel every time. Dug every grave, kept every secret, mourned every misfortune. He loved like no other, like he knew the pain of being cast off.

Shay loved best when he said, *Show me your worst thing. I promise I won't look away.*

When Shay pulled up to the church in a white work van and cut his headlights, his best friend, Patrick, sat in the twilit grass just outside the manse. The two of them were still kids by some measures, high school graduation only a year behind them. Now they had the jobs of presumed adults, even though it still felt like dressing up in their fathers' clothes. Shay and Patrick had wrestled together, smoked together, almost dropped out of school together before Patrick decided to become a cop. He belonged to a family of veteran policemen, all at his disposal, but there was only one person he trusted.

"It's bad?" Shay asked, sitting beside him. The gas station's marquee light flickered at them from across the street.

"Your brother puked all over the bathroom floor."

"Wouldn't be the first time," Shay joked, because the look on his friend's face snagged him like a fishhook. He touched Patrick's shoulder. "Tell me what you need."

"You and I are going to go empty out that shitty attic." Patrick ran a hand down his jaw. His tawny beard was little more than a shadow, and Shay wondered whether he'd grown it just so his fingers would have something to fuss with. "Then we're gonna clean the sanctuary floor," Patrick went on. "I don't want anyone else to see what I saw in there. Or smell it."

Shay stood, extended a hand, and pulled Patrick to his feet. He rose slowly, huskier than his friend and not as spry.

"We're gonna be up all night," Patrick said.

"I know."

Like Shay, Patrick liked to clean. In any other place, it might have been a wonder how two innocents like them were entrusted with such a grim task. Yet Mercury—a shrunken steel industry outpost—had always been a town that thrived on less than it needed. It had no medical examiner, or CSI unit, or even a chief of police. Right now, what this town had to rely on were these two boys. They would have to be enough.

Together, they walked into the dark.

They dealt with the body first, which was doused in rainwater. The friends handled the sopping spool of plastic like it was the Ark of the Covenant. It took both of them to get it down the ladder. It surprised Shay how numb he felt as they loaded the corpse into the back of an ambulance that hadn't bothered to leave the engine running.

Patrick sent the body off to the morgue, then the real work began.

Using a flat broom, Shay swept every last thing out of that attic onto a tarp below. When he'd almost finished, he spotted something that glittered on the filthy planks. He bent to examine it.

It was a ring.

Patrick watched him, a question in his eyes but no words on his lips. Typical, Shay thought, the way Patrick studied him without comment. Sometimes Shay wanted to grab his friend by the shoulders and shake, just to get him to speak.

Shay turned his back as he stuck the ring in his pocket.

Patrick hauled the refuse to the back of his cruiser. Then Shay found the turpentine, got on his knees, and scrubbed the sanctuary's center aisle where plaster and sludge had fallen. It was three days till Sunday, and the church needed to be good as new by then—or as good as it used to be, at least.

Patrick and Shay scrubbed, dried, and scrubbed again. Just before dawn, they finished. Shay sank into a seat along the aisle and eyed the deep purple wave on the ceiling. A bat fluttered about and then disappeared.

"We'll have to paint over those water stains once the plaster is fixed," he said. "And I'll ask Marley to help clean the cushions."

Patrick nodded but didn't leave.

"What's bothering you?" Shay asked.

Patrick's forehead creased. He looked foreign in the low light, and frail. "You mean besides the dead body?"

"Yes," Shay answered softly. "Besides that."

"It's just—" Patrick blinked, then tried again. "There was something rotting here, all this time. And none of us knew."

Shay nodded, though he suspected someone did know, and they'd chosen to say nothing.

Patrick left him alone in the dark of the sanctuary, and Shay lay down in a pew and closed his eyes. He didn't want to return to the house on Hollow Street with this ring burning a hole in his pocket.

Had it fallen off the body? Had it come from somewhere else? Shay didn't know, and he was afraid to find out.

Marley Joseph ate dinner alone that night. She settled into the love seat with her plate of spaghetti and rested her feet on top of Elise's embroidered pillow. Her mother-in-law would have hated the sight—bare toes on the cushions, a plate of food in the living room. Marley ate with a guilt she still couldn't shake.

Waylon hadn't called. Neither had Bay, or their father. The quiet curled around her like a stray cat. She didn't mind being alone, especially when it happened so rarely. Marley didn't even mind that she'd prepared food no one would eat. What she did mind was that the home she'd tried to build for herself didn't belong in this house, and it never had.

Theo had nodded off on the couch with one of Shay's old comic books spread across his chest. Marley still remembered when Shay was young enough to fall asleep in just the same way, on the same plaid sofa. They'd all lived under one roof together for eight years now. What did it mean, Marley wondered, to be married to one Joseph, but wife or mother to them all?

The only thing she'd never been in the Joseph house was a daughter.

She let the leftovers go cold in the pan. Taking the phone into the closet so Theo wouldn't hear, Marley called her best friend, Jade, at her apartment above Mercury's only beauty salon.

"Holy shit," Jade hissed when she picked up the phone. "Did you hear about the church attic?"

"I did. All three Joseph sons got called in."

Then Jade whispered the words Marley didn't want to. "At least it's over now," she said.

Marley pinched her eyes shut. "Tell me we did the right thing."

"Marley," Jade said, a soft warning in her voice. "You know there was never any 'right thing' here."

"I just wish—" Marley paused. "I wish I knew if I should have tried harder to be a daughter, or harder to be a wife."

This was the tender part of Marley that she never let the rest of the Josephs see. The part that questioned her every action, the part that bled. Before Jade could respond, the front door opened. Marley said goodbye to Jade and stepped out of the closet. Waylon stood before her, too weary to ask why she'd been hiding with the winter coats.

He was filthy, his hands painted dark purple. Way lingered in the foyer, looking like a charcoal sketch of himself—fading and blurred. He had black hair like Baylor, green eyes like Shay, and a shopworn heart that was all Waylon's. Her husband had been disappearing for a long time, and Marley had no idea how to bring him back.

She'd loved him not because everyone turned his way in times of crisis. It went deeper than any performance he'd been brought up to give, any debt he thought was his to pay. Waylon had no ego, and he was never too proud to ask for help. She loved him because she knew that under threat of emergency, when Waylon was so often called the hero, there was one person he reached for, and it was her.

Marley went to her husband, did as she'd always done, and made his stains, his pain, her own.

Before

3.

In June of 1990, Marley West and her mother blew into Mercury in their teal Acura with the windows down and the radio blasting. They came from eastern Ohio, where they'd accidentally left their favorite casserole dish and a Blockbuster movie card that had nine punch holes in it. There was no Blockbuster video store where they were headed, only an auto parts shop that also rented out movies on the side.

They hung left off Route 80 East, down an exit that led past a streak of cedar trees to a lone stoplight. On the far side of the road, Marley spotted three men standing atop an empty building, seventy-five feet in the air. Their silhouette cut a virile vista against the trees. The air stank like tar and sweat, and Marley rolled up her window. Tapped her neon fingernails against the passenger's-side window to the beat of Roxette on the radio, crossed her bare ankles on the dashboard.

Marley usually loved the rush of driving into a new town for the first time. She liked to hunt down billboards, ads, even the font on street signs— any static object that might hint at the story behind a city. But here, on the outskirts of Mercury as she and her mother idled at the red light, the only sign she spotted had been hand-painted onto the van parked outside the barren building they'd just passed.

THERE'S NO LEAK A JOSEPH CAN'T FIX

Roofing, Marley thought to herself. *How boring.*

When the light turned green, she had no reason to glance back at those men working on the roof in the rearview mirror.

The next afternoon, she wandered toward the park from the new apartment her mother had recently secured to see what else a town like Mercury might have to offer her. At last, she found wooden signs boasting of local businesses in heavy, white print—Cook's Hardwood, Rotary Club, Joseph & Sons.

She also found lazy summer, relentless sun, and a pitcher on the baseball field. A casual pickup game was underway, where the umpire smoked a stogie and spat tobacco juice from his mouth between every pitch. Marley took a seat on the bleachers' top row. The eager fans cheered when the final out was called, and she watched as two young men in the outfield embraced each other—or what she assumed was an embrace, at first.

"Those Joseph brothers," someone in the stands muttered. "The only boys I've ever seen who fight when they're on the same team."

As she peered onto the field, Marley put two and two together. She'd seen the Josephs the day before, pitching slabs of stony asphalt off a roof as she rode into town.

They could have been twins, with their V-shaped torsos and dark hair, though one was larger than the other. The bigger Joseph—Baylor was his name, Marley had heard from the fans—whispered words that only his brother could hear. The younger one, Waylon, paused. His face blushed like a beet as Baylor strutted away from him. Then Waylon sprinted after him, pinned him to the ground until Baylor punched up, lifting his brother before crashing his body to the ground. Their teammates didn't dare interfere. If there was any talent these boys had beyond baseball, it seemed it was found in their fists.

Marley couldn't believe no one put a stop to it. The people around her busied themselves by tidying a tumble of stray baseballs into a pile by the fence. The brothers grunted and gasped. A boy in the stands in front of her, no older than ten, touched his mother's shoulder and pointed to the outfield. Her head snapped up, and an eyebrow arched with it. The boy brushed a long, blond curl out of his eyes and took a coiled comic book from his back pocket, sliding his gaze over his shoulder toward Marley as if to say, *Can you believe we came all the way here for this?*

As if she were already part of this world.

Marley clambered down the bleachers to climb the fence and force the brothers apart, but the mother's firm hand yanked her back to the ground.

"Boys," she called out toward the field. Her voice belted like the low notes of a bassoon. "Enough."

At that, the fighting ceased. Waylon stood, wiped blood from his lip, and reached a palm toward his brother. That quicksilver moment found in the reaching, just before they joined hands? That was the moment Marley thought she fell in love.

Baylor reached her first. After trouncing his brother, he tipped his bat over his shoulder and caught Marley's eye. He looked surprised, then a little alarmed, and then he tried on a smile that looked more like a sneer.

"You're *new*," he said, as if he'd never heard the word. His eyes were so lavishly blue.

"Maybe." She didn't return the smile, didn't budge from her spot along the railing. Her mother had taught her the importance of caution.

In Ohio, no one kept watch over her. Danger was found in a girl walking home alone past midnight, the moment she stepped into a stranger's car and was never heard from again. How quickly a life could fizzle into a portrait on a milk carton. Here, though, people were already listening. She felt them slinking around her, stepping closer one foot at a time. They'd witnessed Baylor seek her out, and now they leaned in.

"You look like you need a ride home," Baylor said.

"And you look like you're twenty-five."

His face had been so immovably stern that Marley jolted when he started to laugh. His shoulders shook, and his bat fell to the dirt as he leaned on it like a cane. This stoic tree trunk of a human had started to relax, and it was Marley who had done it. She'd never had that kind of power before.

Baylor pointed toward the sun. "That's what happens when you spend the summer on a roof. Turns you into an old man at eighteen."

Marley thought he was joking, but his smile faded. It left no laugh lines behind.

"So," he said. "The ride?"

Baylor's stare turned fragile as he asked the question, framed by the black hair clinging to the thick cords of his neck and the mountainous set of his shoulders. Around him, the women in the crowd—mothers, daughters, sisters, all—didn't spend their gazes trying to slot Marley or wonder why she'd appeared on her own. They didn't look at her and ask who was missing. Instead, they narrowed their eyes at Baylor as if he'd already disappointed them.

The apartment Marley shared with her mother was just on the other side of the cedar trees, and she didn't need a lift. Yet she accepted the ride anyway, because it seemed Baylor very much needed to give her one to earn back some goodwill.

"Sure," she said.

Baylor jutted a chin toward a Chevy in the gravel lot that had a giant ladder hanging out the back and a license plate that had been drilled into the tailgate.

"Fancy," Baylor said as he began to walk away from the field.

"What?" Marley asked.

"That's the name I gave my truck," he answered, tossing the words over his shoulder. "Fancy."

Marley laughed and followed, turning only when the woman who'd stopped Baylor from fighting called out his name in the way only a mother could.

"Baylor," Mrs. Joseph said, somehow already close behind them. Her pleated dress kicked up in the wind, revealing a set of maroon heels. The only colors Marley had seen in the park that day were shades of fluorescent and black, the hues of homemade jerseys and biker shorts. Mrs. Joseph flourished in lake tones, the nutty brown of her shoulder bag like a cattail against the sweeping blue of her skirt.

Marley had never seen someone so beautiful, and also so out of place.

Her blond hair was fastened low at her neck, and the thick coat of mascara on her lashes hadn't smudged, despite the heat. Marley found a bewitching glamour in the way she had styled herself needlessly for a ball game—the unapologetic luxury of it, a defiant indulgence in daring any speck of ballpark dust to make its home on her shoes. Mrs. Joseph didn't appear wealthy—Marley could see she'd stitched a small tear in the sleeve of her blouse—yet she was rich in stature. A line of fellow mothers formed behind her, prepared to vie for her attention once she'd dealt with her oldest son.

Marley's heart quickened at the way this woman commanded attention with a single word. *Baylor*, she'd said, and that was enough. Marley hadn't known many men in her life, and even fewer who would listen when she called.

Marley watched as she took Baylor by the arm.

"You know you can't fight like that with Waylon," Mrs. Joseph said. Her eyes weren't condemning, as the crowd's had been, but beseeching. Invoking a selfhood in her son that others couldn't see. "He won't shake it off the way you do."

She'd scolded quietly, and Marley felt she'd intruded on an intimate moment between mother and child. She took a few steps away, training her eyes to the small billboards by the line of cedars. An arguing couple came into view just behind the Joseph & Sons sign, a man waving his houndstooth hat at a woman who stood in front of him in a long sundress with her arms crossed.

As a girl without a father or a sibling of her own, Marley had studied family arguments like these in beach reads and afternoon movies to understand the shape of what she didn't have. This couple, for example, had one-sided disagreements. The Josephs were the close kind of family that fought in equal measure but didn't know how to make up.

And Baylor was the flinty kind of young man, Marley had started to gather as she watched him looking hangdog before his mother, whom everyone feared and nobody liked. Waylon was likely just the opposite, and the boys didn't get along, sure as they were tied together by blood. Marley, though, didn't fear Baylor. Not when he had a mother who spoke to him like that.

"Sorry, Ma," Bay offered, kissing her on the cheek.

Mrs. Joseph looked to Marley and waved her over. "I'm Elise," she said. "You must be new in town. Are you alone?"

Having been asked this question many times since she was young, Marley still felt the need to stand tall, defend who and what she was, and never bow her head. "My mother is working," she answered.

Slowly, Mrs. Joseph nodded. "Welcome to Mercury," she said.

Marley took Mrs. Joseph's outstretched hand and embarrassed herself by holding it for a beat too long. She felt that same heat from the fierce gaze Elise trained on her boys as it spread between their joined palms, as if this woman could intuit how long Marley and her mother had been alone, and why they'd arrived in Mercury with so little in the trunk of their Acura.

Before, Marley had been a stranger. Now, she was not.

Elise released Marley's grip, a wisp of her blond hair escaping its bobby pin. "Be good," she said to Baylor as she turned away and reached for the hand of her youngest son. "Let's go, Shay Baby."

Shay had been sitting cross-legged in the gravel until his mother called him. When he came to his feet, he looked at Marley with a sidelong grin. Baylor promised Elise he'd be home for dinner. Marley noticed Waylon then, still red-faced and downcast, slouched against the chain-link fence with his glove limp at his side. He'd scored the winning run and caught the ball that ended the game, yet there he sat, defeated.

It gave Marley a savage kind of ache.

Soon, Shay fit himself beneath his brother's arm and ribbed him until Waylon began to laugh. Marley watched them as they followed Elise toward the tan Lincoln parked on the other end of the lot.

Baylor took her by the elbow.

"What did you say to him?" Marley asked.

Baylor didn't answer.

Marley stopped at the Chevy's hood. "What?"

"I said what needed to be said," Bay said as he tore open the passenger door. Then he paused, his fingers still gripping the handle. "Do you ever feel like the rest of the world is trying to save everyone but you?"

Marley frowned. It was a question she'd never considered before. "I'm not someone who needs to be saved," she said.

Baylor slapped a paw against the side of his truck.

"And that," he said, his face near to hers as she climbed inside and he hung his head through the open window, "belongs on a billboard."

The light flecks in his eyes seemed to flicker. He was rugged and misunderstood in ways Marley thought she could comprehend. This was a new sensation for her, the opposite of being overlooked. She didn't need to shout her existence here to be noticed. There was no mistaking the way Baylor wanted her, even if he didn't know her at all.

"What's your name, anyway?" he asked.

"Marley."

He didn't offer his own name in return or ask how she'd discovered it. Baylor Joseph—sexy and severe—was accustomed to being known in just the same way Marley was used to remaining anonymous. Bay hopped into the driver's seat and turned the ignition. Then he circled her wrist with his fingers, drew her slowly toward him until her hand rested on his bare thigh.

His eyes settled on hers with not a question in them but a dare. Marley didn't pull away. The warmth from his leg called forth an animal self out of her, one that was unrepentant and untamed. This, she craved. Closeness, skin on skin. The promise of touch. Fire in someone's eyes when he looked at her.

Marley liked slogans and advertisements because they got attention. They were direct and refused to be ignored. Was it the same to be desired as it was to be seen—to be wanted, and to be understood?

She felt an exultation in finally releasing the burden of loneliness, and when Bay smiled again, Marley bit her lip. She already understood that he didn't give his smiles away freely, and somehow, she'd earned them. Baylor parked in an alleyway behind her apartment and lost no time in kissing her. His hands in her hair, his teeth on her earlobe. His urgency disguised itself as valor when he whispered her name.

Baylor's stubble scratched her throat, and Marley opened her eyes. She spied Elise's Lincoln in the side-view mirror, creeping by with her two other sons in the backseat. Elise looked straight ahead, yet Marley swore somehow she had seen them. Somehow, Elise Joseph had known.

4.

Seven days passed before Marley got an invitation to dinner at the Joseph house on Hollow Street. It was now July, and even in early evening the sun shone through the wide dining room windows, casting angular shadows on the floor.

It seemed there had always been a place for her at the Josephs' table, even before she appeared. She took the empty chair beside Baylor, across from Waylon and Shay, with Elise on the far end. Marley would have been seated next to Mick, but he hadn't come home yet for supper.

The five of them waited silently in their seats for his arrival as the grandfather clock ticked in the corner. Shay drummed his hands on the table. Baylor sighed, angrily. Elise turned off the oven, and Waylon watched at the window.

Ten minutes passed, then twelve. At six fifteen, a man burst through the back door, covered in grime and wearing a short-brimmed hat with a band of houndstooth ribbon around it. He plopped into his chair, looked at Marley askance, and she knew where she'd seen him.

On the day of the ball game and behind a billboard, this man had been arguing with a woman Marley had assumed was his wife.

It wasn't.

Marley stared, and Elise placed a casserole dish in the center of the table.

"Mick," she said. "Your hat."

He took off the hat and hung it on the back of his chair, and Shay tried to pass Marley the stewed green beans. She couldn't look away from Mick, who shared the same fierce jaw as his sons, the same roughened fingertips.

"It's called steep asphalt," Shay whispered to her from across the table, thinking Marley was eyeing the grit on Mick's blackened hands. "From the roof."

There it was: an occupation, a destination, a Joseph family birthright.

"Like, shingles?" she asked.

The whole table laughed.

"Nah," Baylor answered. "We do low slope roofs on commercial buildings. Industrial rubber for mills, hospitals, warehouses."

"Sounds complicated," Marley said, glancing at Elise at the other end of the table, who sat primly in her chair.

"All you need to roof," Mick addressed her for the first time, lifting his gaze from the day's crossword Elise had left by his plate. Then he took a gigantic pause.

"Not this again," Baylor said.

"Please don't say it, Dad," Shay Baby pled.

"All you need to roof," Mick went on, undeterred, "is a pair of scissors and a caulking gun."

"And a crane, and a crew, and a shit ton of gravel," Waylon said into his glass of water, but only Marley heard.

"I saw your billboard at the park last week," she said, snagging Mick's eye and refusing to let go. "I think you were there, just behind it."

The words stopped Mick dead. His face puckered as he held tightly to his fork, its tines spiking the air.

"Who is your father?" he asked Marley, and she heard someone gasp.

"*Mick.*" The name slashed out of Elise's mouth like a whip.

Her sons sprang to life. Baylor slapped a fresh helping of chicken divan on his father's plate. Shay offered to paint the shutters. Waylon cleared his throat and stood to hang Mick's hat on the coatrack.

All this, just to distract the man at the head of the table from saying something inappropriate. Marley had never seen such a feat.

"My father's gone," she answered plainly. "Not dead, just gone."

Silence swept through the room. Elise had stood to fetch a water pitcher from the kitchen, but she didn't move. Baylor looked away, and Mick began to chew.

For a long while, he was the only one at the table who ate.

Then the doorbell rang, and Mick rose from his seat. Once he disappeared into the hall, Elise took a bite. The rest of them followed until Mrs. Joseph stood to clear the plates. When Mick called for Baylor to help him in the hall, Shay took a breadbasket into the kitchen, and Marley and Waylon were left alone.

He inspected her, and he didn't smile. It surprised Marley to realize that she didn't need him to. There was generosity in Waylon's frankness, as if to say—*This is what we are, and I won't hide it from you.*

"I'm sorry," he said. "We try to keep him from saying things he doesn't mean."

The apology felt like a door the rest of the family had left for Waylon to open. He was predictable, and mild, and safe—everything that Mick wasn't. Waylon's eyes were green and adamant as he made amends for his father's potential misdeeds.

"It's all right," Marley answered. "I don't care what he thinks."

And truly, she didn't.

"He never comes to the baseball games," Way added. He fingered the gold chain at his neck. "So you must have seen somebody else."

She was about to press—to lean into the same honesty Waylon had given her. But down the hall, the air filled with a dissonant clang.

"That sounds like someone pounding on a piano," Marley said.

Way stood. "I think it is."

She followed him toward an open room off the foyer. A Victrola stood by the entrance next to a wingback chair that had a clarinet sitting on top of it. The burgundy rug at Marley's feet had been upturned. Sure enough, at the far end of the room, Mick sat at the helm of a battered piano. He'd put his hat back on, tilted to one side.

"Mick," Elise said, coming up from behind. "The floor."

The wooden planks beneath the rug had been scuffed as Mick and Baylor dragged the small piano in from outside. Mr. Joseph didn't respond to his wife. Instead he ran his fingers along the keys, from the highest register downward, the notes cascading like a waterfall. It was out of tune, and brassy, and the keys buzzed each time Mick's foot hit the pedal. But as he started to play "Moonlight Serenade," his whole body leaning into the lilt of his fingers as they slid against the ivory, the music beguiled the entire room.

Mick closed his eyes, his face intent on the swell of the song. Here, he listened. Here, he felt no need to speak. Could this be the *real* Mick, Marley wondered, and not the angry man she'd seen at the park? Elise rested her head against the doorframe, and Shay settled beneath the piano, his body caught in the instrument's thrum. Waylon took the clarinet from the chair so Marley could sit, and when the final chord hung in the air, floating like snowfall even after Mick's foot left the pedal, Marley felt a split so deep in her chest at the beauty of the sound that she had to look away.

It was then she saw that Baylor had slipped into the hallway and sat on the stairs, his back to them all, his elbows crossed over his knees—troubled by either the new presence of the piano or her own, Marley couldn't tell. Baylor, who had sought her out at the ballfield only to ignore her once she stepped into his house, chose to remove himself as a member of the family at the very moment Marley started to become one.

August arrived, and Marley began eating dinner at the Josephs' home every night. She figured the open invitation meant she and Baylor were dating, even though the only places he'd ever taken her were his family's dining room and the passenger seat of his truck. Marley didn't mind. The great house seemed to have endless rooms and hallways to explore, one giving way to the next. It could never be fully understood, not in the way Marley's one-bedroom apartment declared its simplicity. Easy to move in, easy to move out—just as she and her mother wanted.

Her mother, Ruth, was a nurse, and she worked a long day shift in addition to overtime to cover their expenses. The commute was long, but the rent in Mercury was cheap.

"Seems like a place we could stay," Marley's mother had said when they first drove through town. But for the Wests, "stay" usually meant a year and not much more.

Ruth loved to tell Marley about all the wild things she'd done as a teenager—how she'd hitchhiked to the Newport Folk Festival, how she'd dyed her hair blue. Now she never missed a bill payment, and she kept an old coffee can of change by the microwave so her daughter would be able to find enough lunch money in the mornings. Ruth didn't date much and didn't complain; she still listened to Stevie Nicks on vinyl and sang "Rhiannon" into the fake microphone she made of her fist. Marley admired her mother for it all—her resolve, her foresight, her ability to jump-start her life over again and again.

Their story before Mercury wasn't different from many others': a single mother, a father who didn't stay. A new beginning always beckoned at every city limit. To Marley, her mother was a god who never tired, had an endless wellspring of love for her child, and served late-night bowls of popcorn in front of the TV for dinner.

Marley would never admit to wanting the mundane objects that signaled a stable life: a mailbox, a library card. Yet she felt a constant pull toward the Joseph house, which was full of things not so easily moved. For Ruth, who was queen of all women—and for Elise, who seemed to rule all men—Marley would eat dinner twice.

It had been a sultry summer—Mariah Carey's "Vision of Love" on the radio, Arsenio Hall on late-night television, power outages spreading across the country due to the heat. After July had passed with nights spent fooling around in the Chevy's passenger seat, Baylor wedged between her and the parking brake, Marley attended church with the Josephs for the first time.

It was Shay who invited her.

"You can sit next to me," he'd said. "And count how many times the preacher says the word 'sin.'"

Congregants made way for them as they filed into the sanctuary, Mick at the head of their train and Shay Baby just behind Marley at the rear. They squeezed into the second-row pew, all six of them in a space that was meant to fit only five. The AC was on the fritz, and Elise folded a fan out of her paper bulletin. Together, they began to sweat.

More than once, the pastor said the magic word and Shay made a tally mark on the back of the pew with a tiny nail. More than once, Elise stilled her husband's jiggling knee and wrapped her arm through his to keep Mick from adding his own thoughts to the sermon. Marley tried to catch Baylor's eye, but they'd entered the chapel in such a way that Waylon had ended up between them.

She felt Bay sulking as he slumped into the cushion, remaining there from the call to worship, through the offertory, to the benediction at the service's end.

As soon as Elise stepped into the aisle, a band of women surrounded her to thank her for the casserole she'd dropped off, for the ladies' Bible study she'd organized, for the winter coats she'd donated to the local shelter. She placed a firm hand between Marley's shoulder blades and brought her into the fold.

"Let me introduce you to my best friend, Ann," Elise said, tapping the person to her right on the shoulder.

Ann wore a linen Laura Ashley dress and twisted her hair with a rhinestone clip. She was just as stylish as Elise, yet without any of the clout. Ann crossed her arms tightly as if she were freezing in the room where everyone else was sweating, and there was no doubt about it.

This was the woman Marley had seen arguing with Mick at the park.

"Are you a Presbyterian?" Ann asked, her voice like a robin's in a birdbath.

Mick stood at a distance, casting his aloof stare in the opposite direction.

"I—I don't know."

Marley was flustered and couldn't think of an answer. Her mother had told her they belonged to the Church of the Holy Comforter, which meant they used their Sunday mornings to sleep in. Marley had never been swayed by religion before. But as the bell tower above them struck noon and everyone in the sanctuary paused at its force, she felt for the first time the amnesty that religion might offer to someone with a damning secret, the respite from some constant, gnawing need.

Baylor, though, felt no such pull toward faith. After barely speaking to her at church, later that evening he appeared outside her apartment door as the sun disappeared in the sky, drove her to a hill that overlooked the ballfield, and slid a palm up her shirt.

Marley stilled his hand. The greedy glint in Baylor's eye reminded her of the hunger she'd felt all around her that morning as the church prayed from Psalm 51 and asked God to grant each of them a clean heart. Baylor wanted something, it was clear. She was no longer sure it was her.

"What do you want, Baylor?" she asked.

His head reared back, though Marley couldn't see his eyes in the darkness. "What do you mean?"

"Tell me what you want."

He tried to laugh but coughed instead. "I want exactly what you think I want."

"I don't think you do."

She tilted her head and waited. Marley's mother had taught her that what people say is often not what they mean. *Are you alone*, Elise had asked her. *Are you a Presbyterian*, Ann wanted to know. *Who is your father*, Mick had demanded.

Marley didn't want to be someone who could ask a question and yet not offer her own truth. She wanted so much to use the right words, to line them up, to let them self-declare.

"I think," she said slowly, "that no one in your family says what they really want."

"Oh?" Baylor's lip curled. "You're an expert now, is that it?"

"Tell me, Baylor."

"I want—" He paused, gripping the steering wheel with his fists. "I want you to want me."

The admission rattled him, and he stared at her, wild-eyed, like a rabid dog caught in a snare. He screwed the truck's ignition and they flew down the hill, not stopping until the brakes squealed in front of Marley's apart-ment building. She asked no questions as she stepped out. Before she even had a chance to shut the door, he'd driven off into the dark.

Baylor had never taken her on a date. Never bought a milkshake with two straws, never tucked two movie ticket stubs into his pocket, never even called her on the phone. Somehow he knew how to find her only when he wanted to, like hunting down a doe on the first day of the season. He knew how to cinch a wound with his hand and stitch it up with his mouth—but he didn't know what to do when someone told him he was bleeding, too.

After that night Baylor stopped picking Marley up, only a month and a half after they met. Stopped finding her on the far side of the cedar trees or driving through the alleyway where she lived. He hadn't found someone new, as far as she could tell. He was nowhere. Bay had towered above her like thunder on horseback that day they met, and just as briskly, he'd gone.

As much as Baylor might have needed someone to miss him, Marley didn't. She missed the family dinners instead.

5.

Marley didn't see any of the Josephs for the rest of the summer. School began, and the first day of Marley's senior year left her lonely. She did everything a new student should—found her classes, her locker, a place to sit at lunch. Marley had done it all before, but it was harder now that she'd earned, then lost, a spot at the Josephs' dinner table. Ruth had always thrived on the moments when the two of them got to start over, but Marley was growing tired of living the beginning of the same story again and again. She wanted to take this place and write an ending for it—fill its empty billboards, find a seat at a table of her own.

Late afternoon bent into evening, and the final clutch of daylight Marley had always loved as a girl in Ohio became the saddest part of her life in Mercury. The sunset looked different here, always coated in a haze that had never reached the rich rose and gold tones she'd seen along the lower curve of Lake Erie. Or perhaps it was Marley herself who had changed. Once transient and smooth, now she felt listless and hot. She sat alone in front of the television in her apartment, her stomach growling. Marley didn't know whether she was welcome at the Josephs' table without Bay's demanding space for her. It was the emptiest she'd felt since she arrived at the beginning of June.

When three days of school had passed, it had been a full two weeks since Marley had set foot in the Joseph house. Then, at five thirty on Thursday afternoon, someone knocked on Marley's door. She put down her drafting pencil on top of her rough sketch of Mercury's church steeple and opened the lock. There stood Elise, her hair perfectly swept and pinned into a chignon, her calico apron smooth at her waist.

"There you are," Elise said, hands on her hips, as if Marley had run off and hadn't been able to find her way back.

She knows, Marley thought. *She knows that I know about her husband.*

They stared at each other. Marley waited for Mrs. Joseph to call the secret out, but she didn't.

"You hungry?" she asked instead.

Marley was starving.

"Mrs. Joseph," she said, glancing at the tear-shaped diamond ring on Elise's finger. Marley felt that familiar ache in her chest from the night she'd last seen Baylor in his truck, the one that urged her to find the right words to speak.

"Why would you come here," Marley asked. "When Baylor won't?"

Elise was silent for a moment.

"Would you believe me"—Elise twirled her wedding ring, and Marley noticed a faint scar along her knuckles, one that looked like a burn—"if I told you I'm tired of being the only woman in the house?"

A story hid behind those words, one Marley would have asked about if it had come from her mother. Elise, she couldn't read.

"Truly?" Marley answered. "I'm not sure if I'd believe you or not."

Her honesty gave Mrs. Joseph pause. She took in the Wests' apartment in front of her, and Marley saw it through her eyes for the first time—the dull tile, the sofa that converted into a bed, the cold oven where Marley stored her textbooks.

Elise placed a hand on top of Marley's, which was still clutching the door. "I'm willing to bet," she said, "that you're just as tired of being the only woman in your house as I am in mine."

Marley tightened her grip on the doorknob. "My mother is better than anyone—"

Elise raised a hand to stop Marley from speaking. "You will never, *ever* hear a criticism against your mother from me. All right?"

Marley felt streaks of red all over her skin, like rain smearing a windowpane. She blinked, then took a breath. "All right."

"So," Elise said. "Are you hungry, or not?"

"I'm really hungry," Marley admitted. "It's meat loaf tonight, isn't it?"

Elise tilted her head toward her car. "Come on."

Marley had never been a fan of meat loaf, or meat in general. She liked popcorn and spaghetti with jarred sauce and diet pop. Elise's meals weren't perfect or prepared like a spread in a Betty Crocker cookbook. But they *fed*. Those who gathered at her table were eager for a mouthful of heat that felt like an embrace, that dripped down a chin, that sated a longing.

Marley couldn't wait.

They drove past the park and through the main part of town, where Elise slowed the Lincoln as people began to wave. First Ann, who was out watering the pachysandra in her front yard. Then Pastor Hollis waved from the porch of the manse where he lived alone. The owner of the funeral home at the corner of Hollow Street was the last to greet them, with a brief salute. It took Elise twice as long to get through town as Baylor, even though he was the one who acted as if he never wanted to return home.

"Listen to me," Elise said as she pulled into the driveway of the great house. She waited, even though the windows in the car were rolled up, and the air had gone stale.

Marley thought this might be the moment Elise would ask her what she'd seen that day at the baseball game.

"Baylor is a lot like Mick," Elise finished.

The car hummed around them.

"I'm not sure what you mean," Marley said.

Elise kept her gaze straight ahead, her face chiseled and feline. Marley felt the thread of some hidden truth stretching between them, one that began when Mrs. Joseph had knocked on her door.

"What I mean"—Elise cut the engine—"is that he's already in love."

"Oh," Marley said, trying to find a name for the flatness in her chest that had nothing to do with Baylor.

"Not with any woman," Elise continued. "With that." She pointed upward, toward the sky.

Marley began to understand. "With the roof, you mean."

"With being a Joseph. The risk, the labor, the dirt. Tearing something down and rebuilding it." She paused. "It will always come first."

"Mrs. Joseph," Marley said. "Baylor and I aren't—"

"I'm not talking about Baylor," Elise interrupted, and then halted. "What I'm saying, truly, is that you have a seat at our table, and you don't need to date one of my boys to earn it. It's yours."

Somehow, Marley felt both grateful and small. "Thank you," she said.

Elise batted a hand, stepped out of the Lincoln. Adjusted the backs of the pearl earrings she wore before heading into the house. Shay ran to the bright porch, which was dressed in geraniums, and called out when he saw her.

"Marley!" he yelled.

She peered through the screen door, toward the dim foyer of the house, and spotted Waylon's silhouette there, leaning against the wall. Pushing hair from his eyes, he opened the door. Then he caught Marley's stare and held it. She felt no flash of heat the way she did when Baylor locked eyes with her, but a slow burn instead. For the first time, and to her shame, Marley imagined what might have happened if Waylon had driven her home that day at the ballpark, instead of his brother.

Baylor didn't attend dinner that night. As it turned out, he intermittently disappeared in late August every year because he was a prized member of Mercury's beloved high school football team—which Marley had exactly zero interest in. Bay never apologized for the way he'd run away from her in the summer. She grew to expect his disappearances at the great house as the maple leaves turned crimson. Often, she preferred them.

On a rainy night in October, Mick was antsy at dinner because Baylor hadn't been able to help him on the roof in months. He swirled his chili with his spoon, not noticing when it slopped over the side of the bowl.

"Let Baylor play." Waylon handed his father a napkin. "He's good enough to get a college scholarship, Dad."

Mick laughed flatly. "Baylor is too stupid to get a scholarship. He'll be a roofer, just like the rest of us."

A small tick of Way's mouth was the barest of signs that he'd disliked what Mick had said.

"What about you, Waylon? You're applying to college, right?" Marley asked, and then wished she hadn't.

"Waylon will run the business." Elise's voice was sharp as her eyes shot toward Marley, hot with warning. Waylon reached a hand toward his mother's and tilted his head just slightly, as if to steady her.

"Waylon will be fine." Mick waved an arm in the air, ignoring the words from his wife. "As long as he stops puking off the sides of buildings."

Elise opened her mouth, then shut it. She unfolded and refolded her napkin. Whatever she'd wanted to say, she decided to keep to herself.

At the kitchen sink after dinner, Elise dried the dishes after Marley did the washing. Marley could feel her displeasure in the urgent squeak of the dish towel against the drinking glasses.

"Marley." Elise wiped her hands and dropped the towel on the counter with a thwap. "You cannot substitute one of my sons for the other."

Marley dropped the sponge. "Mrs. Joseph, I—"

Elise held up a firm hand. "Waylon needs to run the business when he finishes with school. Don't put any other ideas in his head. Do you understand?"

"I understand."

Marley had been holding out hope that on one of those nights after dinner, Elise would sit beside her on the sofa and ask about how she was faring as the new girl at school, or what she missed from her old town. Elise never did. She was forever consumed by the needs of her four men— feeding them, cleaning up after them, correcting them.

Compensating for them.

Back in Ohio, when Marley had been old enough to ask her mother why she wasn't married, Ruth had only replied, "Men do things, and women apologize for them." Marley had never understood what that meant until now. Since the summer, she'd witnessed Elise, night after night, place a plate of food in front of her but never offer anything more.

Baylor is a lot like Mick, Elise had said after Baylor had started to ignore her.

Marley believed Mrs. Joseph had wanted her company that afternoon she'd come to the apartment to bring her home for dinner, but she hadn't. Elise was only trying to make up for what her son had done.

6.

On a Friday night in mid-autumn, Waylon's elbow touched Marley's as they washed dishes in Elise's narrow kitchen. The air was warm and smelled like gravy; the oven still ticked from the heat of the pot roast. Marley knew she should have stopped coming to dinner after Elise had chastened her. She'd even planned to complete her homework during the dinner hour so she wouldn't be tempted to go. But every night around five thirty, her stomach started to growl. Hunger, she thought, was such an easy need to meet.

If only she could be sure what she was truly hungry for.

Marley's arms were slick with soap as Way dried the gravy boat with a dish towel. She liked this silence they shared, while staring at the blue and white tile on the wall as the sounds of a piano melody thumped softly from the music room.

Marley went on washing, but when she lifted a glass to hand to Waylon, she found he was watching her.

"What?"

"Nothing," he said, taking the cup.

Mick began to play the opening run from "The Entertainer." The lights were low in the kitchen, and the moon hadn't yet come out.

"How come you don't play?" she asked.

"Piano?" Way laughed. "My father isn't a good teacher."

"He taught you to roof, didn't he?"

Waylon reached to place the glass on a top shelf. "The difference is, he wanted to teach us to roof. He likes being the only one who can play the piano."

The air between them turned thick, and an owl hooted from a distant perch. Waylon cleared his throat.

"Listen," he said. "Do you have plans later?"

The rest of Mercury would be at the stadium for the homecoming football game Baylor was playing in.

"I don't want to go to the game," Marley said.

The piano had gone silent. The front door opened, then closed with a crack. Mick and Elise had just left for the game with Shay. Waylon and Marley were alone.

"Do you want to come somewhere with me?" Way asked. His eyes looked deeply green against the lock of dark hair that had fallen across his forehead.

It was an earnest question, one that Baylor had never offered her. He'd assumed it all—the rides, the dinners, the kisses, even his absences, and Marley had let him.

"Wait a minute," she said. "You're not trying to apologize for him, are you?"

Way frowned. "For who?"

"Baylor."

Way began to laugh, his shoulders shaking hard enough that the dish towel hanging there dropped to the floor.

"Marley," he said. "If I ever need to apologize to you, I'll just say it. Okay?"

"Then yes," she said, for what felt like the first time in her life.

They climbed into Elise's Lincoln and drove toward the outskirts of town. Past blank billboards, past abandoned buildings, past fields where the horses had been brought in for the night. The rest of town had packed into the stadium, leaving Waylon and Marley to wander the deserted landscape as if all of Mercury served as their own private haunt.

After ten minutes down a dark road, Way turned in to the dirt lot of an old graveyard. Headstones appeared in the tunnel of his headlights, and then everything went black. He took a checkered wool blanket from the trunk and led Marley to the top of a hillside. The inky night enveloped them for a moment, and when the clouds cleared, Marley saw the outline of a large stone building with a ladder leaning against its facade. They walked toward it, and Waylon placed her hands on either side of the rails.

"After you," he said, and pointed to the roof.

Marley went up, and Way followed. The view was shabby and gloried as an aging oak tree cast the shadow of its branches over the graves.

"Look." Waylon pointed down the hill, past an iron gate. A drive-in movie theater beamed just beyond it, the screen playing *Guess Who's Coming to Dinner* with Katharine Hepburn.

"We're a little late." He took a small radio from his pocket and turned the dial. "Hopefully we didn't miss much."

The film's dialogue flickered into range, and Marley heard herself sigh. Waylon leaned back against the flat roof and closed his eyes. Smoky cords of his breath escaped into the chill. His jaw pulsed, and Marley saw his shoulders strain against the seams of his flannel. His hands were rough and large as they spread across the plank of his abdomen. He knew she was staring at him, drawing her eyes around his every tendon.

This was the first of Mercury's secrets that Marley had all to herself: Waylon wasn't weak. He possessed the same strength as his older brother. Baylor had the kind of muscle that intimidated; Way's was the kind that sheltered.

Marley shivered and pulled her coat closer, though she wasn't cold.

"Why aren't you watching?" she whispered.

"I've seen this one," he answered. "Three times."

"Then what are we doing here?"

"I figured you hadn't seen it." He smiled. "You'll like the end."

Her heart began to pump, and warm blood spread through Marley's limbs. It was a small thing Waylon had promised her, and yet she knew it would keep.

Marley and Waylon watched a movie every Friday night for weeks. The weather turned colder; leaves skated to the ground. Waylon fell asleep almost every time. His long, black hair shaded his face, the bottom of his pink lips peeking out from beneath the fringe. No one could deny the brotherhood between the Josephs—the wide mouth, bold brow, heavy shoulders. All those features so fierce on Baylor went soft on Waylon. He was easier, kinder, gentler. She hated that she compared them, and yet she couldn't stop.

A study in desire, brother to brother: Baylor wanted quicker, while Waylon wanted longer, and in secret. Occasionally, Marley caught Waylon watching her. Baylor floated among them as the weeks passed, sometimes caring, sometimes not. He still thought of Marley as his—even though she rode in the cab of his truck less and less.

He still drove Marley home when he wanted, and she let him.

Mercury's football team went undefeated; the season extended into November. The final game fell on the same night as the last drive-in movie of the year. Soon, snow would blanket the hillside and cover the graves. Soon, Baylor would have his Friday evenings free.

It was quiet that night, the kind of cold where even the wind couldn't move. Marley sat with her knees to her chest. She didn't want to feel sad. This secret between Waylon and her—this trust that belonged only to them—had found its rhythm because it lived outside the house on Hollow Street. At the Josephs' table, she felt like a sister, a side character in the family fable, and she liked it. Thought she needed it, even. Only here, when it was just the two of them, did she look inside herself and find a heroine.

She stared at the screen, but she couldn't bear to watch. Marley and Waylon had existed in a pocket they were about to grow out of—like these old movies, timeless and of their time, both. Waylon would not go up against his brother. He wasn't built for it. And Marley would never come between them—not when that elemental bond between siblings was one she'd longed for herself. The closest she could come to it would be nightly dinner at the Joseph house. She could keep that communal ritual, or she could have this private act with Waylon. She couldn't keep both.

Marley lay back on the checkered wool blanket and stared at the stars. She found a shape among them, like a rolling wave. Like a woman riding horseback. Like a dagger piercing the dark.

"Tell me something," she said. "Do you want to roof for the rest of your life?"

Waylon tucked his arms beneath his head. "Can I tell you the truth?" He paused. "My father—he's brilliant. The smartest person I've ever met. But he's terrible with people."

"What?" Marley thought he was kidding. "Everyone here loves him."

Even as she said it, she started to see it wasn't true. The long lines of people at ball games and after church. The waving at the center of town. The person everyone loved in Mercury wasn't Mick. It was Elise.

"He has these grand ideas, right?" Waylon went on. "He wants to invent his own pottery kiln. He wants to start his own newspaper. He also wants to run for state senator. If it were left up to Mick Joseph, he'd burn his whole life to the ground just by chasing his own imagination." Waylon sighed. "Can I roof for the rest of my life, like he wants? Sure. But that isn't what he needs."

Marley turned to face him. "What do you mean?"

"I mean he needs someone to take this string of jobs he keeps and make it into a business. Something my mother can rely on." He smiled, like he'd never felt the weight of the burden placed upon him. "She calls me the responsible son."

Marley nodded, remembering the keen glare Elise had given her when she asked about Waylon's future. Marley saw how he'd made a habit of studying his father—not so he could judge him, but so he could care for him, and care for the rest of the family in turn.

She wondered whether he'd studied her in the same way.

"Do you examine everyone the way you examine him?" she asked.

He looked sly and sure in the distant light. "Like you, you mean?"

"Yes, like me."

"I think you're the best thing to happen to this town in a long time."

"Stop."

"I'm serious, Marley. You jump in with both feet. You look at someone and love them right away, see everything they could become."

"How could you even know that?" she asked.

He didn't look away. "Because I watched you do it with Baylor."

"Waylon," she said. "You don't need to flatter me."

"This isn't flattery." The whites of his eyes shot through the night. She was close enough for him to touch, and yet his hands stayed at his sides. "This is me telling you I wish Bay hadn't gotten to you first."

Brazen, she ran a finger across his cheek. He closed his eyes for a moment and held his breath. Slowly, he moved her hand away, like it hurt him to do it. "Baylor won't want you forever."

Another truth shimmered there between them. Wanting had a time limit to it, an end date.

She put her hand in her pocket. "What will you do for the winter?"

Marley meant to ask what *they* would do, but she couldn't bring herself to say it. Not when he'd pushed her hand away.

"Wrestle," Waylon said. "It keeps me out of the house when it's too cold to roof and my father has nothing to do."

"So you'll be busy, then."

"Practice is every night at dinnertime."

Like a knife to her sternum, this loss. Marley didn't know whether she wanted to eat dinner with the Josephs without Waylon across the table, talking into his glass of water. They sat in silence for the rest of the movie, then he drove her home and didn't kiss her good night.

Marley felt like a pickpocket who had lost something she'd stolen. The next Friday night at dinner, Waylon's chair sat empty. Baylor, freshly done with football, slung his arm around her after he'd finished with his plate, like he'd earned her for dessert. Elise watched them in silence as Shay went on about his snare drum, and it made Marley feel dirty, as if she'd traded one son for another, which she had.

Somehow, Elise knew. Or Marley swore she knew because of the brusque way Elise began to clear the dinner plates without asking her for any help. After dinner, Baylor grabbed his keys to take her home, as if he'd been around all this time, as if he hadn't set her on a shelf for the last month and a half.

"I don't want you to do that anymore," she said, standing at the bottom of the wide staircase.

Baylor laughed. "Drive you home?"

"Any of it. Drive me home, put your arm around me, ignore me whenever you feel like it. I'm done waiting around for you, Baylor. Mrs. Joseph said I'm welcome at the table, no matter what."

He was surprised, if only for a beat. Then he got mad.

"*Mrs. Joseph said*," Baylor mocked, and cocked his head. He didn't care for being refused, and he made Marley feel it. "Seems like my mother's got a soft spot for strays."

He spoke a truth that had lingered like a tiny bird, nesting just beneath the wooden frame of the house on Hollow Street, waiting for someone to snatch it.

Marley reared back and slapped him. "I'm not a stray."

Baylor clenched his teeth. "Get out," he said.

Elise stepped into the hall, eyed the pair of them. "Marley," she said. "Are you well?"

The question made Marley want to lie down on the floor. Mrs. Joseph always used such weirdly formal phrasing with her. As if they didn't share the same planet, as if they had nothing in common at all.

"I was just leaving," she said, her own eyes burning. "Thank you for dinner, Mrs. Joseph."

Marley walked out of the house and hid behind an evergreen in the yard next door. *A soft spot for strays*, Baylor had said. Marley already knew Elise hadn't cared about her but had pitied her instead. She hadn't thought Baylor could see it, too.

It was cold, and she didn't want to go home. She wanted only to see Waylon, who would soothe her and make her feel star-gazed and lovely again. Marley didn't want to wait for him to come to her. She feared he never would. So she scaled the ivy trellis that ran up the side of the great house next to the porch and climbed on top of the overhang just below Waylon's window.

It was nearing nine o'clock, and he ought to be home soon. Mercury was quiet but for the church bells that rang on the hour. The tip of the golden dome on the courthouse pierced the night as Marley watched one light after another go out. Smoke from every chimney twirled into the air, and Marley felt none of their warmth. She blew into her hands and counted stars until she saw the headlights of Elise's Lincoln turn the corner and slow down toward the driveway. His silhouette emerged from the car. The slap of the car door filled the cold air, and the creak of the porch steps beneath him. Marley held her breath and tracked the seconds it would take him to mount the stairs toward his bedroom.

She waited another hour. He must have had to shower, eat dinner, and perhaps help Shay with his math homework. Marley was losing sensation in her fingertips. At last, a sliver of light pierced the darkness. When Way had shut the door and turned on the lamp, she tapped on the window. Marley wished she could have paused a moment to inhale the sight of him in the center of his room, shirtless in a towel and dripping from the shower. But she was freezing.

And she was hungry.

At first, Waylon looked confused. When he squinted past his own reflection to see her on the other side of the glass, he raced toward the window. In a single motion, he pushed it open and pulled her inside.

"What are you doing here? It's freezing out."

She tried to tell him she'd been waiting for him, not just tonight but for a long while now, but his arms were around her, and he felt so warm, and her heart stuttered so fast, that all she could do was press her head into his chest.

"What's wrong?" he asked as he traced his hand along her spine. Then he went rigid. "Baylor," he said. His voice turned low and angry. "What did he do?"

"This isn't about Baylor," she said.

Marley looked into his eyes and found such thirst there, such an empty decanter of a heart. His mouth was so close. She could barely get out the words—*I missed you*—before his lips were on hers, and he pulled her to him, and she felt herself melting into his bare skin.

Waylon kissed the line of her jaw before dragging himself away. "Wait," he said. "I need to talk to Bay first."

They were both trying to catch their breath, and he couldn't tear his eyes away from her.

"Waylon." Marley pressed her lips against his neck. "I don't need you to save me. I spoke to Baylor myself."

His hands found her ribs beneath her winter jacket, then her waist. Her hips. "When?"

"Today." Lightly, she pressed her nails into the meat of his shoulders. "But I already chose you, a long time ago."

His eyes went dark as he pushed her gently against the wall.

"Marley," he said into her cheek. "What do you want?"

She bit her lip to keep herself from calling out as he pressed himself against her and ran his nose along her collarbone. This was a side of Waylon she hadn't seen: desperate, controlled. Wanting her.

"You," she answered. "I want you."

He brought his eyes to hers. "Are you sure?"

"Way," she said. "I never slept with Baylor."

He shook his head. "You don't have to tell me."

"Yes, I'm sure."

"Marley." He leaned a thumb into the hollow beneath her neck. "I have wanted you since the night I took you up on that roof in the graveyard."

"And I wanted you back."

Later, it would be said that Marley had wormed her way into the Joseph house by luring its members, one by one. This was not so. Each of them had sought her out on their own—first Baylor, then Elise, then finally Waylon. The only Joseph Marley had gone after, rather than follow, was standing in front of her.

The towel Waylon wore fell to the floor. He stumbled toward his bed and undressed her, his hands shaking as they undid the buttons on her shirt. Then they tangled themselves together until it was impossible to tell where one of them ended and the other began.

7.

With his arms around her, Waylon fell asleep. Marley looked at their skin side by side, how tan he remained from last summer's sun, how well their hands fit together. She felt content and dreamy, as if in the past hour this bed had become her entire world, like a snow globe with bits of glitter that never lost their shine. Marley had found it, finally. She was no longer caught in her story's beginning.

But she couldn't stay—not when Elise or Baylor or Mick might discover her. Besides, her mother would worry. She slid herself from Way's grip and put on her clothes. Found a scrap of paper and drew a heart on it. *See you—M.* Then she climbed out the way she'd come and walked alley by alley in the freezing air until she reached home.

Her mother was awake, watching a rerun of *Designing Women* beneath a comforter she'd taken from the bed to the couch. When she heard Marley turn the key, she lifted an edge of the blanket for her daughter to scoot under. Her mother smelled like vanilla and butter, and Marley had always found comfort in it. The smell of home and safety.

After Ruth drew an arm around her, she spoke.

"You were with Baylor?" she asked.

Marley hedged. "Waylon."

Her mother's brow lifted. "Well."

They watched the television in silence until a commercial for Keebler cookies appeared. Marley and Ruth had always liked their company slogan, "Oh, Fudge!" They recited it to each other when it rained, when the Cavaliers lost, and when Ruth decided it was time to move.

"How was work?" Marley asked.

"The usual." Ruth laughed. "Piss, shit, and blood."

"Do you like it here?" Marley asked. "In Mercury?"

"I like the cedar trees," she answered. "The row of Victorian houses on Hollow Street. The smell of burning leaves."

"Those are all things, Mom," Marley said. "You haven't met anyone here."

Ruth took her daughter's hand. "I've made friends at work, baby. Don't worry about me."

Marley wondered whether it was possible to love someone and not worry about them. Her mother—who had the same auburn hair as her daughter, same pouty lips, same penchant for cheating at Scrabble—had taught Marley to be tenacious, honest, and self-sufficient. Marley might have been those things, once. Now she wasn't sure.

"Do something for me," Ruth said. "Sign up for an activity at school that's just for you. A club, a class. I don't care what it is."

"You think I'm spending too much time with the Josephs." Marley pinched the comforter between her fingers, remembering first the rush of Waylon's hands on her, and then, with shame, the prickle of Baylor's stubble against her ear. Yet it wasn't only the Josephs who had a hold on her. Marley liked who she became around them—someone who spoke her mind, someone who saw the truth of them and loved them still. Someone who was, however briefly, a member of the family.

"It's good to say yes," Ruth said. "If you're saying yes to the right things." She took her daughter's hands to her mouth and kissed them. "What do I always say?"

"Head on straight, heart on straight."

"That's it." Ruth smiled and placed the bowl of popcorn between them.

After the show ended and the credits began to roll, Marley felt her mother watching her. Not with eyes of judgment, as Ruth had suffered enough from such glances when she was young—but with a shadowed gaze of old loss for the privilege Marley still had that Ruth once did, too: a certain freedom to offer that "yes" when she wanted, how she wanted, in a life free from the consequences of other people's choices.

When Monday morning came, Marley took out her favorite friend-making weapon from her pocket as she approached the girl whose locker neighbored hers. Her name, she'd heard around, was Jade.

"Hey," Marley said, proffering a silver stick. "Do you want some gum?"

Jade's brown eyes rocked toward hers. "Depends. It's not Wrigley's, is it?"

"If I wanted to chew cement, I'd get it from the sidewalk." Marley laughed. "It's Extra."

Jade took the stick. "Spearmint?"

"Is there any other kind?"

Jade put the gum in her mouth and dabbed her lip gloss in her locker's tiny mirror. "You know what is the actual worst, though?"

Marley didn't miss a beat. "Tic Tacs."

Jade nodded. "Tic Tacs are the worst. The plastic box! The orange! I can't."

The bell rang, and Marley grabbed her calculus folder. "Hey," she said again. "Do you know of any clubs I might join?"

"Join the one I just started," Jade said, pulling her curly dark hair into a ponytail.

Marley needed to get to class, but instead she stood still as her locker hung open. She'd asked the question and gotten an answer, simple as that. How had she spent her first three months in a new school watching for Baylor, then avoiding him, then seeking out his brother? She didn't want to be so narrow, to spend all she had by placing only one bet.

Jade had been there every morning, her nails a fresh shade of neon, fruity lip gloss swiped across her mouth. She had a highlighter in every color on the top shelf of her locker and a pair of knockoff Chanel sunglasses tucked into the collar of her sweater, even though Mercury hadn't seen the sun for months.

"You'll love it," Jade said.

Marley frowned. "It's not 4-H, is it?"

"God, no." Jade laughed. "Let's meet after school today in the supply room so I can steal some Post-its."

And that was how Marley became the second member and vice president of the Mercury chapter of the Future Business Leaders of America.

Later that afternoon, Jade and Marley met conspiratorially beneath a single light bulb in the large supply closet at the west end of the school, whispering even when there was no one to hear.

"You seem like someone who should be running the student council," Marley said. "Why the FBLA? I always thought it was for rich kids."

"And that's exactly it, isn't it?" The light bulb cast a golden filigree around the crown of Jade's head. "It's about money."

Jade explained that the Mercury chapter of the FBLA managed the school's entertainment budget for dances, parades, and the fundraising to go with it. If the club went well enough, she could enter herself into a contest to receive a grant from the state for the salon she dreamed of opening on the town square. She attended cosmetology school at night, ate dinner in her Dodge Neon, and had the kind of low, scratching voice that could convince just about anyone to do as she bid them.

"How did you know that you wanted to open your own salon?" Marley asked. "I can barely pick a shirt to wear in the morning."

Jade slipped a wad of Post-its into her back pocket. "I want something of my own, you know? Something with my name on it. My mother is stuck in an unhappy marriage because my dad makes all the money while she raises all the kids. She's his employee but doesn't even get paid. I don't want that life."

Marley nodded. Ruth had shown her over and over that the ability to leave could define a woman in a small town like Mercury, as much as her choice to stay.

"Even though we just met," Marley said, "I know you can do it."

Dismissively, Jade waved a pack of index cards in the air as if to say, *We both know it's a long shot.*

"I'm serious." Marley fished in her pocket for the twenty-dollar bill she'd gotten for babysitting right before she and her mother left Ohio. "Here," she said. "Consider me your first investor."

Jade dropped the cards into her bag. "For real?"

"For real."

Jade's hand hovered over the cash. "But what should I do with it?"

"I don't know." Marley thought on it. "Use it to send out some post-cards with your services and prices. I'll help you."

Marley took an index card and a felt-tip pen from the shelf. Then she drew a pair of scissors that doubled as a palm tree, with leaves sprouting from the top. Beneath it she wrote, *Life's a beach. Get your hair done.*

"It needs work, but you get the idea."

Jade smiled and took the bill, along with the drawing. "Did you just offer to help me launch a hair salon?"

"Yes," Marley said. "I think I did."

Jade beamed. "We'll start with a pop-up salon for prom in the spring."

Marley said a silent prayer that she and her mother would last in Mercury that long. She'd never been able to make a friend like Jade—fun, friendly, alive—in any of the towns they'd once lived.

"I bet you could get local businesses to donate to the pop-up," Marley suggested. "So you can offer the first five bookings for free."

"You're dating Baylor Joseph, aren't you?" Jade asked, and handed her a stack of envelopes. "Mick's always buying stuff in town. Maybe you could get him to donate."

Marley start to feel hot. "Mick Joseph doesn't care what I think," she said.

"Says who?" a voice called from the doorway, and the two froze.

It was Waylon, after a wrestling match, sweaty with his singlet hanging around his waist. Jade looked from Marley to Waylon and back again. Marley hadn't had a chance to deny it: as far as everyone knew, she was still Baylor's girlfriend.

"Can I talk to you for a minute?" Way asked Marley.

"I'm busy," Marley said. "Can it wait?"

"Please?" he asked, looking to Jade.

Jade fanned herself and nodded consent.

Waylon pulled Marley into the choral closet next door, which was stocked with sheet music and drumsticks and a keyboard, none of which they could see because neither of them turned on the light when the door clicked shut behind them.

"Did you draw that sign for Jade?" he asked. "It's real good."

"We were just messing around."

"You should have woken me up on Friday night," Way said, taking her wrist. "I wish I'd driven you home."

"You looked so peaceful," Marley said as she felt his lips on her neck. "I didn't dare."

He laughed. He felt so good against her. "Will you come to dinner tonight?"

It was too dark to see his face. She stepped back, and her shoulders grazed a ukulele that hung on the wall. "No," she said. "Baylor is really angry with me." She feared Elise would be, too.

"Do you regret it?" Way's voice was tight as his fingers stilled the ukulele strings. "What we did?"

"I—" Marley began, and then stopped. She wondered how her mother divined it—how she knew when the moment had come for leaving, and how she'd ever decide when it was time to stay.

Waylon waited for her to answer.

"Maybe I should regret it," Marley said. "But I don't."

"I know," Waylon whispered. "Me, too."

He kissed her cheek and left her there in the closet, wondering how she'd become a person who kissed two brothers instead of one, someone who stood to leave a room when a man called her out of it. Yet it was Waylon who had wanted to bring them both out into the light, and she had stopped him.

He was more than a secret to be kept, but that was what she'd turned him into. She wondered what good could come from hiding, or whether she and Way were cursed simply because Baylor saw her first. It didn't stop the wanting, though. Couldn't keep Marley from climbing the trellis at night and tumbling into Waylon's bed. They were going to get caught, but they were young, and it was winter, and one body will want another when it snows.

On a night in December, they lay in bed together. Marley's skin was cast in a red and green glow from the Christmas lights Mick had strung above the window. Waylon stretched beside her, safe and warm, tracing the light's pattern with his finger. Giving her everything he had and asking for nothing in return.

"Tell me," Marley said, lacing her hands through Waylon's hair. "Why all your names rhyme."

"Bay, Way, and Shay, you mean?"

Marley nodded.

"It's to rhyme with my father. Mick is short for McKay. It was his mother's maiden name."

"The rhyming was Elise's idea?"

He laughed softly. "Doubt it. I think she wanted to name one of us Theodore."

It was incredible to Marley that Elise had not discovered her yet. Then again, she was starting to suspect Elise was practiced at willfully ignoring things. Marley hadn't attended dinner since she broke up with Baylor. She'd wanted to call Elise and apologize for her empty seat—but she hadn't found the courage. Elise had sought her out once before, and Marley didn't think she'd do it a second time.

Downstairs in the great house, a door opened and shut. Marley and Waylon held themselves still at the groan of feet on the stairs. Another door closed, then silence followed.

"Marley," Way said. "I don't like this."

She felt cold. "What?"

"This sneaking around. It's not fair to you. Come to dinner tomorrow. We'll tell everyone together."

"But Baylor—"

"I'm not afraid of Baylor."

Marley wasn't afraid of Baylor, either. She was using him to stall, so she could find a way out of the triangle she'd created. She'd ended things with Baylor, but what she'd truly lost was some illusory kinship with Elise, and now she consoled herself with Waylon. How desperately Marley had wanted to be a part of this family's story—but being a part of something meant becoming part of its mess, too. Being culpable.

"What *are* you afraid of?" she asked.

"For real?" he said. "Being a shit roofer. Disappointing my family."

"That's it for you, isn't it?" she asked. "Your worst fear is letting them down."

Waylon didn't answer.

"You're not a bad roofer, Way," Marley said. "That can't be true."

He lifted a shoulder. "It isn't untrue. Baylor's born for that kind of risky work. He gets off on it, and I never could. I can do it and do it fine. But I'll never be jumping through the rafters without a safety lanyard, thrusting myself out on unsteady beams just for the fun of it."

"But that's safe. It isn't wrong."

"I'm scared, Mar." Waylon raised his voice, then quieted. "That's what they can't forgive. Every time I go up on a roof, I'm scared."

"I think you're right to be scared."

"No such thing."

Even as he said it, Marley knew there *was* such a thing, because the Josephs relied on it. They needed Waylon to be frightened because it kept all of them steady. Fear made him sensible, resolute. Responsible, as Elise had called him. Waylon worried that Mick couldn't earn a reliable paycheck, so he agreed to run the family business. He knew Baylor would feel betrayed if Way took Marley for himself, and so he'd asked her to wait. Only she hadn't. She'd pushed until he couldn't resist, and now he was ready to upend everything his family counted on, just because he wanted to be with her.

Marley had turned Waylon into someone he wasn't, and she feared it would be the Josephs' undoing.

"I can't do it, Waylon," Marley said. "This will ruin everything between you and your family."

"It won't."

"It will. They won't just be angry with me, Waylon. They'll be angry with you."

Marley couldn't ease the dread rising in her chest. It occurred to her that she'd been ruining Waylon slowly, bit by bit, ever since their first movie night. Had she considered his well-being, even once? She'd been treating him the same way his family did, taking all she could from him because everyone believed Waylon Joseph would always be all right.

It would be best if she removed herself, just as she'd done many times before.

"It's my fault we rushed into this," Marley whispered. "It was my mistake."

She slipped out of Way's bed for the last time, even as he called out her name. Even as he begged her not to go. She ran through the dark streets like someone was chasing her, though nobody was.

When she reached her apartment, she yelled out into the quiet.

"Mom," she called, but Ruth was not home. "It's time for us to move."

Then Marley fell into her own bed. It was cold, and she slept through her alarm the next morning. She skipped school the next day, and the day after that. Later that afternoon, Jade showed up at her door.

"You missed our meeting about prom," she said, bursting into the kitchen, where Marley held a bag of hot popcorn, fresh from the microwave. "I need an update on the funds, and you said you'd help with my pop-up hair salon."

"Listen, Jade," Marley said. "You're better off without me."

"Hey," Jade snapped, snatching the bag of popcorn and tossing it on the counter. "I'm not some boyfriend you can just decide to leave."

And there it was—the cost of what it took to remove herself, which Marley and Ruth had never stuck around long enough to see. Already it had happened. Already, Marley hadn't come through. She didn't want to be someone who only thrived at beginnings.

Marley croaked out an apology, and the rest of her woes spilled out right after. Baylor, Waylon, Elise, and back again. Jade stayed with her until Ruth came home. After Jade left, Ruth pulled Marley's head into her lap while Marley lay on the couch.

"Baby," Ruth soothed. "I've never seen you like this. Are you sick? When is the last time you had your period?"

The panic in her daughter's eye told her that she couldn't recall. After a trip to the pharmacy and a disposable test tossed into the trash, Marley looked her mother in the eye and told her she was pregnant.

8.

To be pregnant in a new town was not unlike getting pregnant in the old one, Marley figured. The same phrase persisted. *That girl got herself knocked up.* As if, by some miracle, she'd achieved it without the aid of a man. Ruth was well acquainted with it, having gone through it herself eighteen years before. This was the reason Marley so deeply feared changing people like Waylon—because she'd already done it to her mother.

Ruth sat once again with her daughter on their worn, tiny couch, a hefty blanket over them. Marley couldn't remember why she'd ever wanted to leave the confines of this safe space. There was food in the fridge and a mother who loved her, and at that moment Marley swore she'd never needed attention from any young man, let alone two brothers.

But that was never really what she'd been after, was it? She'd wanted permanency. Her own story to complete.

"Well," Ruth said, clasping her hands together.

Marley began to cry.

"First things first," Ruth carried on. "A baby is no reason to feel shame. Remember that."

Marley nodded.

"Second." Ruth's face was cast in blue undertones from the television light, making her look careworn and far older than thirty-six. "The best you'll ever be in a town like this is a charity case. When married women have children, it's a celebration. Baby showers, casseroles, balloons. When you're unmarried, it's an indictment. A cautionary tale." Ruth paused. "It's not right, and it isn't fair. So you've got to find your own center, and hold fast to it."

Marley had no idea how to find an anchor when everything inside her was shifting. She shook her head, once again seeing her mother's life anew. The hours Ruth worked, the lack of sleep, the cutting corners to keep the heat on. "I'm not strong like you."

"You can be," Ruth said. "But tell me this first. Think about your life in five years, or ten. What do you see?"

Marley thought on it. This must have been what Ruth had done when she was eighteen and pregnant; she'd weighed her options. Marley was just a possibility then, a dream, a myth, barely a whisper.

In that tiny apartment, her future barreled toward her.

"I wish I knew," she answered.

"Try."

Marley had ideas, at least. She liked advertisements and art. Like Jade, Marley wanted something of her own. It seemed impossible to imagine herself at twenty-seven. That person, whatever version of Marley she might be, was an imprint in the sand of a shoreline about to get washed away. Still, she knew one truth would remain.

"What is it?" Ruth asked.

"It's silly."

Ruth took her hand. "I promise you, it's not."

"I want to love someone," Marley said. "I know it's not enough—but that's what I see. Maybe it's a man, maybe it's a child. I don't know."

"Maybe," Ruth spoke softly, "it's you."

Neither of them spoke for a while. Snow fell outside their apartment window, and they heard the scrape of a plow as it flew down the road.

"What was it like when you told my dad you were pregnant?" Marley asked.

They'd never discussed it before, and Marley wished she hadn't waited so long. She felt that precious time slipping away from her, when all she had to be was a daughter.

"He told me he didn't love me," Ruth said. "The future he saw for himself didn't have you and me in it."

Marley's chest ached. "That must have killed you."

"It did. But it made me realize I didn't want to spend the rest of my life with him anyway." She took a breath. "You, I did."

Ruth's life, Marley knew, had been given to making those three words come true.

"You don't have to tell Waylon until you're ready," her mother said. "Or, he never has to know. You can raise the baby on your own if you want, or not at all. This is your choice, first and foremost."

Marley hid her head under a pillow. Ruth placed a hand on the small of her back.

"For just a minute," she said, "I'm going to be your nurse instead of your mother. All right?"

Marley remained still.

"If you don't want to be pregnant, we can try to find a clinic. It will be a long trip because there's no doctor within at least two hundred miles that will do the procedure safely, as far as I know. So if we're going to take that trip, we need to take it soon. All right?"

From beneath the pillow, Marley nodded.

"If you need more time," Ruth went on, "there are plenty of adoption agencies nearby with people who would cherish a baby of their own. No shame in that, either."

Marley looked inside herself for words to describe her mother's fortitude, but she found none. When Ruth was young and in need of help, she didn't have the kind of tender mother that Ruth turned out to be. Marley's life hadn't been the only one Ruth created out of nothing. She'd done it for herself and was doing it still.

"One more thing." Ruth's voice was muffled from the other side of the pillow. "Tomorrow, you need to go back to school."

Marley obeyed. The next morning, she skulked around the halls. Waylon roamed one end of the building, and Baylor the other. She slouched through English, then typing class, then accounting, where it was her turn to present a profit and loss statement. At lunch, she waited in a bathroom stall. In gym, she hid at the end of the at-bat line in a kickball game. After school she flew to the supply room, where Jade was color-coding the paper. Marley grabbed her arm, yanked her next door to the choir closet, and shut the door.

"Two things," Marley said, leaving off the light. "One. I have the prom fundraising stuff in my bag. I'm all in. Let's plan your pop-up shop."

"And two?"

"I'm pregnant."

"Oh, shit." Jade whistled. "Baylor's?"

"Waylon's."

Even in the dark, Marley could see Jade's eyes go wide.

"Oh, *shit*," she said. "Does he know?"

Marley shook her head. "No."

"How are you feeling?" Jade asked.

"Stupid and scared."

They shared a silent moment. Jade took her hand and twined their fingers together.

"Do you want to keep it?" Jade whispered.

Marley wanted to run away and leave her body behind. "If I didn't want to, where would I even go?"

Jade's voice caught. "I don't know," she said. Together, they sank to the floor.

"Listen," Jade said. "This has happened to two of my aunts and three of my cousins. People will be shitty now, but they'll forget. You just have to ride it out."

"Did they also date two brothers who argue endlessly?"

Jade paused. "That, I haven't seen."

Marley softly banged her head against the wall. "I'm leaving town and never coming back."

"Oh, God." Jade took a big breath. "*Elise.*"

"She'll kill me."

"Marley." Jade hit her arm. "You know you're not alone anymore, right? You have me."

Just then, a cough rattled through the air above them. They froze, and Jade flipped the light. The room was empty. Together, they stared up at the vent by the ceiling, which connected to an air vent in the neighboring supply room.

"Oh, shit," Jade said, for the third time.

Someone in the supply room had heard them.

"Wait a minute," Marley whispered. "Could you hear Waylon and me when we were in here a few weeks ago?"

Jade nodded.

"Why didn't you say anything?"

"Because it was private," Jade hissed.

The time for privacy was short-lived. In small towns like Mercury, information transmitted like a germ. By the end of the following day, everyone in town—including Elise Joseph—heard that Marley was knocked up with Waylon Joseph's kid.

Marley knew enough to stay home from school that day after her mother left for work. She busied herself with mailers for Jade's prom pop-up salon, coming at the end of May. They'd made flyers just the right size to slip through girls' locker slats, and cream envelopes embossed with a *J* sent to their mothers in the mail. Marley loved the simplicity of it—the clean lines, the promise of a very good thing. Her hands needed an occupation while she built up the courage to ring the Josephs' doorbell.

She'd intended to get to Waylon first before he heard the news. But on the night she'd planned to climb to his window, she'd fallen asleep with her head on her mother's lap at seven thirty.

Now, standing on their porch, she didn't need to ring the bell. She heard shouts erupting from the living room, and she pushed through the screen door. Two brothers, tangled up, plummeted in front of her into the hallway and landed at the mouth of the stairs. A litany of shoes, usually neatly placed on a mat by the front door, were scattered across the foyer. Waylon's elbow was coated in white dust from the hole he'd made in the drywall. Together, the brothers gazed up at her, and all the guilt and shame she'd been harboring flew right out of her. She had not done this; Way and Bay had.

Elise was nowhere in sight. Marley stepped in and held her ground.

"Get up," she ordered.

The brothers stood, sheepish.

"Marley," Waylon finally said. "Can I speak to you in private?"

"*In private.* Can you believe this?" Baylor exclaimed to no one. He looked fresh off the field, with his hair askew and red streaks screaming across his cheeks. "Waylon, you've not had one thing in your life that wasn't mine first."

"Stop it, Baylor," Marley snapped. "I was never yours." She walked back to the door and cranked it open. "Waylon, I'd like to go for a drive."

Way nodded, fished for his keys, and they drove toward Mercury's outskirts in silence. Snow slushed beneath the tires; the gutters of every house they passed had icicles dangling from the edges. No one seemed to be out—it was too cold to go for a drive. The car fishtailed beneath Waylon's grip on the wheel. He eased up on the gas, plodding forward until they pulled up to the old graveyard where it had all begun. Or had it begun farther back, when Way glanced up at Marley from the rim of his dinner glass, or farther back still, when Waylon watched her walk away from the ballfield to his brother's truck?

Neither of them had seen the loyalty forming slowly between them, the kind that threatened everything Way had already promised to his family.

Waylon let the engine run.

Marley stepped out of the truck fast, tripping through a snowdrift toward that stone building with the ladder on its side. She scaled it and found herself lying back like a snow angel with arms beneath her head and her eyes to the sky.

Not long after, Waylon followed. He lay beside her, careful not to touch her hand.

"So it's true?" he asked.

"It is."

She didn't know why she was crying. It wasn't shame, or fear. It was heartbreak. She'd liked the open question mark her life used to be. Marley hadn't even gotten a day to hold this secret within herself before it already belonged to everybody else.

Way reached a hand toward hers. "Can I?" he asked.

She nodded, and he pulled her to a seated position. Then he brushed the snow from her back and sat behind her, his legs on either side of hers, her back against his chest. She breathed along with him, watching the sky turn white beyond the field.

Steady, steady.

"Marley." Waylon tucked his chin against her shoulder, asking what he once did at the start. "What do you want?"

"I'm keeping it," she said, without thinking much about it, without realizing this was the first time she was admitting it to herself. Before that moment, she didn't know whether she loved Waylon or not, but she felt herself tumbling toward him, even though she'd tried to stop it. Even though it had happened in the wrong way. She didn't love him because he was reliable, or gallant, or strong. Marley loved Waylon for his questions, and the way he listened for her answers just the way her mother did.

She could have made grand statements. Could have said she wanted to have a child on her own at eighteen, and that she wasn't trying to trap him—all the things her mother had said to the man who fathered Marley and then skipped town. But Marley didn't have the strength for it up on that rooftop. She couldn't say what she would do or wouldn't. She couldn't see farther than the edge of an old graveyard where a signpost for a drive-in movie theater had stood before the snow.

Way was silent and watching the stars come out.

"I need you to tell me what you're thinking," she said.

He turned toward her, his face clear-eyed and wet. "Marley," he said.

"I feel like I won the fucking lottery. I swear to God, six months ago I thought you'd end up with Baylor because he got to you first."

"Then why are you crying?"

"Because I don't want you to feel stuck with me. Because I don't want your whole life to play out this way just because of what we did. Because the last time I saw you, you said you didn't want to be with me anymore."

"I never said I didn't want to be with you." She touched his cheek where his skin was still inflamed from the fight. "And I don't feel stuck. I'm afraid."

She wasn't afraid of Waylon, or even a baby. She was afraid of reentering the labyrinth of the Joseph family that had Mick at every corner, and Elise at every end.

"Marley." He took her hand. "Do you want to get married?"

She laughed, thinking him ridiculous. Marriage, Ruth had said, was never the answer to anything. "Do *you*?"

"Of course I do," he said, as if it should be obvious, as if they hadn't known each other for only half a year. "You're the only person in this town who has ever asked me what I wanted and actually listened to the answer. When I think about the future, all I see is you. I don't care if I roof, or if I leave Mercury. We can go anywhere. Do anything you want."

"Way," she said. "I can't marry someone who still gets in fistfights with his brother."

"Today was the last. I promise you."

It soothed like a cigarette, to dream in this way. "Where would we live?" Marley asked. "How would we have money?"

"I'll roof. We can live at your house or mine until we can afford our own place."

"I can't live with Baylor."

These words caused Waylon to wait a beat, as he thought as a husband instead of a brother for the first time. Here were the Joseph family loyalties again, cracking right down the middle.

"I understand," he said.

Marley had one more question. "You think you're ready to be a father?"

They hadn't needed to say it because everyone else would. They were teenagers, naive, and likely to fail.

Way stood and pulled her up to meet him. "It doesn't matter if I'm ready. It's happening, isn't it? I'd rather do something I'm not ready for with you than waste my life waiting for things to be perfect. Look at your mother—she did an incredible job raising you."

Marley could see what he was doing, how he was selling her on a life together. How much he meant every word of it. This was where Waylon thrived: while painting a picture. Making a benevolent future real, an object she could curl her fingers around. Waylon had once said that Baylor loved the risk of working on the roof, but Marley could see now that Waylon fell for the promise of it. He understood how to take what someone already had and make it better. If Waylon used this same dreamy-eyed candor with potential customers, Marley knew everyone north of the Monongahela would want one of his roofs.

"You were right," she said. "You are good with people."

"Is that a yes?"

"Yes."

"I love you, I love you, I love you," he said.

And that day, Marley loved him back.

9.

After he dropped Marley off, Waylon drove home with the windows down, even though bits of snow skated across his face. He'd never felt so proud. For the first time, he looked at the rest of his life without wanting to flinch. Waylon hadn't realized until Marley came to Mercury that he'd been dreading the rest of his life since before he could remember. Now it felt as simple as he wanted it to be: he'd marry his first love, he'd have a baby, and he'd roof. If there was something else he dreamed of in life, he couldn't begin to fathom what it was.

He skidded to a stop in an icy patch around the back of the great house. Waylon considered himself a student of each of the Josephs, and he knew when Baylor got upset, he made himself a mug of Campbell's soup and headed to the garage, where he was restoring his beat-up, canary-yellow Camaro. And there he was, blasting Black Sabbath and spitting on the cement.

His soup had gone cold on the tool bench.

"Baylor," Waylon said loudly. "I need to talk to you."

Baylor turned up the stereo, turned his back, and disappeared under the hood. Waylon shut off the music, and Baylor spun around with fresh rage in his eyes. He tossed his wrench and made a fist with his hand.

Remembering his promise to Marley, Waylon offered his palms in surrender. "I wanted to say I'm sorry."

Baylor sneered. "For what? Embarrassing me? Making sure I was the last to know?"

"For all of it. I'm in love with her, Bay."

Way tried on a weak smile. Baylor's face remained unmoved.

"Please tell me you're not this stupid," he said.

"Why should it be stupid for me to love somebody?" Way asked. "For her to love me back?"

Riled, Baylor laughed. "This has nothing to do with love, or Marley." His lip arched as he said her name. "What were you thinking, bringing somebody into all of that?"

He pointed at the house with a wild gesture, as if it held some great meaning. Waylon had no idea what it was.

"Baylor, you're the one who brought her home first."

"We both know I'm not the reason she stayed."

Waylon felt like he was slipping over a stretch of ice, wanting so much to grab hold of his older brother, even when the garage was dry. "Tell me what you need, Baylor," he said. "Tell me how to fix it."

"Promise me this won't fuck with the business," Baylor said, wiping grease from his hands.

"Of course it won't." Waylon still couldn't understand. "Why would it?"

"Just promise me."

They held each other's stare for a minute that spanned a lifetime of arguments. Relics of their childhood lined the cinder-block walls around them: bicycles, baseball gloves, and plastic sleds all three of them used to fit on at once. They couldn't see eye to eye, even as they both reckoned with what kind of men they would become, each needing to release the last slipshod ends of their boyhood.

"I promise." Waylon put forth his hand, but his brother didn't take it. Instead, Bay turned the stereo back on and picked up his wrench. That was as close to forgiveness from his brother that Waylon had ever gotten, and he knew enough to take it.

Inside the soft warmth of the house, the air smelled like roast turkey. Waylon pulled open the oven door in the kitchen. Elise left dinner there when one of her boys or her husband missed the family meal, until everyone had eaten. That night, the oven was cold and empty.

"Waylon." Elise's voice emerged from the dining room, where she sat in the dark. "Sit down."

He came and took the chair at the opposite end from her, where she sat like an empress. The room was chilled; Elise had opened a window and the wind howled through it. Once he settled, she rose from her seat and strode toward him. Her witchy silhouette glided until she stopped short in front of him and slapped him across the face.

"Waylon," she said again. He still couldn't see her eyes. "Where do you think all this comes from?" Her finger twirled in the air. "The house. These clothes. This life."

She waited but did not want an answer. "That car you drive? It's not yours. The dinner you eat? Not yours. Your bed, your books, even your haircuts. You cannot pay for one cent of it." Her fist pounded the table along with each word. "What kind of life can you give Marley?"

"She loves me, Ma," Waylon answered stupidly.

"Oh, she loves you? You took away her *choice*, Waylon. Marley will never get it back. She has no choice now but to marry you. Don't you see?"

He thought he might reason with her. "If that's what happened between you and Dad, I can promise it's not—"

"Shut your mouth," Elise whipped. "You want to hear about your father? Then hear this. We were married the day before he left for Vietnam. He refused to sleep with me that night because he worried that if he died over there, he'd leave me pregnant and alone. So think long and hard before criticizing any of your father's conduct over your own."

This was a portrait of his father Waylon hadn't heard. He wondered when Mick had fallen so far in Elise's esteem, now that he was falling, too.

Waylon had never fought with his mother before. She saved her ire for Baylor, her indulgences for Shay, and her pride for Waylon. Just like he had in the garage, he felt himself beginning to slip. Who was he, if not the son who made her proud?

"Ma," Waylon said. "I'm sorry."

"Don't be sorry. Do everything in your power to make that girl happy. Do you hear me?"

"Yes."

"Good."

Then she stalked out of the kitchen, up the steep stairway, into the bedroom she shared with her husband that had housed two separate beds for as long as Way could remember. He'd once heard Elise say while talking to her sister on the phone that this life was hard on two people who loved each other. He'd assumed she'd meant the constant risk of working construction, the dry seasons with no leaks to create any work, the wet ones with too much work to finish. They lived not paycheck to paycheck, but by taking one sum and splitting it into two, then four, then eight. Then they gasped at the meager amount left over.

Elise had never meant that money had grown scarce between her and her husband—love had. Affection. Trust. But Waylon didn't know any of that yet, even as he'd determined how different his life would be.

10.

In the weeks before the wedding, the air had never been so tense at the great house on Hollow Street. Elise hadn't spoken to Waylon since she'd throttled him in the dark of the dining room. Baylor started staying out all night, and Shay Baby asked for an explanation no one wanted to give. Even Mick—who played the wedding march on his piano as a joke exactly once—stopped short when Elise's stare threatened to slice him in two.

She declared the extended Joseph family in Pittsburgh, whom Waylon hardly ever saw, wouldn't be invited to the ceremony. Ann and her husband would attend, and so would Jade and Ruth. It would be small and understated, with no ring bearer or flower girl, just a set of matching engraved rings that Mick had gotten as payment for one of the jobs he'd done at a jewelry store. The members of the house planned for a life that included Marley—her eventual presence at Christmas, her body squeezed into the family pew—even though she hadn't set foot inside its walls since the day she found Baylor and Waylon fighting over her on the foyer floor.

Elise made a habit of delivering chicken soup and bread to the door of Marley's apartment, but she left it in the hallway without bothering to knock. Way caught her in the act while watching her through the peephole in the apartment door. She hunched, her basket of food low to the ground; she gingerly placed it on the welcome mat before making her escape. Waylon had never seen his mother make herself so small. She performed an act of kindness without any trace of love in it, and it left a cold chill in its wake.

Waylon didn't know what it would take for Marley to become one of the family now. Elise never extended Marley another invitation to her table after she'd stopped coming, and Way began having dinner at Ruth's instead.

He and Marley attended their senior prom a few weeks before their wedding day, a taffeta princess dress resting airily over Marley's middle. Jade, cat-eyed and decorated with bangles, was crowned queen as Heavy D's "Now That We Found Love" thumped from the speakers. Their chapter of the FBLA had enough money left over in the school fund to hire a photographer for the night. Marley and Waylon smiled for the camera, letting the photo capture them as a couple in the throes of first love, gooey-eyed and grinning, and not as two people who were preparing for a wedding, for a marriage, for a baby. Waylon kept the picture in his wallet—thinking of it as proof of how joyful he and Marley were after the hardship they'd endured. He could not conceive of a time when that picture might become a relic of the happiness they had before everything that came after it.

Jade fixed Marley's hair the morning of the ceremony into a long, loose braid with baby's breath running through it. Just as she'd hoped, Jade had snagged a rented storefront right on the town square for a third of the price after water damage had ruined its walls. Waylon offered to help clear it out, and it felt good, especially since Elise had started to refuse assistance of any kind from him. He collected the trash, threw up new drywall, and installed a chair that pumped and spun. Dreams were real now, he saw. Real enough to run them rough on his fingertips.

Waylon and Marley were married in the Presbyterian chapel the day after high school graduation. It rained during the service, fat drops of it pounding against the steeple right above their heads. The sound was hollow and searching, as if there were a hidden cavern just beneath the roof that no one could see.

There were few smiles at the swift ceremony, aside from the couple's, and even fewer glad tidings. There was no first dance, no stuffing each other's faces with the chocolate cake Ruth had made from a boxed mix. Baylor wore gym socks with his nicest pants, Shay carried the rings, and Mick got away with playing the bridal march on the organ, after the newlyweds hadn't been allowed to kiss.

At first, Pastor Hollis had claimed they'd have to get married in the basement. The sanctuary, he said, was traditionally reserved for brides who were not pregnant. Waylon hadn't cared one way or the other. But when Elise heard that news, she laughed. Laughed harder than Waylon had ever heard her, so hard she stumbled backward into a coatrack in Pastor Hollis's office.

"On a cold day in hell," she said. "Will my son be married in a basement."

After that, Hollis gave in to Elise's way of thinking. She shed no tears as they were pronounced husband and wife, threw no birdseed as they left the chapel in the rain, tied no empty cans to the tailgate of the truck they rode away in. The gift she'd given them, in addition to her insistence they be married at an altar, was a tiny meat loaf wrapped in foil and left in the middle of the truck's front seat.

That first summer as a married man was the happiest of Waylon's life. He worked on top of a sheepskin factory with his father and older brother just after dawn, before the river valley towns had wakened, when steel mills had just begun their chatter, when the earth was glowy and wet and the empty highway stretched out before them like a royal carpet. They had a trinity between them in those early days, the Joseph men: Mick, the sun's ball of fire; Baylor, its piercing rays; Waylon, its warmth. They worked in hard hats and aviators, Levi's torn at the knee, work boots laced to the hilt. They stood above factories of chicken fat and coal, textiles and iron and flour and any other good thing that made the country churn. And sometimes, if they were lucky, they could view the point where Pittsburgh's three rivers joined together from the rooftop. They could watch the rising sun hit it just so and feel like they'd witnessed the honeycomb heart of the whole world.

Waylon always clipped into his safety lanyard while he worked, and the other two teased him. Baylor called him a girl, and Mick questioned how such a scaredy-cat could be his son, and no one made any jokes about Way's siring a baby out of wedlock.

On the day they finished their biggest job of the season, Waylon hoped his father and brother would get to witness what Marley had seen on the day he proposed. When Way wanted something—when he believed in it and hatched a vision for it—it could catch on like a fever. He could feel it: the owner of the sheepskin factory loved him. He admired the business cards Marley had designed, and when the time came to settle the bill, Waylon swapped out Mick's usual note for a typed receipt printed on fresh letterhead. Mick had always handed over paper proofs-of-sale in chicken scratch—which lent to his charm. Charm, Way figured, worked just fine in small bits.

Mick's whole face darkened as he watched the factory manager offer the company check to Waylon instead of him. On their way out the door to their van, he yanked the check from Way's hand and stuffed it in his pocket, fisting Way's elbow as they went.

"Call who you want, sell what you want," his voice rattled. "But I handle the money."

All summer, Waylon had worked so hard at being an adult, only to have his father crush him back into being a kid. Mick hadn't seemed to notice that Waylon upsold a new soil stack on top of the roof, which added a few hundred extra dollars to their bill. *It's for Mick's good, too,* Waylon assured himself as he tried to stay the hammering in his chest. *What's good for the business is good for all the Josephs.*

What Waylon sought was a dynasty: every industrial rooftop as far as the eye could see with their rubber guarding it from wind, sun, and rain. This, he thought, was the best way to keep his promise to make Marley happy, as Elise had commanded.

These men did not always get along. Yet they relied on one another, even still.

"See?" Mick said as he drove his boys homeward, his mood having cleared, the setting sun in the rearview mirror of their white van. "Joseph and Sons."

"Joseph and Sons," Baylor repeated, a lit cigarette dangling from his grip out the open window.

"Put that out," Mick said.

"No," Baylor answered, and they bickered as they always did once their feet found the earth.

Waylon worked his ass off every day for one reason. After sunset he returned home to Marley, who waited for him in her mother's apartment.

On rainy days, Waylon made cold calls from Ruth's phone with Marley next to him, her feet resting on his lap. He loved having her close, and he dreaded the calls. Way worked best face-to-face, when he could read someone's expression and figure how best to meet their demands. He knew paying for a roof would never be sexy. It was about security, or the ability to buy something new, or the pride in taking care of a building that had been in a family for generations. Those were feelings Waylon could capture. Those were dreams he could pitch. *Tell me what you need*, he'd say, and then he'd listen.

Waylon knew what to look for because he'd had to learn how to do it with his mother. When she demanded that he run the roofing business, he saw only two words flashing in her eyes.

Save me.

Waylon had pledged his allegiance to his mother so long ago that he still wasn't sure what to do now that he'd disappointed her. In order to keep the promise he'd made to Elise, he had to align himself with his father day in and day out.

Mick had one term for this job: the lowest of the low.

"People will pay good money for us to do what they don't have the guts for," he said.

It was a perfect system, but it only worked in person. On the phone, Waylon couldn't see what his customers feared. Was it spending money, or a roof collapse? And they couldn't see his smooth face, his buttoned shirt, or his clean hands. They couldn't see the duality in him: the worker who could mount a roof in minutes, and the salesman with the white collar. The young man with a wife and baby on the way.

But he made the calls anyway, even though they often ended in dial tones. Then he'd look to Marley, so overcome with love for her that he could barely breathe. As she sat next to him at the kitchen table, Marley highlighted company names in the phone book and addressed letters to every business within a two-hour drive. She ferried them to the post office with such speed that Waylon started to wonder whether she was trying to atone for her sudden presence in his life, for the splintering tension their relationship had caused in his family. He knew how much Marley had treasured having a seat at their table, and because of him she'd lost it.

So Waylon made the cold calls not for his business but for his wife.

Ruth often worked double shifts, determined to pay her nursing school loans as quickly as she could. While she was away, Marley kept highlighting the phone book. Once Waylon made his sales call, she followed it one week later with a letter in the mail, which included an offer for a free appraisal of the roof. Scouting, she called it on Sundays when they'd take a drive through the mill towns and look for buildings in need of repair.

Way considered telling his family that Marley was helping him. Yet he feared their disapproval would tarnish the gleam of those Sunday afternoons, when they were just two. An *us*. Like those old movies at the graveyard, their worth appeared in the secret itself.

And on Waylon's longest, dirtiest days, he left his work clothes in a heap by the apartment door, then showered the layers of grime off him before Marley drew a bath. He climbed in first, and she after him, nestling her back to his front, and cleaning the filth beneath his nails while he kissed her neck, her shoulder, her earlobe. He felt himself wanting her, reaching for her, growling against her as she laughed.

"Easy," she'd say. "You already got me pregnant."

This, he thought, was love. Every need satisfied. This, he thought, was ecstasy—getting all he wanted, when he wanted it, and giving it to someone who wanted it in return. They no longer needed to hide. Whenever a flash summer thunderstorm passed through, Waylon rushed home to make love to Marley in the middle of the day, even as the rain slammed against the windowpane. He luxuriated in taking off every piece of her clothing, leaving them on the floor until she was naked and they could slow dance to any song on the radio. He took her on the couch, on the counter, in the shower, up against a wall. Day by day her abdomen grew, and he wanted her even more. Over and over, he fell to his knees for her, until the rain cleared and he went back to work.

They spent very little money. Ate beans from a can and vegetables from Elise's garden, left by the door. Watched Steffi Graf win Wimbledon on the television. They played cards, and Scrabble, and fell asleep too early. There was no baby shower, no announcement in the paper or church bulletin. Marley found a bassinet and some blankets and onesies at a garage sale. They'd spent Waylon's first paychecks on a used red Chevy Citation—a completely impractical car for having a newborn. But they loved it, even with its alarmingly terrible mileage and horn that sounded like a braying horse.

They dared to be happy, and they were.

A month before Marley's due date, Ruth came home early from work. It was raining that day, the fifth rainy day of the month, and Waylon and Marley were trying to hunt down the extra check Way had earned from adding a new HVAC vent on a chocolate factory in Sharon. He'd been certain he placed it in his work folder before leaving the site, but it must have slipped out. The check amounted to only a few hundred dollars, but their income was weather-reliant. It was still raining, and they didn't have a safety net.

Ruth sank down beside them at the table, cracked open a can of Coke. Then she tugged the elastic band around her ponytail, and her russet hair fell around her shoulders, damp and curled at the ends.

"Kids," she addressed them because that was what they were. "I got laid off today."

Marley looked up from her ledger. Waylon hung up the phone.

"How could that be?" Marley asked. "You work harder than anyone."

"The hospital is making cuts," Ruth said. The hems of her scrubs were dark with rainwater. "Last one hired, first one fired."

"We can help cover rent," Waylon cut in too quickly, even as he was searching for money he couldn't find. "We'll figure it out."

"No, you can't," Ruth said. "This is the job. I have to move where I'm needed."

"But you can't," Marley said. "The baby." The desperation in her voice shook the room. She was only eighteen, and she sounded like a daughter. Not a mother, not a wife.

"You can come with me wherever I go," Ruth said. "But there isn't another hospital that's hiring within a hundred miles. It isn't safe to do that kind of drive every day, let alone after working a double."

She paused before repeating herself. "I need to move, and I think you should come with me."

It took Waylon a minute to comprehend what Ruth was saying. She wasn't one to offer "should" the way his mother did. He wanted to consider how Elise would have handled such a situation, but he couldn't even imagine it. Had she ever been given the right to make a decision for herself? Elise turned in an orbit of Mick's making that she didn't breach. Waylon looked at his own wife, fearing he'd already done the same to her.

The dread in Marley's face knifed through him. They didn't even need to discuss it. If they moved with Ruth, Waylon could find a minimum-wage job—but it would never match the potential earnings that Joseph & Sons could provide if he kept selling new roofs. Way had once said he'd go wherever Marley wanted. It was only months ago—but it was before all the other promises Way had made in order to keep his promise to his mother. He'd staked his claim to every business owner for miles around that Waylon Joseph was whom you called when the lights went out. When water poured through the ceiling. When you were in trouble.

"Rain Down on Us" was the slogan Marley had printed at the top of every Joseph & Sons letter she put in the mail, but it wasn't an "us," was it? It was Waylon alone.

These assurances were reminiscent of the vows he'd given his family in his heart long ago. He wanted to be the one they could count on in a crisis. Marley and Waylon had invested everything they had in this promise of who he was, and Way told himself it would be good for her, too. What was good for the business was good for all the Josephs, wasn't it?

Only now could he see that Marley might pay the price for everything he'd done to ensure she'd be happy.

11.

And so it happened just as no one wanted it to: Marley went into labor in early August without her husband or her mother nearby.

The Joseph men had just left for an overnight job at a silica factory in Aliquippa, with an infrared test planned to detect leaks with a special camera once the sky went dark. Waylon loved that camera so much he spent multiple evenings a week traveling with it, using it to book lengthy sales calls that included a detailed infrared map of the roof. He'd attempted to schedule a gap around Marley's due date so he could be on hand, but with the rain, and the backups, and the need for cash, they'd been working through the weekends to keep their guarantee to customers for new roofs before the first frost.

No one was available but Elise, whom Marley hadn't looked in the eye since she'd gotten pregnant. She and Way had done exactly what Marley asked to avoid. After Ruth packed up the Acura and moved to Maryland for a job at a women's clinic, Marley and Waylon moved into Way's old room with his rank wrestling gear and baseball bats and socks with holes, and Baylor two doors down.

Marley spent almost every waking moment at Jade's salon—answering the phone, painting nails, working the register—because the thrill of Waylon's bedroom had lost its luster. Once seductive and forbidden, now it was tiny, and drafty, and it stank.

She lay in bed the morning the contractions began. The spot Way left on the mattress was still warm. Marley worked at ignoring the pain—like she ignored Elise, like she ignored Mick's blank stares when she waddled toward the bathroom—but when a wave hit her, a low moan leaked out of her mouth. She turned on her side and clutched her pillow, furious that the only object she had to train her eyes on was a torn poster of Three Rivers Stadium tacked to the wall.

She heard a soft knock and tried to close her mouth.

"Marley?" a voice called. It was Shay, ready to walk with her to Jade's salon, where he liked to spin in the chairs and sweep the floor.

"One minute, pal," she croaked, trying to rustle herself from bed.

Anger toward Waylon wailed in her chest. She didn't fault him for needing to work, but she did blame him for his absence. As much as he'd been present when they lived at Ruth's apartment, he was gone now that he'd returned to his own house. There was no way to reach him until he checked in at the motel after the infrared test, which would be past midnight.

She was used to leaving. Not getting left.

Marley fell to her knees as pain came for her, and she stretched like a cat. Another hasty knock sounded at the door.

"Coming, bud," Marley said, but no one could hear.

The door swung open, and Elise stepped into the room. Marley lay her forehead in her hands and pushed against the nap of the carpet, too mad to be embarrassed.

"Oh, no," Elise said, because she knew what Marley feared.

Waylon was going to miss the birth of his first child.

"I can't do it, Mrs. Joseph," Marley said.

"You're going to have to stop calling me Mrs. Joseph," Elise answered. "And just call me Elise."

Pinching her eyes shut, Marley nodded.

Elise pressed a hand on the small of Marley's back. It wasn't a peace offering or pity, but a witnessing of her daughter-in-law's pain.

"You can do it, Marley." She cleared her throat, looking up at Shay, who stood in the doorway. "Let me get my purse."

"Elise, wait." Marley came to her knees, then went down on all fours again. "I'm so sorry."

Elise's eyes darted from Shay to Marley: a warning against saying too much in front of a ten-year-old. She brought her face close to Marley's, brushed the hair away from her temples.

"Look," she said. "There is no need to apologize for a baby."

"It isn't that." Marley shook her head. "I'm sorry I stopped coming to dinner."

"Oh." Elise twisted the pearl in one of her ears. "Your seat is still free."

Marley grabbed Elise's arm so she could stand. The three of them loped down the stairs, halting twice. Shay held open the door, where Marley decided to stop and sat herself on the steps.

"I hate this," she said. "I have nothing to bring this baby back to except a drawer of old tube socks and a broken bassinet."

Elise and Shay peered at each other. "We need to show her, Ma," Shay said.

Elise nodded, and Shay led them around the backside of the house, to the lilac bushes that hid a slim door that Marley had never noticed before. Shay opened it and disappeared into the dark.

"Just one more set of stairs," Elise coaxed. "I promise."

At the top of the third floor, Shay had switched on a light. Marley followed it into an efficiency apartment with a kitchen, a small bedroom, and a living room with a wall full of water-stained paperbacks. In the middle of the space stood a crib, a rocking chair, and a hand-sewn quilt with a *J* on it. It felt decades old, a memory untouched until now.

"I cleaned it out myself," Shay said. "There were a lot of spiderwebs in here."

"We lived in this apartment for almost a year while Mick was fixing up the rest of the house," Elise said. "I put all three of my boys in this crib. Mick built it. It's old, but it's sturdy."

The smile on Shay's face was so wide, and the look in Elise's eyes so filled with a tenderness she'd lost since they first met, that all Marley wanted to do was shower them both with gratitude. Her water broke instead.

"Whoa," Shay said.

"We'd better go," Elise followed.

Forty-five minutes later, they burst into the labor and delivery unit. Marley marched around the lobby, trying to outwalk the constant ache in her back. Shay strode to the front desk to sign her in.

"Who are you," the nurse joked. "The father?"

Shay looked boyishly blond, forgotten drumsticks poking out the back pocket of his Levi's. He was undaunted by her teasing, and deadly serious.

"I'm the uncle," he said.

The coven of nurses tried to shoo Shay into the waiting area. Any other family might have complied in that situation—even Elise was ready to relent—but Shay stood firm.

"My brother isn't here to hold Marley's hand," Shay declared when the doctor waltzed in. "So I'm going to."

A noble pronouncement, unworthy of the doctor who shrugged his shoulders and slapped on a fresh pair of gloves to deliver his tenth baby of the day. He spread Marley's legs like a turkey and didn't once speak her name. She'd expected to scream from the pain of birth; she found herself rendered silent by its force instead.

You'll forget the pain, a woman at the post office had told her. *Just when it's time to have another.*

It was not so. This pain Marley would never forget.

Outside the window, a trio of crows sat on a telephone wire. Elise stood at the side of the bed, where Marley's mother should have been. She looked uncomfortable and refused to take off her maroon pumps, and Marley didn't realize she'd gripped Elise's hand until Elise tried to free herself by offering Marley some ice. The women locked eyes as Marley bit down on her lip, and it felt too intimate a moment—too naked and raw for two not-quite strangers who were now family to share.

Elise had not wanted this. Any of it.

Fifty minutes of pushing, a reddish head, and a broad pair of Joseph shoulders later, Marley had a son. He was chubby, and dewy-haired, and alive. He was hers.

They cleaned him up, and Marley too, and placed the baby on her chest.

"Theodore," Marley whispered to Elise. "For the boy you didn't get to name."

Elise didn't smile, and Shay slipped his pinky into the newborn's fist.

"And you, sir," Marley said to her brother-in-law. "He's going to be named after you, too."

"Me?" he squeaked. "What about Waylon?"

Marley raised her eyebrows. "Do you see any Waylon here?"

Shay blushed and shook his head. The matter was settled. That day, Theodore Shay Joseph became the fifth in line of the Joseph men.

It was three o'clock in the morning by the time Waylon reached the hospital. He'd gotten to the motel just after midnight, when he heard the message that Marley was in labor. Luckily, he'd driven separately from Mick and Baylor so he could make a few sales calls on his own. Way drove Route 79 at breakneck speed, not bothering to watch for the cops just outside Slippery Rock who liked to hide along the berm. At the hospital entrance, the receptionist claimed that visiting hours were over.

"But my wife," he pled. "What if she had the baby?"

"Then you should go home and rest."

Way pretended to need to use the bathroom but snuck into the elevator and pressed the button for labor and delivery. When the doors opened, he heard a chorus of infant shrieks echo in the sterile hall, and he hunted the sound. He was about to knock on a random door when a nurse clamped her arm around his wrist. Thinking he was busted, he tried to explain himself before she cut him off.

"Sir," she said. "You ought to go home and rest."

"But my wife," he began again, and then he heard Marley's voice.

"Waylon?"

He pushed into the room, where Marley stood, hunched and bent at the knees, bobbing a screaming baby. She was covered in cords and sweat. His heart mangled at the sight. His wife had been alone for hours while he'd been up on the roof. He didn't know where to look first, so he hugged them both, and Marley winced, and the night-shift doctor popped his head in to see the source of the fuss.

"Ho," he said. "Seems like it's time for Dad to go home and get some rest."

"No," both Way and Marley snapped.

The doctor backed out of the room and Waylon closed the door. As soon as it shut, Marley began to cry.

"I know you think this isn't your fault," she said, shushing the baby. "But I'm mad at you."

"What do you mean?" He felt himself panicking at the thought of her anger, pawing at his pocket for his Zippo, desperate for a cigarette.

"You've been *gone*, Waylon. In here." She pointed to his chest. "Not just today, but ever since we moved in with your family. It's like you think it's every man for himself in that house."

She was right. This had been the tacit vow between him and his brothers, one he'd assumed Marley understood. Everyone felt lonely in the great house, even when they were together. Waylon wanted to fall to his knees. This wasn't how he'd imagined the birth of his first child at all.

"I'm so sorry, Mar," he said. "So, so sorry."

"I'm *not* doing this alone, Waylon. Do you understand me?"

"You aren't alone," he tried. "And you won't be alone. I promise."

Her exhaustion was a palpable thing in the room, something with its own fingernails and teeth. He watched her sway, her thin hospital gown sliding down her shoulder. Without much thought, he ran his hands under the faucet. Then he saw how filthy they were. He gave them a second thorough scrub up to his elbows, kicked off his boots, and settled on the bed.

"Come here," he said.

She stumbled over and lay down with her head on his chest, his legs on either side of her. The baby finally began to nurse, faintly, before falling asleep.

"Thank God," she said, and Waylon felt her muscles relax.

"Marley," he whispered. "He's beautiful."

"He is."

"Please," Way said. "Tell me everything."

"I named him Theodore Shay," she answered. "Theo, for the name your mother always wanted. And Shay because he held my hand while I pushed."

"Shay was here?"

"He insisted. I sent them home a few hours ago. He'd seen enough for one day."

Way nodded, taking in the smell of her hair—this woman he would love forever, who was now everything she'd always been yet so much more.

"It's a perfect name," he said. "For a perfect baby."

And at that pristine moment, Waylon found himself swaddled in fear. He couldn't top the innocence of this scene, nor could he fix Marley's disappointment in the hours before it. Until now, he'd been dancing from strength to strength. The world a storybook of his own writing. He hadn't cared that his family thought he was a fool for getting married and having a baby at eighteen. Only now did he suspect they might be right.

Waylon had envisioned himself to be better than his own father— emotionally steady and reliable, for starters. Not someone who couldn't be reached when his wife needed him, not someone who needed his ten-year-old brother to act in his stead. Here, he'd already fallen short. How had Mick Joseph, a man who satisfied only his own desires and did what was right in only his own eyes, never missed one of his children's births? Waylon had fashioned his own character out of everything Mick wasn't. Mick was never on time. Never planned ahead. Never took on a lick of anything with even a whiff of domesticity to it, other than making BLTs. Yet he'd outmatched his son right from the beginning.

Way waited for Marley to tell him the rest of the story—the hell of contractions, the race to the hospital, the music of Theo's first cry—but she'd fallen asleep.

The day after tomorrow, Waylon would take them home. He'd try his hand at being not just a father but a dad. He'd rock his boy into his dreams, bathe his skin, soothe his cries. Before that night, Waylon thought he'd been working overtime to prepare for all of Theo's eventual needs. Clothes, food, doctor's visits. College, if Theo was the first in the family to go. Now, as he hugged his wife and newborn close to his chest, he realized those were not the needs of real consequence. Anyone could give a shirt, a bottle, a dollar bill.

Maybe a need wasn't met by what you had but by what you never did. Way never wanted his son to know the gutted feeling laying waste inside him as he sat on that hospital bed—what it meant to try to save someone you love and fail. Waylon never wanted Theo to feel like he needed to save anyone at all.

For tonight, Waylon's family was safe in his arms. Tonight, he could hold close all the things he loved most.

Tomorrow would bring enough worry of its own.

12.

A late August heat wave and drought followed Theo's birth. Waylon did his best not to panic about needing to be two places at once: on the roof while the weather was good, and at home with his infant and healing wife. His lifestyle afforded no sick days, no parental leave. They were losing time before work would need to slow for the winter, and Waylon wanted a backlog of new leads ready to go in spring. Rain was a blessing and a blight—with it, he couldn't finish a job he'd already sold. Without it, no leak could be found for him to sell a job at all.

The contradiction of it felt a lot like the paradox of new fatherhood. When Waylon was gone, he felt he should be at home. When he was at home, he felt like he was in the way. He couldn't nurse the baby, which seemed to be the only thing Theo wanted to do. So he kept up the cold calls from the apartment's private line while rocking Theo's bassinet with his foot. He tried to sell every potential customer on the importance of preventative measures. No matter his efforts, they just didn't bite. By the time Theo was four weeks old, he still hadn't sold any work.

Way had gotten into such a funk about it that Marley finally shoved him out of the house with the baby carriage.

"Take a walk around town to clear your head," she said. "A *long* walk."

It was a sunny afternoon, and the lavender phlox in Ann's flower bed smelled like honey as Waylon made his way along the bumpy sidewalk. He headed toward the car dealership Joseph & Sons had redone last spring, and then the post office, and then the pizza place that had closed a few years ago, and that was when it hit him. This was the first time Waylon had been alone with his son.

Waylon was a father.

He stopped beneath an oak tree and bent to get a closer look at his baby. Theo gazed up at him, his eyes like two black marbles. Waylon wasn't certain Theo could see him, but he felt the keen disappointment in Theo's stare, even so.

"I'm trying, pal," Waylon said. "I swear."

Then Way kept on, taking a left past the Presbyterian church that badly needed a new roof, but the members couldn't agree to spend the money on it. Waylon saw Pastor Hollis gazing unhappily out the sanctuary window, the crosses on his cuff links glinting in the sun. He startled as Waylon strolled by with a newborn in tow.

The preacher watched him a moment, and Way knew how strange he appeared, pushing a stroller while dressed in his work clothes without a job prospect in sight, smack in the middle of the day, when less than six months earlier, if someone had seen him in the street they would have phoned his mother to tattle that he'd skipped school. There was unmooring freedom now, and responsibility, and a tangible awkwardness when he crossed paths with someone from his youth who didn't know whether to treat him as an adult or a child. Way nodded at the pastor and continued onward, past the grocery store they'd repaired about three years back, when he and Baylor had just started helping their father in the summers.

He'd felt such pride then, taking up his father's work. "Roofing," Mick had said to his children when they were young, "is a family thing." Way's father viewed the business as a kind of inheritance for his sons, and his mother saw it as a problem for them to solve. Waylon still didn't know which one it was.

"Listen," Way said to Theo, who had stuck all the fingers on his left hand into his mouth. "You don't ever have to roof a day in your life if you don't want to. Okay?"

Theo popped his fist out of his mouth and beamed at his dad. It didn't matter that he was too little to offer a true grin, or that he'd likely just soiled his diaper. The smile still cracked open Waylon's heart like an egg.

They'd made something good, Way and Marley—no matter how young they were, or how quickly they'd rushed in. Evidence of it appeared right before him. They could do the same for the business, too. Theo cooed in his carriage as Waylon left the business cards Marley had tucked into his wallet at the chiropractor's office and the hardware store, and then he turned toward home. The walk had done the trick to break him of his foul mood.

Waylon often prided himself on discerning what people needed. Turned out, his wife was even better at it than he. Somehow, his Marley had known.

By the third week in September, the rain had come. A hurricane hit near the tail end of the season, spewing heavy winds and rain from Youngstown to the south of Pittsburgh. Mick slapped his thigh and ran out into the street, soaking himself. Even Baylor, who hadn't congratulated Marley or Waylon on the birth of their baby, trudged to the porch's front step to witness the downpour.

Marley watched them from the upstairs window of the apartment, where she trotted Theo back and forth. He didn't love to nap. Marley had only recently stopped bleeding into her underwear every time she paced the apartment with him, trying to put him to sleep. She found herself awake at night, anticipating his cries, hearing them even when he was silent. For all the speeches she'd given Waylon, she felt terrified to let the baby wake him. What if he fell from a roof somewhere, after being up all night? She couldn't stand the thought. Told herself Waylon could take over once winter came, and she'd get a break.

For now, she eyed the phone like it might sprout wings and fly away. *Ring*, she willed it. *Ring*.

"Why do you keep staring at the phone?" Shay asked, who was sprawled on the couch with a comic book.

Elise didn't approve of Shay's obsession with Wolverine, so Marley snagged him a new installment each time she saw one at the grocery store. He hated school, and some days he skipped without Elise's knowledge and spent it with Marley. He filled her in on the comics, they watched *Days of Our Lives* at one in the afternoon, and they ate spaghetti straight out of the pan.

"Your mother is going to find out you're not going to class," she answered.

He tossed the comic book onto the coffee table. "I'll take my chances."

She laughed, glancing away from the receiver. "Why don't you like it?"

Shay tipped his head against the arm of the couch, and a blond curl fell onto his forehead. "Every teacher thinks I'm trouble because of my brothers. They give me 'the look,' like they've already got me figured out. I'm warned against fighting even before I've done anything wrong. If they won't give me a fair shot, why should I give them one?"

Marley couldn't argue. As the daughter of a single mother, she knew what it was to be held down by someone else's uninformed opinion.

Just then, the phone rang. Marley handed the baby to Shay and asked him to go into the bedroom and shut the door. Then she sat at one end of the kitchen table with her notepad, picked up her pen, and answered the phone.

"Joseph and Sons Roofing Company, this is Marley speaking. How can I help you?"

First, it was the chiropractor's office, asking for Waylon to come give them a quote. Then, the phone rang again. The shoe store in the next town over had sprung a leak, and a cookie factory just outside Pittsburgh had water dripping into its batter vat. Marley arranged visits for all three of the Joseph men. She'd pass the information on to Waylon, who would farm it out to his father and brother. He was very careful about not mentioning her involvement in the business to his family, as if they believed a woman's presence might ruin it.

The last call of the day came from Pastor Hollis, who had found—as all three Joseph men had predicted—a leak in the slope of his roof, just below the bell tower.

"I can send Mick or Waylon to take a look next week and give you a price," Marley said.

"I was wondering"—the pastor swallowed—"if you could come instead."

"Me?" Marley sounded aghast, even to herself. "Why?"

"I'll be honest." He sounded tired. "The church building committee is full of women who don't trust your father-in-law. Instead, they mentioned you."

"They?"

"Ann." He sighed. "It was Ann who suggested you."

"I see."

Marley knew it couldn't be her roofing prowess that brought her into Ann's mind. She suspected Ann wanted to catch her alone.

"I'll bring my associate," she said. "This Tuesday at nine."

And just like that, Marley had scheduled her first sales call.

The following Tuesday at eight forty-five, Marley stood on the front porch of the great house, preparing to hand Theo over to Elise just as they'd agreed, with a blanket, a bag of diapers, and pumped breast milk for the fridge. He was just over a month old—with a juicy glut of rolls beneath his chin and dressed in a dashing onesie that had a necktie stitched on the front—and she'd never left him with anyone other than Way. The roofers were out for the day, laying down a fresh tube of rubber on top of the cookie plant.

Stoic, Elise took the baby and the bag. She set the bag down in the hall, next to the pair of low heels she always kept by the door.

"Marley," she said. "I need you to know that I cannot watch your child every week."

Even though Marley had long ago given up on Elise showing her any display of affection, the words still slit her across the throat.

"Elise," Marley said. "I never asked—"

"I've raised my children, and I did it on my own," she went on. "You need to do the same."

Marley was so pummeled by a wave of hurt she'd never felt before that she only managed two words. "Never mind."

Elise had rejected not only Marley, but now her son. She took her boy from his grandmother's arms, grabbed the bag from the floor, and strapped the baby into the Chevy Citation before driving to pick up Jade at her apartment above her shop.

And that was how Theo went on his first sales call, too.

Marley, Jade, and Theo showed up at the church's front door at 8:59 a.m., in matching T-shirts that Marley had ironed letters onto the night before. JOSEPH & SONS, they read across the back, though neither Mick Joseph nor any of his sons were present.

"I know nothing about roofs," Jade said.

"Fake it till you make it," Marley replied.

The pastor appeared at the entryway with a torrent of women around him, all of them displeased. Ann was at the helm, dressed in a sweater that was too warm for the day, a tiny notebook clutched in her hand. Each of the women began talking at Marley, and she braced herself for words of judgment, looks of disdain. She'd grown accustomed to them in town in the last ten months, as everyone watched her uterus expand. Yet those accusatory glances didn't come.

"Marley," Ann said, touching her shoulder. "Look at you, out and about, so soon after the baby."

Her gaze said something entirely different. Marley was ready to find out what she wanted, but then the questions began. A woman with red hair stepped forward.

"Do you nurse Theo when you need to take a work call, or use a pacifier?"

"What do you do when you need to be away for a few hours and your breasts start to leak?" asked someone else.

At that, Hollis looked ready to faint.

"How did you have time to design those fancy mailers for Jade's shop?" asked a third.

These curious ladies, six in total, comprised the building committee. It appeared to be all frilly decorations, Christmas pageantry, baptisms, and the like. This was a reality of women's work that Jade also faced daily in her job as a cosmetologist—it was seen as ornamental, as degraded as it was essential. Now the church women had a leak and they wanted to make a good decision—and they didn't want Hollis's help to make it.

Immediately Marley understood two things. First, she was no longer seen as an unwed mother in this church, as she'd once been. Now she was a lot like them. Second, Marley realized they hadn't wanted to deal with Mick because he treated this place like a building. These women thought of it as a home. And like with a home, they had a budget to keep. No housewife would spend more on repairs than she had to.

Waylon taught Marley a trick on their drives, as they sleuthed for roofs, how pale streaks on a slope revealed the pathways water took, and what cracks might lie beneath.

"It's pretty," Marley had said then.

"It's leaking," Way had answered.

Because of the steeple and the bell tower, Waylon had told her this kind of job was complex enough to net a high five-figure profit when the roof was replaced. But Marley could see they weren't ready to spend that kind of cash.

Together they went out into the churchyard and shielded their eyes from the sun. Marley spotted the problem—the slope in the roof, next to the steeple with the bell, had all the water running straight down its joins. When it stormed, it flooded at the weak spot and caused a leak.

"Is there an easier way to get up there?" Marley asked. It had to be five stories up, at least. Jade held Theo beside her.

Ann nodded. "There's an attic in the back of the sanctuary above the locked counting room. You can get to it from there."

They sat beneath a cherry tree and took turns holding the baby.

"The way I see it, you have two options." Marley parroted words she'd heard Waylon use on the phone, with more confidence than she felt. "That roof will cost at least five figures to replace." The women began to squawk. "Or, I can seal the leak with roofing cement and put up a piece of flashing by the bell tower to redirect the water. It's not a permanent fix, but the patch will buy you some time."

"There's something to be said for patching, isn't there?" Ann asked the group.

"How much?" asked the woman holding Marley's son.

"Five hundred bucks," she answered incorrectly, without a doubt.

Jade's head swiveled toward her, her eyes wide. Marley should have stopped and consulted with her husband. Yet ravenously, she needed these women—Elise's peers and her best friend, Ann—to respect her. She wanted them to coo to her mother-in-law about how sure-footed she was, how clear-eyed. How sufficient, all on her own.

"On one condition," Marley added, to bring home the sale. "You'll hire us when you're ready to redo the whole roof."

They looked among themselves, then back to Marley. "Sold," Ann said, and she pulled Marley aside into the parking lot.

"We'll get you the check as soon as the work is complete," Ann said.

Marley frowned. "Tell me why you really called me."

Ann's neck went pink. "I can't think what you mean," she said.

"I think you can," Marley answered.

Ann blinked, pulled her sweater close. "I know Elise could use the money. You all could."

"And you don't want to deal with Mick."

Ann said nothing.

"Why." Marley spoke the word as a demand.

Ann's mouth pressed into a line. "I know you saw us that day at the park."

"And you're trying to bribe me? Now?"

"I'm asking you to remember the truth often isn't what people care to believe, especially Elise."

"And what is the truth?" Marley asked.

"That I'd like to keep Elise as my friend, no matter how much I have always despised her husband."

This stopped Marley right where she stood. So Ann could also see it— the way all of the Josephs worked to keep this man from falling apart.

"All right," Marley said. "I'll patch the roof."

They shook on it, and Ann touched her on the shoulder. "The Josephs are lucky to have you as a part of the family," she said.

A part of the family. Marley smiled, but there was pain in it. It was the first time she'd heard it said, and it hadn't come from the woman she'd hoped it would.

The next morning, Marley strode across the floor of the apartment. She knew it was creaking, knew Baylor was just below her and probably still in bed. Jade, her fellow entrepreneur, was on her way over to help figure out how the hell to attach flashing to a roof. The bell tower was so narrow, Marley doubted both of them would fit.

She could have asked Waylon for assistance, but Marley didn't want to. She wanted something of her own that wasn't a dirty diaper or a burp cloth, a flag she could plant to prove to herself that she was still visible to the rest of the world.

Truth was, her conversation with Ann had terrified her. Marley couldn't think of even one reason why her mother-in-law would need money. And yet Elise's best friend had gone behind her back because of it. There was such love in the act, and also such betrayal. Could that be true of Marley one day, if she ended up like Elise?

Theo fussed, and she bounced him, and Shay walked through the door in a pair of slippers, parachute pants, and an Air Jordan T-shirt that belonged to Patrick. Marley scouted him like a predatory bird, and he blushed.

"I'll go to school tomorrow," he said. "I swear."

"Oh." Marley came to herself. "It isn't that. I was wondering if you knew how to attach flashing to a roof."

Shay laughed, as if it were obvious. "You could just use a staple gun."

"Could you find one in your dad's workshop? Along with some roofing cement?"

Shay scratched his jaw. "Depends."

"On?"

He grinned. "On whether I get to come wherever you are going."

Shay was so dimpled, so sweetly baby-faced, that Marley hardly had it in her to say no. Besides, she was reluctant to ask any other Joseph for help, let alone her husband. She wanted them to be shocked when she brought in a five-hundred-dollar check of her own.

Elise, especially.

"All right," Marley said. "You win."

Shay flew off in search of some copper flashing and a staple gun. When Jade arrived, Marley broke it to her that she'd be relieved of roofing that day.

"Oh, thank God," she said.

Jade took Theo and his car seat with her to the salon. Then Shay and Marley set off toward the church in her Chevy Citation, where one of the deacons had left the counting room unlocked. It was early yet, and Marley didn't want to draw a crowd. Pastor Hollis hadn't even arrived for the day from the manse next door.

She and Shay pulled down the attic stairs by a dangling string, teetered up with their bucket of tools in tow, and found themselves on a small platform in a musty attic full of new polyester choir robes lying in a nest on the floor. Someone, it appeared, had tried to dye them purple, and the experiment had gone poorly.

"Smells like somebody got a bad perm in here," Shay said. "Why would anyone store these in an attic?"

He pulled the collar of his shirt up over his nose. Slowly, they walked the planks toward the other side of the attic.

"Careful," Shay warned, tapping his foot lightly against the plaster on either side of the beam. "If we lose our balance, we'll fall straight through."

Marley found notches against the side of the opposite wall that formed a ladder to the bell tower, which had a ten-inch ledge for standing along the outside. Shay Baby scrambled up first, popped off the scuttle, and straddled the tower's wooden edges.

"It's tight up here, Mar," he said.

She nodded and handed up their bucket, followed by a thin rectangle of flashing. Then she climbed up next to Shay and clipped him with a cord and a carabiner to a pillar of the bell tower before clipping herself. As she balanced on the rim and gazed down the fierce slope to the top of a cherry tree, she cursed.

"Shay," she said, her palms wet. "This is the stupidest thing I've ever done."

"You're still young," he called back. "Plenty of time to do something even stupider."

Terrified, she let out a hoarse laugh. Then she took the caulking gun filled with cement, stepped onto the roof, and squeezed it into the crack. Shay handed her the flashing, and she bent it into the trouble spot. It reached toward the gutter, where the water could flow right over the soft patch of roof on its way to the earth. She lunged over it, grabbed the stapler, and went to town on the copper. Used a whole sleeve of fasteners, then went through a second. When she'd finished, she caught the dull glint of the sun in the metal, the spread of Mercury's landscape over her shoulder, and she swelled with pride.

"The copper looks pretty," Shay said as they shimmied down to the attic and crossed the beams back to the platform by the hatch.

Now, with firm ground beneath her, Marley let out a scream and pumped her fist into the air. The town looked shrunken from the height of the bell tower, small enough for Marley to hold bits of it in the palm of her hand. Hardly anyone got to see these streets from the view Marley just had, including Elise Joseph.

"I did it," she said, catching her breath. "I fucking did it." She stopped and glanced at Shay. "Sorry. Language."

But Shay wasn't listening. Instead, he'd trained his eyes on the heap of purple choir robes. "Marley," he said. "Look."

She crouched close to the pile but couldn't see a thing out of place.

"No." He pointed. "There."

Next to the pile, against the wall, sat a pair of maroon pumps with low heels. They looked just like Elise's, and the suspicion on Shay Baby's face told Marley he knew she knew it, too.

"Those could belong to anyone, pal."

"But they don't."

He picked up a shoe and examined the sole, which had recently been replaced. Elise refused to throw out any pair of heels. She had them repaired by a cobbler, which was a profession Marley hadn't known existed until she met her mother-in-law.

Marley could have told Shay the shoes might have been tossed up there by mistake, that Elise liked to take them off when she counted the Sunday offering, or that most women in town owned a pair just like them. Shay might have been the baby of the family, but he wasn't naive. He'd always seen Marley in her rawest moments: in the hospital, bearing a son; in a bell tower, fixing a roof. He deserved her honesty.

"You're right," she admitted.

The more Marley looked at those shoes, daintily paired just as they would have been on the mat by the front door to the great house, the more Marley understood that her rooftop triumph had been premature. Even here, in a dusty old attic, Elise had a voice. Even here, near the highest point in town, Marley had been the one to follow.

You think you're doing something so new? those shoes seemed to taunt. *Think again.*

13.

When Marley stopped at Jade's hair salon to pick up Theo an hour later, she had no idea about the cobwebs stuck to her ponytail. She leaned against a box full of Barbicide in the back corner, next to the closet where Jade kept the extra awapuhi shampoo and her collection of pink rattail combs. The cobweb caught the fan's breeze and danced like a thread.

"Foul," Jade hissed, and pointed to the shampoo chair.

Marley slid the car seat where Theo slept to a spot beside the sink and sat down in a cushy vinyl chair. Tilted her head back onto the dip in the cold porcelain as Jade ran her hands through her long tresses.

"When was the last time you had a haircut?" Jade turned on the warm water, and it purred as it met Marley's scalp. She closed her eyes.

"It's been ages."

It was certainly before she met Waylon over a year ago now. All these things she'd done since then—moved to a new town, pitted two brothers against each other, got married, helped launch a beauty salon—and now Marley had the hair of a mother. She'd still felt like a girl when she found out she was pregnant, on her wedding day, and even the day Theo was born. But standing on that rooftop, wielding a giant stapler, she'd finally birthed herself into a grown woman.

Jade shampooed the cobwebs away and rubbed her temples in slow circles. This small act felt like therapy, the balm she used to feel late at night on the couch with Ruth. She missed sitting with her mother, breathing in butter and vanilla. Ruth had visited a few times since Theo's birth, but their time together was never long enough. The hours got swallowed by everything the baby needed now, and not what Marley needed.

Jade added conditioner, and the air filled with the scent of coconut. It smelled like what Marley's life might have been—suntan lotion and magazines left by the side of a swimming pool, fruity drinks beneath a hot sun that cooled her till the last drop. College and parties, dreams and downtime.

"How are you feeling about the salon?" Marley asked.

"Good, mostly." Jade's hands idled in Marley's hair. "But I keep wondering what it's going to take for me to feel secure. I still have nightmares about it disappearing at any minute."

"Do you want to send out another mailer?" Marley asked.

Jade shook her head. "It isn't that. I'm booked solid for a few weeks. I think this just might be what it feels like to set out on my own."

Marley nodded. "You remember what you said to me when I found out I was pregnant?" she asked. "That I wasn't alone because I had you? You have me, too." Marley smiled up at Jade's upside-down face on the other side of the sink. "Besides, you always have roofing as a plan B."

"Somehow I think it would be easier for me to teach you how to cut hair than for me to learn how to roof."

Marley laughed. "Maybe."

Jade rinsed and directed Marley to her chair. It was just the three of them in this small space with a hand-painted sign Marley had helped hang over the door. SHEAR SUNRISE, it read simply, in bold print. Inside the shop, the two of them had painted the walls stark white, with hot pink and gold accents, and black silhouettes of palm trees by the magazine rack. Jade had fought for this place of her own, and Marley fought beside her. Gifts like this could get ruined at merciless speed—by rain or wind, by

recession, by reasons no one could predict. Marley and Jade were both pi-
oneers in spirit and in deed, and neither of them knew how long it would
last.

Jade parted Marley's hair down the middle and began to comb.

"Tell me the truth," Marley said. "Is it time for a mom cut?"

Jade eyed her in the mirror. "If I ever give you a mom cut, I will burn
myself at the stake."

They laughed and Jade began to trim, snipping off the old edges Marley
had before she'd ever met any of the Josephs.

"Jade," Marley began. "I did something kind of bad."

Jade snorted. "You mean other than galloping up a roof today?"

"Yes."

Jade grinned. "Go on."

"You know how I've been helping Waylon with his mailers, just like I
helped you?"

Jade nodded.

"Well, I've been making phone calls, too."

"So?" Jade snipped, and split ends fell to the floor.

"I've been introducing myself as the vice president of the company."

Jade dropped the scissors. "You what?"

"It was the only way I could get the owners to talk to me. A few of the
secretaries told me I'd have a hard time getting through without a title."

"Well, you gave yourself a good one."

Theo began to stir.

"I put it in the letters I mailed, too." Marley hid her face in her hands.
"Fake it till you make it, right?" When she looked up, Jade was gaping at
her in the mirror. "What?"

"I was just thinking how pissed Baylor is going to be."

Jade laughed, Theo whimpered, and Marley glimpsed with dread the
gravity of what she'd done.

"What the fuck is this?"

The same words erupted from two brothers' mouths the following
afternoon. One blasted from the kitchen, and the other from the porch.

Marley looked up at the echo from her spot on the floor of the living room in the great house, where she sat with Theo and his tiny plastic rattle that was shaped like a hammer. Elise had meat loaf in the oven. Mick was completing a crossword in his easy chair. It was cold that day, and Shay had started his own fire in the fireplace with a few logs of oak, a Zippo, and some dryer lint. The heat thrust itself against Marley's back like a burn.

Flanking her on either side, Baylor held up one of her letters, and Waylon hoisted a copy of that morning's local newspaper.

He unfolded it to display the front-page story. It featured a huge picture of her straddling her own flashing on the steep church roof, alongside the headline:

PASTOR HIRES WOMAN TO FIX LEAK

"Oh, no," was all Marley said.

"What were you thinking?" Waylon yelled. He'd never shouted at her before. "You have on no hard hat, no tether."

Marley chose not to tell him that there had been a rope, and his ten-year-old brother had been on the other end of it.

"Christ," he said. "You just gave birth less than two months ago."

Mick sauntered over and examined the photograph. Tilted his head. "Looks like she did a decent job."

"I don't give a shit about the roof, Dad." Waylon's face looked both manic and spent.

"Language," Mick chided.

"Well, look at this." Baylor waved the letter around. "She's been sending this out on her girly letterhead, telling people she's the vice president of Joseph and Sons."

At that, Mick laughed so violently he had to fall back on his easy chair. Marley felt her whole body begin to shrink. She clutched Theo to her chest.

"You." Bay pointed the letter at Waylon. "You told me she would not fuck with the business. Now look."

The brothers started to argue, even as Mick kept laughing, even though

Marley tried to interrupt. It was useless, until Elise sauntered into the room. She was wearing a pair of brown slacks with her hair down—it looked lovely and windswept, almost as if she hadn't bothered to brush it.

"Enough," she said, and the room stilled. "Let Marley speak her piece." She nodded at Marley, stern curiosity in her eyes, and Marley looked to Baylor.

"Where did you get that letter?" she asked.

"From the rail yard office." He sneered at the paper. "It says 'rain down on us' across the top. What a stupid slogan."

"It's *not* stupid," Waylon cut in.

Marley pointed at Baylor. "You were at the rail yard for your appointment today?"

He jeered at her. "Of course, for my appointment."

"Which you got because of that letter."

Theo dropped the rattle to the floor.

"Hold on, now," Mick interjected. "Our reputation speaks for itself."

"Maybe," Marley said, picking up the rattle. "But that's not how you sold the job."

Baylor laughed. "How on earth could you ever know that?"

"Because I called the rail yard secretary, and she put the letter on top of the building manager's mail pile." Marley lifted her eyebrows. "She liked the girly letterhead."

Three men stared at her.

"Same goes for the refrigerator warehouse, the potato chip factory, and the cookie manufacturer. And the church"—she pointed to the paper—"will hire us now when they're ready for a new roof."

"*Us?*" Mick repeated, erupting in laughter again.

"Wait a minute." Baylor scratched his head with the bill of his ball cap. "I thought Way was the salesman."

"He is." Marley shifted Theo to her shoulder. "I've just sold a few jobs of my own, is all. In addition to making sure we get paid so we can balance the books."

"Balance the books." Bay was heated. "Will you listen to this?"

At the mention of money, Mick finally sobered. He regarded Marley with scrutiny in his stare, like a stranger had set foot in his house. Beyond his left shoulder, the clouds cleared and sunlight broke through the window. Marley noticed a film of dust had gathered on the Tiffany lamps at the edge of the room. It wasn't like Elise to be untidy. As if she'd read Marley's thoughts, she took up her feather duster and began to swipe the dirt away.

Before Marley had set foot on the church roof, she'd imagined a more vengeful moment of discovery—one where she could hand Elise the five-hundred-dollar check and say, *See what I did? I did this without you.* She thought she'd feel justified; she thought she'd feel proud. But no one here was going to rescue Marley from the choices she'd made. She'd have to rescue herself.

"You don't think it's important to turn a profit every year?" Marley asked Baylor as she looked away from Elise.

"We do the job, get paid, cover expenses." Baylor ticked them off one by one with his fingers. "Then split the rest three ways. Four, when Shay is eighteen. Is that so hard?"

"Wait a minute, now," Mick said, strutting toward her with his pencil in his fist. He lanced Marley with his eyes. "A secretary is just the thing we need."

"A secretary," Waylon and Marley repeated in unison.

Marley knew she must have felt more insulted at some other point in her short life, but at that moment she couldn't recall it.

"I think," Elise cut in as she tucked her duster into the hall closet, "that it's time for dinner. Marley, help me with the plates."

Something unspoken passed between the two women of the Joseph family—a certain signal that declared there could be only one primary wife and mother in this house. And it wasn't Marley.

Relegated again to the confines of her mother-in-law's domesticity, Marley stomped into the kitchen to tell this woman who'd left her favorite pair of shoes in an attic that these men could fill their own damn plates. She opened her mouth, but Elise spoke first.

"Let Mick call you whatever he wants." She spoke soft and low. "Then you can do as you please. Sell your jobs, call yourself the CEO. He'll never know the difference."

Marley had prepared for Elise's cold manner, a dismissive request to place the silverware. She hadn't been prepared for the two of them to be whispering like a pair of hostages.

"I'm not a secretary, Elise." She didn't know what else to say.

"There's dignity in that job." Elise sliced through the loaf. "Or have you forgotten?"

"Forgotten what?"

"That your sales are because of secretaries."

Elise was right, but Marley couldn't help herself. She felt wounded and she wanted to be mean. "Are you missing any shoes, Elise?" she asked.

If Elise was caught in something, she betrayed no signs of it.

"I used to be just like you," she said instead.

Marley started to feel sick. She had no idea what Elise meant. From the dining room, Baylor moaned of presumed starvation.

"Get your own plate," Marley sniped before escaping with Theo out the side door.

She ate dinner in the apartment alone that night. Waylon was angry, she knew. What she'd done on the church roof was foolish. But hadn't it worked? Hadn't she felt a live-wire jolt of her true self, even for an instant? She hadn't done it for show, hadn't even done it to prove she could. She'd done it because she wanted to belong at the Joseph family table, and she was still trying to earn her seat.

It had felt fair and just, to give to this family instead of take. They hadn't wanted it.

Marley put Theo in a rocker in the bathroom and ran herself a bath. Locked the door. She wasn't entirely sure it was safe to bathe so soon after delivery, but she didn't care. In the mirror, her body looked like someone else's—breasts aching and full, skin that had stretched to make room for a new life and now had nowhere to go. Marley was changing inside, too. She'd felt it on top of the roof. She was pushing to stay where she wanted to be. Fighting to make this story her own.

She tied up her auburn hair and submerged her shoulders, rinsed away the sneers her in-laws had painted on her. It was then Marley realized Shay, her trusted confidant, had been there the whole time and hadn't said a word. Right then, he felt like her only friend in the house.

The apartment door opened, and she heard Waylon call her name. Soon he was at the bathroom door, knocking.

"Can I come in?" he asked.

"No," she answered.

"Please?"

"It's locked, and I got the message from your family, loud and clear." She heard Way sigh. "Please just open the door."

Marley grumbled and pulled the tub drain. Then she wrapped herself in a towel and let Waylon in.

"Theo is finally sleeping," she said quietly as she turned her back. "Don't wake him."

Way nodded, came and stood behind her so he could snag her eye in the mirror. "Did I ever tell you about my first time on the roof?" he asked.

Marley shook her head.

"It was the grocery store. Barely thirty feet up. I puked all over the side, and someone had to come out and clean off the sidewalk."

Marley smiled, but she started to cry. She hated how much of it she'd been doing lately.

"Stop trying to make me feel better," she said.

"Wouldn't dream of it. But please, let me say this. What you did? It took balls, babe. I respect it." He hooked his chin on her shoulder, grazed his lips against her neck. "If you want to sell a job, sell it. You want to use pink letterhead, be my guest. Just tell me."

"The letterhead wasn't pink."

"You get my meaning."

Marley sighed. "Mick and Baylor will never be okay with it."

Waylon shifted his head to the side, considering. "Money has a way of soothing all wounds."

She leaned back into him and closed her eyes. He smelled like rubber and meat loaf.

"If you want to go up on a roof, I'll take you," he said, his voice soft. "But promise you won't do it alone. Nobody should."

"I'd prefer to never do it again," she said. "Trust me."

He laughed and ran his mouth along her shoulder blade. "How long till I can take you to bed?" he whispered.

A memory lived between them of what they'd been before—rain on the windowpane, a tangle of sheets, his hands in her hair.

"A week or two." She reached back and cradled his head with her fingers.

He groaned and kissed her cheek. "I'll see myself out." Way grinned at the sound of his wife's laughter. "And Mar, I'll take the baby tonight. You roofed. You need a night off." He lifted Theo in his arms and disappeared into the living room.

That night, after rocking Theo back to sleep for the third time, Way pushed open the kitchen window of their tiny apartment, stuck his head out, and lit a cigarette. He didn't do it often; Marley would kill him if she knew. But judging by her church roof stunt, she was going to be the death of him one way or another.

Waylon flicked his Zippo open and shut. Open, shut.

He was already so tired his skin hurt. At dinner, he barely formed a coherent thought. His father went on about all the filing Marley could handle now, as if she were destined to wrangle the mess of records in his office.

"I've been trying to get Elise to organize it for years," Mick said, his expression libertine against the flames as he leaned his arms into the mantel above the fireplace. "But she never wanted anything to do with it."

Baylor bitched about the rail yard. "I got caught with my ass out," he cried, after having no idea about the mailers Marley had sent. "Made me look like a wage worker in my own damn company."

He said it as if it were the worst thing—as if it weren't laughable. They already knew what no one had admitted: Joseph & Sons wouldn't pay Marley a dime for what she'd done.

Roofers could make a lot of money and make it fast—but they had to spend a lot, too—crane rentals, materials, insurance, travel. The more they worked, the more difficult it became to tell when, and if, they were breaking even. Waylon had meant to tell Marley that evening in the bathroom, but he couldn't bring himself to. His family had flattened her spirit, and he wouldn't stand for it. Not now, not ever.

He just didn't know what to say, was the thing.

To the rest of the Josephs, Marley was considered part of him. His to corral, his to answer for. Any wages she earned—any commission, if they ever had such a thing—would come from his cut. He would tell her, he promised himself. But not tonight, and not tomorrow, either.

Marley did not go on the roof again. She had no time, even if she wanted to. The older Theo got, the more he fussed, wanted to be held, courted around, eager to see his patch of the world. Already he wanted to crawl to places his muscles couldn't take him. Marley had become an expert on strapping him to her chest and performing deep lunges around the apartment while following up on the letters she'd sent, answering calls on Waylon's leads, and preparing for insurance certification audits. Her dealings at the church had proved that if she wanted any part in the Josephs' way of life, she had to hold it all. Make recompense somehow for her presence and never complain.

I used to be just like you. Elise's words haunted her, along with what they might mean.

Theo had grown accustomed to the constant timbre of her voice, the jostling. After an hour, it lulled him to sleep. Marley knew what all the books said. Put that baby down, in his crib, away from her. Let him cry till he learned. And she understood it—she did. She just didn't have time for it. Couldn't have a baby wailing in the background of every call. She knew she was skirting a line already, at just eighteen years old. She feared customers flocked to the image of a young woman at work, cutely staking her claim like Rosie the Riveter, but they'd flee from the reality of a teenage mother with a baby who needed her. There was endless need everywhere she looked: on the counter, in the sink, at the bottom of a full laundry basket. So she did what she could to appear other than what she was: she made her calls in the stairwell during Theo's brief naps, and she whispered on the phone. Always, she prayed he wouldn't wake.

No one in Mercury was short on advice. *Let him cry. Don't let him cry. Breastfeed. Give him formula. Sleep him on his stomach. Sleep him on his back.* What she was short on, other than Waylon and Shay, was someone willing to give her a break.

She often wondered whether all women were treated this way, as if motherhood were her inevitable blessing and curse, or whether the world was harder on her because she'd become a mother in the wrong way. Yet when she looked at Theo, she knew there was nothing wrong about it. It was everything else that seemed broken and ready to fall apart.

Marley talked to Ruth about it at length on the phone, the only person who could understand. Ruth made the six-hour drive from Maryland about once every six weeks when she had two consecutive days off. Marley ached for her, a young mother who needed her own mother, still.

It was an absence Elise could have easily filled but didn't. She held herself back for reasons Marley suspected had to do with the split loyalties of her second son. Before Marley, Waylon had belonged only to Elise. Now he belonged to them both. Or maybe it was money, or her missing shoes. Elise was a woman who had opened her home and her table, yet not her heart, because she had no room left in it. Her husband and her boys had taken it all.

Marley could see how these men were a whirlwind, tempting her to get swept up among them. And Elise was turning, turning: rescuing Mick's trowel from the floor, scrubbing the tar from his clothes. She kept him from penning editorials for the paper, sending letters to the head coach of the Steelers, banging on the preacher's front door in the middle of the night to discuss Sunday's prelude. It was a full life with so little of Elise in it, save for the romance paperbacks that lined a shelf in the attic apartment, each with a grade written on its spine in permanent marker. A, B−, A+, C, B.

She'd wanted to be an English teacher, but Mick's dreams had come first.

Waylon told Marley his father had come home from Vietnam in tatters—as so many men did that it had already become a cliché. But Elise never treated him like his plight was common, even though it was. To her his pain was singular and deep, whether he spoke about it or not. Mick's well-being would make the family thrive, and so she pieced him back together. She did it so fluidly, so seemingly without effort that Mick assumed everyone else would do it for him, too.

Starting with Marley.

She'd had to start locking the apartment's front door. Ever since Marley's front-page roofing escapades, Mick had no shortage of tasks for her to complete. *Alphabetize my Rolodex. File these records. Order my lunch. Find me some pens.*

A month after her picture had been published in the paper, Mick burst in and yelled for her, even though she was standing right in front of him. Theo wiggled in his bouncer next to her on the floor as she thumbed through an old accounting textbook she'd gotten at the library. Mick slapped a large denim binder on the table where they ate and Marley kept her word processor. Inside it were three hundred water-roughened pages, full of his handwriting.

"This is my ledger," he said.

"Your ledger."

"I want the checks Waylon got for the work we did on the tavern in New Wilmington and the nursing home in Grove City, so I can cash them."

Marley didn't need to open the binder to know the mess that waited inside it. The rest of the Josephs tiptoed around him, fearing the world would end should McKay Joseph ever feel the slightest bit disappointed. Marley felt no such dread.

"No," she said.

Mick had brought her to this point of no return—or maybe Elise had. Marley did not want to bend, and bend, and then break. She could have soothed Mick, or sweetly said, *Let me help you deposit those checks.* But she didn't want to be that version of herself. Not with him.

Do your worst, she wanted to say. *Go ahead.*

"Pardon?" he asked.

"I said no. I'm taking them to the bank."

Mick acted as if he'd never heard the word. His face glowered, anger brewing there for just a moment. Then he blinked a few times, picked up his binder, and slumped out the door, leaving it open behind him.

Marley knew she could push back, and Mick would not explode for one reason. The business, as far as she could tell, was having its best year yet. The weather was turning, they were finishing up the jobs they'd sold, and Waylon had already scouted a string of fresh warehouses on 79, toward Pittsburgh. They'd lined up work through March, weather permitting. The business had a solid salesman, a good roofer, and a man with absurd ideas that sometimes paid off. They also had a woman who did all the tiny, essential tasks none of the men wanted to do—which included telling Mick Joseph no.

Waylon had promised that money had a way of fixing things, and at long last, Joseph & Sons was primed to start rolling it in, hand over fist.

14.

Problem was, they didn't.

Based on the great house and the three vehicles the Joseph family owned, Marley assumed they had a decent amount of cash. More than she and Ruth had ever had, at least. Yet when she went to Mellon Bank across from the courthouse to cash Waylon's checks, she couldn't figure out why there wasn't more money in the business account. The monthly balance was less than they'd brought in for the first half of the year.

Marley had tracked every invoice since she and Waylon were married, as well as the expenses of every job. First, she handwrote every detail in her graph paper notebook. Then she double-checked it with a program on her desktop Macintosh. The answer to the puzzle, she suspected, lay in the tornado of receipts Mick kept in the spare bedroom.

Throughout the fall, she waited for the business account's balance to right itself. It only got worse.

One afternoon, four days before Christmas, Marley took the baby monitor and a notepad with her into Mick's makeshift office during Theo's afternoon nap. The floor was covered in tilting stacks of vinyl records, and

a large wooden desk sat just beneath the window on the far wall, its surface littered with papers. Beside it stood a filing cabinet with every drawer
left open. With trepidation, Marley took a step toward the paper piles.

Mick had developed his own system, strange as it was—totems of invoices and receipts, gathered by year, noted by an index card on the top. It
wasn't disorganized, exactly, but the sheer volume was overwhelming—the
story behind every scrap of paper trapped in the maze of Mick's mind.

Marley sat at the desk and pulled open a drawer. Inside it, she found
two framed photos covered in dust. The first was of Elise and three other
young women who looked just like her—her sisters, Marley figured. As
long as she'd been in Mercury, they'd never come to visit.

The second photo was of Mick and Elise, looking not much older than
she and Waylon. They stood in front of a train caboose with Baylor as an
infant, Mick looking to the right of the camera as if bracing himself for
its flash. There weren't many pictures around the house of them as a newlywed couple, and fewer still of the families they'd come from. What had
happened, Marley wondered, and why were Mick and Elise now so alone?

The receipts waited all around her, like snowdrifts in a storm.

Marley decided to start with last year, 1990, and work her way back.
It didn't take long for the issue to reveal itself. There was no rhyme or reason to the receipts—grocery bills, dry cleaning, Reyers Shoe Store—other
than this: They were all personal. Every single one of them. Mick had been
treating the business funds as his individual checking account, and by the
looks of the room, he'd been doing it for a long time.

At what point had the company income ceased to be Mick's alone and
become something he shared with his sons? Marley wasn't sure.

She became so engrossed in the paper chaos that she didn't notice
someone occupying the doorframe, nor the smell of chicken noodle soup.
When Baylor cleared his throat and Marley glanced at him, she waited for
a snide comment about how she'd need more than pink nail polish to be a
real roofing tycoon. Her face must have been stricken because he offered
no joke.

"What's wrong?" He entered the mess, shut the door behind him, and
placed his mug of soup on the desk.

"Your father," she whispered. "He's been emptying out the business account."

Bay squinted and ran a finger along the scar below his ear. Marley had never noticed it before.

"For what?" he asked.

Marley thought back to her first dinner at the Joseph house, when Mick had rolled a piano into the music room and wooed them all with his songs. It wasn't the only surprise Mick had appeared with in the past year: the old detachable camper he parked in the yard last summer, the pottery wheel and small kiln he'd been tinkering with in the basement. Marley assumed he'd bartered for those things. Mick was always fixing porch steps, whitewashing fences, pouring cement, rerouting pipes. Now, Marley suspected he'd been filching the funds that ought to have been set aside for supplies.

"Bay, with all this money gone, I don't know if we'll have the cash to buy even just the rubber we need for the jobs Waylon's already sold."

Baylor cursed. Picked up his mug of soup, and then set it down again.

"Who has been handling these finances?" Marley asked.

"Dad's buddy from Vietnam."

Marley took out her notepad. "What's his name?"

"Buddy."

She threw down her pen.

"What?" Bay looked innocent. "That's what Dad calls him. Buddy."

"I'm going to need Buddy's phone number." Marley knew that would be the easy part. "Someone has to stop him. Your father."

Baylor grunted.

"I'll talk to Waylon," Marley offered.

Bay smirked. "Waylon won't do shit to stand up to Dad. You know it."

Marley looked at him and waited until Baylor grunted again.

"I'll do it," Bay promised. "But I'm telling you right now he's just going to do it again."

Marley drew a hand through her long hair as she thought. "You could open a second account for the business under your name," she said. "And then funnel Mick's cut to the existing one." She spoke like she knew how to do it, but she didn't. She also remembered how disgusted Baylor had been back in September when she inserted herself into this trinity of Joseph men.

"If you think that's a good idea," she added.

"It is."

Baylor looked so young as he took up his mug again, just nineteen years old, lush-eyed in his thick green sweater and his hair recently trimmed. He stared at her as if he'd recognized something of himself for the first time—that Marley now carried a weight much like his, and it saddened him.

Marley wished she and Baylor could start over. She'd been so concerned with everything she wasn't to him—not his girlfriend or his coworker or even his friend—that she'd never stopped to consider what she was. A sister. Baylor had never had one, just as Marley had never had a brother.

"A new bank account still doesn't solve the problem of the missing funds," she said.

"I'll take care of it," he answered, eyeing a few receipts before folding them into his pocket.

The day after Christmas, a huge repo truck pulled up outside the great house. A crowd had gathered at the obscene beeping, faces peering out of porches from the funeral director's home to Ann and her children standing on their front steps in their pajamas.

Elise wasn't there to witness it. No one had seen her since the night before.

Mick's piano got loaded into the truck, along with two of their ladders, and the camper got attached to the tailgate. Before it pulled away, Baylor handed over the keys to the Camaro he'd spent three years restoring. He scrubbed a hand down his face and coughed, then clapped his hands together in the cold. With Theo bundled in a woolen blanket in her arms, Marley watched Baylor from the far side of the doorway as someone else drove his car away. He tucked a fat wad of bills into his pocket, and the sight of it gutted her.

This was how Baylor loved, she learned that day. It was the only way he knew how. Like it hurt.

Mick sulked in the opposite corner with his arms crossed. He'd left his houndstooth hat inside, and the tips of his ears were red.

"Suck it up, buttercup," Baylor said, slapping him on the back before disappearing into the house.

Waylon found Marley on the porch on his way downstairs from the apartment. Neighbors had funneled back inside their warm houses, and she stared into the empty street. Even Ann had turned away without looking back. Marley could tell Waylon about what she'd seen between Ann and Mick not so long ago, just to have someone to share it with. But why would she, on a day like this—when he'd already found out his dad was a thief?

"Who came to take these things away?" she asked.

Way stood beside her, and she leaned into his warmth. "Baylor knows a guy who takes things for cash," he said.

Christmas that year had become a somber affair. Marley and Waylon returned all their presents, except for Shay's. They'd all chipped in to purchase him a teal drum set—which had sent happy tears streaming down Shay's face when he saw it next to the tree. It had been worth every penny.

Marley knew the whole family needed to save where they could, but she and Waylon hadn't sacrificed the way Baylor had for his father's indiscretions.

"Baylor didn't ask you to sell anything," she said. "Why?"

Way blew into his hands. "Because we have a child."

It had to be more than that, Marley thought. More to what Baylor wanted to spare them from.

"That's hardly fair," she said.

"Life isn't fair." Waylon tucked his fists in his pockets. "My dad always used to say that to us when we were young. He'd do things like give Bay a five-dollar bill, and me a quarter, or vice versa, and say, 'Life isn't fair, boys. Better you learn now.' It was shitty, and we knew it was shitty even then. Baylor would never take the money. He felt the manipulation of the whole thing, even without the words for it. That's the worst thing you can do to Baylor—make him feel like he's been played. This is him telling Mick he'll be damned if he can't put his own money down."

"Do you think Mick gets that?"

"No, I don't." Waylon sighed and pulled up the hood of his jacket. Then he felt around for his Zippo and tried to light it, as he often did when he felt unsettled, even though he promised Marley he was done with cigarettes. The wind was too strong for the flame to catch.

"I think your father is dangerous," Marley said.

She'd thought it for a long time by then, but that day was the first time Marley said it aloud. A blackbird called out as it crossed the sky.

"He's harmless," Way returned, as if he didn't believe it, as if he didn't already know that Mick had two older sons who would bail him out, no matter what he did.

Winter came, and life fell silent. Marley and Waylon stayed away from the inside of the great house. They played Monopoly—Marley liked to use the Scottie dog game piece, and Way the top hat. They rocked Theo to sleep. They laughed at how much Baylor liked chicken noodle soup. And they fell into bed to have sex as quietly as they could. Their mattress sat right above the bathroom the rest of the Josephs used on the second floor, and it squeaked. Marley bit into Waylon's shoulder to keep herself from crying out, and he liked it. Did everything he could to get her to break. It was a game they played, Waylon pushing her to the edge until she could no longer keep it in.

"Shhh," he'd say as he kissed a trail down her stomach. "You'll wake the baby."

And then she'd call him an asshole, and they'd wrestle, and he'd let Marley pin him, and the game began again.

The walls and the floors were thin, even though they pretended the attic was a hundred miles away from the rest of the great house. On cold nights, Marley heard creaks, constant and slow, like someone was pacing through the halls after midnight and into the early morning.

She wondered which of the Josephs was kept awake. It could have been any one of them—Baylor's restlessness, Mick's infinite appetites, or Elise's need to sate them. Even Shay Baby, who slept with his drumsticks, had reason enough for a sleepless night: brothers who had gone before him, setting a path with ditches too deep to ford. Sometimes when Patrick slept over Marley could hear the two of them creeping down toward the chest freezer in the basement, where Elise kept the ice cream.

Marley herself lay awake often while Waylon slept with his arm curled around her. His gold chain glittered in the night, his eyelashes fluttering slightly. She carried so much love in her heart for those who slumbered just within arm's reach—a husband, a son. It frightened her to need them, and to be so needed, even as this was the very kind of love Marley had hoped for. Yet she felt the fragility of it pressing in on her. Life would not always be this serene—not even in the morning.

She had a secret gnawing at her, and it had split itself in two. There was the truth of Mick and Ann, yes, but there was something else. Something all Marley's.

She carried a true hate in her heart for her father-in-law, and it shamed her. It was a secret she harbored, but it was there all the same, whispering her to sleep at night and rousing her at dawn. He'd seen terrible wartime atrocities; she had no doubt. But it wasn't fair, or right, that witnessing such things allowed him to build his own dreams on the backs of his sons. Marley felt this with more conviction than she'd ever had for anything.

She and Waylon needed to get out of the great house. Not because they needed their own space, or separation from the business, but because Marley hated Mick Joseph so much she couldn't stand it. By the end of the year, she'd tell Waylon, they needed to be in a place of their own. Marley clung to that hope, the way Waylon clung to her in his sleep.

15.

Spring of 1992 was wet and busy. The men often worked straight through dinner if the light held. Marley found herself wishing for more cloudy days. She kept up with her mailers and her bookkeeping as Theo began to crawl. He found the dust balls hiding just beneath the oven and pulled Elise's paperbacks right off the shelf. He'd grown plump and jolly, and he loved to roll from one end of the room to the other. Before Theo could even walk, he was trying to climb every chair in the apartment. It became harder to make phone calls, to answer them. Theo always had so much to say. Adorable to the mother in Marley, frustrating as hell to the entrepreneur.

The apartment felt like a cupboard. Too dark, too many items that could tip over and break. Marley drove to Jade's shop every day for lunch just to see another adult. Theo had his own walker there, and he scooted around while Jade cut and colored.

Marley felt more at home between bottles of shampoo and vials of nail polish than she ever had on Hollow Street.

It was lonely sometimes, being a roofer's wife. Way was gone at least one night a week now—for sales calls, for infrared tests, for jobs that needed his attention. *I miss you so much, Mar,* he'd say late at night when he called from his hotel room. *It's killing me.* He felt terrible about it, but they agreed. They needed a place of their own. And for that, they needed money.

Marley had offered to help Jade settle her books for free, so she could practice what she'd read in her old textbooks. Shear Sunrise had a simple setup—one proprietor, rent, supplies, utilities, insurance. Jade had a fine rush of clients just before Christmas, when she'd frosted the heads of half the people in Mercury. When the New Year had hit, Jade declared it was time to put the perms of the 1980s behind her. She perfected the art of feathered bangs and pixie cuts, blond highlights and body waves. Every woman in town had one of the new styles, especially after Jade threw out her crimping iron.

"No more," she said to anyone who requested it. "This fad is done."

Jade was born and raised in town, and her clients trusted her. Mercury had no therapist; Jade was as close as it got. Marley loved watching her best friend work—a boss and a beautician who made hearts new at any hour of the day. While Jade's customers didn't always follow her dating advice—which usually came down to *leave him, for God's sake*—what she told women to do with their hair, they did. And they kept coming back. On a cool April afternoon with "Back to Life" by Soul II Soul playing on the stereo, Marley checked Jade's credits and debits and declared her first year would be a success. It was the little jobs that added up—the lip waxing, the eyebrow tinting, the updos.

"A few more blowouts and you'll be on your way to Jamaica," Marley joked.

The affluent women who frequented Jade's shop every other week to get their hair blow-dried into sleek spheres had husbands with salaried jobs closer to the city, pensions, and reliable paychecks. These ladies did not wear jeans; they wore slacks. Never sneakers, but penny loafers. They had a kind of security neither Marley nor Jade would ever call their own, and yet they wouldn't trade it. The two of them wanted to bet on themselves, just as the Joseph men did.

"You really ought to hire a sitter," Jade mocked, as she'd heard her customers instruct Marley more than once. "One night a week, so you and Waylon can go out to dinner."

Marley handed her half the turkey sandwich she'd brought from home. "With what money?"

Jade took a bite as she leaned against a silhouetted palm tree on the wall. She looked just the same as she had when Marley first offered her a stick of gum almost two years ago, her lush curls piled in a ponytail on top of her head. "You do deserve a night out, though. Let me watch Theo for you."

Marley tried to nod. She longed for a night alone with Waylon. But Theo was so attached to her. To her breasts. He loved to nurse, wouldn't take a bottle, and—despite all the advice she'd received—she nursed him when he was upset. Now it was the only way he knew to soothe himself. Theo gazed at her with his doughy face, reaching a hand to touch her cheek. There was such unfailing love in that gesture, such faith in her. She understood Theo—his moods, his cries, his joy—in ways no one else ever would, the same way Ruth understood her. Marley had yet to disappoint her baby, and she felt it looming.

Jade knew somehow, without her having to say it. "Your anniversary is in about two months. Let's aim for then."

Marley could have kissed her, this friend who cared for her in ways nobody else did. Jade, who believed Marley was capable of anything and yet never expected her to make it on her own.

"Shouldn't you be the one going out on dates?" Marley asked.

"In this town?" Jade scoffed. "I'd rather be alone."

Marley must have looked hurt because Jade set her jaw. "Being single isn't a punishment, you know."

"I know," Marley said. "I just want you to get everything for yourself that you give away."

Jade took another bite of her sandwich. "That reminds me," she said. "You need to let me start paying you for keeping my books."

Marley waved her hand. "Free haircuts and babysitting? I'm getting the better end of the deal." She slipped her arm through Jade's. "Will you give me a perm, though? For old time's sake?"

"Absolutely not." Jade tugged one of Marley's long amber locks. "We are never changing this flower-child hairdo of yours. I don't care if it's out of style."

They laughed, and Theo scooted, and there in that tiny shop on the corner of the street in a forgotten Rust Belt town, Marley felt like she was home.

Marley stayed at Jade's longer than usual that day, and Theo fell asleep in his car seat. She didn't want to go back to the great house, back to her apartment, back to the land of the Josephs, where Elise probably already had dinner warming in the oven. Marley planned to pick up Shay from school at three, so she drove around town and let Theo sleep.

Mercury was becoming home to her. Marley looped past the post office where they let her drop her mailers through the back door, the library where she took Theo for story time on Tuesdays, and the sharp elbow turn in the road that always flooded after a thunderstorm.

Spring was breaking through in lilac buds and daffodil shoots, but winter held on. Tufts of dirty snow clung to curbs, and porch steps, and parking lots. The heat had stopped working in the Citation, and Marley shivered. Theo was bundled in the backseat; she caught a glimpse of him in the rearview mirror. Then her eye snagged something else behind her— someone limping from a snowbank into the intersection. Marley slowed to a stop and turned around.

It was Elise, crossing the road without any shoes. Marley hung a U-turn and stopped right in front of her before jumping out of the car.

"Elise," she said. "What are you doing?"

"I'm out for a walk." Elise looked down. "But I lost my shoes."

Marley stared as Elise stood still in the dirty, cold street. Her jacket buttons were mismatched, as if they'd been done in a hurry. "Where?" Marley asked.

Elise watched her, and blinked, and Marley took her arm.

"Let's get you in the car," she said.

She helped Elise into the passenger seat and saw that Elise's stockings were soaked from the snow. A car honked behind the Citation before swerving around. Marley grabbed an extra blanket from the back and tucked it around Elise's legs and feet.

Something was not right.

"Elise," Marley said. "How old are you?"

Elise huffed. "You already know how old I am."

"Humor me."

"Forty-six."

"And what's your address?"

"That house with the bad bones on Hollow Street?" She approximated a laugh. "Really, Marley. I just stepped out of my shoes. That's all. A fluke thing."

Marley knew, though, that it wasn't the first time.

Because the car had idled too long, Theo began to fuss. Marley pressed the gas, headed for the elementary school. "I'm going to drive for a bit, just so Theo will settle."

Elise did not respond.

They toured the streets of Mercury in silence—the church, with Marley's bit of flashing holding tight. The air smelled like cocoa as they passed the chocolate shop where Marley and Jade liked to sample the mints, and as they drove Marley kept an eye out for Elise's shoes. Elise watched it all, looking caught somewhere between troubled and serene.

Marley had been too frazzled with work and Theo to realize that when she was alone because Waylon was working late, Elise was alone, too. They didn't have dinner together if their husbands weren't present. When Patrick came over, he and Shay ate ravioli with Marley on the couch in her apartment while they played *Duck Hunt* on the Nintendo. Elise never joined them. Marley understood the desire for solitude. What she couldn't grasp was her mother-in-law's need to disappear.

Elise didn't cook for herself, as if she wasn't worth the trouble, and the sadness of it struck down Marley's anger. She ached for dinners together, for what could have been.

"You know," Elise finally said as Marley pulled up into the pickup line at the school. "When you look back at this time, once Theo is grown . . ." She smoothed her blond hair, and Marley noticed how the foundation on her face had settled into the crevices just below her eyes. Slowly, her mascara had begun to bleed.

Marley waited for Elise to say what everyone always said. *You'll miss this.* People called it out to her in passing, as if they'd fallen down a well and the words were just an echo. Marley already felt life slipping away from her, every day a reminder that she no longer called her body her own.

But that wasn't what Elise said.

"When you look back, you'll have so much pride in knowing you did all this yourself."

The line inched forward, car by car.

"Pride." Marley felt herself fume, even though the car was frigid. She started to pick at the French manicure she'd just given herself that morning at the salon.

"Yes." Elise ran a finger against the condensation gathering on the window. "You'll have done it all without any help."

Marley gripped the wheel so hard that bits of it began to pill against her palm. "Is that what you think, Elise? That there's a reward at the end of this? A trophy for my independence? There is no prize for not having any help, I promise you. All I have is constant fatigue and a daily dose of resentment."

Elise appeared unmoved as she watched children file out of the building. Shay and Patrick, who were huddled together over the latest issue of *Wolverine*, separated when Shay spotted Marley's car.

"You have a husband who loves you," Elise said. "That's more than most can say."

Elise had placed Waylon on a pedestal just for being decent. Marley wondered when her standards had sunk so low. She could have argued back, could have claimed Mick loved her, in his own way. But Marley truly didn't know whether he did, or whether he loved anyone but himself and his grand ideas. She'd never even seen Mick truly look at his wife.

Shay swung open the door to the backseat, rocking his green eyes back and forth between Marley and his mother.

"What's wrong?" he asked, and Elise answered without looking his way.

"Nothing, Shay Baby. Now tell us about school."

"Mom," he said. "Your shoes."

Elise's toes were curled against the car's black floor mat, her stockings dirty and wet.

"Oh." Her voice was flat. "They'll turn up."

Marley had never seen Elise's feet. She always wore slippers or pumps. It felt like witnessing something indiscreet, a great embarrassment she wanted to conceal. Shay caught Marley's eye in the rearview as she pulled out of the lot. He was worried, and she was worried, and the rest of the Joseph men were far away from them, up on a roof.

By the time Marley and Waylon's first anniversary arrived, Theo had started sleeping through the night. He dozed with his hands over his head, his face tilted to the side with a profile that looked like Waylon's. Seven straight hours of sleep felt like crossing into some unforeseen paradise that made Marley partly human again. As promised, Jade took Theo for the evening in her apartment above the salon. She had a playpen, a rocking chair, and three different Sade albums she wanted to play for the baby. Jade also ordered them not to call. Waylon pulled Marley out the front door.

"I have a surprise," he whispered into her ear—four words just enough to get drunk on, just like she had the first time he'd asked her—*what do you want?*

All of Mercury was decorated for high school graduation with blue and white balloons, streamers, and signs of congratulations from local businesses. One of which was from Joseph & Sons, which Marley had posted herself. It felt foreign to her, this rite of passage she'd crossed only a year ago. Marley had swum oceans away from the girl she'd been, and she didn't miss her. She liked the woman she was becoming—brave, selfless, smart. What Marley missed was a life without claustrophobia, without the guilt of needing to feel grateful for her in-laws' charity, without the worry over what to do about Elise and her missing shoes. These were burdens Waylon didn't know, and Marley carried them on her own.

It had started with one small secret, and it became easier and easier to keep another, then another. To just not say anything at all. Ruth had taught Marley the importance of taking up space, of speaking her mind.

Why did such things come with a heavy cost at the Joseph house? But here, now, in Waylon's truck, it was just the two of them. This was how they worked best.

Way drove south on 79, his hand out the window. It was hot, but there was a breeze, and Patty Smyth and Don Henley sang a duet on the radio. They passed a flurry of construction cones, each flying by in an orange blur. It felt like being born again: heading somewhere new instead of staying put. They were still young, the two of them. So much life still to be had.

Waylon took an exit before the bridge that led to downtown Pittsburgh. He didn't need a map; he knew these streets as well as the back of his hand. They pulled into an empty parking lot in front of a blunt gray building, and Marley noted it was not a restaurant or a movie theater or a hotel.

"Way," Marley said. "What is this?"

He handed her a hard hat, and she put it on. "Come on," he said. "You'll see."

He took her around the back of the building to a wrought iron ladder attached to the side. It led all the way up to the roof.

"Waylon," she said. Her palms began to sweat.

"After you."

She took one rung, then the next, and the next until she was about ten feet off the ground, but it felt like thirty. Marley promised herself she wouldn't chicken out, and she made it to the top with Waylon behind her.

Once she set foot on the roof, she felt firm rubber and slag beneath her feet. The stench of tar mixed with something sweet in the air.

"I know what this is," she said, taking off her hard hat. "It's the cookie plant."

Waylon nodded. "Your first big sale. Other than the church, of course."

He smiled, she blushed: an unspoken memory between them. Way pointed to the far corner by the chimney stack. He'd set up a blanket with some sandwiches from Marley's favorite deli, sugar cookies, and two cans of Rolling Rock.

"How did you do this?" Marley asked.

They hadn't gone on a honeymoon. They'd not saved a piece of the wedding cake that Ruth had made. The only anniversary token they had was this business they poured into, the baby they'd left behind for the night.

"I had help," Waylon answered. "The secretary here likes you."

Marley bent to run her hands through the stony slag. The rubber beneath it was hot in the sun. Here, away from the great house, she felt proud of the Joseph she was, who had aided in the construction of something so reliable and sturdy. She and Waylon sat together at the building's edge and watched the sun set.

"That one, that one, and that one." A manufacturing cityscape stretched before them as Waylon pointed out the roofs they'd redone. The Josephs had sinew in this town now, in its outline and silhouette, its defenses against the seasons. Seeing the rough black stark against the tawny sky, the orchid corona of an ending sun, Marley knew she'd never see anything more beautiful, more private, more infinite for the rest of her life. They'd made Theo, she and Waylon. And they'd made this, too.

"That." Waylon pointed to the view. "Is the best part of this life. You deserve to see it."

She opened her mouth to say thank you, but the words didn't come. This wasn't what she had imagined for her future, and yet she'd grown up in it and made it her own. Marley wondered, though, whether she could be called to a life she had never meant to choose.

Whether she needed to thank her husband for giving it to her, or whether she'd given it to herself.

"I know this year has been hard," Waylon said. "But it's the happiest I've ever been." He brought her to her knees, eye to eye with him. He was so handsome and young, so strong and soft—yet hesitant like the graveyard Waylon, the one who was afraid to take what he thought belonged to his brother. Relics of who they were then floated around them like cinders.

She felt it, that pull between them, even stronger now.

"I love you so much it hurts." Way took her hands in his. "But are you happy?"

"What do you mean?" Marley's heart fanned out before her, wide enough to hold an entire city. At times, her own happiness felt just like this fading sunset, a far-off view that she beheld but did not own.

"I mean this was *my* life, my career, my family. You took on all of it."

Way felt guilty for what he was, for all the miracles he couldn't see—and should he? In her heart, Marley felt she'd paid a price as a young mother that Waylon hadn't. But Marley felt it was wrong to measure such a thing. What could love become once it was compared?

You are the one who is telling this story, she reminded herself, and she was proud of it. *You are the Marley who stayed.*

"Maybe we didn't do things the right way, according to anyone else. But Waylon, there is nothing I'd rather be doing than this. All of it, with you." She put her head on his chest. "You have to trust it."

"I trust you with my life," he said.

"And I trust you with mine."

They meant it because they were starved for each other and young and the clock was running out on their freedom. They wanted to bottle the feeling of possibility, to capture their own potential before it turned into regret. Way lifted Marley's arms over her head and removed her shirt. Her bare skin pricked in the soft breeze. Waylon ran his thumbs along her rib cage, kissed her neck, and whispered her name. Marley felt herself floating, tethering herself to the rooftop by dragging her nails down Waylon's back. They tumbled to the blanket, and they were alone, and could take their time, and they never got around to finishing their dinner.

That night Waylon had given her a gift: she got to be as loud as she wanted. Nothing about them that night was hushed, or rushed, or secret. Way could take her again and again, and it would never be enough. He rocked her until she cried out, filling every open space with her voice. Then they fell asleep, and Waylon woke her just before dawn so she could see the sun rise over their city.

16.

Waylon and Marley were married two years, and then four. Their relationship settled into itself the way sand sinks into a jar before it calcifies. Sturdy like a rock, and unable to move. They were in love—no doubt about it. Yet inertia set in toward the life they'd planned to have. Marley's first deadline for moving out passed, and then her second, and a third. Could an existence outside the great house truly be so much better, or would it just be different? With a small child, a young business, and a lifetime of roofing jargon to learn, Marley was no longer sure she had the energy to find out.

Theo grew into a boy who loved brushing cattails with his fingers and tossing rocks into the pond by the baseball field. Marley cherished this private time with him, like she'd had with Ruth. She and Waylon saved their pennies and made sure to eat family dinner on Sundays. Elise's door was never locked. Marley still felt afraid to use it. Elise loved Marley dutifully through food and free rent yet remained unavailable in her affections.

It was a rift Marley knew would come to a head. Soon, Elise would stop holding back. Surely, she'd reveal what Marley had done so wrong.

Mick had taken a liking to Theo, sat him on his lap on the porch on warm days and let him fill in letters in his crossword. His hand looked so delicate next to Mick's colossal paw. Once, when he was three, Theo discovered a den of baby bunnies beneath a holly bush by the downspout.

"Look, Grandpa!" Theo was so elated he took one of the babies into his palm so he could pet it.

"Don't touch them," Mick chided, taking Theo's wrist and shaking it until the bunny fell into the grass. "Their mother won't return if she smells you."

Theo was now at the age where he believed in eternal permanence—every thoughtless scrap was a treasure in his eyes. He cried when Marley threw away straw wrappers or he outgrew a pair of pants. She could sense the threat of him never forgiving himself for making it unsafe for a bunny's mother to come home.

As Mick let go of his arm, Theo's eyes puddled, and he reached for Marley. She saw such a hollow-hearted resolve in Mick's face as his boot hovered over the tiny bunny, such an urge to hasten the inevitable that it frightened her. *Doing what no one else had the guts for*—wasn't that what Mick had built Joseph & Sons upon, the tagline his whole life had created? Marley held Theo close and turned his eyes away. She didn't know Elise had materialized from the shadows of the house until she spoke.

"Mick," she hissed. "Don't you dare."

Mick's boot retreated. And just as smoothly, Elise was gone again.

Marley had never told any of the Josephs about the day she encountered Elise and her missing shoes. They were already so worried about the roofing business, and there was always something to panic about—from the flash fire they'd had when the lid popped off their boiling asphalt vat at a department store in Hermitage, to the cereal aisle of the market in the next town over that had gotten soaked during a flash thunderstorm while they were patching a hole in the roof.

Yet Marley suspected they used the stress of owning a small business as a proxy for honesty. The Joseph family didn't talk to each other the way she and her mother did when Ruth visited every other month. Rather than speaking truth of any kind, the Josephs talked about roofs instead. Marley was becoming one of them not just by name but by her silence. And she wasn't sure she liked it.

Other signs continued to appear, suggesting Elise's mind lay elsewhere. Occasionally, she put sugar in her meat loaf instead of salt. She left the faucet running. She drove to the grocery store, only to return without any bags.

In time, Marley determined it was Elise who paced the house at night. She grew accustomed to the lope of her footsteps. The syncopation of it lulled her to sleep. Elise had retreated to a palace within herself, an act done to her or her own doing, Marley didn't know. She did wonder why Elise's husband and adult sons didn't seem to take note, or study her the way Marley did. Perhaps the simplest explanation was that Elise didn't want it. Her men didn't notice Elise because she'd trained them not to. A certain freedom came with not being seen and going where she pleased.

Marley understood the weight of family life and the toll it took. The "Mom, could you . . ." until there was nothing left. A mother got turned inside out until all she had was spent on the floor. And shouldn't Elise be afforded a moment or two of forgetfulness without it serving as an indication that something was wrong? Marley often wondered what those nighttime hours spent pacing the floor gave Elise that she wasn't getting from her husband, or sons, or even from Ann. Whatever it was, it belonged to Elise alone.

Marley, though, wasn't the only one who noticed. Shay did, too. He'd never said as much—it wasn't his nature to talk about someone he loved as if they couldn't speak for themselves—and yet he watched them all closely. Marley could see it in the way he rolled his favorite piece of beach glass around in his palm any time his father or brothers started to speak. In the Joseph family, Mick aimed for the impossible, Waylon hoped for the best, Baylor planned for the worst. And Shay? Shay Baby was all right, always. Like the mail coming every weekday at four, like Lake Erie freezing over in January.

But after Shay had seen Elise in the snow without any shoes, he started to ask Marley for things he needed: a signed permission slip for a field trip to Phipps Conservatory, assistance in picking out his first stick of deodorant, packed lunches with the chicken salad he liked from the deli on the corner. Help with algebra and science projects. Together, they'd created a trifold display on blind spots and hand-painted the anatomy of an eye onto a kickball.

"'That eye is ugly as sin," Patrick had said hours after the science fair had ended, as Shay and Marley kicked the eyeball back and forth in the street.

"You're not wrong," Shay said, and they laughed.

It might not have escaped Marley that she was giving Elise's youngest son exactly what Elise had denied Theo, but she was too enamored with Shay to see it. She loved his quiet strength and wry sense of humor, how he'd dunk Theo's diapers into the trash and hang his own shirts on a clothesline. Slices of Shay appeared between tapestries of white in the backyard, his blond curl catching the breeze as he held a clothespin in his mouth. Nightly, he banged on his teal drums while he listened to Stevie Ray Vaughan, and everyone else in the house hated the noise. It filled Marley with joy. Always, she would give Shay Baby everything he needed.

So it made sense that when the principal called during the spring of Shay's ninth grade year in 1995, it went to the apartment phone and not to the great house. Marley had long been the name on every form, the contact in case of emergency. Which there never was, of course. Shay was careful in a way his brothers never learned to be—not on the roof, but with people.

She was in the middle of pressing a new vinyl logo of a steel mill skyline onto work shirts for Waylon and Baylor when the phone rang. She'd wanted to print RAIN DOWN ON US on the back, but Bay complained that it sounded too much like a Phil Collins song, so she'd designed a skyline instead.

"Mrs. Joseph," the school secretary said. "You need to get here right away."

Marley barely remembered to unplug the iron after she hung up, and it left a dark ring on the board and a charred stench in the air. She buckled Theo in the car and raced to the high school on the other end of town.

When she burst into the building, it was eerily silent for the middle of the day. The hallway smelled just like it had when she was a student there—a glut of Lysol and a little bit of vomit. Marley's Keds squeaked as she hauled Theo to the main office. Inside, she found Shay sitting in a

chair, holding an ice pack to his eye. He was small for fourteen but mus-
cled and kind and filled with hatred for school.

"Shay," Theo called out, and he turned his head.

"Shay Baby." Marley winced after calling him by his family nickname.
Her tongue grew thick in her mouth. "Are you all right?"

"I'm sorry, Mar," he said. "They wouldn't let me leave without calling
you. I'm fine. Just a bit beat up, is all."

He spoke words Marley knew were lies. She could tell by the way his
free hand fisted his beach glass. Her little love was haunted, and sad, and
weary.

Marley was ready to pounce.

A clerk pounded away on her typewriter in the corner, and the happy
clacking made Marley want to throw her car keys against the window.
How could this woman go about her duties, undisturbed, while Shay sat
there with a gash on his head?

"Come on, pal," she said, struggling to sound calmer than she felt. "Let's
get you home."

"Hold on a minute." The principal turtled out of his office. "Can I see
you inside, Mrs. Joseph?"

Marley left Theo with Shay and closed the door behind her. The room
was just like the inside of a briefcase—bland and male and stuffed with
paper.

"Tell me what happened," she said.

The principal stroked his mustache for a minute as he attempted to
place her. She'd only been a student here as a senior, four years ago now,
but she wasn't the hero of any story told about her since then. Waylon was
the famed brave heart between them. Waylon, the principal knew. Marley
could have been anyone.

"There was an incident in the locker room," he said.

Marley felt her claws come out. "An *incident*?"

"Shay got into a fight, and as I've told his brothers on many occasions,
fighting is not tolerated on school grounds."

"Did he get into a fight, or was he punched?" Marley spat the words. "I
only see one kid out there, bruised to hell. Mine."

She shouldn't have said it. Shay wasn't her son. And yet she inserted herself, just as she'd done when she titled herself vice president of the family business. She'd only wanted to help then, as an outsider might. Now she was ready to defend her own.

The principal looked like he was going to try to settle her down, then thought better of it.

"We asked Shay who threw the punch," he said. "But he wouldn't say."

"I see." Marley stood. Out the office window, she saw a silhouette of someone who looked like Patrick, trying to get a glimpse inside from the other side of the street.

"Are you accusing Shay of something?" she asked.

The principal sighed. "Not at this time."

"Then I need to take him home."

He nodded and called her name when she turned her back.

"Mrs. Joseph." The principal cleared his throat. "I think you ought to keep him home tomorrow, too."

"With pleasure," Marley snapped.

She strode down the hall and stuffed her boys into the Citation. Without a word, she drove to Lickety Split, the ice cream stand across from the grocery store, and ordered three twisty cones. The oak branches above the shop shook in the wind. It was too cloudy outside for ice cream, Theo's dripped all over the backseat, and Marley did not care.

"I didn't start a fight." Shay looked stricken. "After Way and Bay, Mom always told me to never fight back."

"Never is a strong word," Marley seethed. "But go on."

He closed his eyes as a school bus thundered by, and Shay sank into his seat. "You don't want to know."

"Try me."

Shay's breath caught, and his cone melted onto his hands.

"Listen," she said. "Waylon is going to see your face. But I won't tell him what happened if you don't want me to."

Shay looked out the window. "If I'd only gotten punched, I wouldn't care. But that's not even the worst part. I swear to God, Mar—after his fist hit me, I had him on the ground with my arm against his neck before

I even realized what I was doing. It wasn't until his lips went purple that I got myself to stop. Just like Baylor and Waylon used to do."

Marley felt all of herself spilling out, trying to find a way to comfort this perfect child, to keep him intact, to break apart so he wouldn't have to. As Shay's mother, Elise should have been the one to take the call, to comfort her son and take him out for dessert. For the past four years, Marley had felt so slighted by everything she wasn't receiving from Elise that she hadn't stopped to consider that Shay wasn't getting what he needed from her, either.

"You know I'm here for you, right?" she said.

"Stop, Marley. Yes, I do. Okay?"

"Do you want to go back to that school?"

He laughed. "No."

"Then you're done."

Shay nodded, exhaled, and closed his eyes. The sky darkened. A crack of lightning lit the sky, and three beats passed before thunder chased it. Marley turned the Citation's ignition, remembering what it had felt like to return to that same school building the day after everyone in town discovered she was pregnant. She had no right to make that decision on Shay's behalf, but it had been made, and there was no one who would stop her.

"What the fuck?" Baylor yelled, predictably, when he saw Shay's face later that evening after he returned home from work.

Shay had tried to bypass him on his way up the stairs to his room.

"It's nothing," he called back, refusing to turn toward his oldest brother. "It's fine."

It had started to rain outside, and a shushing sound poured over the house. Marley watched as Baylor took the stairs three at a time.

"Who did it," he said flatly.

The flare in his eyes caused Marley to see why Shay hadn't told anyone who punched him. He didn't want Baylor to know. Baylor, who made sure Shay got an equal cut for every day he worked on the roof. Baylor, who knew how to speak love with only his wallet or his fists.

"Marley," Bay barked when he got no response from his brother. "Who was it?"

Marley chose her words carefully. "Shay can tell us when he wants, if he wants."

Baylor grunted.

"But I was wondering," Marley ventured. "Do you think it might be best for him to do school at home?"

She felt a little sick as she said it. Shay glanced down at her. This, she'd seen Elise do a hundred times with her husband, her sons, yet never with her. Marley fed her own opinion just so, until Baylor thought of it as his own.

Bay sat down on the steps. "I—" He pressed his fingers into the scar beneath his ear as Marley watched him deflate. "I almost failed out of school. I can't teach you, Shay."

"You can teach me how to roof," Shay called over the banister. "I'll go with you in the mornings." Outside, the cedar trees moaned in the wind. "Maybe Marley will work with me in the afternoon? She's the smartest of all of us."

These two Josephs looked at her so earnestly that she could not refuse. *Give, Marley, give*, they seemed to say, and she wanted to.

"Of course," she said.

Shay held a bag of frozen peas to his eye, and Bay stood. "Let's give it a month," he suggested. "To see how it goes. Marley has a lot of other shit to do."

They shook on it, Marley nodded, picked up her son, and shuffled up the outside steps to her apartment. Once she shut the door behind her, soaked and shaking, she promptly threw up in the toilet. That day she had acted—and felt like—not only Shay's mother but Baylor's wife. The intimacy of it rattled her, the slippery way she moved in and out of these roles that weren't hers. How easy it was to act in ways that couldn't be undone. Theo came behind her, rested a small hand on her back as she hunched over porcelain.

"Mama," he whispered. "Are you okay?"

Marley didn't think so. Here she was, already lying to her son.

"I'm fine, pal. But if I keep puking like this," she tried to joke, "I'll be as bad as your father."

Baylor had been home that evening, but no one else was. Waylon was nowhere to be found. Perhaps he'd gotten stuck on a sales call before the rain came, while Elise was fetching things for dinner, the single ballast to her day. Mick might have been hunting God-knows-what supplies for whatever project he'd recently hatched. The seven of them lived together, worked together, and ate together, yet so often Marley had no idea where anyone had gone. She and Baylor had decided what was best for Shay, which was no special act. Humans came preloaded with opinions. The grievous truth was that she and Baylor both knew neither Elise nor Mick would likely even notice what they had done.

Way, however, did.

He blew into the apartment after stopping by at the great house for dinner—Elise's chicken soup and biscuits—and threw his mapping wheel on the floor.

"Marley," he said. "Shay needs to go to school."

The thunder had passed, leaving a soft and constant rain in its wake.

"Baylor told you?" she asked.

Angry, Way laughed. "Of course he told me."

Marley had just given Theo a bath, and they were selecting a book from his tiny shelf in the cove of the living room where he slept. He still didn't have a place of his own to sleep, and they still hadn't moved out, and there were still plenty of empty bedrooms they could inhabit in the great house.

Marley eyed the tar-caked wheel until Way picked it up and placed it in the stairwell outside the door.

"Hello to you, too," she said.

"I'm serious, Mar. If Shay doesn't go to school, he'll be trapped with them all day."

An unspoken truth hid beneath his words that Marley knew Waylon wasn't ready to admit. He thought it was safer for Shay to get in fights at school than to stay at the great house with Mick and Elise.

In bright red pajamas, Theo ran to his dad, who picked him up and held him close.

"Hate to break it to you, babe," Marley said, "but Shay doesn't go to school much as it is."

"Dad," Theo said. "You're dirty."

Waylon realized his own filth and set down his son. "Shay doesn't go to school? Why?"

"He hates it," she answered. "The judgment, the boredom, the rules. He always has."

"Hating it isn't a good reason to quit. As if we all didn't fucking hate being a Joseph in that school."

Waylon was crusted with dust, his shirtsleeve had torn, and he was just as soaked as Marley. They both looked a little wild. There she stood, arguing with her real husband instead of his brother, and she'd lost the patience for it.

"He isn't quitting. The school is the issue, not Shay."

"He could have gone to college," Way whipped, as if it were already denied this boy of fourteen. "He could have been better than us, Marley."

The tension held as they stared at each other. Waylon's words stung. He'd never faulted Marley for the strain they both felt living in that house, yet their marriage had still crossed into darker territory now. Or it had long ago, when neither of them had noticed it. Waylon saw Marley as capable of blame not only for her own choices, but for his.

How long, Marley wondered, had Waylon looked at their life and wanted better for his brother?

"He already is better than us, Waylon," she said.

Marley whisked herself into the living room and folded back the sheets of Theo's small bed. Waylon hadn't yet had enough.

"Not to mention," he called after her, "that you and Baylor made this decision without me."

"And that"—the words bit as Marley spun around—"is really why you are upset. Tell me, since you're such an expert on Shay's life—what is his first-period class? Which subject is a struggle for him? What time does he need to be picked up from school?" She smiled, irate and riding her horse high. "Let's start with this. What's his best friend's name?" She waited. "Any friend?"

His face fell. Marley had wounded him, and she enjoyed it. Waylon had nothing to say, and it was just as well, because there was a knock at the apartment door.

Marley yanked it open, figuring it was Mick, ready to tell them to keep it down. But there stood Patrick, head hanging and rain-spattered, hands in his pockets. Marley had seen him earlier that day, his dark eyes shifting along the windowpane as he'd tried to see inside the principal's office.

"Patrick," she said. "It's late."

His skin had mottled in the cold. "I know."

"Shay isn't here."

Waylon crowded Marley out from the doorway. "Are you the one who punched him?"

"No." Patrick looked at his feet. "But I caused it."

"So you want to apologize, then," Marley said.

"I do."

Marley didn't trust that Patrick was telling the whole truth. Still, Shay deserved to have something good on this horrible day. She wanted it so bad she could scream. So she instructed Patrick to wait on the couch while she fetched Shay, and Waylon bundled up Theo so they could go on a long walk.

It was kaleidoscopic, the way shortcomings and fear and loneliness each masked themselves as secrets in the great house. If Shay hadn't been punched, and Patrick hadn't wanted to make peace, and if Marley hadn't been so bent on proving to Waylon that Shay deserved his privacy, she might never have left her apartment that night after a heavy rain, looped around the side of the porch, and spied Elise in the wet dark without a jacket, sitting on the roof.

17.

Elise didn't know that Marley had seen her sitting on the roof after the rain, and Marley chose to leave it that way. She planned to save it for the impending blowout that loomed between them, the time when they'd lay it all out once and finally—the roof, the shoes, the attic. Marley didn't want to use any of these as a weapon against her mother-in-law, but as an offering. A means by which to say—*I see you. Even when you think no one does.* Marley vowed to ask Elise whether she was all right once they found a private moment.

Truth was, Marley had no time to spare. Office duties, an almost four-year-old, and now homeschool for a teenager. She and Elise were never alone. Elise preferred it that way. Marley wished things hadn't grown so strained between them—didn't like what it portended. Was this what lay in store for Marley, after half a lifetime of working side by side with the people she loved most? It had hollowed Elise out, Marley feared. It turned a family into strangers.

Marley and Waylon walked the empty streets that night after Patrick came by, while Theo fell asleep in the stroller he'd outgrown. Drops of water glistened on the courthouse lawn's hydrangeas as they walked past, and Theo stretched his arms above his head. It reminded Marley of when he was an infant, and she and Waylon had taken turns rocking him to sleep. Whatever it took: a trip around the block, a lullaby, the sound of the dryer running nearby. Waylon must have been thinking the same.

"I miss it," he said. "When Theo was young."

Marley wanted to protest and claim their boy was only three, but she understood what he meant. How fast she could lose this one heart she used to encompass, how it happened little by little each day until he wouldn't need her anymore. She and Way hadn't made up after their fight, and she wasn't feeling charitable toward him. He was sore and still filthy from the roof, rolling his shoulders and wincing as they bumped over the sidewalk. His faded Levi's hung off his lean hips—jeans she loved, had washed, had taken off him too many times to count. Marley felt an ache that drew out the noble parts of her, the ones that brought out the best in him.

"Do you want another child?" Waylon asked softly.

They'd never talked about it before. She did, she didn't. She could, she couldn't. "Tonight is not the night to ask me," she said.

They turned left at the church, where steam rose from the freshly mulched flower beds after the storm. Marley gazed up toward the bell tower, to the slick patch of shingles where she'd once stood triumphant. It seemed so far away now and beyond her reach.

"You don't need to save everyone, Marley." Waylon looked stern, and disappointed, and wounded. "You didn't need to do that for Shay."

It felt like a scolding. He was reminding her that Shay was not hers—as if Waylon had drawn a Joseph family line and she was outside of it, as if that would free up some unoccupied space in her heart. Yet Way reserved a reckless kind of intimacy for Marley that had no place in the great house. Way said things to her he didn't dare say to his mother. Marley had filled the gap in a house full of men who needed a shepherdess, and Way was blaming her for it.

"If you want another child," she said, "then move us out of the house. I won't have another baby there."

It was fair, what she said. And unfair, too.

"Are you really so unhappy?" His voice wavered. "Being with me?"

Words stalled in Marley's throat. She thought of Elise up on the roof, waiting out her life. There must have been a time when Elise had hope and it had gotten chiseled out of her, shard by shard. Marley felt herself tumbling into these well-worn grooves before them—as went Elise and Mick, so went she and Waylon. What other example did they have to follow? Marley had to stop it. Run from it with every breath in her body and pull it up by its roots.

"The problem," Marley said, finding a part of her honesty if not the whole, "is that I'm not with you as much as I'd like."

Waylon stopped them in the street. He took her hands, kissed her palms. "We can fix that."

She pulled her hands away. "Please just listen."

He nodded.

"You forget that you get to escape to the roof and leave this whole family behind. I have no escape. You *get* to escape because I can't."

Waylon leaned against a streetlamp. Ran a thumb along his forehead. The slick road ahead looked flecked with gold. He was trying to understand her, even if he couldn't.

"This is all I know how to do, Mar." He sat on the curb and rested his chin in his hands. "I don't know how to do anything else."

Maybe he was talking about roofing, maybe he was talking about being a son, or a brother. In the great house that Mick built, they were all the same.

"What we have is so good," she whispered, looking backward toward their darkened home. She and Waylon were partners. When she had an idea, he let her lead. He had no interest in reducing her to someone else's idea of a woman: a mother, a wife, a sister. To him she was simply Marley, always. When they'd first married, she feared the people in Mercury would never see her as anything other than a pregnant teen. Now, just as Jade had predicted, she'd found a way to define herself for the whole town to see—as a businesswoman, as a citizen, and as a friend.

"I don't know how to keep from losing it," she said.

Waylon was quiet for a minute.

"Did you ever want to go somewhere else, just the three of us? Where no one knows me or my father?" He looked up at her, his eyes a pearlescent green in the soft light. "Start over?"

She did think of it, and often. But what would it do to Waylon to take him from his home? She walked toward him and threaded her fingers through his hair. It was thick and soft, finely dusted with loose drywall. He rested his head against her thighs, breathed her in. She felt his weariness seeping from his body into hers.

"I've lived that life," she answered. "The problems you have in one town follow you to the next."

He nodded, sighed, and stood on his feet. "I'm sorry I got so mad about Shay."

"I shouldn't have made the decision on my own." She paused. "I still think it was the right one."

Way began to push the stroller toward Hollow Street.

"I think—" He took a breath. "I think we should split the homeschooling. Maybe you take math and English, and I'll take science and social studies?"

Relieved, Marley nodded. Waylon still saw her, she told herself, and all the things she carried. He would not let her break.

He stopped again, took his Zippo from his pocket. Flicked it open and shut. "Do you know what happened to Shay at school?"

Marley shook her head—a bit of a lie, but mostly the truth. "What I'm worried about," she said, "is that he feels like he can't tell us."

Waylon considered it. "He's grown up with five parents instead of two, I guess."

Marley laughed because she hadn't laughed all day and she desperately needed something right then to be the least bit funny. Otherwise, she'd crash. She'd admit to being overwhelmed. She'd tell Waylon she wanted her own paycheck. All things she thought would do no good, were they said aloud.

"Marley," Way was saying. "I promise I am looking for the right house. The business still feels so fragile. I swear to you, I'm looking."

He said "the business," but he meant something with far greater risk. Way couldn't give up his role in the family. Couldn't bear to let it go, even for his wife. He needed to be the soother; he wanted to be the glue. He also made oaths too often for Marley to believe them anymore, and that loss knocked the wind out of her.

"I know you want to, Waylon," she said.

That, she knew for sure.

18.

At some point, Elise was bound to discover her youngest son was not attending school any longer. Even though Shay rose early in the morning and disappeared for the day with his father and brothers, the secret wouldn't keep. It was only a matter of time before a teacher would find Elise in the grocery store or at church, or she'd see Shay headed for Marley's apartment around one in the afternoon. Or Mick—who didn't seem to care that Shay was missing school—would let it slip if he ever had an actual conversation with his wife.

Marley knew Waylon and Baylor stood with her in the decision, but it was Marley Elise would blame. She knew it because of that day almost five years ago when Elise told her she couldn't substitute one of her sons for the other, and still Marley had. It had cast all of Marley's actions with a veil of deceit. She carried that truth with her everywhere she went—to Jade's shop for lunch, to the grocery store for extra buns and carrot sticks, to the pediatrician for Theo's busted lip after he tried to do chin-ups on the fireplace mantel and fell. No matter what she accomplished, Marley had never felt like a grown woman in Elise's presence, nor a daughter. She'd felt like only a girl.

Shay was a thoughtful student, slow to answer, surprising in the depth of his writing journal after he'd read *Macbeth* for the first time. March gave way to April, and Mercury came back to life again after another long winter. The high school hosted spring dances, spaghetti dinners, and tryouts for the track team. Shay didn't seem sad to miss any of it.

School went on at home for a full month of book reports, equations, and discussions of colonialism before Elise called Marley in the middle of the night.

The ring shook her from her sleep, and Marley scrambled for the phone. Waylon was a deep sleeper, but Theo was not.

"Hello," she whispered into the receiver, dragging it into the bathroom by its cord.

"Marley," the voice said. "It's Elise." The line crackled. "I need—"

Marley had so prepared for this eventuality that her speech dribbled out of her mouth. "Shay is happy and thriving, he—"

"This isn't about Shay. I need—"

Marley heard Elise's voice catch.

"I need your help."

Dread tickled the back of Marley's neck. Never had Elise asked her for anything. "Where are you?" she asked.

"I'm at the church."

Marley hesitated. *The roof, the attic, the shoes.* The time she'd been waiting for had come.

When she arrived at the church ten minutes later, it was past one o'clock in the morning. A storm threatened in the distance. The street was dark, the building like a haunted house with no light. Marley tried the front entrance and found it unlocked. She hadn't thought to bring a flashlight and discovered that she didn't know the church as well as she thought. Sweat slipped down her back as she felt her way to the stairwell, calling out Elise's name.

"Elise?" Marley called but received no answer.

For four years Marley had been calling, calling, and not once had Elise responded. The wall beneath her fingers was made from brick, and Marley remembered the way she'd skated her hands across it on her wedding day. How it had rained. She'd been scared then, and happy, and young.

When she reached the sanctuary, the sweat on her skin cooled as a chill set in. She called for Elise again and found her there, seated in the last pew, a spare light from the stained glass window casting her monstrous shadow onto the aisle.

Marley crept in beside her and sat down. Waited. The air around them smelled sour, and all sound had fled. Elise watched her own silhouette, and Marley felt afraid to speak. Elise finally did.

"I used to be like you, you know."

Marley still didn't understand what those words meant, and she didn't want to.

"Before I knew that my whole world relies on the myth of the good man," Elise went on, "of which there are none."

"Elise," Marley spoke slowly. Her mother-in-law was toeing some ledge, readying to leap. And she'd called Marley to pull her back from it. "You've raised three wonderful sons."

"That's not the point."

The features on Elise's face, usually so crisp and certain, looked as if they were trying to slide toward the floor. Marley had known her mother-in-law to be impatient. Disappointed. Distant. Even kind, years ago. Yet here was an emotion she'd never seen, until now.

Elise was sad.

"Can't you see?" she said. "This life is unmerciful to mothers. Always has been, always will be."

"I'm part of this life, too," Marley said, still fighting for purchase in Elise's mind. Still wanting to belong. "I've tried to love you."

"But you shouldn't even be here." Elise's voice went coarse. "I tried to warn you away from all this. I took pity on you that day at the ballpark, and I regret it."

"Has it truly been so terrible, having me as a daughter?" Marley asked.

Elise said nothing, and Marley rose to leave. She didn't deserve to be chastised for wanting to be part of this family. Not after everything she'd given to become a Joseph and to love each of them as her own.

Elise clamped a hand around Marley's wrist.

"Sit down," she said.

Marley shook off Elise's hand, and then she sat. The woman next to her was family, and yet she'd always been a stranger, too.

"Elise," she said. "Are you all right?"

Elise's eyes went black and wet, like twin seeds that had drowned. "You mean my mind. How it comes and goes."

Marley nodded.

"Funny, how you're the only one who's noticed."

It was tragic, was what it was. Who could know what to search for in a mother? Children were trained to look at her and see their own needs instead.

"Dementia is what they're calling it. Losing my mind, they say."

The words hit Marley like a wrecking ball.

"But it's made me see things in brighter relief," Elise went on. "I can see now what a blight it is that all I've done for most of my life is serve the men in it."

Marley opened her mouth to offer a consolation—*No, Elise, you have me now, too*—but found she couldn't. Elise never wanted Marley. Despite the differences between them, Elise had never lied to her. Now Marley wouldn't lie to her either.

Elise tucked a stray blond hair behind her ear. She wore a slouchy sweater, a pair of leggings. Clothes Marley had never seen before. And she was barefoot.

"Now I can't help but wonder what all this was for," Elise said. "I did everything right. I was a virgin when I got married. Sent letters overseas and saved paychecks while my husband fought in some war. I gave him sons and kept a clean house. Collected all the pieces of a man who came back shattered. It's not his fault—but why was it my responsibility to fix it, when I didn't know him at all?"

"Elise," Marley whispered. "Let me take you home."

"Mick kissed me on an altar, and my father promised me my best days were ahead." She showed no emotion, shed no tears. "Am I a cliché, Marley? People look at me like I'm unoriginal, like I missed my shot. Martyrs aren't that unique, it turns out."

"Elise, you need to see a doctor."

"I've been."

Marley searched for words of comfort, but none came. Elise was right—Marley shouldn't be here. Not in this church, not as a witness to Elise's private undoing. She could think of only one person who might offer solace. This was not a wound a husband or son could soothe. She needed a friend.

"Do you want me to call Ann?" Marley asked.

Elise looked bewildered. "Why?"

Marley thought of all the times Ann had stopped by, how she and Elise shared recipes, and summer roses from their flower beds, and paperback novels. "Because she's your best friend," she said.

Elise laughed. "Let's be honest. She's not my friend. Ann feels a repulsive pity for me because she knows I'm married to a selfish fool. All I've got is *you*."

She threw away the word as if it disgusted her.

"If we're being honest," Marley shot back, "you and I are not friends either, Elise. You don't need to pretend to love me."

"I haven't been, any more than I could pretend to love my own reflection in the mirror."

Marley gripped the pew cushion with her fingers. She recalled Elise's curse once more, the words she'd offered when Theo was a newborn.

I used to be just like you.

Elise saw her daughter-in-law as an adversary, of sorts. A ripple effect. A looking into what might have been, and what already was.

"Tell me why you called me in the middle of the night," Marley said. "What do you want?"

Abruptly, Elise stood and disappeared into the counting room behind her. Inside it, a bald light bulb fluttered to life. The attic door already hung down from its thread. Its spider arms stretched out before them, limp. Beckoning.

Elise climbed, and Marley followed. There, at the mouth of the stairs, atop a heap of loudly purple choir robes, was the preacher, naked and dead.

All of it—the disappearances, the shoes, the lamps left undusted—had been leading to this.

Elise looked to Marley. Marley stared back. Her hands fumbled against the wall, but she couldn't feel her fingers or her feet. All she felt was panic roiling in her stomach.

"We—we need to call an ambulance." The words sat like stones in Marley's mouth.

"Useless. He's been dead for over an hour." Elise's fingernails bit into the meat of her palms. "God forgive me, but I look at him and all I can think is that I've already been dead for years now."

The words seared the air like a burn. Elise was reckoning with her own mortality, something she'd lost, like a trinket on a chain.

"You found him like this?" Marley asked. She couldn't stop looking at the preacher's eyes—half-closed, milky. Afraid.

"He died on top of me. Heart attack, I'd wager."

Slowly, Elise's absences began to make sense. She'd been sleeping with Hollis in the attic. And at least once, she'd left her shoes behind.

All those nights Marley was alone while the men were working, she'd thought Elise was alone, too. But she wasn't.

"What do you expect me to do about it?" Marley asked. "I have never, *ever* been good enough for you. What makes me good enough now?"

Her words were heartless, but her heart ricocheted in her chest. A corpse lay before her: monumental and immutable. A whole life turned into an object. Why had Elise done this to her? Why had she done this at all?

"We need to move him," Elise said simply, refusing to blink.

"We can't move him. He's too heavy. You should have called Baylor."

Elise laughed. The sound was raspy and somber. "He can't know," she said. "None of them can. They're fragile, our men. Surely you can see that. No telling what they'll do if they discover I'm not the saint who feeds them supper."

Marley twirled her wedding ring around her finger. Here was the moment she'd been waiting for, and she wanted to give it back. She'd never truly wrestled with what it cost her to be part of this family until now.

"They're going to find out, Elise."

Elise's face went blank. "They can't. That's why I called you."

"*This* is why you called me, finally?" Marley backed toward the ladder. The body lay before them like a bomb. Marley twisted her wedding ring again, trying to keep her voice even. "We could have had something so much better, you and me. If you'd let us."

Elise marched toward her and gripped Marley by the shoulder. "I was angry with you."

Marley pushed back. "Why? If anyone could understand your life, Elise, it would have been me."

"That's just it!" Elise shouted. Marley had never heard her yell before. "I never wanted you to have to understand!"

The strength of her voice echoed around them, ringing like a bell.

"That day I came to your apartment and invited you back to dinner," Elise spoke softer now, "I wasn't lying when I said I was tired of being the only woman in the house. It was the truest thing I've ever said to anyone. I told myself it was an act of kindness, but I didn't see until it was too late that all I'd done was use you as camouflage. My sons needed very little from me when you were around, and I took advantage of it. Went where I wanted, did as I pleased. I could finally be something other than a mother."

Elise leaned against the wall and tilted her chin toward the dark ceiling. "And then you got pregnant, and we both ended up stuck in this life I never wanted. I used to be just like you—smart, bold, eager. Now you're just like me. Stuck. And it's the worst thing I've ever done to anyone in my life."

Marley had never felt more wounded than she did as Elise's confession hung in the air. She'd grieved the absence of Elise's affection in her life even more than her own father's. Always, Marley thought Elise was judging her shortcomings. But truly, Elise hadn't been thinking of Marley at all.

"Elise," Marley said. "What are you asking of me?"

Elise remained stolid and crow-eyed, but she slid to the floor. "I'm asking you to consider what you would do if you were me. If you were married to a man who has never once said he loves you. If you were sleeping with another who asks you every day to run away with him. Has a letter of resignation signed and ready in the top drawer of his desk. And every day you think about leaving."

Marley thought back to her wedding ceremony, how Elise and Hollis had fought over her right to be married in the sanctuary. *On a cold day in hell,* Elise had said, *will my son be married in a basement.*

"Wait—" Marley began, and then stopped.

"What?"

"I thought you and Hollis didn't like each other."

"We didn't," Elise said.

"You have to give me more than that, Elise."

Elise gazed down at the body. She was close enough for Marley to see that the golden backing of her pearl earring had fallen off, and the jewel hung there like a raindrop.

"It started with these ridiculous choir robes." Elise closed her eyes briefly. "Hollis got them on sale four years ago. They were white back then. Every woman in the bell choir had a fit over it because they'd be so hard to keep clean. They said he'd never have done something so stupid if only he had a wife. So he got this ridiculous idea to dye them purple, and I caught him in the act in the church basement. The robes had dried into this terrible neon color, and I walked in with a casserole for the youth group and saw him clutching them, looking like he'd just robbed a bank."

Marley waited for Elise to cry, but she didn't.

"He was *trying,*" Elise continued. "With earnest. For me to see someone caring, really caring about something so trivial and having it collapse, it—I don't know. It made me feel like not everything is dying."

Marley remembered how Elise had rescued the baby rabbit from the heft of Mick's boot, the way she watered her garden in the early morning and plucked out the weeds, one by one. The way she did the same for her war-haunted husband.

"And you know what?" Elise went on. "I laughed. I swear to you, I've never laughed that hard, and it felt so good that I wanted to chase that feeling down. Force it to stay."

Elise couldn't drag her eyes away from the preacher's face.

"Hollis asked me to help him hide the evidence," she went on. "We couldn't throw the robes away. Someone would surely see them in the trash, and call Hollis incompetent yet again. So we threw them up here in the attic. My feet were hurting, so I took off my heels and sat down on the pile of them when we were through. Hollis sat beside me, we both got stained with purple, and we just kept laughing. I know how silly it sounds, but it was salvation. There was no stopping it between us after that. I was so taken up with the idea of having something to look forward to, with someone finding me funny, someone telling me I looked beautiful with my hair down, that I didn't realize I'd driven home in my bare feet." Elise shook her head. "You'd think that should have been a warning sign to me then, especially after I forgot my shoes more than once. I wasn't ready to see it."

Marley wrapped her arms around herself. "Did you love him?"

"No." Elise took out the pin in her hair, and it fell around her shoulders. "For so long I'd thought something must be missing from my life, but Hollis made me see that I'd missed the whole thing entirely."

"How can that be true? Your life has so many good things in it."

Elise's lip curled at Marley's question. She was frustrated, lonely, and desperate to be understood. "There's this story in the book of Matthew," Elise said. "The parable of the sower. Do you know it?"

Marley shook her head.

"It's about a farmer who buries seeds in different places—some in rocks, some among thorns. Only the ones the farmer plants in good soil have a chance to survive. All the others die. I'd always thought of myself as the sower in my own story. Someone who planted her seeds well—my children, my husband. Even you."

Elise paused, and Marley waited.

"Now I see I was never the farmer at all. I was the seed all this time, tossed on bad earth. I never stood a chance."

In the attic, Marley found it hard to breathe. The air filled with the chemical dye on the polyester robes and the musk of sex. Here was this dutiful woman, so mighty in Marley's mind—and in all of Mercury's—brought to her knees by her own misery. Her own loss. Elise had looked upon Marley's need once and refused to make Marley's mess her own. And now she wanted Marley to grant her the kind of company she'd always withheld.

"Leave him here," Marley said, "and let's go home. Someone will find him."

Elise fanned her hands out in front of her. "My fingerprints are here, my hair, all of me all over him."

"So clean it up."

Marley's voice cut so sharply she could barely recognize it. Her patience for Elise's apathy had worn thin, but then Elise told her the truth.

"My memory spells. There's no telling when they'll hit." Elise pointed to her heels in the corner, as if Marley needed a reminder of the day she'd found her barefoot. "If I'm up here alone, I'm not sure I'll know how to get home. That's why I called you."

The simple need she revealed—the desire to reach home and not knowing how—broke Marley's bitterness. Marley had loved this woman once, before all of this. And she loved her still. It was not a feeling she could give back, or trade in, or ignore.

"Here's what we're going to do," Marley said. "I'm going to Jade's shop for bleach and ammonia and some sponges. We are leaving *everything*"— she looked to the corpse—"as it is. We're just erasing you. Someone will find him here tomorrow."

Elise nodded. Didn't say thank you, didn't cower in the face of what she'd asked of her daughter-in-law. An incredible feat to witness, this absence of empathy. Marley was certain Elise once had that emotion. Now she wondered where it had gone.

Marley used her key to the salon's back door and crept inside. The black palm trees on the wall looked like witches' fingers in the dark. She flicked the light in the storage closet. The door hit a broom; it fell to the floor with a clatter. Marley held her breath and turned off the light. Waited. When she bent to take a pack of sponges and a jug of generic-brand ammonia, she felt something sharp in her back.

"Stay where you are," Jade said, turning on the light.

When she saw Marley, she dropped her kitchen knife. Dressed in plaid pajama pants and an Exposé T-shirt, her hair in a side pony, Jade leaned against the wall and rubbed her eyes to survey the contents of what Marley was stealing.

"Shit, Mar. If I didn't know better, I'd think you were burying a body."

When Marley just held her gaze, speechless, Jade said, "Oh, shit," and grabbed her coat.

For the next two and a half hours, the three of them scrubbed Elise's presence from that hidden upper room. A mighty act, three women cleaning. Erasing skin and flesh and blood, as if they knew inherently what it took to make something un-exist outside the walls of memory. These women knew how to give life, how to sustain it, and how to starve it, too.

When they finished, Elise used a gloved hand to shield the preacher's body with a choir robe.

"I don't want to speak of this again," she said, her eyes darting back and forth between Jade and Marley. "We're leaving it in this attic. Believe me—silence, more than anything else, is what it takes to be a Joseph."

Marley could think of no response. She was exhausted, and dirty, and frightened. She'd never been closer to Elise, and she'd never felt so far away from herself. Elise took her maroon heels, and the three left the way they'd come: with the attic hatch left open and the light on. They went home just before the rain and did not fall asleep.

The next day, an insistent guilt nested in the great house as its women waited for the phone to ring, for police cruisers to appear. For Elise to confess what she knew.

Yet here was what they didn't know: the church was scheduled for a paint job that day, a Tuesday, so it would have plenty of time to dry before Sunday's coming service. The painters went to the counting room and gave the entire space a thick coat of glossy white paint.

It just so happened that the painters were Patrick and Shay, whom Mick had hired for half the price Pastor Hollis had promised for the job. It was early, Patrick had skipped school, and so preoccupied were they with words they hadn't said to each other that they didn't foresee any consequences in swiping thick swatches of paint onto the ceiling, right over the closed attic door.

Later that afternoon, Mick Joseph realized he had yet to be paid for the work Patrick and Shay had done. He drove his Astro van to the church but couldn't find the preacher anywhere—not in the sanctuary, or the manse, or the basement. Not one to get skimped, Mick was eager to handle his own money, to cash a check in his name and imagine its possibilities as his and only his. He pawed around Pastor Hollis's office, looking for a box of petty cash. Elise had used it once or twice to buy baptism sheet cakes and the like. He didn't find the box, but what he did uncover was a signed letter from the pastor himself, stating he'd resigned and had run off to Florida with the love of his life.

Mick arrived home early in the evening to spy his wife making his favorite dinner, and he relished in sharing this prime cut of town gossip he thought he was the first to know. Elise was so shocked she spilled his Salisbury steak on the floor.

It was about this same time that Marley realized she couldn't find her wedding ring. She'd forgotten she'd tucked it into her pocket before they cleaned the church attic, where it had fallen out as she bent down on her hands and knees to scrub the floor. Marley tore each room in the apartment apart as she searched for it, but she would never find it, as it had slipped off her finger and landed silently in the soft harbor of choir robes that had never been worn.

The ring was sealed tight into the church's upper room, along with Elise's secrets, never to be found as long as Marley's feeble piece of flashing along the joins of the steeple held strong.

19.

Elise was never the same after that night. Her daily routines remained unchanged, but her gaze no longer settled on what lay in front of her: a face, a tree, a book. Either her eyes flitted between one object and the next, or they sank into themselves—open, yet unable to see. But it was far worse than that, too. Her presence once felt at the dinner table, the love Elise channeled into her pot roast, the drip of salty gravy down a chin, the bite of a warm biscuit like being welcomed in from the cold, was gone. If it was illness or guilt, Marley would never know, but the men in Elise's life could no longer ignore it.

It wasn't the food they missed. It was her.

Marley felt relief not to bear the weight of it alone, but another sadness took its place. She hadn't been prepared for their faces, so afflicted and concerned. Crushed. Briefly, she'd considered telling the rest of the family what she'd seen in the church attic, but she couldn't bear how it would wound them. They were already losing the mother they believed was impenetrable, and Elise's three sons were laden with disquiet. Shay began to help with dinner, his hands shaking as he rinsed the lettuce. Waylon washed the floors and the dishes. He washed her sheets. Baylor drove

Elise to the doctor and sat with her in the waiting room. They stopped going to church, even as the congregation was left stunned by Pastor Hollis's sudden disappearance.

The only person who didn't notice or care how his world was starting to chip was Mick. He went about his daily business of roofing, painting, playing the small piano he'd bartered for, and doing the crossword. Marley watched Mick's sons bend around him, contorting themselves so that he could remain the same.

By summer—what ought to have been a roofer's busiest season—Elise was more often gone into her mind than not. She sat on the porch while her geraniums yellowed and her maroon heels waited by the door. Her sons took on less work than they had the previous summer, in 1994. They cut back on spending and decided not to buy their own crane, took their chances on putting off the huge job Waylon had sold at a hospital in Greenville until the fall.

Way drew a heavy hand down his face as he struggled with the decision. "That was my biggest sale to date," he said. "We'll never be able to afford our own crane if we lose the job."

Baylor stood next to him in the dim kitchen, holding his mother's apron in his grip. "Fucking cancel it, Waylon," he said. "Cancel it all."

Waylon carried this weight everywhere he went, even as he slept. Marley did what she could to shoulder it. It never felt like enough. On a late night in June, they lay in bed together as a soft rain beat down against the screen of their open window. The air smelled like moss and Marley lay naked, Way flush against her back. His pack of Salems sat half-empty on the windowsill. Marley didn't press it. Any other year, they'd be talking about the rain itself, what jobs it would delay, what others it might create. But that night their hearts were shot through, and they were hunting for respite, and they found it in each other.

Waylon's hands traveled the land of Marley's skin. He whispered her name, and it sounded like the rain, and she wanted to drown herself in him. They were facing too many lasts for being so young—the last family dinner, the last time Elise would remember Theo's name, the last time she'd ask Mick to play "Moonlight Serenade" on the piano—and it had turned them into seekers. They hunted each other down at night, leaving no part of themselves unturned. Waylon kissed Marley's jaw, her neck, her shoulder, her hipbone. She wound her hands into his hair, and he held fast as he called out her name again.

"Marley," he said, breathless. "I think we need to move into the great house."

She stiffened at his words. Even Waylon, her ever-hopeful love, was beginning to fear the worst.

"Not forever," he promised. "Just for a while."

Marley knew his meaning, and it reached forward into a future where Elise wouldn't follow. Marley would never wish for it. She didn't care whether Elise had never loved her. Marley had never wanted to steal Elise's life away—she'd wanted only to separate her own from it. Already, people in Mercury asked after Elise in a different, careful tone—at the grocery store, in the post office, on the sidewalk. They'd found Elise's shoes, they'd seen her looking lost on her own street, they'd helped her home.

"How *is* Elise?" they'd ask Marley, and she never knew how to respond.

They wanted to know how long the end would take, how excruciating it would be, and really, the question on everyone's mind—how on earth this indomitable person could cease to exist—had no answer.

"Tell me what I can do," Ann said each time she dropped off a basket of rolls and strawberry jam.

So much went unspoken between them at the threshold of a house where Ann still wouldn't step inside. If Ann wanted to know what she could do for Elise, or what she might do to atone now for the secrets she'd kept from her, Marley was too weary to find out.

Waylon, when asked about his mother, always answered that the family was already doing everything it could, as if love might be powerful enough to stop what had found them. Marley saw him grasp at that hope with the same fervor he gave her at night.

Beside Marley in bed lay the man who had all her heart, wildly stretched between the loyalties of being both a husband and a son. Even though they were both tired, and sad, and scared, she didn't stop wanting him, aching for the rhapsody of their bodies locked together, the intensity with which

Waylon held her stare as he brought her to the end of herself. This was everything to her—their closeness, their bond. They'd built this life on it, and she needed it to sustain them now. Marley soothed him with her touch, turning in to her bedsheets with Way behind her, above her, around her. His hands clutched her hips, pulled her to him, and she begged him not to stop—words so bare and true, surrendered so Waylon would know that with Marley, he could be strong. With her, he could fall apart. And they fell together, and then fell asleep.

The next morning, they moved out of the apartment Elise had fixed for them when Theo was born, never to return.

Elise did not get better. She also didn't get worse. That summer of 1995, Shay Joseph's fifteenth birthday came and went. Marley baked him a cake. It had taken her all day, and somehow batter had ended up splattered on the kitchen wall, with Theo holding a beater in each of his hands. Shay had forgotten he'd told Marley how much he liked the apricot jam she'd put in his sandwich once, and she used it in the frosting. The smallest details about him were never inconsequential to her. Not his love of beach glass from Lake Erie, or his pocked drumsticks, or even his favorite citrus scent of Lysol he liked to use while cleaning the sink. Shay's cake was a bright, peachy hue, and even Baylor—who had the voice of a hound dog—sang before they ate it. Baylor, who thought he wasn't smart enough to educate Shay but had helped him make a wooden puzzle with a jigsaw so he could satisfy his industrial arts requirement for school.

Elise hugged her youngest son, called him good—a sentiment given far too late to be useful now—and Patrick did not come. A stupid thing for a fifteen-year-old to be hurt by, Shay told himself. It was time for him to grow up.

One morning in mid-August, Mick announced he was taking Elise to her doctor's appointment. The clanging of three brothers eating their cereal stopped at once as they looked to their father.

"Like, today?" Baylor asked.

Mick nodded glibly, as if he were taking his wife to the county fair. Shay thought it was strange, as Mick hadn't done so much as even one load of laundry to help Elise, and then he chastised himself. Of course his father wanted to take her. Of course he loved his wife.

All three of Mick Joseph's sons unclenched as the screen door shut and their parents drove away toward Route 62 in Elise's Lincoln. The day ahead felt fresh and steady without Mick around. He was unsafe on the roof. Like Baylor, he refused to wear protective gear, but he was also absent-minded. Just last week he'd teetered near the gutter of the auto parts store in the center of town, balancing on spindly two-by-fours as he pivoted and knocked a bucket of roofing cement onto the sidewalk.

Without Mick to babysit, the brothers finished their work before noon. They'd ripped out all the old roof plies on top of a dwindling cassette tape factory, and the grimy dust of coal tar pitch caked their every crevice. Laugh lines, knuckles, the bends in their knees. The brothers planned to return the next day to patch up the roofing deck, lay down the insulation and rubber membrane, and finally top it with gravel to keep that rubber from cracking in the heat. The sun, it turned out, could be just as damaging to a roof as a terrible storm.

Together, they ate the lunch Elise had packed for them in a cooler. Shay's sandwich had the lid of a tuna tin can stuck in it. He peeled it off and set it on the ground before them. The three watched it and didn't move. They sat beneath the shade of a hickory tree that whistled slightly in the hot wind. Beyond the tree line, they could hear tractor trailers as they sped down the highway. The brothers resembled a string of paper dolls: matching faded Levi's, work shirts with the sleeves cut off, deeply tan from days beneath the sun. How long Shay had wanted to be like them, and also didn't want to, now that they were all stuck on the same sinking ship. Each set of eyes trained on that tin can lid, afraid of what it prophesied.

"She's going to be all right," Baylor coughed. "She will."

Baylor wouldn't have offered such a platitude if it were only he and Waylon. It made Shay angry that they still treated him like a kid. *Let me be like you*, he thought. *Just once.*

"Stop it, Bay," he said. "You don't have to lie for me."

"She's so young," Way cut in, too worried to soothe or try to fix it. Shay preferred him this way. "What the hell is happening?"

Bay spat in the dirt. "Doctors don't fucking know. But shit, if I had to be married to that man, I'd lose my marbles, too."

A joke that wasn't funny, but sad. Shay wondered whether one person could cause an illness in another. If that was how life passed by, trading wounds through handshakes and family dinners and regret.

"Fuck this." Baylor came to his feet. "We're going swimming."

They packed up Mick's van and drove back roads away from the city, past the strip mines, speeding like it would never hurt them. The truck lurched to a stop at an old strip pit that had closed years ago when the ground had no more coal to give. It was fifty feet deep, the bottom of it like a junkyard of wire coils and metal. They could get arrested for swimming past the hazard signs. Baylor took off his shirt and jeans and cannonballed off the edge. He looked like Wolverine, brutish and woolly and also a little bit lost. Way followed, and Bay held him under, and they splashed and laughed the way Patrick and Shay used to do in the creek behind Patrick's house.

Patrick, whom Shay hadn't seen since they painted the church white and couldn't look each other in the eye.

At the edge of the water, an old rope hung from a retired crane like a noose. Not to be outdone by his older brothers, Shay stripped to his underwear, pulled the cable back, and got a running start before sailing through the air. He held on until his arc reached its peak, and he released. For just that one moment, it felt like flying instead of falling. Like living instead of dying. He exalted these treasures that lay in the empty spaces where the earth had been hollowed out—hidden coves and deadly precipices and the seams of coal running deep in the ground. He crashed against the water and dared open his eyes into the pit below, full of mineral and dirt and sweat from lives long ago.

When he came up for air, Baylor had grabbed the rope and took a swing. They laughed when Waylon tried it and did a belly flop. His skin burned bright red against the golden chain around his neck. Later, Shay would remember this portrait-in-motion of the Joseph brothers—fifteen, twenty-two, and twenty-three—one a father, one who swore he would never marry, and one who feared he never could. They had very few pictures of the three of them, so often together that they forgot it was special. This was the best memory Shay had of his brothers, that August moment when they flew through the air and felt like kings.

Shay couldn't sleep that night. He was tired of being the only brother left awake. Waylon, the luckiest of them all, never had any trouble drifting off. And Baylor often snuck out after dark. Shay knew Baylor loved best by the way he hid—he still waited for Elise's light to turn off before he headed for the bar called the Crow on Route 58. There was never any alcohol in the house, and Bay respected the rules. Kept his sins, as Mick might call them, outside their four walls.

Since he was young, Shay knew everything no one wanted him to. He'd collected all these Joseph family riddles—the ways each of them tried to appear other than what they were—because he was desperate for one of them to care enough to solve his own.

Past midnight, he heard a fierce rustle. A pinprick of silence, then a soft thrashing.

Insistent, urgent.

Shay crept to the open window. The street sat quiet in front of him, the tar and stones aglow beneath the streetlamp. The noise shuffled again, followed by a hoarse cough. Shay flipped on his light and stepped into the hall. The sound was coming from inside the house.

It could have been any one of them. Yet Shay knew who it was.

He ran for his mother. Elise lay in bed clutching a pillow she'd cross-stitched, her body ramrod straight. She couldn't breathe. The room was silent as she clawed her throat, her feet flailing at the tight hospital corners of her sheets. Her eyes shot to him, terrified, and Shay couldn't tell whether she recognized her youngest son. His face was not the one she wanted to see—that much he knew for sure. She was horrified by it.

Shay should have run to her, dug into her mouth with his fingers. That piercing look she gave him—like she knew all his scars—undid him. Like that had been what kept them apart all this time, and it always would be. Shay did the only thing he could. He called for his brother.

Please be home, Baylor. Please.

"Bay," he called out once, twice, three times.

His voice chirred, the sound of a child he thought he no longer was.

Like a giant bat, his brother flew in and lifted their mother into his lap. Bay looked like Waylon then, his face dripping in fear. He prodded, squeezed, pumped, begged. Shay had never heard Baylor Joseph beg for anything a day in his life.

Until now.

"Please, Ma," he said over and over, an incantation. "Not yet. Please."

Marley startled in Way's old bedroom to the bracing sound of someone's scream. She stumbled over a herd of Matchbox cars in the hallway toward Theo's room. She swung open the door where she found him fast asleep. Then she ran to Elise in an old T-shirt and underwear. Her legs buckled when she saw Elise lying limp in Baylor's arms.

Shay froze by the door to his parents' bedroom, the phone in his hand, his stare fixed on his mother. The oval mirror on Elise's vanity crashed on its side as Baylor tried to shake her awake. Marley couldn't hear herself scream for Waylon to get up. She couldn't stop. Shay's voice jolted her as he spoke to the emergency operator.

"It's my mother," he said into the phone. "Please come quick."

Elise lay on the floor, slumped against Baylor, who thumped her chest with his fists. Then he dug his fingers into her mouth.

"Fuck," he yelled.

Marley shoved his hands aside. "Mine are smaller," she said. "Let me try."

She did, but it changed nothing. Baylor squeezed Elise around the middle, then waited, then tried again. How silent this motion was, even as Waylon rushed in.

"Do something," Marley ordered her husband, gripping him by the shirt.

Elise's eyes settled right in the middle of Shay's chest. Unblinking, unseeing. Baylor pressed for a pulse. Marley heard a low moan. It was Waylon, down on his knees next to his brother. Only then did Marley realize Mick had been standing in the room by the vanity, a shadow of himself.

Baylor erupted.

"You motherfucker. What did you do?"

"Nothing could be done," Mick said, staring at the woven rug. He was still dressed in work clothes, white paint spattered across his hems. "This was inevitable, and you know it."

Baylor sank deeper into the floor with his mother against his chest. A paramedic burst in. He used a suction to free the paste of pills from Elise's throat. He coursed an electric current through her body. He started to sweat. Then he cursed, too. It was no use.

Elise was gone.

They pronounced her, *time of death, 1:03 a.m.*, and a gristled wail clawed out of Baylor's mouth. The sound haunted the empty halls. Shay reached for Marley's hand as Waylon remained on his knees next to his older brother. They looked like a pair of supplicants, begging for what they wouldn't get back. The only person not capsized by shock was Mick, who stood by the window, lifting the curtain to watch the ambulance lights twirl.

"Dad." Waylon barely got the words out. "What happened?"

"What do you think?" he snapped. "She got what she wanted."

Mick Joseph swore it was true. But had Elise Joseph ever gotten what she wanted?

The paramedics took the body, and just like that, the house had no Elise in it. The gurney wheels squeaked on the sidewalk, and none of her children went to the window to witness it. Baylor had not moved from his spot on the floor. Mick sat on the edge of his bed, a husband now separated from his wife. They'd been a family of seven at the beginning of the night, and now they were six.

Marley towered over her father-in-law. This anger inside her was meteoric and primed to explode. That moment marked a turning within Marley, the wheel of some ancient ire, some constant loss.

"What did you give her?" Marley demanded.

"Sleeping pills," Mick answered. "Prescribed by the doctor."

"All at once? How many?"

He hedged. "Elise had the bottle. I can't be sure."

Marley dug the empty bottle from where it had rolled under the bed.

It had been filled with twelve pills, and none were left. She threw it on the mattress.

"So did Elise do this herself, or did you give them to her?" Marley thrust her face into Mick's. "Which is it?"

"She needed help." He looked at her, that imploring expression like the one that had captured her the night she met him and his fingers held the final chords of "Moonlight Serenade." He'd seemed trapped inside the romantic notion of the song then, and now he acted as if he were caught in it still.

"*Help?* She wasn't lucid enough to ask for your help." Marley didn't realize she was yelling until she felt Waylon's hand on her back. "She *never* asked for help."

"Theo is next door," Waylon whispered, as if she didn't already know where her child was. She shook his hand away.

"Elise did not want to live like this." Mick pointed to the empty spot where her body had lain. "Sliding in and out of her life. Waking up next to a man she sometimes couldn't recognize."

His chin puckered, and Waylon swayed, and Marley was horrified by the sight of it.

"I understand, Dad," Waylon soothed. "I see."

He hadn't soothed anyone since the day he found out his mother was sick.

"I loved her," Mick declared.

"I know." Waylon wrapped his arms around his father, and Marley waited for him to turn to her, to show her he understood what Mick had done, to say with his eyes that they'd fix things once they were alone.

Instead he looked at his wife askance as if to say: *Is this proof enough for you?*

It was not. Waylon had watched the entire scene and chosen to side with his father. This wasn't Elise's doing; Marley felt it in her bones. And it wasn't an accident, either.

"Did Elise tell you that she wanted to die?" she asked.

Four pairs of eyes shot toward her, as if they couldn't believe she'd said it aloud.

"I didn't need her to tell me what I already know." Mick's own eyes were sharp. "We've been married for almost thirty years."

"I'm calling the police," Marley said.

She reached for the phone on the floor, but Waylon took her wrist and pried the receiver out of her hand.

"Waylon Joseph." She clenched her teeth. "Take your hands off me."

He did and dropped the phone to the floor. "If you call the police, my father will spend the night in jail."

"God forbid."

"He just lost his *wife*, Marley." Way pawed at his pockets, looking for a lighter that wasn't there. "What the hell is wrong with you?"

Mick sat on the bed like a forlorn lamb, and Marley didn't pity him. She felt a great tearing through the house, fiber by fiber, loyalty by loyalty.

"Baylor?" she called out to the stricken creature on the floor, who could only look at her and shrug.

Marley began to nod. "I see," she said, and she did. Here was the violent awakening of what Elise had said to her that night in the sanctuary, what Elise had tried to warn her of. When it came down to allegiances, these men would always choose each other.

Mercifully, Theo began to cry. Marley slipped into his room and locked the door behind her. Then she gathered her boy into her arms. She hadn't rocked him to sleep since he was an infant. He was too old for it now, and Marley didn't care. Theo, this life of her life: the heart that had to be left beating at the end of this, no matter what. Marley understood it then. She'd pay any price to give her son a capstone to lean on in this house of broken men, just as Elise had done.

Theo fell asleep, and she didn't put him down. Marley stared into the darkness until dawn stretched its fingers into the crevices between the blinds.

After

20.

Marley was the only woman left in the house.

It was cold. No matter how many sweaters she put on, no matter how much the August sun shone through the windows, Marley couldn't get warm. Shay sat beside her in his room the morning after Elise died, recounting what he'd seen the night before.

"My dad just stood over her. Doing *nothing*. She couldn't breathe, Marley. It happened so fast. I didn't know what to do."

His drumsticks lay in the corner of the room, next to a desk. It had been ages since she'd heard him play.

"You did everything you could, Shay Baby." Marley wrapped an arm around him and inhaled the scent of clean cotton. "You're not alone."

But alone was exactly what they were. After Elise's death, the Josephs did something they'd never truly done. They separated.

Over the next two days, Baylor roamed the house at night the way his mother once had. His footsteps sounded like fat stones falling on the stairs. Waylon hid in his childhood room, which now also belonged to Marley. They slept back-to-back—not touching, not speaking. And Mick sat at the dining room table, staring at a pile of crosswords he hadn't begun to fill in.

None of the Josephs came to the door when Patrick's father, a cop, stopped by to say he'd spoken with the coroner, who had ruled Elise's death an accidental overdose.

"She was ill, we understand?" he said with willful pity in his eyes, and Marley didn't know how to answer.

How much of it was illness, and how much of it trying to survive?

She and Patrick's father watched each other as he waited for her to confirm what he already believed, which had fallen directly from Mick's mouth: This death was inevitable. Already set in motion. Nothing anyone could do.

Marley wanted to rail against that version of the story with every atom in her body. But she thought about the other secret she was holding, the one Elise had asked her to keep, and she questioned her own loyalty and what it meant to honor it now. To prove it, even after Elise was gone. And she swore she could hear Elise's voice, clear as her own.

Just answer the damn question.

"Yes," Marley answered. "She was ill."

Her response shook her so deeply that after he offered his condolences and Marley shut the door, she slid down against it and couldn't catch her breath.

She didn't know what to do, so she did what Elise would have done. She stepped into Elise's kitchen, fingered her weathered, handwritten recipe for chicken divan, and started to cook. Marley placed meals outside each closed bedroom door, with a gentle knock to signal a casserole, then chili, then turkey sandwiches. She and Theo ate alone.

"Mom," he said, as he pushed his pudding aside. "Why is everyone mad at us because Grandma died?"

Even Shay didn't come down to sit with them. He barely ate at all.

"They're not mad, pal," Marley said, even though she thought maybe they were. "They're sad."

Marley couldn't see that she was grieving, too. All she could feel was anger. Anger that it was Elise who died and not Mick, fury that she'd loved the mother-in-law who had never loved her back. She couldn't compare her loss of this intrepid, infuriating woman with that of her sons. She had no name for it. So she began planning instead—a funeral, a burial, a wake, a repast. All these things, tangential to a life. Marley shouldered them all.

This is what it means to be part of this family, she said to herself. *Even when no one can see.*

When Jade visited on the third day to bring a tray of baked ziti, she took a hard look at her friend. Saw the bags under her eyes, the piles of dirty pots in the sink.

"Marley," she said. "You hate to cook."

Marley smiled weakly. Then Jade told Theo to get his sleeping bag.

"Come to the salon for a few hours," she said. "Just for a break."

"I can't." Marley heard the edge in her voice. "This place is falling apart."

She could see it wasn't just the dishes, or the pile of mail on her desk, or the dead plants on the porch. It was the way the Josephs had so swiftly abandoned one another now that the person who had first brought them together was gone.

"Look at me," Jade said, and Marley did.

A conversation passed between them without their needing to speak. Marley was trying to fix what couldn't be fixed, and Jade knew it.

"I'm taking Theo for the night," she said. "So you can rest."

Marley realized then that she hadn't showered since Elise had been alive. After Jade left, she crawled into the tub beneath the scalding stream without bothering to turn on the bathroom light and sobbed into her hands.

Four days later, the Joseph family held a memorial and a meal. The service was packed and perfunctory, hosted at the church—where Hollis's body still hid—and presided over by an aging interim pastor newly assigned by the presbytery, because everyone still believed that Hollis had abandoned them. Lavender dahlias spilled off the pulpit, the casket, the piano. Pastor Lennox had not known Elise, nor was he under the influence of the primrose aurora that surrounded the Joseph family in Mercury.

"Can you tell me about her?" Lennox asked right before the service.

"Honestly?" Marley answered. "I wouldn't know where to begin."

She preferred it this way—the distance of anonymity without the intimacy of lies. Marley had lived with the Josephs for four years, and it took only one night to prove she didn't know any of them at all.

Lennox recited the highlights of Elise's life, and Marley grew even colder. Graduated top of her class, a legendary cook. Loved to read. Donated most of her money and time to the church itself. Baylor tried to speak about his mother. Shay declined. All three Joseph sons sat in crisp suits, in addition to Theo's, that Marley had ironed herself. It had been Elise's iron, and Marley felt gutted to hold it. Death had threaded into the latticework of every object in the house—even Waylon's old necktie. Marley hadn't seen him wear one since their wedding day.

Baylor stood at the pulpit, looking blank-faced between the bouquets. His eyes sagged, his lips were chapped. He ran a hand down his chin, whispered "fuck," then "ah, shit," when he realized the microphone had captured his cussing, and then he sat down. He shot Waylon a glare and threw up his hands. Slowly, Waylon stood.

He strode toward the lectern, his shoulders heavy. He took a break to steel himself and looked toward the crowd. Then Waylon, the comforter, swept in and displayed all the shiny, heartfelt emeralds his brothers couldn't.

"My mother was a saint," he began.

Marley wanted to scream. Waylon had always been so honest. Why was he failing now?

She felt herself flying away toward the rafters, toward that sealed upper room that hid just above them. The body lying there that never had a funeral. She felt dizzy from it, this secret she never asked to be hers. She could have told someone now that Elise was gone, but she didn't want to. Marley would never give Mick the satisfaction of ever feeling even the least bit justified for what he'd done. Elise was no saint, as Waylon had declared. But she didn't need to be a saint to be missed. To be loved.

Waylon manned the podium, and he sounded so far away that Marley could hardly hear him.

"The last thing I want to say," Way said, looking out into the crowd where Elise's three sisters from Illinois sat, dressed in black, "is that my mother once invited a young woman who was new in town to have dinner at our table, and that's how I met my wife."

His eyes locked onto hers, and Marley felt a great burning.

"I think—" Waylon paused, a tough swallow working its way down his throat. "I think my mother was disappointed in me when she died."

The room was already quiet. Now it felt haunted.

"I made her a promise a long time ago, and I haven't done a good job keeping it." Way shoved a hand in his pocket, then pulled it out again. "But that's what loving someone is, isn't it? Knowing you're going to let them down. Having to live with it."

Waylon left the pulpit, looking thoroughly cleaved, and sat next to Marley in the front pew.

"Well," Baylor whispered. "That took a turn."

Marley hadn't stood in the same room with Way for days. He glanced down at her left hand, and for the first time saw no wedding ring there. His face paled, and she whispered his name, eager to tell him it wasn't what he thought. But Waylon shook his head, turned away, and before long he, his brothers, and his father were carrying Elise's casket down the center aisle.

At the repast in the great house, Marley hid in Waylon's old bedroom. Remnants lay around her of the sex they had the night Elise died, when Waylon had gently cupped his hand over her mouth to hold in her cry. How close they'd been, how fervent. How innocent. The sheets were still soiled, her underwear was still on the floor. Marley hadn't had time for cleaning—she'd organized the catering, printed the memorial programs, and paid the funeral home across the street. She couldn't stand one more condolence, couldn't repeat "thank you for your kind thoughts" even one more time. The Joseph men knew how to be gracious. Elise had raised them as such—or to appear that way, at least. *Let them*, Marley thought. She only wanted to be alone.

But she was never alone in the great house, try as she might. The doorknob turned, and she expected to see Waylon. Her heart leapt at the thought of him taking her into his arms, pulling her close. But it wasn't Waylon seeking refuge and quiet.

It was Baylor.

"I can't fucking stand it, Marley," he said. "Not one more thing."

She nodded, and together they looked out the window at the mass of cars clogging their street.

"Did you see her sisters?" he asked.

Marley had. Elise's three sisters—from the photo hidden in Mick's desk drawer—had arrived the day before. They traveled through the house in a tight pack, each one as grim-faced as the next.

"They look just like her, and they never talk." Baylor pressed a palm into the window. "It's freaking me the fuck out."

Marley didn't respond, and Baylor touched her arm. His fingers felt rough and warm.

"Marley," he said. "Are you all right?"

She couldn't help the tears that fell. She cried for Elise, cried that Baylor had been the one to check on her instead of her husband, cried that she even expected Waylon—who had lost his mother—to check on her at all.

"You know what my mother always used to say to me?" he asked, and Marley wiped her eyes. "Don't turn out like your father."

Bay leaned his forehead against the glass. The lights in the funeral home had all gone out.

"Baylor," Marley said. "You are nothing like Mick. You know that, right?"

A faint smile appeared on his face, plaintive and beat. He smelled like whiskey. "You and I might have been good together." He touched her cheek. "If I wasn't such a shit."

They stood side by side, not quite brother and sister, and not quite anything else. Bay took her face in her hands. Before she could pull away, he'd buried himself in her neck.

"Baylor," she said. "Stop."

She pushed her hands against his chest, but he circled her tighter, sinking his mouth onto hers.

"Stop," she said again, loud enough for someone to hear, trying to wrench herself free.

The door flew open and Waylon shot into the room. His hair was dirty and flat, his eyes rimmed in red. "What the hell are you doing?" he yelled as he ran for his wife.

He wrested Baylor's arms from her and shoved him to the ground. A picture frame fell off the wall. Baylor came back for him, full force, but Waylon caught him around his middle, preparing to tackle. Bay lost his balance and swung so violently at his brother, and missed, that he struck Marley's eye with his elbow and sent her flying into the footboard of the bed.

"Oh my God, Marley," Baylor cried.

Waylon hadn't had his fill. He dragged his brother back to the floor, where they tussled until Jade appeared. She took them both by the suit collar and shoved them toward the door.

"Out," she said. "*Now.*"

They obeyed. Jade ran for some ice, returned to Marley's side, and locked the door. Marley curled herself into bed with her best friend next to her. She held the ice to her eye as Jade walked to the window and shut the blinds.

Jade looked ready to kill.

"Marley." Her voice quivered. "Are you safe here?"

It wasn't Jade's habit to pose a question when she could give her opinion instead. She was pushing Marley toward some truth she wanted her to acknowledge on her own.

"I—" Marley began but didn't finish.

Jade had offered her four words and left so much unsaid. She knew how much Marley had always wanted a seat at the Josephs' table, that she was still trying to earn it, even when she felt she'd never be enough. Now they both saw how this depth of wanting could become a very dangerous thing.

Jade said nothing more until Marley fell asleep. Then she stood, found her friend's son, and took him home for the night.

At half past two in the morning, Waylon crept into the room. Marley woke to a throbbing head and a burr of blood in her mouth from biting her lip when she'd flown into the footboard of the bed. Her body clenched, and she turned away from him.

Way came and knelt before her, touched her swollen cheek. He was tender, generous, and unable to be present with the truth as Marley saw it, the way she wanted him to be.

"Marley," he said. "I know you're angry with me."

She couldn't look at him. "You promised me no more fighting."

"I know I did. I'm so sorry, Mar."

It struck her then, how adept he was at apologizing, how earnest, as the son of two people who didn't know how to do it at all. He'd learned from the absence of it, how to fill that empty space with what he'd needed but never received.

Marley and Waylon were both fixers. They'd built a marriage on it, and a business, too. Elise's death was the first time they didn't agree on what truly needed to be repaired.

"Why did you lie?" Marley asked.

His eyes were skittish. "What do you mean?"

"During the eulogy. Calling your mother a saint."

Marley felt the heat vibrating off him. The hurt. "It doesn't mean she wasn't a good mother, just because she was disappointed in me." His whole body wilted. "She's been disappointed in me since the day she found out you were pregnant."

The sorrow in his voice broke her. Waylon hadn't had his mother in a very long time.

"Can I stay?" he asked, just above a whisper. "I know things aren't all right between us, but please, Marley. I can't sleep without you. Not tonight."

Not after he'd buried the first woman he'd ever loved. Not after he'd soothed away his father's misdeeds. Not after he'd become a motherless son. Marley felt wrung out and unable to refuse. She nodded, and he took off his shirt. She saw the lines where the sun had kissed him, the scars that roofing had left. The muscle, the heart.

He climbed in beside her, wrapped his arms around her, and Marley knew there was something deeply wrong at the root of this family. As if he could read her thoughts, Waylon spoke.

"My father—he isn't right in his mind. Not since the war."

"But what does that mean, Waylon?"

He said it to offer an explanation. To inspire compassion. It only inflamed her. Mick was not the center of this story, no matter how the rest of the Josephs behaved. Why should he receive all the mercy, all the second chances, and Elise none? The arc of a mother's life shouldn't have self-sacrifice as its inevitable pinnacle. Once again, Marley relished that she'd chosen to keep Elise's secret. Sometimes a secret was all a woman had to call her own.

"Don't you get it?" she said to Waylon. "You claim your father hasn't been in his 'right' mind in years, but no one fed him a fistful of sleeping pills. No one questioned his utility, his right to live."

He opened his mouth, the words still caught in his throat.

"What if she wanted to die, Mar? And he loved her so much he granted it to her? That would shatter anyone."

"You don't really believe that's what she wanted, do you?"

He shushed her, which Marley loathed. "Don't," she said. "You're making both parents seem better than they are, and it's killing you."

Immediately, she regretted it. Now wasn't the time. He twined his fingers with hers, and she felt the wounded compassion in his grip. Each of them had tried to reach the other, and yet they couldn't.

"Please," he said. "Not tonight."

Marley relented, though she was ready to argue that it was already to-morrow. Her head swam, her body ached, but soon, she felt Waylon relax against her. There were so many things Marley didn't know, couldn't understand, and one thing she did. She didn't want to be the only woman who lived in this house. She couldn't stay here without Elise. Marley had shoved herself into Waylon's childhood spaces for long enough. She'd been quiet, compliant, useful. She'd been the helpful version of Marley, trying to earn her spot, with Waylon as her guide.

He had no idea about the role he played in his family. It came to him as easily as breathing because he'd never been without it. In this house, Way could not act as a husband ought, because he would always be a son. The walls were marred with holes from his old posters, his socks stuffed in the drawer, still paired by Elise's hand. Marley could even still smell the beaten leather of his baseball glove. And part of Waylon wanted it just that way. Here, memories of the mother who cared for him still lived.

Marley couldn't get Jade's question out of her mind. What did it mean for her to be safe here now?

Just before dawn, she slipped herself from Waylon's embrace. She staggered through the room as she silently threw her clothes into a duffel bag along with one of Way's T-shirts, then crept down the hall and did the same for Theo. She took the quilt Elise had sewn for him and his favorite bedtime book, *The Runaway Bunny*. Last, she knocked softly on Shay's door. When she entered, he lay awake, fully clothed and on top of his sheets, staring at a barely turning ceiling fan.

"Shay," she whispered. "Pack your things. We're going to stay at my mother's."

He groaned and shifted. His crumpled suit jacket lay at his feet. Shay covered his face with his hands.

"You don't want to?" Marley asked.

"I want to, but I can't. Not now. Not when—"

Shay didn't finish his thought, but Marley finished it for him. Not when these men were so wrecked.

"They're not your responsibility," Marley said. "Your brothers. Your father."

This was why she wanted him to come—to spare him. If Marley left alone, Shay would care for the family the way Elise did, giving away what he'd never gotten from her.

"You want to stay," she said softly.

Marley couldn't force him because he wasn't her son.

Shay nodded, but he didn't move. The fan above them clicked as it spun. Marley took a sheet of paper from his nightstand and wrote her mother's number on it.

"Call me every weekday at two. We'll keep up your lessons once school starts." She bent over him, kissed his head, and he held her tight, like she wasn't coming back. "When you want me to come and get you, Shay Baby, just call."

She was so certain he would.

Shay wiped his eyes and her heart broke fresh, just when she thought it couldn't break any more.

She padded down the grand staircase into the foyer and stopped with her hand on the doorknob. That's when she spotted Mick, seated at his new piano in the music room next to the window that faced the street, his shadow looking like a mudslide in the half-light. She tried to escape his notice, but he spoke without moving his eyes from the glass.

"You think I killed her," he said plainly.

Her hand left the knob. "I do."

"She took the pills herself."

Marley stepped into the threshold of the music room, her feet on Elise's plush carpeting. "Mick," she said. "How much did you know about your wife?"

"I knew plenty, same as her." His eyes dogged her. "She knew I'd do what no one else in this house had the stomach for."

Marley was no closer to understanding the secrets Mick and Elise shared, and she never would understand. All of death's fanfare had gone; there were no winners left.

"We are never going to agree," Marley said.

He turned away, looking tired and alone. She left the great house, packed up her Chevy Citation, and counted the small amount of cash in her pocket. The air in town was humid as she drove through it. As the streetlamps ticked past, she pressed the gas. She no longer wanted to be the Marley who stayed—she wanted to return to who she'd been before she met the Josephs and got caught in all their transgressions, the Marley who left. She picked up her son from her best friend, promised to call when she arrived, then drove south and reached the highway before the sun came up.

21.

A few hours after Marley arrived at her mother's condo, she began to bleed. Ruth's place was crisp and white, situated next to a grove of magnolia trees and down the street from a shopping mall. It was the nicest home she'd ever had, now that she'd been living on her own—and Marley couldn't help the mess she spilled all over it. The bloodshed wasn't like her monthly period; it was urgent and clotted and woeful.

She recalled the chills she had the night before, the way her muscles coiled. The pain was so blindingly precise that she crawled into Ruth's very white bathtub and could not get out. Theo knocked on the door and she couldn't answer. Trees outside the far window swayed in the breeze, casting their shadow across the floor. Marley counted to ten. The swells of pressure piercing her middle were just as fierce, just as insistent as they'd been when Theo was born.

Marley had no idea she was pregnant. And now she was losing it.

She tried to call out for her mother but could make no sound. When Ruth finally found her, the pain had ebbed for a moment. She was pale, flagging against the back of the tub. Ruth looked at her, at the pool of blood circling the drain.

"I'm calling Waylon," Ruth said.

"No," Marley shouted, her voice loud in the small space.

"Come now." Ruth rarely sounded so sharp. "No fight is worth this."

Marley swirled at the words, wondering whether her mother had said them to a girl, a woman, a wife, a mother, or a daughter. Which one was she now?

Ruth went for the phone.

"Mom, don't," Marley said, but her voice drowned in her own exhaustion. She passed out, right in the tub, and dreamed that her torso was being flattened in a vice. When she woke, her mother stood over her with another woman at her side.

"This is Dr. Perry. She's a friend," Ruth said. "She's going to help clean you out."

Marley's back arched. They were three women, and each of them knew what it meant to be clean. More pain was on its way.

"No," Marley said. "It hurts."

"I know," Dr. Perry said. "I'm here to help you."

She looked to Ruth, and Marley understood. If she went to the hospital, there would be questions to answer from men. They would call her husband without her consent. There would be a huge bill, too. Marley nodded and tried to breathe. Dr. Perry put on a mask and a pair of gloves.

"How far along are you?" She helped Marley lie down on the cold bathroom floor.

"Two months? Maybe three."

"Marley," she said, and Marley started to hate the sound of her name. It was always a precursor to things she didn't want to hear. *Marley*, Elise commanded while baring her secrets. *Marley*, Jade whispered before asking whether she was safe. *Marley*, Baylor repeated when he feared he was just like his father. But what about Waylon, who had always asked her questions and waited for the answer—when was the last time he'd said her name, and it had mattered? Marley knew it must have been before the night Elise had died.

"You run the risk of infection if I don't get everything out," Dr. Perry said. "All right?"

Marley squeezed her eyes shut, spreading herself on top of her mother's good towels so the doctor could work. The pain was so magnificent that Marley left her body, found the tops of the magnolias, and built herself a nest there. When she descended and found her skin and a trash can full of what she'd held inside her, she was helped into bed and given an antibiotic. She slept, then cried, then slept. Marley considered calling Waylon a hundred times.

One reason, more than any other, kept her from making the call.

When Baylor had knocked her into the footboard of the bed, the corner of it clocked her right beneath her abdomen. Twelve hours later, she'd started to bleed. Marley suspected it was Baylor's fault that she lost the baby, and she knew that Waylon would never forgive him.

It comforted Marley, living with her mother. As in: she didn't have to care for any men. So little drama, so few mouths to feed and clean up after. Marley remembered how much she treasured being a daughter. Elise had never truly treated her like one. Marley and Ruth cooked, listened to Linda Ronstadt on vinyl, and watched Theo rescue worms from the sidewalk and place them in the grass. He asked endless questions about why Waylon hadn't come along, and where Elise had gone, and why, why, why they'd left the only house Theo had ever lived in. Marley answered as best she could— that she needed some time away, and that often, life didn't make any sense when you lost someone you loved.

"I want Dad," Theo said after Marley scolded him for trying to stand on the back of Ruth's couch and leap off it.

It was the kind of thing she prohibited, and Waylon encouraged. She understood Theo's longing; she had it herself. She still hadn't washed Way's shirt. But Marley wasn't sure whether the husband she'd left behind was a man she and her son should trust.

"I know, pal," she said, running a hand through his soft, auburn hair. "Me, too."

When Ruth worked long hours and Theo napped, Marley found time for herself. Hours to think her thoughts, to wonder what might have been if she'd said no to Waylon's marriage proposal instead of yes. Marley didn't regret it, but she still felt the loss of that unknown, what-if life. Who she might have been if she'd wandered instead of remained. She waited for Way to come after her, to call. To do what he did best and fix it. Day after day, he didn't. One week became two.

Shay was set to start his homeschooling in late August. He called the night before his first day and spoke in hushed tones.

"Waylon enrolled me at the high school," he said.

On her end of the line, Marley started tapping her fingernails against the Formica counter. She'd painted them dark blue, and one of them chipped. "Is that"—she took a breath—"is that what you want?"

"It's fine, Mar. It'll be fine. You okay?"

She looked at Theo, who was sitting in a time-out after coloring a library book with a pen. She could tell he was listening. Worry drenched his tiny face over how often now his mother got upset. Marley looked to the forest beyond Ruth's window, where trails wound through black oak trees. She had split into two Marleys—one who loved the Josephs, and one who loved herself. "I'm good, Shay Baby. How are things there?"

Shay didn't answer right away. "It's—" He stalled, called out something muffled Marley couldn't decipher. "I gotta go, Mar. Way's coming. He doesn't . . ."

Marley waited. "He doesn't what?"

Shay had already hung up the phone. Marley paced the floor so doggedly that Ruth's downstairs neighbor began poking the ceiling with a broom handle. By the time her mother returned, she was flint-faced, tight-fisted, and stirring a vat of linguine on the stove.

"What's all this?" Ruth asked, referring to the stream of laundry Marley had strewn about in her wake.

"It's Waylon. He put Shay back in school."

Ruth nodded and took over the stirring. Marley had spilled dry noodles on the back burner of the stove.

"Is that so bad?" Ruth asked. She spoke softly, as if Marley were a riled cat who needed to be coaxed down from a tree.

"He's doing it to punish me."

At that, her mother looked up and put down the wooden spoon.

They'd ventured into new territory, as one mother speaking to another, as two people who were learning that grief is rarely coherent.

"It's possible he's doing what he thinks is best for Shay," Ruth said.

Marley smirked, just to hide how much she missed this boy who didn't belong to her. "I doubt it."

Ruth took up her stirring again. "It's all right to miss them, even if you're angry."

Marley picked Theo up as a shield. "Are you trying to get rid of me?"

She'd asked because it had been weighing on her. Marley hadn't managed to find the independence her mother had, and it embarrassed her. She'd been working in the Joseph family business since before Theo was born yet had no money of her own. She could get a minimum-wage job in Maryland, but it wouldn't cover the cost of childcare. Marley had made a career for herself in Mercury, one where Theo could remain at her side. And she'd left it behind.

She felt freer here than she had at the great house on Hollow Street, and somehow just as trapped.

"Did you ever want to get married?" Marley asked Ruth as she set Theo down on the floor and he ran into the living room.

Ruth drained the pasta in the sink. "No. I didn't want a husband." She glanced up at her daughter. "But didn't you?"

The emotion lived not so far off, this memory of wanting to be Waylon's wife, of feeling called to his family. It was buried beneath a grave of hurt, beyond Marley's ability to dig.

"Do you think I chose wrong?" She'd been wanting to ask her mother this question for a long time, but only now had the courage.

"Do you mean about getting married or having a baby?"

"About all of it."

Ruth's stare needled her. "I could never answer that," she said. "I can't even answer it for myself, as if I could ever wish that you didn't exist— even though I'd change the circumstances if I could."

Marley asked the next question she was afraid to face. "Take Theo out of it, then. Did I ruin your dream for me?"

"Don't you see?" Ruth's forehead creased. "I just wanted you to dream for yourself. I wanted you to have a choice, and I'm still not sure that you did."

To that, Marley had no response. She knew she couldn't choose between what she had now and what might have been. She also knew her mother had never gotten that choice, either.

"How do you always know?" Marley asked. "When to leave, when to stay—what to tell me when I'm upset. You always knew what to do as a mother, even when I screwed up. Even when I disappointed you. Even though I must be disappointing you now." Her eyes fell to the floor. "I don't think I've ever felt that even once."

But that wasn't quite true. Marley had known what to do exactly one time, when she escaped the great house with Theo in the middle of the night.

"I never knew, and I still don't," Ruth said quietly. "My worst mistakes have been the ones I made as a parent."

"Mom," Marley said. "That isn't true. Look at everything you did on your own."

"I had help here and there, Marley. Not enough, but I had it." She shook some salt onto the linguine. "I didn't do it all by myself, and you don't have to, either."

Marley picked up a jar of pasta sauce and ran her fingernail down the length of the paper label. Just last week she'd made this meal for the Joseph family, but she'd done it alone.

"I want to give Theo everything you gave to me," Marley whispered. "And I haven't figured out how, even with all those people living in that house."

"Most of what I did was just trying to survive," Ruth answered. "And making sure you knew you were loved."

Marley set down the sauce and reached out a hand toward her mother's. "I knew."

The moment held them as the pasta hissed in the strainer and Theo ran his Matchbox car across the floor. Outside, the early-evening sun spread across the woods.

"I want to tell you something," Ruth said, and Marley squeezed her hand.

"I used to think it was my job to make your life easier." Ruth squeezed back. "But I failed."

"Mom," Marley protested, but Ruth went on.

"It wasn't until I failed at it that I realized what you really deserve— and what I'd give you if I could—isn't an easy life, but a full one. And now I think that's something you have to give yourself."

Marley stayed silent for a minute.

"Is that what you have now?" she asked. "A full life?"

"Let's just say," Ruth answered as she dropped Marley's fingers and poured the drained pasta back into the pot, "I'm working on it."

"Mom," Marley said again as she met Ruth by the stove and leaned into her mother's shoulder, her warmth, her very self. "I wish I knew what to do."

"I guess what I'm trying to tell you"—Ruth wrapped an arm around Marley's waist as she dropped half a stick of butter into the pot—"is that it's all right if you don't."

After five weeks, the green leaves of the magnolia trees began to turn gold. The weather cooled, and Marley found herself missing Mercury in autumn—the sound of a distant bass drum from the marching band on a Friday night, the haze of burning leaves. Mostly, though, Marley ached for Waylon. Ached for the way he watched her while she spoke, for the way he held her when they slept, for that depth of connection she couldn't get anywhere else. Ached even more that he hadn't come. So when from her window she saw a white construction truck with the Joseph & Sons logo stuck to the side pull into the parking lot, she ran out to greet it, barefoot and hair down.

Yet it wasn't Waylon who hopped out of the truck, not Waylon who had come to see her.

It was Baylor.

22.

Marley stopped short in the grass, tucked her arms around herself in the chill. The last time she'd seen Baylor, Jade had towed him out of her bedroom by the collar, Waylon's blood all over his fists.

"I know I'm not who you want to see," he said, staring at the sidewalk.

His hair was shorn down to the scalp. Bay looked fragile and wooden, like he'd exhausted himself practicing what he wanted to say. "But I had to come. I fucked up, Marley, I know that. I'm so sorry for all of it. Please, though. You have to come home."

She'd never heard Baylor say so many words at once.

"What's wrong?" she asked. "Tell me."

And he did.

Things were not well in the great house in Mercury, Baylor said, after she'd welcomed him inside and poured a cup of tea. Mick had started asking every widow he knew on a date. Half of the church directory had been scandalized. Shay was back in school and miserable. He was also attempting to cook dinner every night and sending most of it into the trash.

Waylon fared the worst: not eating and smoking to the hilt. Not quite making it to his bed before falling asleep in the hallway. Hadn't made a sales call since before Elise had died.

"The business is in the shitter, Mar. We have work we still haven't finished. The invoices are a mess. I have no idea what money is coming or going. Look," he said. "I can roof the hell off a building, but I'm not a salesman." He stood before her, hands faintly quaking. "It's not fair, Marley, but we need you. All of us. Everything we've worked for? I'm telling you, we're about to lose it."

It was everything Marley expected would happen, and she found no satisfaction in it.

She had never once buckled beneath the burden of the Joseph family name. There was power in it, and there was suffocation. Baylor felt it, too, this birthright that felt like a razor and a salve. Marley couldn't return to the old Marley now, the one who always left without looking back. And she couldn't keep being this new Marley—the one who wanted to stay, no matter the cost. She had to find a way to be both.

"Two things," she said, and Baylor nodded. "First, do you want me to come home for work, for the family, or both?"

Baylor didn't hesitate. "Both."

"Then here's the second thing. I want a paycheck," she said, looking at him squarely.

He blanched. "We can't afford it right now."

Marley took a sip of her tea. "Sounds to me," she said, "that you can't afford not to."

A wry smile fanned across his mouth. "Well, shit," he said. "The lady has made her case."

They laughed, and he looked pained. "I'm so sorry for—" He paused, unable to finish, and grabbed the back of his neck with his palm. "I was drunk the night of the funeral. It's not an excuse, it's just—I don't measure up to the person my mother saw in me."

"But you might."

Bay shook his head. "Don't hold your breath."

Even in his refusal, Marley caught a glimpse of what Elise had seen in her oldest son. He didn't need Marley. Baylor could strike out on his own, put slate on residential roofs, restore old cars, eat soup out of tin cans—if he only cared for himself. Baylor wasn't here for Joseph & Sons. He was here for his brother.

Bay bit his lip. "So you'll come home?"

It was not the way she wanted to be asked, and not by whom. And yet, she wanted to go.

Marley and Theo arrived around noon the following day. She'd gotten up early to pack up her Citation before she lost her nerve, and then she hugged Ruth in the dark morning.

"What do I always say?" Ruth asked, holding her close.

"Head on straight, heart on straight."

As she drove away with her mother shrinking in the rearview mirror, Marley understood a bit more of what motherhood meant, this continual opening of every door for children to pass through, stay a while, leave, and return.

Even from the curb of the great house, Marley could tell that the men were still at sea with grief. The gutter hung askew from the side of the roof, which no Joseph would have stood for before Marley had left. Elise's geraniums had grayed in their pots. Marley could smell the stench of whatever dinner had burned in the oven the night before, all the way from the sidewalk.

All this, she expected. She wasn't prepared for what she saw next.

Waylon lounged on the porch, leaning against the railing and smoking a cigarette. His shirt hung off his lean frame, and his eyes looked overcast and dulled. He glanced up when Marley cut the engine, locking stares with her. She found an expression there she hadn't witnessed before: part despair, part wrath. They had been married for over four years, yet Marley knew now that marriages were not measured by time. They were tracked by disappointments, by hurts. Betrayals and apologies.

Her hands started to shake.

"Mom," Theo said. "Can you let me out?"

When Marley unbuckled Theo from his car seat, he flew out and ran into his father's arms. Way swept him up, and laughed, and disappeared with him into the house. She knew then she wouldn't see them until dinner.

Hollow Street was empty, a dog barked, and no one came out to greet her. Marley felt a bit like the stray she'd been that night she'd first climbed to Waylon's window, waiting to be let in.

This time, she was using the front door.

She sighed, steeled herself, and hauled her duffel bag up the stairs toward Mick's room of records, where the real work began.

Marley found unexpected calm as she set about organizing the cluttered office. No one had tidied it since Elise's funeral. A flat bottle of Crystal Pepsi lay sideways on the floor next to a petrified peanut butter and jelly sandwich. Her pack of bright green gum still sat next to Mick's Rolodex. Even though it was cold, she threw open the window, found her ledger, and began a great purge. Before she'd left, Marley had let Mick's records stand. She'd forced herself to work within his arbitrary system, but not anymore. Now she was doing this her way.

She'd sorted through all the outstanding work orders and potential leads on the answering machine by the time Shay came home from school. He stepped into the kitchen, saw her at the stove, dropped his backpack, and ran to her. Marley had been gone two months, and he looked older, stronger, lonelier. Her boy picked her up and twirled her around.

"Oh my God," he said, a tension in his throat. "I thought you weren't coming back."

She touched his curls. How she'd missed this Joseph and his humming-bird heart. "How was school?" she asked.

He lifted a shoulder. "It's fine, Mar. Swear."

She watched him until his eyes shifted to the counter. He'd grown up that summer; Marley could feel a heat rising off him, a new heaviness to his gait. She had missed too much already. Couldn't bear to miss even one second more.

"I—" she started. *I wish I hadn't left you.*

"Let me help you cook," he said at the same time.

Then he reached into the bowels of the refrigerator and handed her a can of Diet Coke. No one else in the house drank it. Shay had kept it for her, even when he thought she wasn't coming home.

Marley took the can. "I hear you've been feeding the whole house."

Shay groaned. "I'm the worst. It's why Waylon is so thin."

"Don't worry about that. Leave Waylon to me." She said it more confidently than she felt for this man who loved her not so long ago but hadn't fought for her at all.

At the 6:00 p.m. chiming of the grandfather clock, the Joseph men gathered at the table—sitting idly like crows on a telephone wire, unsure whether they should wait to be served. There was no tablecloth, no clean silverware, no fancy goblets. Newspaper littered the table, along with a crowd of dirty paintbrushes. Mick looked wily, Baylor worried, Waylon withered. Marley strutted in with her hands on her hips to look at the lot of them.

"Now, then," she said. "You can serve yourselves, if you like."

Mick stood, and she thrust a hand in his direction. Marley noticed he'd poked a new hole in his belt to help pull his pants in. No one had been eating in the house, it seemed.

"Just a minute," she said, and Baylor's eyes found hers. *Now's the time,* they seemed to say.

"Sit down," Marley said. "Please."

Mick sat.

"Tomorrow Mick and Baylor are going to finish the job at the cassette factory. The rest of your supplies will be delivered by midmorning. I've already called and apologized for the delay. Waylon." She felt nervous as she said his name. "There are a lot of leads left on the answering machine. I picked three that are right off Route 80 near Clearfield. It should be a simple enough task for tomorrow. Can you do that?"

Waylon looked to his brother, his father, and then to her. She'd never spoken to any of them this way before. "I can," he said.

"And Marley's gonna start getting paid," Baylor spoke up. "Starting today."

This brought Mick to his feet again. The glasses perched on the top of his head fell to the floor. "Paid? For what?"

"For all the shit you and I can't do," Baylor said, and he and Mick both waited for Waylon to speak.

Way's jaw rocked back and forth, covered in a fine stubble that Marley once would have liked to feel rough against her shoulder.

"Fair's fair," he said.

Marley didn't thank them, and she didn't ask for past money she was owed. They ate disjointedly while Theo told them about the trees he climbed in Maryland.

"Mom wore your shirt the whole time," Theo said to Waylon, and specks of shame dotted Marley's skin.

Way ate nothing. When Theo finished his plate, his father swooped him up again, leaving the rest of them cheerless. Waylon was the thermostat in this family. No one knew how to behave when he was boiling. For the third time, Mick stood from the table.

"You've got dish duty tonight, old man," Baylor said. "I'll take tomorrow."

Mick didn't argue. He collected the plates and set about washing them in the sink. Before, he would have been playing "Moonlight Serenade" on the piano by now. Before, Elise had done all the dishes herself. Now, everyone knew they had to be better men than they were.

Marley sat at the dining room table as the sun went purple and set over the far silver maple trees. The emptiness she'd felt the last time she stood in this house still hunted her. It had waited for her return. Elise was still here, and yet she wasn't.

Shay finished his geometry homework next to Marley, then disappeared into the garage to play his drum set. Marley felt the house's beams bracketing her. The immobility of grief had set in: for Elise, for a pregnancy, for the innocence of what she'd had with Waylon that was tarnished now. She'd tried to outrun it all and failed.

At eight o'clock, she rose to put Theo to bed. The stairs were dark as she climbed them. When she reached Theo's room, his door was already shut. The sounds of Way reading a book wafted through the wall, and Marley leaned against it.

"I missed you, pal," she heard him say, such tenderness in the words.

She didn't want to be standing there when Way came out. Where else could she go but down the hall, into the room they'd shared? It was autumn now; the sun had set long ago. A chill curled in from the open window, and Marley felt the maleness of this space once again—his dirty clothes on the

floor, an unmade bed. What had happened the last time she was here, the fight and the fall, was a memory Marley would circle for the rest of her life.

She also felt another sadness. She couldn't feel her own absence in this space because she'd never belonged in it. This was Waylon's territory, and Waylon's haven. Either Baylor hadn't told him she was coming, or he didn't care. Every inch of her was hurt by him—there was no place she kept that he hadn't smeared. What had she done that had caused their marriage to part from love and turn into pain? She'd done nothing, in her mind, but try to defend Elise.

She needed to get out, to the roof, as Elise had done. There, she could think and remind herself of why she'd returned—of the family worth fighting for. The family that was hers. Marley placed a foot on the bottom of the windowsill and stuck her hands on either side to hoist herself. The wind bit and made her feel alive. Before she stepped out, someone grabbed her arm and pulled her backward.

Waylon.

She could tell by the way his chest fit against her back, the heat of his hands on hers. The smell of his shirt that she'd missed. He spun her slowly, and Marley imagined he wanted to kiss her. End this strife.

He lifted her left hand and asked, "Where is your wedding ring?"

She didn't recognize this voice, this man. *Where are you*, she wanted to say.

"I lost it, Way. Before your mother died." These were the truths she could tell. "It must have slipped off my finger."

The angles of his face hardened in the dark. "You should have told me," he said, as if her withholding it had been the match that lit this fire, as if the truth would solve all the hurt that lay beneath it.

"When? As I was planning the wake? Arranging the funeral? Picking out a dress for her to be buried in?"

Way released her hand and stepped away. "Don't do that," he said. "Don't play the martyr."

"What have I done but try to help you? What did I do that made you hate me?" Her voice spilled around them like a waterfall. "Just because I

didn't go along with your father's story about loving his wife so much he killed her?"

"What did you *do*, Marley?" He stepped toward her, and she inched her back against the wall. Emotion pulsed from his body in waves—anger, lust, hunger, need. "What did you *do*? You took my son from me. That's what you did. I can think of nothing more heartless than waking up after my mother's funeral to find you gone, with Theo, leaving no note behind. I lost all three of you at once—my mother, my wife, my son. That's what you did."

To that, Marley had nothing to say. How had she forgotten her own ability to inflict pain? She hadn't seen Waylon cry since the day he found out she was pregnant.

"What did *I* do that deserved that, Marley?" He leaned his head out the window. "Why did you come back? For me, or the business?"

"What does it matter?" She dug her nails into the flesh of her arms. "You didn't come after me, either way."

He acted as if he hadn't heard. "Well, now that you've got your own paycheck, you don't need to stay here."

"Don't say that to me." Her voice lost its strength. She saw her husband in his grief, how it had razed him. It had taken all of Marley's mettle for her to come back into this house. To choose it. To say it was right when she knew such a thing didn't exist.

"I get why you want your own money. I do." The words flattened Waylon like an old tire. He turned toward her, helpless at the sight of his wife, his best friend, and leaned his forehead into hers. "Everything I have is yours, Marley. All of this, I did for you."

"Who's the martyr now?" she asked wistfully, because all the venom had leaked out of her.

Way wiped his eyes, and cursed, and then left Marley alone in the room that had never been theirs.

Marley stayed. Baylor's words from long ago floated around her like driftwood. She was a stray, hoping to be taken in. Yet she was also the wife who had left. Both versions of herself felt true: she'd needed to leave, and she'd needed to return to rescue a part of herself.

Marley might not have stepped into it so willingly if she hadn't run out on them in the middle of the night. It shamed her that either she hadn't thought of how hurt Waylon would be if he woke to find her gone, or if that had been her aim from the start. Had she wanted him to feel the pain of being the one not chosen, the way Waylon had chosen his father over her?

Still, though. Marley wanted to atone for what she'd done.

Waylon was so practiced at the art of apology, Marley couldn't recall a time she'd made amends first. He always jumped out ahead of conflict, like a deer trying to head off a car. It frightened her already, the ways she was becoming just like Elise. The martyr, the cook. The woman of the house who resented her husband. Marley didn't want to be someone who couldn't admit when she was wrong.

Waylon didn't seem ready for it. He quivered around the first floor like a wraith, only turning human if he saw his son. When he entered the upstairs office to take a work order from Marley and their fingers brushed, he drew back like he'd grazed a flame. Marley had been sleeping on the floor in Theo's room. Waylon, in his stupor, had lost his sense of gallantry and hadn't offered his bed. Baylor would have, she knew. He was often out all night anyway. Marley disliked the strain in her marriage playing out as theater for the rest of the Josephs to watch. It felt claustrophobic, perhaps the way Elise felt in everyone knowing she and Mick kept separate beds. It had sent her to the roof, to another man's arms.

Marley didn't know what to do, so she went to ask Jade, who had an answer at the ready for anything.

This time, it was Jade who needed her.

23.

Marley had been back for nearly a week and had yet to see her best friend. She feared Jade would think less of her for returning to Mercury, hadn't dared mention it during their weekly conversations on the phone. When Marley entered the shop, she found Jade standing on the counter while water poured out from the utility closet onto the floor.

Five inches of water spread across the whole salon, at least.

"Marley." Jade's eyes were red, and she was soaked. "Don't come in."

"What happened?" Marley yelled over the swell.

"The hot-water heater burst, and the electricity is still on. I'm scared there's an electric current in the water."

Marley took a step back and yelled down the street for someone to call the fire department. Mercury didn't have its own; it would take them at least a half hour to arrive. Then she went to the trunk of her car, pulled out the rubber waders she kept there for all of Theo's pond adventures, and went in to rescue her friend.

"Climb on my back," she said to Jade when she reached her on the other side of the salon.

"Marley," Jade said. "I'm half a foot taller than you."

"Just do it."

Jade climbed on, and together they made it out the door, where they sat on the concrete and watched Jade's shop fill with water while they waited for the fire department to arrive.

"What are you doing here?" Jade asked. Her manicure had started to peel, and her hair was coiled in knots.

Marley took off her boots. "So you *do* think less of me for coming back."

Jade put her head in her hands. "I didn't want you to have to come back, and I've never been so glad to see anyone in my entire life." Water seeped out the door and started a river toward the gutter.

"Marley," she said. "What am I going to do? I don't even have enough in my bank account to cover the insurance deductible for this."

Marley took hold of her arm. "We're going to let the fire department turn off the water, and then tomorrow we're going to clear out the damage. Okay?"

Jade acted as if she hadn't heard. "I built my whole life around this salon, Mar. I don't have anything else."

Marley could have said that Jade had her, but she knew that wasn't what Jade meant. It was almost a privilege, Marley's ability to leave. Jade couldn't pick up and travel to Maryland without losing everything she'd built. She *was* this place.

The fire department arrived; they shut the water valve. Made sure the electricity was off as well, and then they left Jade and Marley standing in a flood as it crept up the wall. The trunks of the black palm trees they'd painted began to blur. Jade's rattail combs floated around them, and everything smelled like a sewer.

They each got a push broom and shoved the extra water out the front door. When Marley's framed drawing of palm-tree scissors from their first meeting in the school supply room floated out onto the sidewalk, Jade stopped and leaned against the counter.

"Marley," she said. "I don't want to be alone anymore."

"Okay." Marley propped her broom against the storefront window. "Do you want to add another stylist here, or do you want to go on a date?"

Jade rubbed a hand against her forehead. "I don't know. Neither. Both. But I'm going to need to repair the shop first."

"Well, the extra stylist I can help you with. Payroll and all of that." Marley paused. "As for the shop—I'll ask Baylor to come with the wet vac tomorrow. Once everything's dry, he can patch the wall."

"You're not serious." Jade looked like she'd been slapped. "Do you remember what he did to you?"

Marley had told her about the kiss, the pregnancy, all of it.

"I forgave him."

Troubled, Jade laughed. "I haven't."

The sound of dripping filled the space around them.

"Maybe he deserves a second chance." Marley felt silly saying it, even though she believed it was true.

"Do you hear yourself?" Jade said. "You've given those men plenty of chances. Sure, they'll sell a car for you or propose marriage on a whim, but do they have any emotional backbone when it really counts?" Water trickled down the wall, and Jade looked tired and defeated. "You always say yes, Marley, and I love that about you. But I'm saying no. I don't want their help."

Marley knew her friend was saying things she otherwise wouldn't if her shop hadn't just flooded. Even so, it was clear that her best friend had examined Marley's life and concluded she'd never want it as her own.

"Do you think forgiveness makes me weak?" she asked.

"No." Jade took Marley's drawing and set it on a shelf. "But it puts you at risk."

Marley knew she wasn't wrong. Together, they watched the water swirl.

"Listen," Jade said. "I know Waylon loves you, and he'd die just to keep what you have. But he's got to live for it, too." She picked up a sodden box of paper towels and tossed it out the door. "You need to tell him about the pregnancy. You already have enough secrets you're keeping on your own."

Marley and Jade barely talked about what they'd seen, then concealed, in the church's upper room half a year ago. A whole summer had passed, and still that body remained where it lay. No one had come searching for it, and no one had missed Hollis. The tragedy of being forgotten was too brutal to abide. It wasn't as if Marley and Jade believed that if they didn't speak of it, then the truth of that body didn't exist. It was precisely due to the actuality of its decay that they didn't. Always, they waited for Pastor Hollis to be discovered.

Marley wondered, though, why that body had betrayed no sign of its presence. Who had shut the attic door without first checking to see what hid beyond it? Sooner or later, someone would have to enter that attic. She and Jade had done what they'd done, and Elise had shown no remorse for bestowing them with its fallout.

"Tell me," Marley said. "Do you think I'm wrong about Mick—and the sleeping pills?"

Jade sighed as she took up her broom again. "I don't think you're ever going to know."

She began to sweep, and Marley followed, and then Jade stopped. "It's worth mentioning, though—Mick has left not one, but two messages on my answering machine, asking me out to breakfast."

Marley paled. "He didn't."

"He did."

"That's appalling."

"It is."

A laugh escaped Marley's mouth, then another, and then she couldn't stop. She doubled over as Jade joined her.

"Jade," she said. "What if he comes by?"

"I wouldn't worry." She pointed to the corner. "I have a big metal bat."

Marley laughed again, but she was shaken. "Jade, I'm so sorry. I'll tell him to stop."

"Don't sweat it." Jade looked at herself in the mirror. "But I do hope it's not too long before I get asked out on a date by someone else."

Marley took Jade's wrist. "I vow to hunt down the man who is good enough for you."

Jade bent to pick up one end of a soiled floor rug, and Marley grabbed the other. "You can start your hunt just as soon as you settle things with Waylon." Jade caught her eye as they hefted the rug out into the sunlight.

Marley nodded and wiped her hands on her jeans. "Consider it done."

They lugged over a fan that was plugged in next door to air the salon out, and it felt holy, this friendship that was worth returning to Mercury for. It was just as strong, just as sustaining as any other—the kind a whole life could be built upon.

That night, Marley waited in the kitchen until everyone was asleep. A full moon hung in the October sky, and the porches on Hollow Street were decorated with corn husks and jack-o'-lanterns. The men in the great house rose early and went to bed early, too. It gave Marley the pleasure of outlasting them, of keeping guard long after they'd tired. She read through her dog-eared textbook, thumbing through a chapter on payroll software, beneath a single overhead light.

When the clock chimed eleven, she shut the book, darkened every lamp in the house, and climbed the staircase. Outside Waylon's room, she paused. Marley imagined him sleeping, dreamless on the other side. Her hands itched with how much she wanted to slide her hands across his shoulders. Feel his heat beneath her palms. She didn't knock, but entered and knelt next to his side of the bed.

"Waylon," she whispered, not knowing why it felt easier to apologize in the middle of the night. But it was more than that, too. She longed for him to see her, to meet her after they'd broken apart. To know her in this new way.

Moonlight from the window hit his profile, casting an amber crown around his face, and Waylon opened his eyes. He jolted out of slumber, his hair askew.

"What? What is it?" His eyes ricocheted around the room. "Is Theo all right?"

Marley remembered only then that the last time she'd woken him, his mother had died. It was almost two months ago now. He sat up, bare-chested and heaving. Marley still loved sleeping in his old shirts, and the way he showered the day off him just before climbing into bed. How he smelled like honey and mint.

"Everything's all right," she said. "I wanted to apologize."

"Jesus, Mar." He swiped a hand across his eyes. "Now?"

This was already not going as Marley had hoped, and she felt the tinder she'd lit within herself begin to go out. "I," she said, then stopped. She tried to stand but couldn't find her balance.

"Babe," he said, touching her wrist where her hand had fisted his sheets, and she felt him soften. There was her Waylon, mostly heart and hope, shimmering on the surface of himself. "What is it?"

She pressed a hand on top of his. "I shouldn't have left without telling you. And I shouldn't have taken Theo like that. It wasn't right, and I'm sorry."

Slowly, Waylon pulled his hand away. "Were you planning on coming back?"

"Yes," she answered, and she knew it was true. "Always."

He nodded, but he didn't reach for her. She felt the sadness rolling off him in waves, hated that she was about to add to it.

"There's something else I need to tell you. I was pregnant when I left." She swallowed. "And I lost it."

"Marley," Way said, a little too loud, and she couldn't tell whether it was an admonition or a consolation. "You should have called me."

She hated the "should" that accompanied this kind of news. She'd gotten one from Ruth, too—as if there were a right way to have a miscarriage, as if it weren't something she'd had to fight just to survive.

"I didn't want that to be the reason you came," Marley said.

His mouth hung open. "Was it"—he searched for the right word—"painful?"

She nodded. "Terrible."

"Does it still hurt now?"

She tried to answer and found she couldn't. Can a body heal and still hurt? She knew it could, because hers did. "I don't know how we fix this, Waylon," she said. "Any of it."

He leaned his head back against the headboard. "Neither do I. I wish I did." Way played with the chain around his neck. "But leaving definitely doesn't help."

Marley wanted to tell him that she'd felt she had no other choice, that he'd first abandoned her by taking up alliance with his father, and that she couldn't stand to stay in that house one more minute. And that deny it as he might, Waylon was not prepared to care for Theo without her.

Instead, she said, "I don't want to sleep in Theo's room anymore."

He turned toward her. "I don't want you to sleep in Theo's room anymore."

Way pulled back the covers, Marley slipped off her clothes, and she climbed in bed beside him. She waited for him to reach out for her, to wrap his body around hers. He lay on his back, eyes open, hands behind his head. Marley remembered the rooftop vows they'd made to each other on their first anniversary, how they'd sworn to trust each other with their very lives.

It was one thing to save a life, and another to share it with someone.

Marley feared this meant that Waylon loved her but didn't want her as he once did. That he saw her body as the site of an accident, a loss. Were they bound together now, more so by grief than by happiness? It was a force that could fuse two people together, as well as drive them apart. She wondered how many times Elise and Mick had weathered just such a tragedy, and how long it was possible for two people who loved each other to hold on.

24.

But hold on they did. Through a rough year-end, where Joseph &
Sons lost more than it made due to all the work stoppages at the
height of the busy season. Elise's death resounded in both an emotional
and economic free fall. They ended up losing the huge job Waylon had
sold at the hospital in Greenville to a competitor. Way put his necktie back
on and traveled west on I-80, ready to sell whatever he could, even though
he'd lost his shine. Marley learned how to do payroll without the aid of a
vendor for the roofing business, and for Jade, too. She stayed up late into
the night, studying OSHA regulations, insurance policies, construction
terms and conditions that still made little sense despite how many times
Baylor explained them.

She took her stand where she could. On a cold day in January, after
Elise had been gone five months, Marley sat the men around the table and
stated that they needed to have a talk.

"About the toilet," she said.

"Is it broken?" Way asked.

"The seat's always been loose," Baylor added.

"I'll get the plunger," Mick offered as he stood.

"There's nothing wrong with the toilet," she cut in. "It's all of you. You need to piss *in* it. Not around it, not on it. In it."

The men blushed like schoolboys. They hadn't known of their own mess because Elise had always cleaned it. They tried as much as they could to correct themselves. Marley could tell Waylon was trying to please her, like he had with his mother. Elise was someone, Marley was beginning to see, whom Waylon had loved but didn't trust. She wondered whether he trusted any of them—even her.

As Theo grew, so did the business. By the time he started kindergarten in 1996, Waylon had sold their biggest commercial job to date at a refrigerator manufacturer in Pittsburgh. No longer did Waylon focus on a building's potential instead of its problems. He diagnosed what he saw and declared when it was fatal. He mastered the upsell to people who had money to spend.

By the time Theo finished second grade in 1999, Shay had graduated from high school and joined Joseph & Sons full-time. He hated it but never complained, and still had Patrick over every Friday night for a horror flick and ice cream. Marley was proud to be so often mistaken for Shay's mother, even though she was only seven years older.

Mick, as ever, did as he pleased. Marley marveled at his ability to start three different projects at once, spinning them like plates in the air, not caring which of them dropped: fixing the front door of the manse, mowing the high school football field, laying down fresh sidewalk around the courthouse. He didn't worry about where money came from, or whether it would stop.

Marley and Waylon, however, worried enough for them all. The more she learned about the business, the more precarious it felt. Waylon bore that weight for his brothers and father. It was a constant, relentless exhaustion, this fear that they were one bad accident or one failed roof away from having to declare bankruptcy. The two of them made excellent business partners, mostly because they'd forgotten how to be husband and wife.

Way and Marley often dreamed of what the future could hold, but it was always for Joseph & Sons—an actual office space with a warehouse, a crane of their own, a new GMC Sierra—and not for themselves. She longed for the days when they were first married, and Waylon was hungry for her and not ashamed of it. He still came for her from time to time, furtively and past midnight when he couldn't sleep.

Marley could sense the shift in him, how he wanted her yet felt guilty for it. Gone were the words he once spoke when they made love, gone were the famished eyes that used to feast on her as she got undressed. Now he looked away. Now they communicated only in apologies. *Sorry for these messy receipts, sorry for missing dinner, sorry for blocking you in with the truck.* Marley feared she'd grown less lovely to Waylon as a result of everything that had happened—or because some days he felt like her boss, and other days she felt like his.

It flayed her heart, over and over again.

He wouldn't let her in. Her Waylon had grown distant and roamed through his own mind. He refused to be present, to see her for the miracle that stood before him: self-taught as a wife, a mother, and a roofer. Marley did yet again the only thing she knew how to do.

She lived.

Marley lived in Mercury, just as Elise had done. She made the town her home. She and Jade coached Little League in matching hot-pink jerseys with the Shear Sunrise logo on the back. They started a book club and watched *Melrose Place* while breathing silently together on the phone. Jade never fixed the water stains along the bottom of the salon's walls, but she did add a part-time stylist who focused on nails and makeup. Jade and Marley attended Tupperware parties and never bought anything and had picnics by the courthouse in the grass. If anyone remembered Marley had once been the unwed mother, an object of scornful pity, no one dared mention it. Theo was beloved, Marley spun daily miracles that kept her house and her business safe, and her husband noticed none of it. Marley was so very tired of wanting more than she was wanted in return.

It was almost as if in order to move on from the past he had to forget the present, too. Just as Marley did when she kept Elise's secret, and every time she thought about that body in the attic.

Bookend
Boys

25.

It cast a pall over the Presbyterians of Mercury when they discovered that a body had been long hidden in their church. Some swore they'd always known the attic was haunted. Others reconsidered their faith entirely, each memory of sitting in a velveteen pew now turned grisly by the knowledge of what, or who, had lain above it. All of them felt the inevitability of loss, how it twined so tightly with life itself that there was no hope of ever pulling them apart. The notion of such holy and violent things dwelling together turned the town into a stranger no one could trust.

No one here was who, or what, they seemed.

Shay Joseph was not shaken, for he'd always found both beauty and horror everywhere he looked—in the great walnut tree with roots like the knuckles of giants, and in the owl carcass laying waste inside it. In the bodies of young men running loose on a Friday night, ramming into each other on a football field until their lips went rosy with blood. In the bottom of a pool of water, where Shay would let himself sink down, down, holding his breath right until the moment he feared he'd close his eyes forever. In his father's gaze, when Shay saw him stare at his own wedding photo on the wall, and he wondered whether Mick remembered what had befallen his wife.

Mostly, he felt it while high up on the roof, looking down onto the tops of tallest trees, dwarfed by his height. That beautiful, gamey stench of rubber and sweat, of a day's hard work, of dirt caught in the creases of a forehead. That moment of communion he, his brothers, and his father shared when they'd finished a job and the sun slayed all the city's bridges, and they looked out over it and felt immortal. It was the closest he ever felt to them—close enough to crave but also to run and hide himself in the great house's old apartment, away from these men who had known him since he was born and yet didn't know him at all.

He was dreaming of just such a sunset when he woke, late morning, to a view of the walls he and Patrick had painted in shades of elephant tusk years ago. It was the morning after they'd cleaned a corpse out of the attic, he was crammed into a church pew, and his feet were resting on a stack of hymnals. The air still smelled like mold and turpentine. Shay's first thought was for Marley. She'd saved him a plate for dinner, and she'd be worried. He kept to his routine so she'd find respite in the predictability of it, and so nothing would happen to her like what had happened to Elise.

Shay's second thought from the bed of his pew was that someone stood nearby. He felt it from a slight shadow against the light pouring in from the open sanctuary window. It couldn't have been Patrick. Surely he'd returned home to wash the stench off him. And then Shay had his third thought of the morning. He stank.

There was a coarse clearing of a throat, and Shay sat up to find the old interim preacher holding forth a cup of coffee.

"It's bitter," he said. "But it gets the job done."

He was portly, and he eased down beside Shay, and the pew creaked. That creak was such a familiar sound of Sundays past, like a baby being rocked to sleep. Shay drank and coughed. He was nineteen and hadn't yet developed the taste for coffee or liquor, which he was still not allowed to drink in a country that counted him old enough to go to war and die.

Mick wasn't a drinker, but Shay had heard that line from him a hundred times. No one listened to Mick Joseph anymore except for his youngest son. This was why Mick covered for Shay's absences on the roof and sent him on odd jobs instead—so he'd always have someone close by to hear him out.

"Whose body do you think it is?" Shay asked Pastor Lennox because he didn't feel ready to go home, where Mick would be waiting.

"I have my suspicions," Lennox answered. "But I also wonder how a young man such as yourself became the one who got called in to clean up such a thing."

Shay shrugged. "I don't scare easy."

"Seems like a lesson hard learned."

The preacher's wavy gray hair fell into his eyes. Patches of loose skin hung beneath his lower lashes. This man, Shay figured, also had a poor night's sleep.

The two of them had never spoken. Shay stopped going to church when his mother died. It wasn't because he didn't want it or need it. He figured that the church wouldn't want him. Yet he felt an odd pull toward this man who had padded in with coffee, wearing his slippers and a Pitt sweatshirt with a snag at the collar. The room around them was a mess. The ceiling was still purple, and there were bat droppings running down the center aisle. The body was gone; its wreckage remained.

"What are you going to do?" Shay asked.

"I'm thinking of canceling church this week."

Shay's mouth dropped. All his life, this church had never shut its doors—not even during the terrible blizzard in 1996. "Can you do that?"

Lennox laughed. "When a corpse shows up in the sanctuary, I figure it's okay with God for us to take a pause. Besides, there's the bats."

Together, they looked toward the ceiling, where a flock of them hung in the corner. It was Shay's turn to laugh, even though so little about this circumstance was funny.

"I like you better than the other guy," he said. "The one who ran away."

Lennox took a sip of coffee from a mug that had Johnny Cash's face on it. "Don't be too tough on him. It's hard, this job. It takes a whole life."

Shay nodded. "Like roofing."

He said it because he'd been taught that roofing was the bucket he could dump all of himself into—his emotions, his pain. But he didn't find the job hard at all—or that it needed to take a whole life, like it did for the rest of the men in his family. Everyone spoke in metaphors and no one said what they truly meant. Roofing hadn't taken a life; Mick had freely given it. It was Elise's life that had been taken, though by whom or what, Shay would never understand.

"I imagine so," Lennox said.

Just then, the sanctuary doors burst open, and Patrick strode in with the shirt of his uniform untucked, his firearm banging against his leg. Something about his expression made Shay squint, as if his friend were standing too far away.

Whenever they were alone, Shay felt no distance between them. He and Patrick sank into each other when they watched *The Texas Chainsaw Massacre* on the couch in the great house, tackled each other when they searched for beach glass along Presque Isle's sandy shore, found each other when swimming in the creek behind Patrick's house and testing who could hold their breath the longest. Shay always won because he knew how to give himself less than he needed. How to grasp that smooth piece of green glass in his palm and hold on.

"Shay," Patrick said.

There was so much in the sound of his name in Patrick's mouth: Longing. Lust. Loyalty. Love. Patrick cocked his chin toward the exit.

Patrick knew Shay would follow, and he did. Outside in the parking lot, a yolky sun beat down. Shay shielded his eyes.

"What were you doing in there?" Patrick asked. "Confessing your sins?"

He'd tried to joke, but it came out sad because of his rangy glare, his body like a windup toy that had been turned too tight.

"Sins are like butterflies." Shay kept his cool. "They all began as something else."

Patrick looked like he wanted to burst out of his own body, become something entirely fresh and unsteady and inhuman, like a foal. "Why did you shove that ring in your pocket last night when we were cleaning out the attic?"

Shay felt around his pants. He'd forgotten that he'd found Marley's wedding ring, with a feather engraved around it.

"Hand it over," Patrick said, grasping Shay's fist until he pulled free.

"It's Marley's," he explained. Shay wasn't sure why, but he felt the need to defend her. "She lost it years back, probably when she and I were up there fixing the flashing to the roof."

By his reedy stance, Shay could see that this prospect gave Patrick no joy. It did give him an object of obsession, something that lay beyond himself to draw his eye ever outward.

"Are you sure about that?" Patrick asked.

"I am." He wasn't.

They stared at each other. It wasn't the first time they'd disagreed on something—just the first time they'd argued about it out loud.

"Just give it," Patrick said. "If it ends up having something to do with the murder, you don't want to be implicated."

"Murder?" Shay repeated, dropping the ring into Patrick's palm.

"Fine. *Suspected* murder."

"You sound like a detective."

"So what?"

"Is it what you want?"

Shay had been trying to get Patrick to say what he wanted since they were fifteen, and he never answered. Not with words, at least. A breeze tossed up Patrick's downy hair, and he looked just like his younger self, raw-skinned and dejected after trying out for the high school wrestling team every year and never once making it. Shay didn't care about those things, but Patrick did.

"We have to do something," Patrick said. "We can't just bury the body and let it go."

"So this is it?" Shay asked. "This is the thing you finally want to do something about?"

Irritated, Patrick sighed. The wind died, and his face returned to that of a long-suffering rookie cop, costume and all. "You're a lot to deal with sometimes, Shay. You know that?"

It stung because Shay worked tirelessly to be easy as butter melting in a hot skillet. Why was it so wrong to ask his oldest friend what it was he wanted, unless that very thing was truly something Patrick could not say?

This had been Shay's life: finding the words no one wanted to speak. It had started with his mother, who didn't tell him what had happened to her shoes. Shay wanted to believe Elise had loved him as much as she loved her two oldest sons, but there was so little of her left to spare by the time he came around. Mick enjoyed Shay, but only in the way a dog jumps for joy at seeing himself in a mirror. The dog thinks someone has come to play, someone who resembles him and stares deeply into his eyes, waiting for this newfound reflection to blink. What Mick never said but meant: *I don't love you. I love the likeness of me.*

Then there was everything Marley hadn't said when she disappeared from family dinners almost nine years ago, only to turn up again, pregnant. Back then, Shay had asked Baylor more than once how it had happened, but Baylor only grunted angrily in response.

There was also all his father hadn't said about the war, a topic he and his brothers were taught to revere and never broach. And then there was his own truth, one he dared not even utter when he found himself alone.

Shay had fallen in love with his best friend a long time ago and was scared to death of ever outgrowing him.

To live this way was a certain kind of death. He could remain in Mercury with a loyalty to his family, to the town, to some masculine illusion that made him miserable, or he could leave for places he knew Patrick wouldn't follow him to. Both seemed an impossibility, so here he remained, nineteen years old and fearing he may never get the chance to love someone who would love him back.

When he was fourteen, Shay could have sworn he and Patrick were one. They both liked AC/DC and Guns N' Roses, both devoured *A Separate Peace* only to finish it, look at each other, and wonder what it meant. To be a boy was to stretch himself in a constantly tender arabesque—having a body with a mind of its own. Seeing the delicate wings of a fly and being taught to smash them.

Mick Joseph believed a man loving a man was a sickness. He also thought feeding his wife sleeping pills when he got tired of caring for her was an act of mercy. Shay was no fool. He knew such a person could be no arbiter of what was good, and what wasn't. Besides, loving Patrick had always been such a part of Shay that he'd never learned how to hunt it down as a separate entity. It could not be sequestered, or removed, or stitched up. It hid in every place inside him. And also? He didn't want to let it go.

Patrick was different. All Patrick wanted was to let it go, and he tried every convention to rid himself of it. He flirted with girls, played football, lifted barbells, and—dare Shay admit it—Patrick became a cop. Anything he could slap a badge of masculinity on, this sad, narrow, quicksand view of what it meant to be a man. Patrick was as trapped as Shay, in the end, though it didn't keep him from trying to free himself.

All Shay could think to do to stay afloat, to avoid getting swallowed by a tide of everything unjust in his life, was to keep a list of everything it meant to him to be whole. A short list, one tucked behind the driver's license in his wallet.

1. A whole person loves well.
2. They keep their promises.
3. They tell the truth.

There ended the list, because Shay wasn't sure he'd told the truth a day in his life. Honesty wasn't safe, and he blamed the world for making him live as less than he was meant to be.

But what of the world had he truly seen? Shay's earth was defined by the three-minute route from Patrick's house to his, through the great house's back door behind the lilac bushes, up the stairwell, inside the apartment. It had never grown beyond this map and its ever-shrinking borders.

This, Shay supposed, was exactly what drew him to the interim preacher that morning after the body was found. Pastor Lennox was one of the few in Mercury who hadn't watched him grow since he was an infant—hadn't revered Elise or witnessed how his brothers liked to fight or how Mick worked miracles with his hammer and caulking gun—and therefore might have no opinion on what Shay ought to be.

Shay had woken to a fresh realization after a restless few hours' sleep in an old pew, as he held the memory of fetching a dead body from the church's upper room. This mystery of what had happened to Pastor Hollis only drew the eye away from where it ought to look. It wasn't the true mystery, the real crime. Something far greater hung in the balance.

Patrick didn't even realize how he was complicit—that years ago, he and Shay had sealed that body inside. Shay had felt Patrick's exhilaration at the potential of a murder, and there was the wound. Patrick would rather uncover a murderer living among them than admit that he was in love with his best friend.

Shay wanted someone—this preacher, or anyone—to tell him how on earth he could survive such a betrayal.

26.

Even after Shay left Patrick standing in the church parking lot the morning after the body was found, he could feel the velvet of the pew running soft against his cheek. He hadn't sat in a sanctuary since the day his mother was buried four years ago, and he could still recall the last vision he had of her as she looked at him nakedly in her terror.

You did this to me, that face seemed to say. *It was you.*

There was no way Elise could have known Shay's secrets—not the way Patrick did. His mother wasn't in her *right mind*—whatever that meant, and whoever decided it. She'd seemed very lucid, perhaps understanding the world in a way the rest of them didn't. Yet her face haunted him. At the funeral, Shay had sat in his pew as Lennox offered a benediction, trembling with rage for the father who sat to his left. He hated Mick Joseph, and he blamed Elise for it. Why had she looked at her son with the contempt that should have gone to her husband? All this felt like Mick's fault, yet for it he paid no price.

After the burial, Shay had wanted only to run. He didn't care that his family watched him, or that all of Mercury saw him sprint down the hill in his suit and tie in the soft rain, through the elbow turn in the road that would certainly flood, past the florist where he'd picked up the dahlias that morning, past the church where he thought he'd painted his mother's shoes up into the attic.

And there it was—the belief he'd hidden just one of his mother's tiny indiscretions, only to find out it had been so much worse.

As he ran out of the cemetery, bloody pieces of himself lay everywhere he looked. Shay wanted to be brave like Baylor, eloquent like Waylon, selfless like Marley. He couldn't forgive himself for being young and sparrow-hearted, for still not understanding what it took to feel whole. He ran to the empty apartment on the top floor of the great house with a hidden staircase twisting up its side. His old comic books still sat open-faced on the small kitchen table. Trapped in a moment in time when his mother was still healthy, no matter how much she ignored him. He'd spent so many days here, basking in Marley's glow when Theo was a baby. He went to the small kitchen window and opened it, even though a torrent of rain blew inside. Without anyone living in it, the apartment stank like must. Shay flung his shoes by the door, left his wet suit jacket in a heap, fell on the dark living room floor, and wept.

He must have fallen asleep. When he woke, a figure hovered over him. Shay blinked as the shadow came into focus. It was Patrick, in his own suit and tie, his flaxen hair parted and combed to the side, calling out his name.

"Leave me alone." Shay covered his eyes with his arms. The last time they'd talked, the two of them had painted the sanctuary and tried to pretend that nothing between them had changed.

Patrick sat down. "Don't be a dick," he said. Then he softened and lay down beside his friend.

Together, they stared at the ceiling. Patrick took his hand.

"Don't do that." Shay pulled away. "You're too chickenshit to do it in front of anyone else."

On the day Shay had gotten punched last spring, he'd sat close enough to Patrick on the locker room bench that their thighs had touched. It had never bothered Patrick before, but in front of a crowd of boys, he'd recoiled. *What's wrong with you*, he'd sneered, pushing Shay away until one of Patrick's cousins began to throw his fists.

In the apartment, Patrick sat up. His lips were pink and soft as they trembled. "Don't you get it? There's no 'out there' for us." He pointed to the window. "In here, the two of us, is the best we're gonna get."

Shay was so tired of surviving on so little. "And that's enough?"

"It has to be."

Shay longed to experience what it felt like not to be a burden. To be celebrated. Elise had carted him everywhere—he, the shopping bag she had to set down to deal with her two oldest sons. It had worn her out, raising them, and Shay had paid the price.

"I'm sick of always being someone else's leftovers," Shay said. "My brothers got every good thing out of my mother, and they squandered it. I don't want to be your leftovers, too."

"She loved you, Shay. You know that, right?"

"You can love someone even though they let you down." Waylon had said as much in his eulogy. Shay had felt it plenty in the Joseph family. "I was the last person my mother saw before she died. And I swear to God I saw the disappointment in her eyes. Patrick, I swear to God she knew."

"She didn't."

He looked doubtful, or worried, or both. Did Patrick mean it, Shay wondered, and did it even matter? It was the only consolation he could offer now that Elise was gone.

Shay slipped his hand back into Patrick's, and it felt like coming home, like stepping into a hot shower, like laying himself bare.

Patrick touched Shay's cheek with his fingers. The sensation flickered, sensual as a butterfly, soft as an eyelash. Shay wanted to sway toward him, take Patrick's pink fingertips and bring them to his mouth, but instead Shay turned away. Patrick took hold of his arm. Then he leaned in and brushed his mouth against Shay's before drawing back, wild-eyed. Shay felt white-hot, molten, reborn. Patrick did it a second time, then a third, before Shay took him by the shoulders and pulled him in, opening Patrick's mouth with his own. It was sloppy and innocent and intoxicating and scary as hell.

Patrick kissed him, and Shay kissed him back. They didn't know what they were doing, and they didn't care. Tangled, they lay together until past midnight, and Patrick left. Only then did Shay see the river of water the open window had left on the floor.

He carried his wet jacket up the dark staircase of the great house, pausing on the bottom steps when he saw Marley creeping down the hall to Theo's empty room. When she shut the door and turned on the light, he hurried past and climbed into his own bed, not quite getting a chance to close his eyes before Marley stepped in and asked him to escape with her.

Pack your bags, she said.

He desperately wanted to go. In that moment, Shay never wanted to see his father again. Didn't want to hear his brothers bemoan the loss of a mother he'd never had. But Patrick. Shay couldn't leave this boy he loved behind. For him, Shay would be the last lamp lit on the street, the final candle left burning.

"I can't leave—" he began, and decided to fight for a way to tell Marley the truth, to hand over even the smallest bit of this weight so he wouldn't have to hold it alone. She'd misunderstood and assumed he meant he couldn't abandon his fragile father, the man everyone was so worried about and no one blamed.

In the moment he declined Marley's offer for escape, and in every moment after, Shay wondered whether he'd been wrong to choose Patrick over her. Over himself. What unlived life echoed against the one that kept him tied to this house? Would Marley have returned to Mercury if he'd gone, or would they have left all of this behind?

He missed her every minute she was gone in Maryland. He didn't miss her food or her rides home; he missed the way she beamed at him when he hadn't seen her all day, the gasping sound she made at the television when they watched *Party of Five*, how she'd turn to him during a commercial and say, *Shay, can you even believe it? Who even writes this stuff?*

Then he went back to school. Shay watched as Patrick ignored him. He witnessed the men in his family self-destruct without Elise or Marley to anchor them. And he ran, and he roofed, and he raged with his drum set until the day he stepped into the kitchen and found Marley cooking spaghetti at the stove as if she'd never left. He knew there were other reasons for her return, but he liked to think she found the most joy in returning to him.

Somehow, he'd been granted a second chance to get it right.

Over the next four years—before the body was discovered in the church attic and the friends cleaned it out in a way they'd never come clean with each other—Patrick came to Shay when he wanted. Always, they met in the apartment. The space became a fever dream, one with its own rules and ecstasies and confidences. Always, Patrick told Shay it had to be the last time: when they finished high school, when Patrick graduated from police training, and anytime there was a thunderstorm so bright it lit the entire sky.

In the apartment, they were childhood loves—though never any more than that, because they'd never done anything more than kiss. Shay knew how much more Patrick needed, could feel it, but above all else, Patrick stayed loyal to the idea of what he thought he ought to be.

Shay believed he couldn't live without him, that clandestine meetings were all his heart was worthy of, even though they made him so perilously sad. He had never made love—not that he minded the wait. What he minded was that the reward for patience might never come, that he might die without knowing what it meant to love and be loved in that intimate way. That like for Elise, it was his destiny to be misunderstood.

Patrick seemed so satisfied in his ability to compartmentalize himself into public and private. Shay wondered how he saw himself before God, because Patrick grew up in the same kind of pew that Shay did. He was content with letting God love only half of him, the way he gave himself to Shay: in pieces. Shay longed for a God who would take all of him, and this was how he loved his family—exactly how he hoped to be loved in return.

In public, before all of Mercury, Patrick and Shay were partners, of sorts. A partnership made their union feel honorable, which Shay didn't need but Patrick did. It began with Patrick's early days as a night-shift cop when he got stuck making the rookie rounds around the courthouse square that no one else wanted to do. Dispatch phoned one night while

Patrick was on call, lying on his back next to Shay in the apartment. A cat stuck on a roof, the message said, and Shay had laughed so much he forgot to be quiet. Then he threw a ladder into Mick's truck and followed Patrick to climb the residential rooftop and get the cat to safety.

Rescuing a cat became the making of a small-town hero, it turned out. Shay got a reputation for being able to clean what folks in Mercury had soiled—not as a preacher, but as a kind of compassionate janitor. Perhaps this was why he felt an instant kinship with Pastor Lennox. It was the same, what they did, in offering a kind of promise. Problem was, people mistook Shay for the promise itself—as if he were its origin. Its home fire.

When Old Lady Hanley died a hoarder, and her house got condemned and deemed a health hazard, Patrick and Shay went in to clean it out. When the grocery store burned down and all that was left was the rubber roof his brothers had put on, Shay pawed through the wreckage, Patrick at his side, to uncover the safety deposit box that held all the cash. He'd been in attics and bell towers, basements and alleyways. He saw people at their worst and didn't flinch because he knew how devastating it was to have to hide.

Both of Shay's brothers considered themselves the son who had to clean up Mick Joseph's messes. Shay was the only one who knew they both had failed.

"A natural," everyone called him. Shay could fit into any space, reach his arm into any slim crevice. There was no darkness he would not tread, because this, he felt, was the easy work of life. This required so little bravery at all.

When Patrick appeared that next morning after they'd shucked a dead body from the church sanctuary, thinking only of Marley's wedding ring and not this rotting carcass of a hidden truth between them, he figured it must be for show. It couldn't be that after all they'd cleaned up in town, after all they'd concealed, and all they'd shared, Patrick believed no one else but he had a right to harbor their own secrets. This was Marley Patrick was accusing, Marley who had left and returned, who had chosen Shay twice when his own mother had never chosen him at all.

Shay started to suspect he didn't know his best friend as well as he thought. *Who are you,* he wanted to say. *And since when are you so concerned with the truth?*

They had pulled opioids out of mattresses in the town square department store, shooed robins from the rafters of the very high school whose principal had urged Shay not to attend. He cherished the chance to meet needs without asking anyone to explain themselves—to give what he had never been given. He felt such depth of compassion that it became hard to tell where one person's regret ended and his began.

And it was in this way more than any other—not his blond hair or his dimpled chin—that he favored Elise. Shay had been so worried about Marley meeting Elise's end that he couldn't see he'd been the one running straight for it. He hadn't caused the terror on his mother's face the day she died. Shay recognized that emotion because he'd felt it so many times himself. Elise hadn't detected his secrets; she was reckoning with her own.

She had never cared what her secrets would cost everyone else.

27.

The morning after her husband puked on the church's bathroom floor and returned home with purple hands and his ghost-town heart, Marley sat down at her oak desk on the second floor of the great house to listen to the Joseph & Sons answering machine messages and finish sending off her quotes for the day. She had three file folders to her right—one for outstanding work orders, one for invoices, and another for leads. To her left she had three more file folders for Mick, Waylon, and Baylor. She popped a fresh stick of spearmint gum in her mouth, and a Diet Coke sat cracked open at the ready by her favorite blue pen.

Then there was a knock on the front door.

Marley found Patrick on the front porch, trying very hard to look official with his hand caressing his firearm. She hadn't liked him much ever since that night he came to her apartment in the rain, and he hadn't cared for her much, either.

"Patrick," she said, noting how young he looked. He was just about the same age she'd been when she became a mother. "Shay isn't home."

She said it even though she knew he hadn't come for Shay. When he did, he never used the front door.

"I know." Patrick fished around in his pocket and presented a gold ring with a feather engraved on it. "I came to see you."

"My wedding ring." Marley's heart quickened as she reached for it, only for Patrick to pull it away.

"I've been looking for that ring for years," she whispered.

It was only when Patrick said "I think you'd better come with me," like he was some authority she hadn't fed spaghetti and root beer floats on a hundred different nights, that she felt certain the ring had fallen from her pocket in the church attic by mistake.

All this time it had been there, sealed in with a dead man.

Damn you, Elise, Marley thought. *For leaving me with this.*

They drove through town in the cruiser, lights off, with Marley in the front seat. Patrick attempted to guide her into the back until she fixed him with a glare that would make good on the threat to call his mother. She caught him flush beneath his aviators. Patrick was so fair and golden-haired that he could not camouflage his nerves.

Marley might have found some compassion for the thankless role Patrick filled in town, but she had none. Shay had an endless vial of patience and loyalty that Marley respected, but she hated that Patrick treated him like a puppy who knew no other home. Even so, she buckled herself in and rode the two minutes to the police station, which was not a true crime headquarters of any kind, as it shared the building with the local library. And yet Patrick had taken this on as his mystery to solve.

Let him, Marley thought. *We'll see how far he gets.*

She still felt uneasy. Patrick would enjoy tarnishing her, if he could. He perched before her in the empty station at a desk that bore his nameplate next to a smooth piece of beach glass. From Shay, Marley knew.

Patrick slid the ring across the table.

"I have one question." He paused, anxious, trying hard to dig at some truth as if it might solve one of his own problems. "Why were you in the church attic?"

"I haven't been there in a long time. Soon after Theo was born."

Marley had thought many times about what she'd say when she found herself in this position. It had nothing to do with the body itself, but with

the nature of her secret with Elise. Marley had never feared punishment; it was the rest of the Josephs finding out that worried her. The opportunity it would create for Mick to receive more mercy, as if his actions might be justified toward an unfaithful wife.

But that was before she knew she'd left her ring in the attic.

"It was when I patched up the roof," she said.

Patrick jotted something down. "Were you alone?"

He asked in a way that suggested he already knew the answer. Could he mean Jade? Impossible. Patrick looked smug, and then Marley realized that he meant Shay. He always did.

Marley carefully treaded the fault line between her secret and his. "I think you know I wasn't."

Patrick, after clearing out that disgusting attic late into the night, was in no mood. There was a new edge to his voice, a gruffness to his manner. Slowly, Marley watched him realize that she knew what Patrick and Shay had never told anyone.

"Watch it, Mar," he said. Her Joseph family nickname went sour on his tongue. "I know you only look out for yourself."

Marley's jaw dropped. "How can you say that to me?"

"Because you left him. Shay. Right after his mother died."

She was about to fight back—then it struck her why Shay had truly stayed behind. It hadn't been for Mick or his brothers. It was for Patrick.

"He didn't want to come with me," she answered. "Because of you."

"Shay knows I'd never leave." He spoke as if this were a triumph, but a river of sweat swamped the seams of his shirt.

"What's really bothering you," Marley said, leaning in close, "is that you're afraid you weren't worth staying for."

It came out harsher than she meant. Maybe she should have told him there was another body he should investigate instead, but Marley didn't want him looking into Elise's death, either. It would reveal things about her that Marley had promised to hide.

Patrick flared red again and threw down his pencil. If only he hadn't felt like all he'd done was get to play pretend cop rather than be a real one, or live a pretend life instead of a real one, if only their town weren't small

enough for people to expect him to rescue their cats, if only Marley hadn't known him as a pimply faced wrestling team reject, he could have behaved with decorum instead of spite.

They were both angry at other absences, other injustices. But here, the confrontation found while sitting across from each other, was the only one they got.

"Fine," Patrick said, hoisting his keys. "Have it your way."

And that was how Marley Joseph found herself locked alone inside a Mercury jail cell on a Tuesday afternoon.

Waylon was browsing for a Phillips head at the hardware store near the town square when the door jangled behind him. He knew he shouldn't be spending the money right now, and yet here he was, hoping a new tool might grant him some courage. The shop was small, and the argument between a mother and her daughter in the next aisle about which spade was best for their garden rippled through the tiny space. The day had gotten off to a slow start. Waylon had woken to an empty bed and a headache. He still felt a bit queasy from catching a corpse the night before, but it was the closest his wife had held him in a long time, so he considered it a wash.

Truth was, holding Marley tight had roused something in him, and he realized it while holding up a screwdriver to the light. This fluttery feeling was a newfound desire for his wife. Not the girl she'd been at eighteen when they'd fallen in love, but the woman she was now.

It surprised him, and Waylon had not been surprised in a very long time.

A rough hand bumped his shoulder, and Way turned to see Patrick, who looked like he'd just boxed with the devil.

"You all right?" Waylon asked, eyeing the pink splotches on Patrick's neck.

"It's your wife," he said, humorless. "She needs to be picked up at the station."

Suddenly, the shop grew quiet. Way felt the women in the next aisle listening in, just as a motorcycle zoomed by on the street.

He frowned. "Why?"

"She's a person of interest regarding that body you—"

Waylon held up a hand. "I know what body you mean."

Any other husband might have been hit with shock or worry. Waylon felt neither. Marley had never needed him to rescue her. Instead, he started to laugh. It was impossible for Marley to be involved in such solemn dealings, especially when they'd both been kept up the night before by the reality of it. A body, unclaimed, had existed for so long in that upper room without anyone to mourn its presence. How much rot must exist in one place before it was finally detected? What willful ignorance must have infiltrated them all for no one to notice? It chilled Way's blood to picture it.

When Patrick didn't join in his laughter, Way remembered what he couldn't after he'd found the corpse and puked in the bathroom. He'd known it was a person, tightly wrapped, because he'd spotted something he recognized tucked into the cuff of a sleeve, right where the side of a fleshy wrist would have been. It was a presbytery pin, a cross with twin flames, the one he'd seen through the sanctuary window on one of his long walks with Theo and his stroller when he was a baby.

"I know whose body it is," Waylon whispered. "It's that preacher. The one we all thought skipped town."

Patrick sobered as he relayed a detail of his own. "Waylon," he said. "Shay found Marley's wedding ring up there."

Her wedding ring. The one she'd sworn she had no idea where it had gone.

Way stared at the row of screwdrivers until he started to see double. He remembered his words to Marley that day they'd discovered she'd gone up on that church roof eight years ago. *I don't care what you do*, Way had told her then. *Just tell me*. It was all he had asked of his wife, and even that promise, she couldn't keep. Waylon felt he was drowning in a ferocious sea of all the vows he'd made, and here Marley had done as she pleased.

And she'd left him out of it.

He might have had empathy for the woman awaiting him in the jail cell, but he had little to spare. It had been years since he'd felt much at all beyond this viscous longing. For now, Waylon Joseph was just plain mad.

Waylon made Marley wait another hour before sauntering into the police station, where she sat in the quaint little cell, her head resting against the bars. She looked tired and annoyed and lovely and alone. Not to mention trapped—just as his mother had been, and just as they all were by this family business, this business of the family.

The air smelled like vanilla beans. There was no one at the reception desk to greet him, no one guarding the holding cell. At the end of the hall, three women who worked in the records department were eating a sheet cake and wishing a very happy birthday to someone named Susan. The real correctional facility lay just outside Mercury's city limits, and it was a stolid place even Patrick wouldn't go. He'd only put Marley in time-out simply because he could.

She hadn't heard Waylon come in, so he made sure to speak loudly when he called out to the barren building.

"Ladies and gentlemen, my wife," he said. His voice bounced around the room, between the cinder-block walls and back again. "The jailbird."

Lazily, her gaze found him and she pressed her lips into a thin line. "Finally," she said. "I've been in here for hours."

"What's that?" He held a cupped hand to his ear. "The great and powerful Marley has been keeping her own secrets, all these years? I'm astounded."

"Secrets?" She smirked, though her eyes darted through him. "You think I don't know about all that money missing from our account? Let's start there with our secrets."

Way panicked, but only briefly. "Let's not."

Marley was not amused. "You're being an asshole," she said.

"I know."

He walked toward the bars and touched his thumb to her chin. Held her stare even as she tried to look away. He wanted her to see that he *knew*—not that she had things she'd never told him, but that they kept missing each other when they spoke—after Elise's funeral, and after she returned from Maryland, and in everything they hadn't said since. Now, when they both feared there was nothing left and they stood in the quiet of the holding cell, they heard the same beating heart between them, the one they both wanted to keep alive.

Way pulled a chair in front of the cell and scanned the empty room.

They were still alone, so he cradled his hands beneath his chin and said, "Now spill."

And she did.

"Let me see if I've got this right," Waylon started slowly, after Marley had finished telling him what had happened in the church attic. "For four years, you've been holding it against me that I 'chose' my father over you. And here I find out you've been covering for my mother, all this time. How is what you did any different?"

"She didn't murder anyone, Way."

He threw his hands up. "We don't know that my dad did, either. *She* took those pills, Marley."

Marley grabbed one of the steel bars in front of her and tried to rattle it. "Look at me in here," she said. "I'm the one in a jail cell. Do you think Patrick or anyone else has the balls to do this to your dad?"

It was a child's game they fought, petty and privileged. Marley covered her face with her hands. "I can't do this again. I can't rehash this with you one more time."

One of the women from the records department appeared from a back room to lick frosting off her fingers and announce that her shift was ending. Way recognized her as the one who'd given them a marriage license, as well as Theo's birth certificate.

"You can process your wife out of the holding cell over by the front door," she said.

"We're not quite through," Waylon called.

"Yes, we are." Marley stomped her foot. "What about Theo?"

Waylon remained calm. "He's with Jade."

"I wasn't kidding," the records clerk repeated. "I don't get paid overtime, and it's my birthday. Clear out now unless you both want to be locked up for the night."

"Are you even allowed to do that?" Marley asked.

"Do you see any cameras in here?" The woman twirled her fingers around. "I can do just as I please."

Waylon grinned, and a look of horror shot across Marley's face.

"Don't you dare," she whispered.

"We have to fix this, Marley. Now."

The gate unlocked, the door swung open, and Waylon stepped inside. She was about to rush out, and Waylon wanted to grab her, hold her, keep her. But that wasn't what Marley needed. If she wanted to leave, he needed to let her go. He stood to the side as she pushed past him, but she paused when she saw he wasn't trying to stop her. He wanted Marley to choose.

"I want to stay," he said. "Do you?"

Marley closed her eyes and nodded. The gate locked again with a clang, and the clerk left with the rest of her birthday cake in tow. Quiet spread throughout the small-town police headquarters, where a body hadn't been known to be missing until it was found. It was shocking for all of Mercury, but it shouldn't have been for Marley and Waylon. They'd lost the lifeblood of their marriage in much the same way, and neither one of them knew where it had gone.

There was nothing to shield Marley and Way from each other anymore. No pounding of a piano, no banging of a drum, no ringing on the roofing business line. This was the first time in years that Waylon was truly alone with his wife. He took her in now, how effortlessly sexy she was in her tank top and cutoff Levi's, how miserable.

"This is a joke to you," she said. "But it's been hell for me."

He didn't move closer, didn't want her to spook. Marley so rarely confided her feelings to him anymore. He longed for the days when they were teenagers and he'd wooed her slowly over old films on a rooftop. They were sharing themselves then, like shedding clothes in a graveyard Eden, never ashamed of their simple nakedness. By the time Marley knew what Waylon was doing, she'd already fallen in love with him.

"Why didn't you tell anyone?" he asked gently.

"I promised I wouldn't."

There was more waiting for him beneath those words. Waylon could feel it.

"What do you get for carrying that secret to your grave?" he said. "What reward?"

Marley began to pace around the cell. "Of course there was no reward," she answered. "I knew even then it was only a punishment. I did it because it was your mother who asked."

Waylon didn't miss a beat. "She shouldn't have put that on you."

"That secret was all she had left. I owed it to her, even after she died, because of what your father did. It wasn't right, Way."

Waylon began to burn inside. "That's just it," he said. "Aren't you tired of deciding who's right? I spent a slew of Sundays in a church pew and there's one thing that stuck. *Judge not, lest ye be judged.* I don't want someone else's damnation on my conscience, Marley. I don't want to be the one to decide if what he did was wrong. Do you?"

Surprised, Marley laughed. "You're not judging Mick, but you're judging me. You think it was wrong for me to keep your mother's secret. To side with her. Can't you see it? You offer your father the kind of forgiveness you've never offered to anyone else."

The words might as well have been a spear headed straight for Waylon's heart. He hadn't even seen it until now. All of his mercy had poured out into his father, over and over until he had nothing left.

"This isn't about whether I kept Elise's secret or not," Marley said. "It's about why I had to."

A tear formed in her eye, and she let it fall. "I wanted someone to care what happened to Elise. You have only thought about *him*. This never should have been Mick's story, this whole life with his name all over it. It should have been hers, too."

She was angry for this woman who had labored her life in secret and died. It was also a cry for Marley herself. A violent wish to be seen, to be granted a voice of her own.

"I don't know how to fix this, Marley." Way's voice was strained. "All I see when I look around us is decay."

All his faults, his failure, his folly.

Marley stood in front of him and pointed to his chest. "Decay is all you can see because that's what's in here. Every time you defend your father, it grows."

Waylon sank to the floor. He'd been so caught up in whether he could trust his wife that he'd never thought she couldn't trust him. She hadn't felt safe. Way had never seen himself as anything like his father, and he found comfort in it. But it struck him, then—Mick Joseph was not the only kind of danger out there. Waylon had created one, all his own.

"I shouldn't have stopped you from calling the police that night," he said. "I don't know why it's my gut reaction to cover his mistakes."

Marley spoke softly. "I wanted to cover your mother's mistakes, too."

Way reached up a hand and pulled her down next to him on the floor.

"Do you ever wish we were still eighteen, sitting up on that graveyard roof?"

"No." She pulled her hand away. "I want you to give me the chance to love the person you are now and not only the person you were then. Give me the choice, Waylon. Don't make it for me."

"I need you to know," Waylon said, "that I marvel at you—at everything you pull off, at home, at work, and for our family. Every single fucking day."

"Marveling isn't enough, Waylon." Marley moved toward him. "We need to move out."

"I know." He opened his mouth to let out another of his promises, but it didn't come. This was it—his chance at honesty, and he took it.

"I wasn't sure you wanted me anymore," he said.

She collapsed against him—slowly at first, then all of her body resting against all of his, and Waylon felt everything he'd been longing for. She was trusting him with her burdens, if only for a minute. His wife—his brilliant, unflappable tempest of a woman—still wanted him, just as he wanted her.

"Marley," he said. "I need to tell you something."

Just then, the station door swung open, and Patrick and Baylor stepped inside. Light filtered in, and Waylon's older brother looked pissed as summer fireflies swarmed his head.

"You two"—Baylor pointed at the cell—"are the biggest pains in my ass."

Patrick unlocked the door, and Marley and Way were free. They poured out into the night to face the secret that Waylon had been keeping.

◆ ◆ ◆

Baylor did not follow them home. In fact, they didn't go home at all. Waylon drove away from the great house to the other side of town, turning down a side street next to the old dry cleaner's. Way pulled his truck into a notch of grass. He pointed ahead of him.

"There," he said. "This is what I wanted to show you."

"It's a construction site." Marley peered through the dark. "They want you to roof it? I never got a call."

"No." He gripped the Zippo in his pocket, and then he let it go. "It's a house. Our house."

Her fingers dug into the truck's console. "How?"

"I know the builder, and it's ours." He bit his lip. "If you still want to be with me."

Marley stared at the structure before her. Her hair caught the breeze from the truck's open window.

"I'd been looking out in the country," he went on, "but I figured you'd like to stay walking distance from Jade." Way watched his wife and couldn't read her expression. "And Shay can come, too, if he wants. Mar?"

She acted as if she hadn't heard.

"It's a refundable deposit, mostly. You know, if you don't—" He cleared his throat. "Do you want to see it?"

She nodded and almost fell out of the truck. Marley was tired, Waylon reasoned. He should have waited to tell her. But all he'd done was wait. He'd waited for Baylor to be over Marley when they were young. Then he waited for Marley to come around after she'd left the great house for Maryland. She'd returned all the way back then, but she hadn't truly come home. Neither had he. Marley had needed her own home to return to as much as Waylon needed to leave the one he had. He was waiting, still, and he was sick to death of it.

"The windows are in." He jogged up behind her. "No electricity yet."

The street had gone dark, and he rooted around for a key hidden beneath a fake rock. When he found it, they stepped inside. The air smelled like fresh sawdust, coating both of them in that new-house high, the one that came with a promise for a future. Marley took in the brick fireplace where Christmas stockings might hang, the thick wooden banister Theo could slide down. The possibility of a whole life lived between the kitchen and the living room. A swing set in the yard. Then Marley looked at Waylon like she was full of dread.

"So this is where all the money went that we'd been saving."

He nodded.

"What if this doesn't fix things?" She settled on the floor. "What if it's just a new house, and that's all it is?"

Way knelt before her, took her hands. "When you got pregnant with Theo, I promised my mother I'd do everything I could to make you happy. I've tried so hard to keep it, and I—I forgot that you needed to trust me first. I didn't give you a reason to."

"Waylon, Elise shouldn't have done that to you," Marley said. "She shouldn't have done this to either of us."

His face looked silvery and frayed. "Do you regret it, though? All of this?"

He meant the marriage, the business, the family, their life—every portion they shared that could not be divided and judged by its own merit.

"The only thing I wish," she said, "was that I hadn't believed your mother when she said I had to be silent to be a real member of your family."

The thought of Marley living with his mother's secrets took the breath out of him. "Please tell me," he said. "Do you like the house?"

She stood slowly and took a spin around the room by the wide windows and the sliding door into the backyard.

"I love the house," she said as she pressed a hand to the windowpane. "But I don't want you to buy it to make me happy."

Waylon went to her side, feeling desperate to start over with her again and get it right.

"What do you want, Marley?" he asked quietly, curiously, just as he had that first night in his bedroom when she appeared at his window. The question that began this love and was begetting it still.

Maybe it was the bare rasp in his voice, or the silhouette of his shoulders against the moonlight, or the fact that he still cared enough to fight with her in a small-town jail cell. That night, standing in a new and empty house, Marley had one answer to his question. What did she want? It had nothing to do with promises, or a house, or a business, or a dream.

She wanted Waylon, her husband, to want her. Not like he had since his mother had died, shamefaced and penitent, but like he had on the roof when he undressed her against a city sunset, like he had when he felt he had nothing to lose because he'd already spent every emotion, every bead of sweat, every tendon on her. Like he had to make it count for a thousand nights, like he could never get enough.

Marley couldn't bring herself to say it. She felt embarrassed by how dirty it sounded—the way she wished Waylon would take her up against a wall. What had happened to her over these eight years? Her body had grown and shrank, held life and given it away. She'd never been a prude, had never ascribed to the myth of the submissive, innocent wife. Why did it feel wrong, then, to crave her husband just as much, and more, as she had when they were eighteen and had no idea what was coming for them?

Marley feared it was because he didn't want her back, not now that she was a mother, and a liar, and a secret keeper, and a Joseph. She was still that young woman yearning for him to notice her, to see all her wonders deep within—and yet she'd become so much more than that, too. Since she'd met Waylon, she'd been the Marley who stayed, the Marley who left, the one who helped, the one who hurt. Marley wanted to be known by her husband, and she never wanted him to be satisfied with just a piece of who she was.

She looked at Way with such stark need, without an answer on her lips but a rush of blood to her cheeks, and Waylon knew. She could see it in the way his eyes went dark, the way he set his jaw. He knew she wanted to see him undone by her, for them to come undone together. Gently, he leaned her against the door of their new house and hitched her up by her hips. Marley's breath caught, and Waylon took his teeth to her throat. Then he reached for the strap of her tank top as she pushed herself against him.

"Marley," he said, taking her shirt from her shoulders, kissing one collarbone, then the other. "Do I still know what you like?"

She smiled at him and clasped her hands behind his neck. They fell to a drop cloth on the floor as he climbed over her, and she whispered, "Let's find out."

When it was through and they were left speechless, sweaty and clinging to each other in a film of sawdust, Marley knew it had never been better than this. After the hurt, the silence, the space, the pissing off and the making up, only to do it all again. These were the contours of the love they shared.

This was the beginning of a life Marley was building, all her own. She'd told her mother nine years earlier that what she dreamed for herself was to love someone, but she'd cast too narrow a vision. Her days were abundant with all that she loved, and the only thing left to do now was to claim it. Claim her home, claim her work, claim her people, claim herself—with her own voice, as loud as she wanted.

"Are we still good together, do you think?" she asked Waylon, her hand splayed beneath her head as she lay naked next to him.

He reached down and kissed her hipbone. "Fuck yes," he answered.

And they drove home and fell into bed, so ecstatic to have reached a denouement in their own story that neither of them stopped to wonder why there were no other Joseph men in the house. After some time, when Marley had almost fallen asleep, Waylon sat up and looked at his wife.

"Wait a minute," he said. "If you wanted Pastor Hollis's death to seem innocent, why did you wrap him in plastic and shut the attic hatch?"

Marley rubbed her eyes. "We didn't."

"If you didn't do it"—Waylon's voice was slow—"who did?"

His eyes went to the open window. Soon, Marley's followed. Together, they looked out into the empty street.

28.

On the night Baylor Joseph bailed Waylon and his wife out of jail, he was itching for a haircut. The sensation tickled the length of his body, beginning at the nape of his neck and ending at the base of his spine. As a boy, his mother used to give him a trim when his hair began to curl beneath his ears, snipping one coiled strand at a time, her fingers pinching his hair into a straight line as she went. She kept at it long after he'd grown, fastidious with her blade in just the same way she behaved as a mother. Hers was not a violent nor careless love, but thorough, the breast-bone that remained after a life had been picked clean. Once Elise's mind started to stray, she nicked him with the razor. It startled her, but she kept on, and Baylor couldn't remember a time she'd ever done it. Her hand had always been so steady.

Bay didn't want her to know that he noticed. At the time, it seemed right to grant his mother her privacy because truly, what else could he give her? Baylor couldn't imagine even one thing his mother might want. He did know—after seeing her hack into a mangled butterflied chicken as if the fowl had betrayed her—not to let her near his neck with a set of shears. Elise was time-traveling through her memories, setting up camp within them, and Baylor understood what strife he brought on the family as the firstborn son.

As the oldest, Baylor held the weight of knowing past lives, other truths, different selves. They had not always lived in the great house. He'd witnessed Elise and Mick transform from people who could not agree on how to live together into parents who could not agree on how to raise their children.

His mother had never wanted to live in Mercury. She'd never said as much to her son; it leaked out of her as she and Mick used to argue about money. What they meant to fight about was parity of sacrifice. As Elise gave, so should Mick. And yet he didn't.

At first, their debts had nothing to do with cash and only what they owed each other when neither of them was content. This was the ledger of transgressions they kept: Mick had taken Elise from her family farm in Illinois so he could return to the outskirts of a city he loved that couldn't love him back—not when steel mills were closing, and every outsider declared that Pittsburgh's glory days were gone. No western Pennsylvania native would ever agree to that, Mick included. He was a good soldier and kept to the script.

We leave no one behind.

This meant the city itself, and besides—there was nowhere else for them to go. Elise had become a stranger here, so that Mick could thrive in the land he was known.

Thriving, to Elise, had not meant earning a wage only to piss it away. Mick didn't spend his cash on alcohol or cigarettes, but possessions. Tools. Instruments. Then he bought flowers and chocolate for a wife who refused to cut her own lilies from the yard, lest she have to watch them die. Mick Joseph couldn't see that he was extravagant in all the wrong ways.

Baylor learned early on that money might have been the cause of their arguments, back when they still cared enough to fight, but it was not the root of it. The root lay in Mick's erratic habits of mind. He was obsessed with the notion of starting over, of wiping his own slate clean with his fist, and therefore saw no need to sustain even one thing that he'd built.

As a farmer's daughter, Elise knew no other way to live other than to bury a tiny seed in the ground and gently coax its sprouts out of the earth. Her Black Krim heirloom tomato seeds were among the precious items Elise brought along when Mick returned from Vietnam and whisked her away, as if she hadn't been living her own life in the Midwest while he marched through waterlogged trenches so deep the skin of his heels rubbed clean off his feet. Elise had planned to attend school and become a teacher, but she never got the chance.

This was how Elise told the story. Not to Way, not to Shay, but to Baylor alone. Over twenty years later, Baylor would still remember the tales his mother told him of that time.

It was 1972, Mick had served his country, and Elise had served him by bearing him a son. They lived in the forested caboose of an abandoned train at the edge of a dead-end track that belonged to Mick's uncle, while Mick worked out his grand schemes. He'd work in ceramics. He'd go to college. He'd start a newspaper or maybe a construction company, having built houses from scratch with his own father years before. Mick jostled the train car with his pacing, a pencil and newspaper in hand while he jotted down his ideas.

Elise watched him and rocked her son. Once her husband had left the caboose for the day, Elise would look at her boy and say, "You cannot grow up to be like that man." This was the vein in the throbbing heart of all his memories. Baylor had become his mother's best confidant. He also learned to define himself by what he could not be.

Mick claimed Baylor didn't learn to speak until he was three and a half because he was stupid. He treated it like an indictment, but Baylor knew otherwise. From his earliest moments, his mother had wanted him to listen and not talk back because that was what her husband never did. Only later, when Bay was old enough to see that listening had done no one any good, least of all his mother, did he learn the satisfaction of using his own mouth.

Baylor quaked with rage any time his father used the word "stupid" to describe him. He made a vow to himself that he'd prove to his father one day how vocal, how crass, how raw he could be. One day, he would not hold back.

But first, a miracle. In 1973 Buddy—whom Mick had been drafted with in the war—discovered a house in the heart of Mercury that had gone uninhabited since before the time the government started sending young men to Vietnam. No one lived in it because it had a gaping crater in the roof and every window had been blown out. All the copper pipes had been filched. Several autumns' worth of dead leaves lay in tufts on the floor, which had warped and bubbled from snow and rainwater. Rumor had it that a horse had once walked in and took a shit on the living room floor. This, Mick decided, was the destiny of the day. He was not intimidated by filth, or improbability of success. And dirt? Dirt meant work had been done.

This was a home where his wife could raise a family.

They moved into the great house that Mick had bought on a loan, though it was not so very great then, Baylor barely a year and his mother already pregnant again. It was at this house on Hollow Street that the Joseph family fable was born. Mick donned his work boots, tucked a hammer into his belt loop, turned on his AM radio station to Vivaldi, and thrust a long steel ladder against the side of the house. Up and down he went all day, ferrying buckets of tar, swatches of rubber, pieces of plywood to repair the hole in the roof. The air smelled like pitch and lumber. He pried up the rotted beams and threw them into the yard. Stood atop his property, shirtless in his grimy slacks and sweating in the midday sun. It didn't take long for a curious horde to gather. These people were strangers who would turn into neighbors, a young wife named Ann who would become Elise's only friend.

"Look at that, will you," Elise said to Baylor, who hung on her hip at the window. "He loves having an audience."

No sooner had the words fallen out of her mouth than there was a grand tumbling, the deep rat-a-tat-tat of a body rolling off the roof. Elise screamed when she saw Mick's body crash to the ground. The spectators gasped. A car screeched. The whole town seemed to hold its breath. Then Mick stood like a skeleton from an open grave, groaned, and cracked his neck on either side. Dusted the bits of lilac bush that stuck to him and climbed back up the ladder to finish the job. Elise ran out onto the porch, craned her body toward the gutter.

"Mick!" she yelled. "Are you all right?"

"Better than a country girl at a square dance," he said because he'd drawn a crowd.

Later, when the roof was patched and the yard raked, he spent most of the night in a bathtub full of ice.

"You are a fool," Elise said to him, eyeing his naked form in the tub.

But she was laughing, and he laughed, and he figured his luck had finally changed. Bit by bit, Mick transformed the house. He began with the roof, and then fixed up the porch, followed by the main staircase—and everyone in town witnessed it because he left the front door wide open. Mick developed a reputation in Mercury for being able to fix anything. Need your electricity rewired? Check. Want a new porch? Done. Need your doorbell to flash instead of ring? Mick Joseph could do it, easy. Only thing he couldn't do, though, was make things look pretty.

"My God, Mick," Elise said about the contraption he built to make the toilet seat go down each time it flushed. "That is ghastly."

He began his legacy by putting ugly roofs on ugly buildings. They didn't leak, and no one cared about how they appeared. This was also how Baylor grew up—atop an ugly roof. When he was five, he hammered a nail. At six, Mick let him climb the ladder that led to their porch roof. By ten, he knew how to find a leak, attach flashing, and lay down a roll of rubber three times his height. He was strong, and he reveled in it. The reliability of his muscles allowed his mouth to utter whatever the hell it pleased. He had much to say, and he'd finally found the words to say it.

Too bad no one had listened to him since the day Waylon was born.

The brothers were born thirteen months apart. For thirteen months, Baylor had Elise to himself. For thirteen months, he was the most important man in her life. Then, it stopped, simply and finally. Elise was there but not available to him, and he felt the same kind of rancor he'd felt when his father called him stupid. He couldn't aim his anger at Elise, for she was the person on whom his well-being relied. So he turned it on that beautiful infant Waylon, who was pink and dimpled, happy and smart. Who was he, that he could come and take what had been Baylor's simply because he was younger? His crib, his blankets, his mother. This Waylon was a thief, living off what Baylor was owed.

Together, the boys grew, Waylon always nipping at Baylor's heels. Wanting to play with him in the dirt, wanting to mess with Baylor's drawer of private treasures—his hammer, his GI Joe figurines, his baseball cards. What had Waylon ever done that was so original? What thought had he had that wasn't Baylor's first? He'd just found a way of expressing it that Baylor wasn't able to mimic. When Baylor called Elise's meat loaf "good," Waylon called it "delicious." Where Baylor predicted a storm, Waylon found a rainbow. Way was an optimist, but Baylor knew his own pessimism made him wiser than his little brother, if more badly behaved.

From the beginning, Elise and Mick delighted in their second son. *He's ahead of the curve*, they said. *Speaks better than Baylor. More emotionally sensitive. More obedient.* All the things Baylor could have been if he'd been given the time. Even that, Waylon was stealing, eager to surpass him in every way.

Baylor did not joke, and he didn't smooth things over. The only thing he'd ever been good at, the only thing that remained his native language, was being rough. It became so apparent that Baylor lagged even more than Waylon surged ahead that his mother decided to hold him back a year from starting school.

"He's just not ready," Elise explained to her church friends over punch and powdered cookies in the building's basement. It was an explanation she offered to everyone else and not to him. "It will be good for him to be in school with Waylon," she added, as if Waylon were his crutch and not the other way around.

It crushed him to sink so low in her esteem, especially when his body still held the memory of a time when he'd been her favorite boy. They attended school together, and Way was so damn likable that Baylor searched for the means to bring him down, if only by a peg.

It happened at recess when Baylor was nine and Waylon was eight. Shay was a year old, and Baylor had overheard his mother tell Ann that Baylor and Shay were her "bookend boys." The first and the last; "book-ends" meant that Waylon was the book itself, the main part of the story. Baylor wanted to know when Elise decided that everything he did ought to be in service to Waylon. He was used to Mick, but not his mother, put-ting him down.

What was Baylor's story, and when was his moment? What if he'd al-ready missed it?

On that bitter fall day, the third graders were bundled up and taking turns on the slide. They bunched together on the ladder like train cars in a locomotive. As usual, Waylon followed Baylor around like a fly. Baylor slid first, followed by Way, who hit Baylor in the back with his feet, so eager was he to follow closely in his brother's path.

Baylor made a show of it, behaving as if Way had done it on purpose and kicked him right in the kidney. He'd planned only to get his brother in trouble, but so concerned was Waylon for him, so apologetic and puppy-eyed, that Baylor knew he needed a tsunami to get everyone to see that Way was no better than he, despite his pretty face. He took his brother by the collar and tossed him into the grass, held him down with his arms. Mud squelched beneath his head. Waylon looked confused, then betrayed, then hurt, and then, finally, weak. "Weak Waylon" and "Big Baylor," their father would one day call them, as soon as they mounted a roof. Waylon was not strong enough to lift his brother off him, and Baylor relished it. He'd discovered he was stronger and could best his brother in this simple manner. He'd do anything he could to hold on to it.

Both boys were sent home from school that day. Waylon with a bloody lip, Baylor with a trophy hidden inside his chest. Elise ran to her golden son, and Baylor stood with his chin up as she consoled Waylon. Then she sent him to his room with a washcloth full of ice and turned to Bay, her hands on her hips.

"Sit," she said.

Baylor sat at the long dining table as Elise removed her calico apron. It was one of those few things she'd brought from Illinois in addition to her Black Krim seeds, something that had belonged to her grandmother. Sometimes Bay liked to feel the edges of it when it hung in the pantry, this soft calico that held memories of a beloved past. Elise spoke often of Illinois, but her boys had never seen it.

"You'll remember," Elise began, flattening her palms on the table beside him. Her hands looked parched and webbed. "What I told you when you were a boy."

Bay wanted to argue that he was still a boy now, but it wasn't the time. "I remember."

He remembered because of everything Elise's words hadn't been. Not, *I'll love you no matter what.* Not, *You can do anything you set your mind to.* In the dining room, the grandfather clock ticked.

"You cannot grow up to be like that man," his mother said again.

Elise loved her husband, same as she was disappointed in him, and Bay felt the sentiment saddling him. This was the kind of private confession saved for Baylor because Waylon, the chosen, was no one's confidant. Even at nine years old, Baylor knew no one told their sins to an angel like they would a fellow criminal.

"Don't make yourself less than you are," Elise went on. "I know you think you're only a Joseph, but you have good farming blood in you, too. Own it," she said. And then she walked away.

Baylor felt despicable. He wished she had yelled or sent him to his room, anything but holding on to this standard he feared he'd never reach. It only worsened when his father returned from a day on top of the local gas station's pavilion, and Elise forced her eldest to tell his father what he had done. Friction pulsed from every corner in the room as they waited for Mick to respond. No one dared touch their breaded chicken. Baylor braced for the slap, for words of condemnation, but they didn't come. Instead, Mick laughed. He laughed so hard he spilled his milk onto his green peas.

"Cain and Abel, I'm telling you," he said, slapping his knee. "These two are Cain and Abel."

Bay knew it was some Bible story but had no idea what it meant. He finished his dinner with his head down, and then he cleared his plate. After everyone went to bed that night, Baylor hauled the big family Bible off the credenza in the foyer and thumbed through the feathery pages of the Old Testament while holding a flashlight in his mouth until he found it. There, in Genesis, the first brothers who had ever existed in the world were named Cain and Abel. Fitting, as Mick saw himself as an eternal pioneer of sorts, like Adam, no longer entrusted with ruling the earth and blaming his wife.

Baylor read on to discover there was a good son, and a bad son—only one who did right in the eyes of God. Then the bad brother murdered the good, and he got damned to toil the land for the rest of his days after getting shoved out of the family. Baylor shut the book and didn't open it again. He didn't need to guess which son Mick deemed him.

His father had cursed him. He was Cain, through and through.

Being the evil son had its benefits, it turned out. No one expected much of Baylor, so he did as he pleased. He skipped school when he wanted. He saved his roofing cash to buy a beat-up Camaro. He played football, where brutality reigned. Baseball, so Way would be reminded who dominated. He took girls by the waist, took them home, and took them to bed when he thought they might like it. He suffered no illusions of his own goodness, other than this: he was a good roofer, and he took pride in knowing that a Joseph roof would never leak. He was a mighty Adonis when he worked up in the air, only becoming mortal when his body returned to the earth.

Baylor knew most of Mercury was scared to death of him. And Waylon they loved.

By the time Bay was eighteen and had one year left of school to go, he felt so ready for the end of things—sports, midterms, tardy slips, and absentee calls to his mother. All he wanted was to make money, restore his Camaro, and for people to leave him the hell alone because he didn't think anyone could love him just as he was.

What he hadn't counted on was Marley.

She'd come out of nowhere, zipping into town in her mother's shitty Acura, her long hair trailing out the side window. Mercury wasn't a place where new people appeared. Even fewer of them remained. Bay felt sure he was born knowing everyone in town. He'd never even learned how to introduce himself; the whole community was built on the collective psyche of knowing one another better than they knew themselves.

After seeing Marley twice—once driving by the courthouse with her pink-painted toes balanced on the dash, and once at his baseball game with a pair of sunglasses perched delicately on her head—he became infatuated not so much with Marley herself but with the idea of having a clean slate, the very thing his own father loved more than all else. Bay was known as Mick's son and Waylon's brother to all of Mercury. A bookend.

He hoped this might be his moment to have a story all his own.

Things didn't go according to his will, however. During the game, Baylor witnessed the way Waylon caught sight of Marley for the first time. He'd made a masterful catch in the outfield, and like a doting boy looked to his mother in the crowd. There behind Elise sat Marley, fawnlike and nimble, the sun kissing the freckles on her nose. It made Waylon drop his glove in the grass, even as the rest of the team ran to the dugout to celebrate the win. Waylon was heroic but unsurprising. All his life, Baylor had been first in things, with Waylon close behind.

The look of enchantment on Way's face struck fear right in the heart of him—some inner demon whispered that Waylon would reach Baylor's fair shot first. Then this stranger would only see Baylor through Waylon's eyes, and the time had finally come for Way to surpass him as his father had predicted, and this would be the first of many slights. Waylon in a suit and tie, with a pretty wife, and his own set of business cards. Bay drowning his sorrows at the bar in the lowlands outside town, his life culminating in leakless rooftops and one-night stands.

A bookend till the end.

And Bay said to himself, *No. Not today. Not this time.*

So he did something shameful. He didn't care about Way's tender feelings, nor did he realize that all Waylon truly wanted was Baylor's company, but he did know the stab of being compared to a brother and being found wanting.

He grabbed Waylon by the back of his jersey and muttered, "Enjoy this, since you ain't worth shit on the roof," hating himself just a little for knowing it would set Waylon off. So much of him was still that little boy who flew down the slide, only to end up beneath his brother's fist, heartsick with betrayal. Waylon threw a punch, and they thumped into the outfield, tangled like snakes.

"Why do you have to be a dick all the time," Way said while in a headlock.

"Because no one else has the balls to be a dick to you but me," Baylor replied, and just then, they heard their mother's warning knell.

"Enough," she said.

Elise did not tolerate fighting. She didn't yell or grouse. Instead, she was disappointed. Different though the boys were, they both loathed displeasing her. She was the gate that beat back their father's erratic moods: his declarations of new horizons despite a dwindling bank account, his weekly discourse on why the answer may be to pick up and leave. Elise paid his ideas no mind, and she taught her sons to do the same. The boys, unlike the rest of Mercury, had never thought of Mick Joseph as strong. They had one model of strength, and it came forth in their mother who drove a wide Lincoln and cracked eggs two at a time and had birthed their baby brother at home. When Elise called out, the boys fell apart in the dirt.

Baylor wished he'd let it end there, that he'd let Way have Marley from the start. It would have been easier to never get hurt, to vault into adulthood without wondering why he always loved the wrong people—or why whenever he had the chance to give to someone instead of take, he always chose himself.

Marley seemed to fit into his life like rain filling cracks in the sidewalk. She met some deep need in him, though Baylor wasn't certain it was the right one. Elise welcomed her at the table; Shay Baby fell in love with her from the start. Bay longed to parade her around like a gem he'd never have enough money to buy but had found by luck. The rest of town already knew she was too good for him, but Marley didn't. She looked at him like he'd never punched out a window, never cursed, never found spare liquor bottles in someone else's basement and drank them. He thought this might be love—to see past the worst parts of someone, to never see them at all.

He tried so hard to make himself good for her. Baylor kissed her with abandon and fought with the zipper on her jeans.

"Baylor," she'd said on a hot August night when he thought all he needed was to lose himself in her. "What do you want?"

The question caused his hands to stagger at her waist. He'd heard those same four words the evening he'd helped Mick roll in his new piano weeks ago, the first time Marley had eaten dinner with his family. Baylor had been levering the piano on its side with three other men who had come to drop it off, and Mick stood outside on the sidewalk, where Ann had been walking alone.

Baylor had watched his own father reach his fingers toward Ann's cheek, and she recoiled.

"What do you *want*, Mick?" Ann asked, her voice laced in disgust.

Whatever advances he had made toward his wife's best friend were unwanted, and they weren't the first. Bay sensed it in Ann's weary dismissal, the bile in how she spoke. Baylor felt himself plummeting, wishing he'd never seen it.

Wishing he weren't the only one who knew.

While his father serenaded the rest of the family that night on his new instrument, Baylor crouched on the stairs and struggled to breathe. He felt like an outcast for this new knowledge he had, even though this time Mick was the one who had earned the name of Cain.

Long ago, Elise had taught Baylor to look at Mick and see himself, so when Marley offered Ann's same words a few weeks later—*what do you want*—Baylor panicked. Felt a poison spilling from him that he couldn't control. He sped away from her with the truck door flapping open, gutted at the notion that the inevitable had already come true.

Baylor didn't want to let Marley go, nor did he think she should stay. Like with Elise, who had been taught to submit to her husband and inwardly fumed, the only person Baylor's behavior punished was himself. There was no one to see his longing, no one to understand why he avoided the kind of romantic gestures Mick loved so well: the flowers, the chocolates, the presents with satin bows. They were all tools of manipulation. When Mick had done something foolish again, these tokens were the only way he knew to apologize.

Baylor would never be pretty that way. Pretty, you couldn't trust. He talked straight, built ugly roofs, and knew he was a bit of a shit. Anger was a welcome darkness that spread through his body like mold. He couldn't stop it or rip it out. He could only conceal it, for a time.

That time ended when he discovered that Marley was pregnant. Yet again Waylon had swooped in, snatching what was his. He couldn't quell the rage anymore. Baylor couldn't stand the smirk his father gave him, as if he couldn't hold on to his woman. As if Mick had any right. Bay couldn't weather the fact that everyone knew. And he couldn't handle the truth he'd known from the beginning that Marley was too lovely for him, and that one day she'd prefer the good son over the bad one.

All his work, his heart, his sacrifice had been for naught. Marley deserved better than the Josephs, but the Josephs were what she was going to get. *Fuck it*, Baylor thought. *Fuck it all.*

Behind the house, he lined up a row of mason jars on a wooden workbench. Then he took his steel baseball bat and swung at them, one at a time. The crash crinkled through the air, like he'd taken the jars and crushed them with his fist. A holy, desperate, aching crack. He was lining up a second batch when he felt his mother's presence behind him. He turned, caught a glimpse of her pressed skirt, her nude stockings, her maroon heels.

Briefly, he wondered whom she dressed up for. Mick barely looked up from his crossword after the day's work unless he was sticking food in his mouth. It seemed an impossibility that she'd dress up for herself, and so he didn't even consider it.

"Save it, Ma." He choked up on his bat. "I don't want to hear the 'don't turn out like Mick' speech today."

Elise said nothing, and he smashed one jar, then a second, and a third. Finally he turned, feeling spooked by the focused serenity in her glare.

"What?" he snapped.

"That could have been you."

She meant Waylon, the baby, the beautiful girl. He was about to shout back, to finally announce how he hated being the oldest son in this godforsaken family, when Elise opened her mouth again.

"Be glad that it wasn't."

After she disappeared into the house, Baylor felt a thin line of blood trickle down the side of his neck. A shard of glass had sliced him below his ear, deep enough to leave a scar. Bay didn't know fully what his mother meant, but he knew Waylon was now stained. A chill filled the air as Baylor realized that in losing Marley, he'd gained everything he'd ever wanted.

There would be no returning from this, in Elise's eyes. The battle for the good son was over, and Baylor had won.

29.

Baylor did some fine roofing in the years that followed. He sold his Camaro for it, and gave his body to it, one sinew at a time. But what did it give back to him? It didn't show him love, and it didn't keep him company at night. He vowed never to speak to Marley, which he honored briefly and nobody noticed but him. Yet she inserted herself in his life, living in his house, eating at his table, pretending to run his business. Her pastel letters, her phone calls. Baylor saw it as the fruition of what his mother had predicted long ago. Together, Marley and Waylon would prevail with their fancy titles, with their button-down shirts, with their logos pasted on the sides of gray vans. Bay would get lost in the dust of the only thing he'd ever been good at.

It took his mother getting ill for him to see that it had never been about winning for Marley. She'd lost more than she'd gained ever since she first had dinner at the Joseph house, as far as Baylor could tell. Her mother had moved away, she'd gotten pregnant, and she had no house of her own. And yet she treated the Josephs like they'd earned the right for her to call them family, even though they'd done nothing to deserve her. This was how Marley helped, and how she helped was how she loved—like a tidal wave. In time, she took on Elise's responsibilities so fluidly it was hard to detect any change. She cared for Shay, who brightened every time Marley walked into the room. And there was more money in his pocket once Marley took hold of the finances, forcing Mick to let go.

If only money were all he cared about.

Baylor had been livid when he discovered Mick was dipping into the business account. Not because they needed the capital, which they did, but because Mick saw that money as his own. Bay stormed through the house to find his father at his potter's wheel in the basement, absently forming a large bowl. Mick had his own workshop down in the cellar: a wheel, a small kiln, and an avalanche of tools. A silver drain in the ground. Even a standalone toilet off to one side with no lid or seat.

Bay stomped down the steps and thrashed the clay right from the wheel to the floor with his fist. It made a sucking noise as it smacked the cement. Mick sat before him, astonished.

"What the fuck, Dad," Baylor began, because he didn't know what else to say.

"Language," his father chided.

Above them, the kitchen floor creaked as Elise set about making dinner.

"Stop it with your shit morality and listen to me."

That command—*listen to me*—was one Elise had given her oldest son many times, but never her husband. Now Baylor did.

Mick stood, already looking like a wounded, hungry wolf.

"You've been taking money from the business account to spend on God-knows-what," Baylor said, "and it ends today."

"The *business* account?" Mick's lips screwed into a pucker, as if he'd just heard a dirty word. "Have you forgotten that I'm the head of this family? I started this company so I'd never have to answer to another man, least of all you."

This company, this family. How different they were, yet treated the same. Mick turned to leave, and Baylor caught his arm.

"You do have to answer to me. To Waylon. To your wife."

Baylor let the final word hang in the air between them. They'd never spoken about what he'd seen between Mick and Ann, and Baylor hoped his father sensed that he knew about his wandering eye. He knew about so much more, too. The deeper things his parents had weathered. Now he reckoned with the reality that he knew them in a way they'd never known him.

The silence rankled Mick to his core. He swung his arm around in a circle. "Do you see this house?" He thrust his hands out. "These hands paid for it. All of it. We had *nothing* when I came back from the war. Nothing."

Baylor grew madder still. He didn't want to hear any more about what ailed this man. Who was he to say what price had been paid? Mick had bought the house, but who had paid for his behavior—for his outbursts, for his lack of remorse? Always and only his family.

"This isn't about the war, Dad. This is about why you think it's okay to steal from your sons. Why it's okay to stray from your wife."

Baylor stopped short. He couldn't believe he'd said it out loud, and neither could Mick.

In a fury, Mick drew back his hand and struck Baylor on the cheek. Clay spattered everywhere; they were both covered in it. The misshapen pot had started to harden on the floor.

"I'm selling your piano," Baylor said quietly. His face throbbed. "So I can keep food on the goddamn table."

"Return the drum set," Mick spat. "Shay doesn't need it."

The air started to smell like biscuits in the oven, and Baylor saw it then. He and his father had never been alike. Being selfless was not so complicated as Mick made it seem. Bay wanted Shay to have that drum set because it would make him happy, and that was it. The difference between them was so stark that Bay couldn't believe he was only now starting to see it. Mick manipulated, while he shot straight. His mother had bestowed Baylor with an untruth it would take a lifetime to shake.

He shoved his pointer finger into his father's chest. "Don't you dare touch those fucking drums."

Mick stormed up the stairs, and Bay left the clay molded to the cement. Being the good son was not at all what Baylor had hoped it would be.

◆ ◆ ◆

The business grew, Theo grew, and Baylor thought he stayed the same. The only difference he saw in himself was that the back of his hair was no longer cut in a straight line across his neck. It looked like a jagged staircase when Elise was through with it. She was distracted, the tips of her fingers bloodied by the shears. Her mind had flown elsewhere, and for the first time in his life Baylor figured his mother may have better things to do than cut her son's shaggy mop once a month.

One day, not long after Elise had walked through town without her shoes, Baylor stepped into Jade's salon without an appointment.

She was about to close shop for the night, and the lights had dimmed as she spun a broom around, singing along to Janet Jackson's "That's the Way Love Goes" on the stereo. Jade looked sweaty and sublime, the collar of her shirt slipping off her shoulder as she swept hair from the floor. She glanced toward Bay when the door jingled.

"Baylor," she said, not hiding her surprise. "Is Marley all right?"

For a moment, Baylor stewed that wishes for Marley still followed him everywhere he went. "She's fine," he answered petulantly, and then he thawed at her smile. It was bright and warm and reminded him of his favorite part of the year, high summer, when the fireflies came out at dusk.

"So you've come for a haircut, then?" she asked.

He nodded.

"Thank God."

She pointed to the chair in front of the sink, the one that stood in front of a crowd of palm trees painted on the wall, and Baylor grew uncomfortable. Everything in the shop was so very pink and gold. People passed by on the street outside the storefront window, and Bay wasn't sure he wanted to be seen while he was covered in shampoo lather.

"Can't you just cut it?" he asked.

Jade frowned and strutted toward him. Her bangles clinked as she studied his head. He noted the bright green of the spearmint gum she chewed, how her jaw rocked it back and forth.

"How clean is your hair?" she asked.

"Clean enough."

She reached up and feathered her fingers through his thick locks, longer now than they'd ever been. He almost lost his balance when he caught the fresh linen scent of her. A dark curl fell from her shoulder.

"Baylor," she said. "There's paint in here."

He blushed, and she laughed. He sat in her chair. Jade finished her sweeping, then put away her broom. Janet Jackson's album came to an end with "If," and the CD player whirred before beginning the tracks again. Jade came behind him, ran the water till it went warm, and told him to lean back.

"Please know," she said. "I'm charging you for this."

Baylor let out a deep laugh, the kind he didn't think himself capable of. The water sang soft upon his skin, and he closed his eyes. He and Jade had not crossed paths much in high school; Bay was the kind of kid others went out of their way to avoid. He felt embarrassed then at the thought that Jade had once wanted to steer clear of him. Then further embarrassment still at the notion she thought of him at all.

She had always been lovely, olive skin and curly black hair, plush lips. Earrings that jangled as she walked. Bay sank deep into the salon chair, barely aware that he was holding his breath. Jade's fingernails scraped his scalp tenderly, and she ran her hands through his rangy mane in a proprietary way, as if she knew it better than he. The shampoo smelled like island coconut.

His hair fell far past his ears now, gathering along his nape, and as Jade massaged the hair on the back of his neck, Baylor had to keep himself from sighing. He had known privilege in his life, but not much kindness such as this. He opened an eye to peer at Jade as she rinsed. She was so focused, so intent, so skilled at her job that Baylor could not tell whether all her clients experienced this euphoria. It made him wonder about his own faulty notions of men's and women's work—one defying danger, the other providing refuge. With Jade at the helm, Baylor no longer knew which was which, or why it had mattered at all.

She added conditioner, then washed it out and held a towel to his head. When he sat up, the room righted itself, even as the world spun.

"What's it like, being on your own?" He didn't know why he asked it, or where it had come from.

"What do you mean?" Her eyebrow arched.

"You do everything here. You cut, you style, you clean. Do you ever get a day off?"

She laughed. "Probably about as many as you."

"But don't you want a family?" he blurted, and quickly wished he hadn't.

Her face went to stone. "Has anyone ever asked *you* that, even though you run your own business, too?"

"No."

He could feel himself reddening at his stupidity when he lifted his eyes to hers in the mirror, and she gave him a wink.

"Tell me about work," she said as she dragged a comb through his locks and began to cut. She hadn't bothered to ask what kind of style he wanted, and he found that he didn't care.

"I went inside a library today," he said. "It had one of those spiral staircases that led to the roof hatch." He watched her blink, the deep brown of her irises flashing.

"That sounds like a job Marley must have sold," she said.

He laughed. Twice in one night. "It was."

Jade pulled taut the hair on top of his head and began to snip. "They let you in there with those work boots on?" Her eyes flitted to his dirty shoes, caked in plaster and old leaves and roofing glue.

"I wore booties," he explained. "The kind that look like hairnets."

She stopped, looked at him in the glass, and giggled. "Now that, I'd like to see."

Baylor felt a warm sensation flood his middle, and he could not recognize this chatty man who appeared before him in the beauty shop mirror. Jade finished, brushed the stray strands from his neck, and scrutinized his appearance.

"Can I put gel in your hair?" she asked.

"No."

She sighed. "Suit yourself."

Jade rang him up at the cash register, and he paid her twice what he owed.

"Next time," she called as he went out the door, "make an appointment." And he did.

It was unfortunate, falling for someone off-limits to him. Jade was not only unavailable because she was Marley's best friend. In any other family, it might have worked quite nicely, but Baylor Joseph knew from his failed experiment with his brother's wife not to shit where he ate. Also? Jade was wholly uninterested in him.

He always booked the salon's final appointment of the day and arrived to Jade's symphony of washing the makeup from her face and throwing her hair into a topknot while Bryan Adams's voice rasped on the radio. She listened to Baylor's stories about pulling dead birds out of roof vents or carrying boiling buckets of tar up rickety ladders, her breasts so close to his eyes while she cut the front of his hair that he could only conclude she saw him not even as a friend but as her friend's brother-in-law.

It denoted a distance between them that he didn't feel was true in his heart. Didn't they share the same struggle of what it meant to put your own name on a business and do everything you could to keep it alive? A younger Baylor would have pulled up beside her in his truck, given her a ride to wherever she was going. But Baylor had changed, even though he couldn't quite see it.

After witnessing his father steal from their own funds, and the price he paid to account for the loss, Baylor had begun to take a hard look at the things he'd stolen, and what they'd cost. He'd stolen kisses, glances, dances, phone numbers, Friday nights, Sunday mornings. Mick suffered from a kind of cannibalism, Baylor had realized, one that feasted on his own blood to survive. He thieved from the flesh of his flesh and bankrupted himself. Baylor did not want to steal from Jade—or from anyone—the way his father had stolen Elise's happiness, scrap by scrap.

He'd not had words for it until the day he realized Mick was capable of emptying the business bank account and feeling no guilt. At the same time, his mother had started to lose shavings of herself across the plane of her life. It was Mick Joseph's fault, Baylor knew. Again, his mother's words haunted him.

Do not become like that man.

So, Baylor drank. In that regard, at the very least, he and Mick were nothing alike. The bartender at the Crow knew he liked his Jameson straight and did not like to talk. Baylor only did his talking in a salon chair, it turned out. The stool beside him at the bar was often left open, and women filled it from time to time. He did not converse, he did not buy drinks, he did not want to appear friendly. The thought of a woman assuming he expected something in return—as he'd once done with Marley—sickened him.

He was under no pretenses about the kind of person he was, good son or not. All he could do was minimize his reach by keeping to himself. He walked the mile home after closing time to sober up, to feel the wind claw his face. As in the words of a love song, he took the route that passed by Jade's shop. Just to check that all was safe, he told himself. Always, the street was empty, the lights gone out. He imagined her sleeping soundly in ways he couldn't with Elise roaming the halls at night.

He could move out at any time. But this loner did not truly want to be alone.

On a spring night in 1995, Baylor loped through the town square. He peered at the church bell tower from the lawn below, barely able to make out its edges in the overcast sky. Lightning fluttered, far off. Bay had a mind to stay right where he was and wait out the storm. The rain driving into his skin was preferable to the empty feeling squatting in his chest.

Behind him, down the street from the church, Jade's shop sat dark—until it didn't. The light burst, like a train emerging from a tunnel. Drunk and on high alert, Baylor flipped up the hood of his sweatshirt and crept across the street.

From just beyond the door of the shop, he could see two figures moving around. He swore Jade almost spied him as she grabbed her jacket from the coatrack, but he'd blended into the shadows. Then he heard Marley's voice. Baylor hid in the alleyway until they exited, hands full of jugs. He couldn't help but follow them.

After they stole past the red light, Baylor advanced from a safe distance behind. They hung a right into the church parking lot. Before Baylor could catch up, they were gone.

He sat in the shadow of the manse for a long while, waiting for them to appear. Old and greasy, the church roof next door taunted him. Marley's bit of flashing shone against the spare moonlight. And just like that, Baylor swore he had it all figured out. Marley's flashing must have begun to leak, and she'd rather repair it under cover of night before the coming storm than admit to the Joseph men that her plan had failed.

Marley felt she needed to hide, and it was Baylor alone who made her feel that way.

The roof, at least, was something he could fix. He imagined the church's upper room rotted with rainwater, the rank satisfaction he'd get from ripping it out. His illusions lived a short life when the church door creaked open, and not two women but three snuck out. Baylor saw his mother tiptoeing like a cat burglar, clutching an extra pair of her shoes.

Baylor's head fell into his hands. Here was Marley again, helping where he wouldn't. His mother was not herself, and some indignity had transpired that proved it. It made clear sense. If Baylor were to find himself in a similar dilemma, he'd call Marley, too. He decided not to tail Jade on her way home, like a creep. Beside him, the church beckoned.

He snuck inside just the way they'd done, and he took care to leave his boots by the door. Up the stairs, around the corner, in a building so dark he couldn't see the hand in front of his face. Baylor couldn't shake the image of a flooded attic, and that's where he headed. When he reached the counting room at the back of the sanctuary, he found the door wide open, the light on, and the attic stairs extended before him.

The one thing he did not expect to find was what awaited him—the town preacher, dead and naked on a heap of choir robes.

30.

"Well, shit," Baylor said.

Obviously Hollis must have lured her here and forced himself on her. Why else would Marley abscond in the middle of the night, Jade at her side? In his limited imagination, it was more plausible that Elise Joseph had committed murder than willful infidelity. Baylor had tried for a long time to save his father from himself, and what good had it done? He figured it might be time to try saving his mother instead.

Baylor knew the shit-for-brains Mercury had for law enforcement. They'd shuffled him home on many a cold night he'd spent on these streets.

"Only man I've ever seen who has a roof over his head and still acts like a vagrant," one of them had said, caring little whether he heard.

His mother would be entangled in this death for the rest of her life. The room stank of bleach. Marley and Jade had shown up here, fancying themselves Charlie's Angels, thinking it would be enough to erase Elise's presence with a few sponges. Baylor thought he knew better. If a body appeared, it wouldn't take the townspeople long to start hunting for the person who must be linked to it.

Gallantly, Baylor decided to move the body out of the attic. Realistically, the body was too heavy. He was still drunk. It had started to rain. He could hear the drops of water pricking the steeple roof. So Baylor did what he would do anytime something needed protection from the elements. He made that body watertight. He spooled it in industrial-grade shrink-wrap from Fancy, his truck parked in front of the great house. Then he stapled his package shut and left it among the robes. His last act was to lift and shut the attic door before grabbing his shoes and hurrying home just before daylight.

It appeared to the rest of his family living in the great house that Baylor had risen early the next morning, choosing to take a shower before work rather than after. He remained beneath the hot stream twice as long as he ought, with Mick banging on the door about the water supply. Baylor thought back to the body he'd hidden and wondered whether this was how you truly loved someone—to look upon their worst act and never let them know that you had seen it. He hadn't done the same for Mick when he'd gotten caught stealing because he'd never loved him the way that he loved his mother.

No matter how much water fell, Baylor could not wash the night away.

Of course, his mother worsened. Ann had started taking her to the grocery store because Elise couldn't always remember what she'd gone there to buy. Baylor worried she'd out herself about Pastor Hollis before he could stop her. After he sobered up, he questioned the wisdom of his actions. He watched his mother with a trained eye, imagining what she was capable of. Elise went about her daily activities, and it shook him to his core. It took such a lack of effort for her to ignore things that Baylor wondered what else she might be concealing, and when exactly he'd stopped being her favorite confidant.

Baylor hated feeling philosophical. What a worthless pursuit. Yet the quandary invaded his thoughts. His sleep. Two days later, he took his cares to his monthly appointment with Jade, who he knew already knew what had happened that night. He also knew she wouldn't tell him. Baylor Joseph had never been worthy of anyone's trust.

Jade usually radiated warmth with her throaty laugh and smooth rock on the radio, but that day Baylor sensed the tension in her. She washed his hair absently, getting rough in a way he didn't mind but knew she didn't intend. He sat in her chair and watched as she stared at her scissors. He couldn't stop himself.

"Tough week?" he asked.

On command, she brightened. "It's that obvious? I'm sorry."

"Don't be. I like that you can't hide things with your face."

Her nose crinkled, and he grew hot at the weird compliment he'd given.

"What I mean is," he tried again, "I hope you're all right."

She dropped her smile, stuck her hands in his hair, and looked at him in the mirror. The same heavy secret pulled them toward each other, though their motives had been different. Jade had done it out of love for Marley, and Baylor out of love for Elise. They were alone, together, in the knowledge of what hid inside the church steeple. The ghost that haunted them had nothing to do with the body left behind, but the loyalty they kept for the living. For a moment, the contradiction felt so pure, so bare, that Baylor swore Jade knew his part in all of it, even though he hadn't said a word.

"I hope you're all right, too," she said.

Baylor shocked himself with the strong impulse to grab her and confess that he wasn't all right, that he didn't think he'd ever been, and it had nothing to do with his mother's mysterious misdeeds.

"Can I ask you something?" he said instead.

She pulled her eyes away and began to trim. "Go ahead."

"Do you think it's possible to spend your life loving the wrong people?" He thought of his brothers, Mick, Elise, Marley—the marrow in the bones of home, and yet he didn't understand anyone who lived in that house. They'd all chosen their alliances with someone other than him.

Jade considered it. "I think it's more likely that we love the right people in the wrong way."

Her words ached inside Baylor's chest, the way the truth does. He said nothing the rest of the cut. His hair fell around him like heather. She brushed off the stray strands with her fingers. When he moved for his wallet, she stayed his hand.

"Don't," she said.

"Why?"

"You've paid me double for every haircut I've given you."

Baylor started to feel cold. "So?"

She watched him and did not falter. "I think you're trying to say something with your money that you ought to say with your mouth, and I'd like to know what it is."

He froze. Here this so-very-right woman stood, and he was terrified he'd love her the wrong way. That there would be no second chance.

"Baylor," she said.

"Shit," was all he could manage before he fell back against the door and fled into the street.

When Baylor took his mother to her slew of doctor's appointments that summer, the experts proclaimed she had early-onset dementia. No telling how bad it would get, or when, and there was little they could do.

"But where did it come from?" Baylor asked, and no one could give him a straight answer.

Hereditary or circumstantial, there was no fixing it. Baylor wondered what use doctors were when they handed over bad news he already knew. He didn't need more than a high school education to see his mother was not her meticulous self. All he had to show for it was a medical bill the sum of a mortgage payment.

He also didn't believe that all his mother had become was this illness. Her life amounted to more than how it would end. Mick, however, could not see past his wife's diagnosis. If it was valiant or self-serving, Baylor couldn't say. All he knew was that his father was afraid, and it caused him to start living as if Elise were already gone.

Mick started to mutter absurd things. He talked about moving to Arizona to get into the construction boom, along with his desire to start another business in ceramics. In piano tuning. In an inventor's guild. He was always talking, tossing around outrageous words, and his family had stopped listening long ago. Elise had taught her sons to let Mick talk and do as he pleased.

A month before his mother's death, Baylor found Mick in the basement tinkering with some tubing that came in through a small window from the outside. It connected to an air duct in the ceiling that circulated through the second floor. Mick had built this house with all its funny mazes, a tangle only a son could comprehend.

"Dad." Bay touched the ducting. "What the fuck is this." He asked in a manner that wasn't truly asking because he already knew.

Mick glanced up at him, then continued with his work. "The truck's running right outside. This pipe will connect the exhaust to the air vent in your mother's room. She'll pass while she sleeps."

It was so ridiculous, so maniacal, that Baylor laughed. It was a moment he'd come to regret for the rest of his life. He grabbed hold of the silver tube and yanked it down with one hand.

"I know you like to play God in this house," he said. "But you ain't Him."

He chose his words carefully, in a language Mick would understand. Mick dropped his wrench, and it stuttered against the cement.

Baylor pointed to the ducting. "You need to stop this."

"I don't want to watch her die."

And there it was—Mick's motivation for everything he did. He was trying to avoid pain, to cut off his own loss at the pass.

"Then move out," Baylor said.

In that moment, Bay hated his brothers. They were too cherubic, too wispy to speak to their father this way. It had to be Baylor, who did not care to be kind. Mick stalked out of the basement, and Baylor punctured the tube with his pocketknife.

There remained truths about his father that only Baylor knew, thanks to Elise. He knew Mick suffered a mental breakdown in the weeks before Waylon's birth, that Elise had called the hospital and had him carted away. He was nearly catatonic, she'd told Baylor when he was ten, as she warned him yet again not to become like his father.

When Baylor was just a year old, she said, Mick was claustrophobic and inconsolable. They didn't have words for what he suffered then, though as an adult Baylor could follow the pattern of life-defining triggers: the impending birth of a son, the looming death of a wife. Back then, the hospital pumped him with electricity and sent him home. Mick and Elise awaited the arrival of their second son like it would fix things, because Baylor had been their first disappointment.

He remembered his mother whispering about the mental hospital into the phone, years after they'd moved into the great house.

"It was the saddest thing," she said to her sister. "I went to pick him up, and there was a man standing on the curb in a suit and tie, watching for his family to arrive. Mick got into the car and said that man had been waiting for two days straight. His family just deserted him. If I did something like that to Mick, I couldn't live with myself."

It hounded Baylor to know that Mick could do the same and live with himself just fine. Elise had seen Mick through his darkest time, and Mick would do the same for her. Baylor would see to it.

31.

Baylor assumed it was a good sign when Mick offered to take Elise to her doctor's appointment on the morning before she died, just as Shay had. He rejoiced in his own way, with one swig of Jameson instead of two. That night, he woke to Shay's screams and ran to find his mother having taken all the medicine in the unmarked bottle the doctor had given her. Mick claimed they were sleeping pills while he stood a safe distance away from Elise's body.

Bay knew his father was devastated. Mick Joseph wasn't made of steel; he had bone and heart. What he lacked was self-scrutiny—the strength to ask himself how, in the face of crisis, he would choose to live. How would he forever be changed? That was the bottom of the bucket they were all swimming in: Mick had not changed at all—not on the brink of fatherhood, nor when he was caught stealing, nor when his wife got sick. He was the same man he'd been when he jostled the train car with his fantasies over twenty years ago, never once admitting any fault.

For the first time, Baylor wondered what the Josephs had been building.

Perhaps an ephemeral industrial roofing empire, but surely not any kind of lasting relationship between them. *What is this thing we're doing,* he wanted to scream at his father, *and did it ever mean to you what it has meant to me?*

Mick thought he was collecting an inheritance for his sons, but the truth of his legacy lay dead among them on the floor: a woman who had not survived, her husband convinced it was just as she'd wanted.

Baylor wondered as he held his mother what kind of understanding passes between a husband and a wife as they live side by side. At some point, a marriage must become a junkyard of things, unfinished sentences and earring backs scattered across the floor. Whether the overdose was a mistake or purposeful, Baylor couldn't be certain. All he knew was that pulling truth from his father would be harder than fishing through a ship-wreck. All broken pieces and artifacts, sunk too deep to be brought to the surface.

Bay didn't know what it was like to be a husband, and he doubted he ever would. He did know what it was like to be a son, and he realized that day he'd gotten it wrong. Love and devotion weren't found in disregarding someone's transgressions. The Josephs hadn't found trouble by withhold-ing mercy from each other, but by pretending no one in the family had any need of it. Baylor had known what his father was capable of, and he'd ignored him. He was tired of Mick's antics and wrote him off as a punish-ment that Elise took instead.

In his mind, Bay was as much to blame for Elise's early demise as Mick. He'd tried to honor his mother's one wish that he become nothing like his father. In the end, the good son had failed.

Bay was too aggrieved to remember most of what came next. He didn't remember attempting to revive his mother, nor the moment he realized he couldn't. He couldn't remember the way Waylon and Marley argued, not the coroner's report, nor the visit to the funeral home across the street. He had no idea how a clean suit and tie hung from his doorknob on the morn-ing of the burial, or where it had come from, or why Elise's three sisters stared at every one of the Josephs with contempt. Baylor had forgotten his blunders during the eulogy and the whiskey he drank after the cemetery as he walked home alone.

He did remember spotting Jade at the repast, his lighthouse in a sea of mourners, and how he tried to swim to her but was kept back by a tide. Like trying to speak underwater, he ran out of breath and went unheard. He hated living in the great house, and he blamed himself, and he wanted a haircut.

There was nowhere to run from the truths that turned him sad. He stumbled up the steps toward a soft beam at the end of the hall, away from the crowd, away from his mother's bedroom. There he found Marley, a beacon glowing against the half-moon. Like Jade, she was steering their ship through rough waters while the men around her jumped overboard, and Baylor was flooded with the desire to push the clock backward to a time he could have made himself worthy of her light.

If she'd cast it on him alone, instead of Waylon, then Baylor wouldn't be such a fuckup. He was tired of being told it was too late for miracles, and his head swam, and he thought perhaps he'd fallen asleep and found Marley waiting there in his dreams, where he'd no longer be alone.

He kissed her, pulled from his stupor only when his brother threw him to the ground. Baylor came alive in a mangy way, craving blood spill. Bay couldn't admit to feeling responsible for his mother's death, but he could paw at his brother's perfect flesh, he could throw a punch and take one.

He reared back and swung wildly, the crack of his elbow upon something willowy, like a curtain billowing in the wind. Marley flew back, and Baylor heard himself scream. He was still the jealous boy who had pushed his brother in the mud at the end of the slide, the one who whispered lies in his ear after a winning catch on the ballfield. It had only been a matter of time, and Elise's death had hastened it, before Baylor committed the sin for which he would not be forgiven.

Jade thrust the brothers from the room, and Bay began his descent into hell.

Later, when the house was empty and a large sheet cake was left on the table, Baylor couldn't sleep. Why had someone brought a sheet cake anyway, he wondered. This memorial was not a celebration of a life, but a recognition of their failure to care for it. He knew what he ought to do: check on Shay, whom he had not seen, and apologize to Marley. Instead he wandered past the courthouse and found himself banging on Jade's apartment window. Baylor called out her name, moaning like a baleful basset hound and pounding the glass with his fist. Just as he leaned his forehead against the door, it pulled open only as far as the safety chain would allow.

"So that's how it is now?" he said to the sliver of Jade's face that appeared—an eye, gleaming like a precious stone, the slope of her nose, and the curve of her mouth.

"You need to leave," Jade said, her voice stiff. Gone was the warmth they'd shared beneath the beauty salon's light. "Theo is here."

Bay swore drops of himself were puddling on her doorstep. "Theo isn't afraid of me, Jade. Let me in."

She shook her head, and he caught the message in her glare. It wasn't anger, or grief, or—dare he hope for it—compassion. Jade was a one-and-done. Bay had lost her trust, and there would be no finding it.

"*I* am afraid of you, Baylor," she said. "Now leave."

Jade shut the door and locked it, even though the chain had remained in place. He slumped against it, and for the first time in a long while, he cried.

Baylor awoke in his bed hours later, unsure of how he'd gotten there. He could smell the whiskey seeping out of his skin as he oozed down the stairs. The men in his family stood like chess pieces in the morning sun—a rook, a king, a pawn. Among them, there was no knight.

Marley had fled. The food had congealed, and flies had nested near the open windows. A garbage truck beeped from the street, and none of them left to get the trash to the curb. This was the first time the Joseph men had existed without a woman to shepherd them. Each of them found they could not move.

"Shay." Waylon's voice held a bitter edge. "Tell me where she went."

Shay was flushed and trembling as he held firm. "Marley needs time,

Waylon. Can't you see you let her down?" Shay cast Baylor an angry side-eye. His youngest brother had never looked at him like that before. "All of you let Marley down."

Waylon let out a sad, frustrated roar, and whipped his head to spear Baylor with his stare. Then he stomped out of the room. Mick went into the basement. Soon, they heard the scrape of a spinning potter's wheel. Shay sighed, retrieved a garbage bag, and started to clean. Baylor watched him dump the sheet cake into the bag and didn't summon the strength to ask whether he was all right.

It went on like this for days, then weeks. The great house felt like it had been overtaken by the undead. Vacuous, the four of them wandered aimlessly through the kitchen. The office door remained closed. Baylor hadn't given Waylon nearly enough credit for the sales he brought in. Now Way lazed around the house, and the engine of their business had stalled. Their records were a mess. Unperturbed, Mick went about his daily tasks: building porches, fixing kilns. Doing what he needed to survive while his sons flailed. Baylor knew Mick's life hadn't been easy, yet he'd had plenty of luck. His was the body pulled from the wreckage every single time.

Shay started school and the house felt even emptier than before. After Marley had been gone a month, the doorbell rang. Baylor, who had committed himself to the sofa, slumped to the foyer. On the porch he found Ann, wearing cape sleeves and holding a withered bouquet at her side.

Now that he was unpracticed with society, Baylor's mouth hung open. He felt sure she'd come to retrieve a casserole dish from the repast, maybe that soupy one with the water chestnuts in it, just as certain as he was that every one of those dishes had ended up in the trash.

"Uh," he said brutishly.

Ann's fingers tapped the wide plastic belt at her waist; Baylor felt around for his shirt and pants to make sure he was decent.

"You got a leak?" he finally asked.

She shook her head. "It's your father," she said, words that hit Baylor like wet concrete. That look Ann gave him? He recognized it now. It was the same muted sneer people shot at Elise when they wanted her to corral her husband.

"What's he done now?" Baylor asked.

Quite a lot, it turned out. He'd left daisies on Ann's doorstep and asked her to dinner twice.

"He's been making innuendos for years, but he won't take no for an answer now that your mother's gone," she said, and Baylor knew she expected him to put a stop to it.

Not taking no for an answer: great for business, dangerous with women. Ann's wasn't the only house call Baylor received that morning. Mick had done the same to three other ladies in their church directory. He'd also burst into a town council meeting at the Elk Lodge, offered to act as mayor of Mercury free of charge, and was voted in unanimously. People pitied a widower, yet they blamed his sons. A whole town was out to rescue him on the backs of his children.

This, Baylor could not abide on his own.

He found Waylon in his bedroom, facedown in his sheets, curtains tightly drawn. The pitiful sight made Baylor recall how many nights he'd pulled his own comforter over his head just down the hall after Waylon and Marley moved in. He didn't want to hear their quiet creaks and gasps as they tried to hide their lovemaking. How deeply Baylor had wanted it—not Marley herself, he saw now too late—but that feeling of desiring the person beside him so much that he was ready to burst with more ardor than one small room could contain.

The room stank. Baylor pushed the window open along with the curtains and said, "We need to talk."

"I don't want to talk to you."

"I don't give a shit. Dad is out there, asking every woman with a pulse to have dinner with him." He paused. "He wrote them *poems*, Way."

Mick had written sonnets for Elise more than once, and she'd barely read them before using the paper to line her cupboards.

The bed began to shake. At first, Baylor searched for the source of the quaking, until he saw that his brother was giggling like a hyena. Like his wife hadn't just run away with good reason. He flopped onto his back, his body rigid with laughter. Waylon couldn't stop.

"Super happy this amuses you," Baylor groused.

A necessary melting happened inside him as he watched his brother. When he settled, Waylon wiped his eyes and looked at Baylor.

"Ew," he said.

"Oh, and he's the mayor now," Baylor added. "So there's that."

"Well, shit." Waylon stood and put on his jeans. "Sounds like we've got to go on an apology tour."

He'd come to life so quickly, ever prepared to cover over Mick's behavior, that it made Baylor a little dizzy. This was not a natural kind of love but a conditioned response.

"Wait," Baylor said. "You don't have to fix this, Waylon."

"Mom would want us to." Way ran a hand across his stubble. "Wouldn't she?"

"That's not a good enough reason anymore. Maybe it never was."

Way looked like he had a heavy load he couldn't put down. "What do you mean?"

Baylor thought on it. "She taught us that saving Mick would save the family. And you know what? It didn't work."

Way sat down on the edge of the bed. "So why even bother to tell me?"

"I just thought—" Baylor stopped. He couldn't bring himself to say he simply needed his brother.

"You didn't want to be alone," Way finished. "I get it."

Baylor's eyes fell to the carpet.

"We should talk to Ann, at least," Way said. "Maybe mow some lawns."

"All right," Baylor agreed because he didn't know how to get Waylon to see that his identity as the family savior was mostly an illusion. "All right."

Way threw on a fresh shirt, and together they walked out the front door. The Joseph sons were only just beginning to see all the ways Elise had kept Mick at bay, but one thing would always be true. Anytime Baylor took even the smallest step to lessen the divide between him and his brother, Waylon ran to greet him.

Things were better, but they weren't fixed. Baylor had yet to apologize for kissing Waylon's wife. Marley hadn't returned. The furniture on the first floor of the house remained pushed toward the edges, as it had been for the repast. The business phone rang, and no one answered it. Baylor had given up on finding, and keeping, the love of his life. He couldn't blame it on his father, his mother, his brothers, or anyone but himself.

The day before he left to beg Marley to come home, he gave himself a buzz cut in the bathroom mirror. It didn't look like Jade's portrait of him—refined and cared for. It showcased what he was: rugged and raw.

Waylon sat on the porch steps, shirtless, as he often did now. Baylor sat beside him and put his elbows on his knees.

"Listen," he said. "I don't love your wife." When Way gave him a side-eye, he blurted, "Not like that. What I mean to say is, I shouldn't have kissed her. I got stuck in my own head and I didn't know Marley was at the end of it. I was drunk, and I'm sorry."

Way nodded. "I appreciate it." He waited, then turned abruptly toward Baylor. "Don't you think it's strange that Elise and Mick never learned how to make amends with anyone? I've been thinking back, and I can't remember it. They didn't apologize to each other or to us. Not even one time. I don't know why—I don't think it was pride. Maybe they thought it was pointless."

"Is it?" Baylor had not considered it. His brother had always been so good at apologies, Baylor didn't realize that Way had started to question their merit.

"She took my kid away. Marley." Way's mind jumped from one hurt to the next. "Is that something an apology can fix?"

If there was an answer to that, Baylor surely didn't know it. What he did know was that Waylon was still so stuck on saving Mick that he was about to lose himself. He needed his wife. They all did.

And Bay was the only one willing to go and get her.

Marley came home, but life didn't return to what it once was. How could it? They'd all drawn their lines in the sand after Elise died. Marley had asked for Baylor's backup, and he hadn't given it. Waylon judged her, and Shay disappeared. She had lost her spark, even as a smolder remained.

After that, the Josephs did what they knew how to do. They built their business. They let the work speak for them when they should have let themselves argue. Grieve. The men traveled farther, longer. They took their losses: jobs that never sold, projects halted halfway when the funding got pulled as Pittsburgh's economy took hit after hit.

Marley might have repaired only one roof in her time, but she knew everything else. And what she didn't know, she learned. When the internet began to boom, Marley ushered Joseph & Sons into the digital age. She leapt from dial-up to DSL, from phone lines to routers. She mastered the legal jargon of contracts and insurance audits. If there was proof that a person could remake themselves, it was found in Baylor's sister-in-law. Marley grew, she pushed, she wore a thousand faces, each of them a different side of her. Their family thrived from it. Baylor worried she would break, just the way Elise had. He'd now witnessed two marriages that had evolved into business transactions, though he couldn't say roofing was solely to blame. He knew nothing of these things, anyhow.

Jade never cut his hair again. She never came to the house, never sent him a Christmas card, never sat beside him at any of Theo's school recitals. He still walked past her salon at night and her little apartment above it.

One evening after Elise had been dead for a year, he caught Jade's silhouette in the window. She was lithe and strong and brave, his Jade. His body curdled with longing. He imagined running to her door, falling at her feet, being the kind of haven she needed and deserved. Then he looked up and saw that she was not alone. Another man touched her hair, kissed her mouth, pulled her down to the floor.

Jade fell in love with someone else. Marley fixed her up with a carpenter they'd worked with on a job at an antiques shop the previous spring. He was handsome, and probably never said the wrong things at the wrong time, and he'd built the most stunning wooden staircase Baylor had ever seen. One year later, Jade married him.

And so it was that Baylor Joseph was itching for a haircut the night Marley and Waylon got locked in a jail cell. He was inured by then to the sensation of constant want, of disappointing and getting disappointed. When the preacher's body turned up, Bay was ready for the truth to come out.

He thought he'd saved his mother's dignity that night in the attic, but he'd done it in all the wrong ways. Baylor wished he'd just asked her what had happened. He had no shape to compare with his choices, a shadow box for tracing the silhouettes of what might have been. He and Elise had a communion in her secret now, neither right nor wrong, but one of simple witness where Baylor acknowledged that Elise did not have what she wanted in life, and neither did he.

This was no way to love someone, Baylor knew. And yet he loved, still. The night after Preacher Hollis's body was found, Bay was lurking past the courthouse after midnight when a patrol car pulled up.

"I'm going, I'm going," he said, without casting a glance backward.

When the engine cut, he turned. Patrick leaned against the hood of the cruiser with his arms crossed. He looked fidgety and parched. Briefly, Bay wondered why adulthood seemed to be shriveling him.

"I'm looking for Shay," Patrick said by way of greeting. His eyes skidded from left to right. "Do you know where he is?"

"I ain't seen him."

Baylor kept up his walk, headed away from the entrance to Jade's shop. Patrick followed.

"Any idea why Marley's wedding ring showed up next to that dead body?" he asked.

The question stopped Baylor in one second flat. "Seems like a question for Marley," he said evenly, even as his heart furrowed beneath his ribs.

Everything he and Marley had done for Elise, not a word spoken of it, and all they had to show for it was the dead body of a man none of them had loved while he'd been alive. It was unjust, the way they'd chosen Elise's silence over the truth. And yet, Baylor couldn't regret it.

"I did ask Marley," Patrick said. "She refused to talk so I put her in the cell for a while. She's in there with Waylon, last I heard."

"Wait a minute." Baylor turned around. "You did what?"

"You know how she can get, Bay, even if Shay always acts like she walks on water."

Bay's mouth popped open. It was so obvious; he couldn't believe he hadn't seen it. Patrick was jealous of Marley, the woman who just yesterday had to pour bleach all over their fluffiest white towels after two different men had stained them purple.

In the distance, Mercury's only stoplight turned from yellow to red.

"Do you try to be an idiot," Baylor asked, "or does it happen naturally?"

Patrick pinked, and Bay could tell that envy was eating him alive. Patrick wanted the easy devotion Shay and Marley shared, or something akin to it. And that, Baylor understood.

"I was going to let them out soon," Patrick said.

Bay pointed to the cruiser. "You'll do it now."

Baylor rode with him around the corner to the police station. Every house was dark, but the summer season's fireflies had just started to shine.

The whites of Patrick's knuckles gripped the wheel as he drove.

"You're acting weird," Baylor said. "And it's not the body."

"I just need to talk to Shay, is all." Patrick pulled into the lot. "Before he talks to anyone else."

"Maybe he doesn't want to talk to you." Baylor had been on the receiving end of that sentiment more than once.

After Marley and Waylon were released, Patrick and Baylor stood in the alcove of the empty station. They didn't care for each other, these twin crabs who often found themselves alone and lonely.

"I'm still going to need their statements," Patrick said.

"Let me save you some time," Baylor answered. The fireflies around them blinked. "They ain't gonna say shit that's of any use to you." He paused. "If you want to fix things with Shay, just fucking fix them."

Patrick rubbed his forehead. "How?"

"Damned if I know, but I'll tell you what I do. Not every mysterious death is a murder, and not every secret is a sin."

Patrick's eyes were wide. "What did Shay tell you?"

"Nothing." Baylor had never been one for confessions. "But if I were looking for Shay, I'd start with a roof."

Bay had told the truth. Shay had revealed nothing to him, but it didn't matter. He wanted Shay to have every happiness he never did. Baylor wanted him to have it all.

32.

Earlier that night, Shay went to church. He wasn't hunting for abso-lution. Like Baylor, he had no sin to confess. What he searched for were answers.

He stepped into the empty sanctuary and found the pew his family had occupied when he was young. The tally marks he'd left in the wood with a nail were still there, softer now. Shay still found comfort in Presbyterian liturgy, the creeds, even the stained glass reprisal of Jesus on the cross—garnet and gold and glowing. What he feared was that God had never lived in this place, or that God had left long ago. What a bunch of lost sheep they all were. Did even one of them know how to love someone—really, truly love them without fault? Shay had been taught that God was too pure to look upon sin. And Shay wondered, then, what on earth there was left to look at—if not people hurting each other, misunderstanding each other, missing each other.

He pushed the red velvet nap on the pew back and forth, watching it darken and return. Darken, return. In that moment, he didn't care about dead bodies, lost shoes, or found wedding rings. They were each a secret someone carried, and Shay had been weighed down by them since the day he'd been born.

What he'd seen of his mother, his brothers, even Marley—Shay had longed to hold their darkness alongside them so they'd know they weren't alone. Yet it was Shay who became lonely. *Patrick understands*, he'd told himself since he was fourteen. Now he wasn't certain Patrick did.

Shay heard a throat clearing and glanced up. Lennox, the interim pastor who'd been stuck here for four years, stood in the sanctuary entryway with a flashlight, glasses, and a T-shirt that said, I'M A PRES-BEAR-TYRIAN.

"Sorry." Shay stood. "I was just leaving."

Lennox lit the candles next to the pulpit and turned off his light.

"Please," he said. "Stay as long as you like."

He turned to go with the slow, measured gait of a man who had been walking in and out of sanctuaries since the time of civil rights. The world had changed then. Perhaps it was changing still.

"Wait," Shay called out. "Will you sit with me?"

Lennox nodded and took a seat beside him. Pushed his spectacles up his nose.

"How did you end up here?" Shay asked after a bit of silence. What he truly wondered was why Lennox wasn't desperate to leave.

"I ended up staying in Mercury a lot longer than intended, I suppose. Interim pastors move around quite a bit. There was a need here, though, and there still is."

"What need?" Shay asked.

Lennox's chin dimpled. "People here think God has forgotten them, maybe because much of the world has. But I don't believe that."

"Do you feel at home here, then?"

Lennox sighed. "No."

A wave of sadness pushed Shay back against his pew. "You never found anywhere else you wanted to go?"

Lennox thought on it. "The churches didn't want me to stay, more like." He smiled, wistful. "You don't become an itinerant preacher by pleasing people."

Shay spotted a flicker of his own solitude in Lennox's eyes. "What do you mean?"

"I mean that most people treat church like it's a country club," Lennox said, "and they think I'm the concierge."

Light from the pulpit cast shadows on the wall. Shay ran his hand along the cloth edge of the hymnal tucked into the pew shelf before him.

"What's church for, then?" This was the question he'd had as a three-year-old, then as a ten-year-old, now nineteen. Shay couldn't decide whether he wanted to find his own faith or not.

"I think it's for this." Lennox motioned between them. "A way to work out the lives we're living, to reach for something deeper."

"What if you're afraid of what you'll find if you reach too deep?"

Lennox tilted his head. "You'd be right at home, I'd say."

Shay laughed and looked to the purple stain patterned on the ceiling. "We need to repaint in here," he said.

"I'd heard you did it the first time around."

Shay nodded. "Patrick and I, when we were young." As if they weren't still young, as if they hadn't carried an unspoken burden even back then.

"You did a fine job," the preacher said.

"Didn't know we were sealing a body up there."

"How could you?"

Shay turned to him. Word of the corpse's identity had already traveled through Mercury's streets after a mother and her daughter overheard Waylon at the hardware store. "Did you ever suspect?" Shay asked.

Lennox lifted his shoulders. "Every pastor has dreamed of dropping everything and leaving town, but I never knew anyone who did it. I've thought of Pastor Hollis many times over the last few years."

"You wondered where he went."

He nodded. "I told the police I was concerned. They called me Father Brown."

"Who's that?"

Lennox smiled. "TV priest detective."

"Well." Shay grinned back. "Who's laughing now?"

It wasn't the right response. What Shay wanted to say was that he'd been waiting to leave for years now and that he'd long envied Pastor Hollis for it. The truth was, parts of Shay had already left, and no one had come to look for them. Shay had been hiding, and he couldn't yet say whether he wanted to be found.

"Did Pastor Hollis have any family?" Shay asked softly.

"I wish I knew."

"Do you have family?"

"Oh, yes." Lennox removed his glasses and polished the lenses with his shirt. "Sisters, nieces, nephews, a whole crew."

Shay decided to just say it. "But you never married."

Lennox shook his head. "Not everyone has to—or wants to. Or can."

It was the first time Shay had heard words such as these uttered in this sanctuary. He felt Lennox leading him somewhere—dressing his wounds, washing his weary feet. Showing him that sometimes it was right to hold on to things, and sometimes it was right to let them go.

"There's something troubling you, I think," Lennox prompted.

Shay turned to him. He thought of Patrick, who swore his life would be torn up by its roots if anyone knew the truth about him. Shay had hidden it for him so long that he'd grown up inside of it and was outgrowing it, even now.

"I need you to understand," Shay said. "This is not a confession."

Lennox nodded. "I understand."

"I've been told since I was young that this one essential thing about me is a sin." Shay took a breath. "I don't like women. I never have—not like that. And this person that I've loved doesn't want to love me back because he thinks it's wrong."

The preacher peered at him from the corner of his eye. "That sounds like a hard and lonely way to live."

Shay grew restless. He did not want pity or compassion—he wanted to know how to find what he was looking for, or how to be found instead. He wanted to press a palm to all those religious boundary lines drawn in the sand and wipe them away. To toss all the hymnals to the floor, upend the holy water, spill the communion bread, and then clean up his mess, because that's what his mother had taught. Live how you must and leave no trace of yourself behind.

But hadn't Elise left bits of herself anyway? In the leaden weight of Waylon's promises, in Baylor's belief that he was just like his father, in Shay's practice of giving himself less than he deserved.

"Is it wrong," Shay asked, "if I just want to run away?"

Above them, a bat flapped its wings.

"Not all leaving is running away. Sometimes it's just leaving." Lennox touched Shay's shoulder, then removed his hand. "No one can answer that but you. I can tell you, though—loving someone is not a sin, no matter who it is."

"Tell me," Shay said. "Do you think God is a man or a woman?"

"I'd say God isn't an *or*," Lennox answered. "God is an *and*."

Shay thought about the tiny piece of paper tucked inside the wallet in his back pocket, the list of what it meant to be whole. At the top it read, *A whole person loves well*. And Shay knew he had done it—he'd loved everyone in the great house and they'd loved him back, each of them in their messy, mistaken ways. The only person he hadn't been able to love was himself. No one had shown him how.

"I fear," Lennox said, "that I've been preaching at you."

Shay might have cried if he hadn't already felt a little hollow. "I think I'd like to be alone here for a while, if that's all right."

Lennox stood. "You'll blow out the candles when you're through?"

"I will."

As soon as Lennox had gone, Shay went to the pulpit and snuffed the flames. After this night, he wouldn't set foot in this church again. Shay didn't seek to condemn it, only to find something holy within himself. The police tape that hung around the counting room drooped to the floor. Shay stepped over it into the small room. Above him hung the cord to the attic stairs. He pulled it, and they creaked, and he remembered the way Marley had taken his hand as they made the climb eight years ago—the union they found in it. He took in the cleanly swept platform: the plank where he'd seen his mother's heels, the nook where he'd pocketed Marley's wedding ring.

He climbed the thirteen notches in the wall that led to the top of the steeple, where the bell was set to signal the start of a new day in fifteen minutes. He perched himself on the ledge of the box like an eagle in his nest. He could see Mercury's city limits from this elevation, and beyond them, too.

Down below, Patrick's police car screeched to a halt. Shay was about five stories up, but he could see Baylor emerge from the shadows of the courthouse. Patrick and Bay spoke about things Shay couldn't hear. Baylor walked away; Patrick followed. Shay recognized the keen pace to his step. It meant Patrick was looking for him. Baylor climbed into the cruiser, and they disappeared.

In time, the clock struck twelve. One hour passed, then two. Shay took a step out onto the slippery roof. Covered with moss and damp leaves, it was steep and slick and needed to be replaced. He walked gingerly toward the south side of the town square, to the empty parking spaces by the antiques store. Patrick sat there on the hood of his cruiser, his head in his hands.

Shay stepped, and his foot snapped a twig that had gotten stuck in the peeling shingles. A soft crack filled the air, and Patrick looked up. When he spotted Shay, he stood.

"Come down," Patrick called, as loud as he dared.

"No."

"We need to talk."

"So talk."

Shay had said it because he knew Patrick wouldn't do it—not here, not when people would rush to their open windows at the sound of his voice. Patrick strode toward the church. In minutes, his head appeared in the steeple, just below the brass bell.

"You'd better move," Shay said. "Because that sucker is due to ring."

"You think I won't come out there." Patrick gripped the ledge. "That only a Joseph can walk on a roof."

"It's slippery, but do what you want," Shay said, even though neither of them had ever done what they'd truly wanted.

Patrick slid himself over the edge, then balanced ten paces away from his best friend.

"I need you to promise me you won't tell anyone else about us," he said. His face was dark, and so was the sky. "You never told me that Marley knew."

"Of course Marley knows, Patrick. I didn't need to tell her. She *knows* me."

"I thought we agreed this was only between the two of us."

"Is that all I am to you?" For the first time, Shay spoke as loud as he wanted. "A secret?"

Patrick took a step toward him and steadied himself. "Just promise me."

"Three times we've talked about this, Patrick. After that fight in the locker room, after my mother's funeral, and right now. We're still in the same place we were at fifteen, and I don't want to stay here anymore."

"What are you trying to tell me?" Patrick asked.

"I'm leaving."

Patrick laughed. "Where would you go?"

Again, Shay looked toward Mercury's city limits. "Anywhere."

"But you can't leave."

"You can come." Shay motioned between them, laid a hand flat on his chest.

"You know I can't."

"Why?" Shay asked. "Give me a reason."

The heel of Patrick's boot swiveled on a patch of moss, and his arms flew out from his sides until he found his balance. "Is this because of Marley's ring? Take it. I don't give a shit."

Suddenly, Shay saw why he and Patrick couldn't agree. Patrick was still trying to clean up a mess. He wanted to return the jewelry, solve the case, empty out the attic. All the people Shay loved had fought over ephemeral objects at one time or another—wedding rings, maroon heels, grand pianos, drumsticks. They were so easy to take hold of, to restore to their rightful homes.

"This is because not every mess needs to be cleaned," Shay said, pausing on it. "*I* am not a mess to be cleaned."

"Just you wait," Patrick said as he turned toward the steeple. "You'll see it's no better anywhere else."

He took a step, and the bell tower began to chime. It shook the roof, this reckoning all of Mercury could hear. That clock marked the passing of time, of growing old, of forgetting things no one wanted to know.

The bell chimed a second time, and Patrick lost his footing.

"Shay," he called, but Shay was too far to steady him, the slope too harsh for him to make the leap.

"Easy now," Shay whispered, remembering the times they'd held each other in the dark, and it had been good. It had given him a dream for all his life could become. "Ease your foot back, one at a time, and wait for me."

But the soles on Patrick's shoes were worn, and they would not hold. By the third bell, he began to slip.

33.

Down below, Baylor haunted the streets. He didn't wish to return home, where Waylon and Marley had each other. He didn't want to skate past Jade's window because he knew it was time to let her go. The thought made him want to dig himself a ditch and lie facedown in it.

Then, he looked up.

Baylor was right when he told Patrick where to find Shay—on a shaggy, mossy, Rumpelstiltskin of a roof. He saw the two of them in locked stances on the church's steep slope, like scrawny plastic infantrymen who could not free themselves. He'd never seen Shay that rigid before. He was the family acrobat, able to squeeze in and out of danger by making himself small. But now Shay looked petrified, and Baylor knew it was Patrick's fault.

"That numb-nut," Baylor said. Patrick was about to lose his balance.

Baylor was no sprinter, but he ran across the courthouse lawn toward the church, threw open the doors, then flew up into the attic and into the steeple. He saw how stuck Shay and Patrick had become.

"What the fuck," he cried because it was what Baylor, the brave and rough, would say. Baylor, who claimed to care about no one but himself.

He didn't want these boys to know how much he feared for them. How easily their lives could break apart.

"I'm gonna get him," Shay said. "Just give me a minute."

Baylor looked from Shay to Patrick, who outweighed his brother by thirty pounds. Patrick had slipped halfway down the roof, where he'd landed flat on his ass. His hands groped for purchase as they clawed the slick shingles.

"Like hell," Bay said. "I'll get him."

Shay, his fellow bookend boy, had always done as he'd been told. Had never made a fuss. Had remained in the slender box Elise had placed him in as the third of her sons. Baylor had stopped looking for his own moment in life, and therefore didn't realize he was in it. He didn't weigh the risk; he didn't consider saving himself. This, Mick Joseph had not taught him. This was Baylor's alone.

He pulled himself out of the bell tower, crouching down on one foot, and then the other. The night felt cool from up there, and the stars shone like topaz. Baylor had never done this until now—spent a night on a moonlit roof instead of the streets. It might have been beautiful if he were not so afraid of losing what he loved.

He took the length of belt from his waist and looped it around his hand. "Patrick, when you can, reach back and grab the end of the belt."

With one hand holding a steeple beam and the other extended toward Patrick, Baylor leaned. The bell tower creaked. Patrick didn't move.

"Come on, motherfucker," Baylor grunted. "I ain't got all night."

Patrick turned and reached backward. A crow scuttled through the trees, and Patrick jolted. His boot slipped a second time, and his head thudded against the roof. He tried to squirm upward, but his foot fumbled again, and he skidded down until the toe of his boot caught the gutter.

"Shay!" he screamed in a howl that made Baylor shiver.

Shay scrambled toward his friend, and Baylor saw his dread about to unfold. Shay was going to tip over this edge, trying to rescue his friend.

Shay reached him and balanced one leg on the gutter while he worked to free Patrick's shoe. He loosened his laces, pried out his foot, and left the shoe stuck in the drain. Patrick used Shay's hands to steady himself, and

34.

As the church's bell tower struck three in the morning, Marley and Waylon lay in bed together. They were naked in every way, whispering everything and nothing all at once. There was soft lamplight, an open window, and Waylon tracing the arc of Marley's back with his hand.

"Do you remember that ball game where I first saw you nine years ago?" he asked. "I remember feeling so certain then that I could save my family."

"I had Elise all wrong that day," Marley said. "I watched her, and she seemed like the most confident and content woman in the world. I wanted her secret." She closed her eyes. "As soon as I got her secrets, I wanted to give them back."

Waylon toyed with a lock of her hair.

"Do you regret telling me?" he asked.

"I don't." She sighed. "Being a member of the family shouldn't require silence. I think there's a time for holding on to secrets, and it's over now."

Way figured the same could be said for rescuing his father. The time had passed to repair what Mick had done. Maybe it was time to let things break.

Shay swayed backward. Baylor shot down the slope, slamming the hard metal gutter with his boots. He thrust forward and lent his weight to hoist Shay away from the ledge.

The momentum shoved him onward, and after saving his brother, Baylor Joseph lost his balance and hurtled five stories down, right off the edge of the roof.

"Do you want to tell your brothers about your mother and Pastor Hollis?" Marley asked.

"I don't know." A breeze blew in from the open window. "Maybe."

He moved his hand from her shoulder and shifted to look at her face. "Marley," he said. "Do you want to have another baby?"

He asked because he wanted one so very much. Way knew he was tempting fate, getting his wife back and asking for a second child all in one night. Still, though, he wanted it.

"I don't know," Marley answered. "Maybe."

There seemed to be a shift in the wind. Their nights in the great house were numbered. Way was ready to surrender the hold it had on him. For the first time, he and Marley were about to make a home that was fully their own.

"What are you going to do about your father?" Marley asked.

Waylon sighed. "Nothing."

"Nothing?"

"I'm going to stop apologizing for him, fixing things for him, rescuing him. I'm done," Way said. "He can keep running the roofing business he dreamed of, even if he runs it into the ground."

Marley sat up, a sheet around her shoulders. "Waylon, this hasn't been your father's business in a very long time. It's yours and Baylor's." She took a breath. "And mine."

For eight years, Waylon had watched his wife dig her own roots—in the strength with which she carried herself, in the dedication she brought to her desk, in the love with which she'd raised their son. She was a self-taught expert who helped build a company that had never given her a title. It was past time for Marley to own what was rightfully hers.

Joseph & Sons was not the right name for what they'd become.

He opened his mouth to say as much, but they heard a wail from an ambulance and a scream from the road, nearing ever closer, calling out for them to come.

"It's Shay," Marley said, and they bolted from bed, threw on their clothes, and ran out to meet him.

✦ ✦ ✦

Patrick drove them in the cruiser to the hospital thirty minutes away, where Baylor had been taken. Shay hadn't been permitted in the ambulance. All he remembered was the spread of his brother's body against the lush earth. He couldn't even hear himself scream, not as he peered over the ledge through the cherry trees, not as he and Patrick climbed up the roof and down through the attic, not as Patrick held his face in his hands and said he'd call for help.

Shay ran wild through the streets, past the post office and past the florist, not caring whom he woke as he went. Baylor was not heroic or rash or sacrificial—not in the way of stories and fairy tales. Yet everyone, even Baylor, had a person they cared enough about to be stupid for. Patrick had been Shay's, and Shay had been Baylor's.

Marley held his hand as they took the long drive to the hospital. He could have sat in the front, but he couldn't bear to be separated from his family by even a foot. Shay had run from this closeness ever since his mother died, and now he wanted to crawl inside it like a caterpillar cocooning itself into a moth. Waylon was warm and solid beside him. Shay couldn't keep from shaking.

"What the hell happened?" Way was asking him. His hands were balled into fists. "Why were you up there? You know not to go up without a harness." He spoke into the tight air in the car, as if the notion of safety were something any of them had ever heeded.

"It was my fault," Patrick said, speeding down an empty highway with his lights flashing. "All of it."

When they reached the emergency room, it was four thirty in the morning. The hallway was dim, and the nursing staff was sparse. Bay had been rushed into surgery. There wasn't an inch on him that hadn't been marred by the fall—not his head, his shoulders, his back, or his legs. No one came to reassure them.

Daylight arrived, and Patrick disappeared. Four hours passed, and Jade came with Theo. They didn't speak or eat. They watched the door to the OR and waited for someone to come out.

When Patrick returned, it was ten o'clock in the morning, and he had Shay's father in his cruiser. Mick hated hospitals, and he refused to come inside. Shay hadn't even thought to bring his father along. Why hadn't he come out of the great house when Shay came running? Surely all of Hollow Street had heard his cries.

"It took me some time," Patrick whispered. "But I found him at the graveyard."

As Baylor fell from the church roof, Mick had been sitting up with his wife, dead four years now. Why did it feel longer to Shay, like the remaining Josephs had lived a hundred lives since Elise's death, scarring each other in every single one of them? Mick was still spry in his fifties, could still haul a load of two-by-fours on his shoulder. He fixed doorbells and porches and pipes and roofs, but he hadn't been able to suture the seams he'd ripped through his wife. His children had all tried to mend this shortcoming in their own ways, and none of them could.

Around one in the afternoon, Jade took Theo home with her, and Patrick sat with Mick on the hood of his police car. The day passed, and Shay, Marley, and Waylon waited it out together. Pastor Lennox came with sandwiches, though later Shay wouldn't remember it. He stood and stretched, stumbled over toward the window. His eyes blurred with exhaustion.

The parking lot was stuffed with cars, even though the waiting room was empty. He recognized the bartender's truck, Ann's sedan, the minivans of the players on Marley's Little League team. They stood in a clump together, Lennox among them, waiting outside the hospital, just as the Joseph children were waiting in it.

It occurred to Shay that this was just what would have happened after Elise's death if he and his brothers hadn't each gone running for their separate corners. Hadn't licked their sorry wounds in private. Hadn't been ashamed to step into the depth of their devastation—not only for the way Elise had died, but for the way she'd lived. The Josephs weren't the only family that threatened to crumble because of its hurts. They had people here, blood and not, that ran generations deep.

Marley came to stand beside him at the window. Shay leaned his head on her shoulder.

"For a long time, I thought my mother was angry with me when she died," Shay said, touching the smooth beach glass in his pocket. "But now I think I was the one angry with her."

Marley looped her arm through his. "What's got you thinking about that now?"

Shay let go of the glass and ran his hand down his jaw. "You should have seen Bay on that roof. He just threw himself off it to keep me from falling. I could see it in his face—he wasn't thinking about himself at all, like it was the most natural thing in the world. Like he knew he was always meant to do it." He took a breath. "I've replayed it over and over in my head, and I don't think my mother ever looked at me that way. I think she was always calculating the cost of what it took to love me."

"Shay Baby." Marley took hold of his elbow. "It costs nothing to love you."

"I'm serious, Mar." Shay felt an old, protective skin sloughing from his body, scattering itself on the floor. "I should have left with you for Maryland after Mom's funeral. Then you never would have had to come back."

It was more than that, though. He wanted Marley to know she'd been worthy of his yes then, and she was worthy of it now.

"Don't believe that even for a minute." Marley's voice was quiet and firm. "I was always coming back."

He watched cars pull in and out of the lot. "None of this would have happened if I'd just left. I've been wanting to leave this place every day since then, but I can't figure out how to love someone and still leave them behind."

"Shay," Marley said. "It's okay to choose yourself. Even if Patrick can't understand."

"I'm not talking about Patrick. I'm talking about you, Marley." He turned toward her. "When I think of home, I think of you."

"You can have more than one home, Shay." She took his hand and held it in her own. "We'll always be the people you're from."

Shay didn't know how much he needed to hear Marley say it. He didn't know whether Baylor would make it through, and he didn't know what would become of his family if they lost two sons in one night. All he knew now—after yelling on the roof with his best friend, after watching his brother fight for Shay's chance to live, after baring his heart to the woman who had become his mother and so much more—was that this time, he was finally ready to leave home so he could find it.

Love, Elise

35.

Elise Joseph had not heard, nor would she ever know, that on the cool June night her oldest son fell from the roof, her husband was seated at her graveside. There were many things she hadn't understood at the hour of her death, or before it.

Firstly, she hadn't known what it would mean to be a wife. What it would ask of her, what it would take away. She'd been taught that marriage was the commitment a life built itself upon, more worthy than a vow to a friend or a sister. When she and Mick met in 1969, he'd already received his draft notice. It was yellowed and curled, Mick's name crookedly type-set next to the circular stamp of the Selective Service System. They were spreading like a pestilence throughout the countryside, these cards no one wanted to get in the mail. Some young men feigned illness or drank water till they were about to burst so they'd be deemed too overweight to serve in Vietnam. Others, with money, went back to school. Mick, just twenty-two, did none of those things. Not because he thought of himself as better, or because he was thirsty for blood. He didn't run from it for the inescapable truth that if he fled, someone else would have to take his place. Mick

Joseph hadn't always sought to rescue himself at the cost of everyone else. War would teach him that soon enough.

Mick said nothing about it on the night they met. Elise's church was hosting a barn dance in the style of the Grand Ole Opry as a means for new soldiers to let loose before they flew out to places they'd never been. Dolly Parton trilled about her Blue Ridge Mountain Boy, pretty and forlorn. The night was meant to be full of star-spangled balladry, no hint of the grittier tones from bands like Creedence Clearwater Revival or the Rolling Stones. Soldiers appeared like raindrops on the pavement because of the recruiting center just outside Chicago. Their mossy uniforms were starched and pressed, their badges neatly stitched. Elise's father, farmer of corn and wheat and rye, often bemoaned that he'd had four daughters instead of sons. Once the draft began, and after it didn't stop, and the cherry-faced young men who worked his fields and ate at his table didn't return home, Mr. Jenkins never uttered those words again.

He wasn't the kind to let his daughters consort with strange men on a Saturday night, but as he was a World War II veteran himself, his heart was rent for every last one of those boys. Theirs was the only sacrifice he could see, and therefore he didn't understand the one he demanded from his daughters. His wife dressed their girls in gingham and curls—looking younger than they were, more doll than flesh or beating heart—and they sent them off. That night, Elise would be the only one to find a husband.

Mick had blown into town a few days before like a cowboy on a Chevy steed with his white smile and boxy shoulders. He tilted his helmet as if it were a top hat and banged on the out-of-tune piano in the mess hall, inspiring his fellow surly draftees to sing sea shanties and big-band tunes. Mick told jokes, he tap-danced, he fixed one officer's faucet. He was the throbbing pulse in a holding depot that felt like certain death, and everyone flocked to it—soldiers and sweethearts alike.

There was already a cloud of adoration subsuming him by the time Elise walked into the high school gymnasium. It smelled like old sweat and leathery basketballs. Elise swatted a fly. Church-lady pies lined the back wall; streamers fell from the ceiling like dead limbs. Signs shouted appropriate messages, given the mood—no HELL NO WE WON'T GO, as the protests shouted—but NO GLORY LIKE OLD GLORY instead.

Elise had never been one for dancing, nor was she easily impressed. The things she loved were Sunday-morning hymns on an upright piano and the first signs of a pastel sunrise on the hills of her farm. She ran her hands along the buttons of the blue and white dress she and her mother had sewn from an old tablecloth, and she wished she'd thought to wear something trendier like the other girls in wide headbands and short-sleeved sweaters, Capri pants, and flats. She had no money for clothes like that, anyway. All she had was what she could make with her hands—butter and breakfast, dresses and dinner.

She watched this ham of a man, dressed in camouflage, trounce upon the makeshift stage and act as if he knew the difference between a shuffle and a maxi-four. He did not. *What an idiot*, she thought. His boots squeaked against vinyl, and she sipped her small cup of weak punch. Her sisters mingled, but Elise didn't care for small talk. It was so very useless. She wondered how long she'd have to stay before she'd be permitted to leave and return to the book she'd left on her nightstand. She kept her dime romance novels folded inside cookbooks, where they couldn't reach the outside world. The books were a fantasy in her mind, as she'd never met any man in life as striking as what she found on the page.

Elise turned her back to the crowd and placed her cup on an empty tray. As Loretta Lynn began to sing "Woman of the World," she felt a benevolent pat on her shoulder. Elise turned and beheld the tap dancer, who had a string of admirers behind him.

"Excuse me," he said. "But you look like you're wearing a tablecloth."

She didn't smile; she didn't coo. "I am," she said, and he began to laugh.

The sound swelled over the music and flew out the open door. She, Elise Jenkins, practical and bookish and boring, had made the evening's comedian laugh. She felt it pierce her very center, and a delicious heat pounded out of her in waves. He admired her in a way that, for the first time in her life, made her admire herself. It was the kind of moment a love story was born from. Elise had not been taught how to love well—only that loving her sisters was reserved for girlhood and loving a man would make her a woman.

"Dance with me," he said, and she gave him her hand.

He twirled her across the floor as if she weighed nothing and he hadn't been chosen by his country to sacrifice himself. It seemed Mick Joseph didn't need to follow anyone else's rules, and Elise thought he might be able to offer her the same freedom. *No war could bring this man down*, she thought as she spun. *No earthly or man-made thing could fell him.*

She was wrong.

Mick and Elise had an afternoon church wedding the day before he was due to depart. Elise wore an A-line flared dress she'd sewn quickly from a Simplicity Pattern and a short veil that itched the back of her neck. She'd planned to spend her wedding night with Mick at a hotel in the city and then return home to the farm to await his return.

The wedding was quick, the reception quicker. Elise assumed it was because Mick wanted her in his bed. She'd read about such things in her romance novels—a man so overcome by his own desire for her that he couldn't be polite—and she wanted it, too.

They weren't the only newlywed couple on their gilded hotel floor, love having gained a dire urgency that accompanied wartime, but they were the quietest. Elise emerged from the bathroom in the lacy white chemise her sisters had given her, the slit rising high on her thigh, to find Mick pacing a rut into the floor. His army boots were untied, his shirttails untucked. He peeked at her, then looked away and resumed his pacing.

"I can't," he said to a heart-shaped stain on the wall. "I can't do it, don't you see? If you get pregnant, and I die over there, you'll have nothing to help you."

She gaped at his haunted eyes, the deep grooves in his forehead. The savagery of what this young man was being forced to do. Without another word, he swung his duffel bag over his shoulder and left her alone in the room. He didn't return that night, leaving Elise too embarrassed to go back to the farm until morning. She didn't see Mick again until the day he returned home from war.

♦ ♦ ♦

Mick wrote her letters for the year he was away, and she wrote back—signing each one with *Love, Elise*, as if the act could turn the words true. She started to wear the high heels, belted skirts, and pantyhose of a married woman, even though she still felt like a girl. Should she feel betrayed by the story lines in her novels, she wondered, or had she simply gotten the wrong man? Elise didn't know. She took a job as a stenographer and perfected her shorthand, as she saved money to attend college for a teaching degree. Early mornings, she fed the pigs. Watched the sunrise. Weekends, she studied in the library. Sundays, she wrote letters. And this was how she came to know her husband.

His print was bold and sprawling, taking up twice the space on the page as Elise's practiced script. She imagined him writing under cover of night in the deep of a trench, a helmet strapped to his head and a meager flashlight to guide his hand. The illusion was fraught with a sick kind of romance. He talked to her about anything but combat. He told her of roofs, of the swimming pool his father had dug into the ground when he was a boy, and how he had once lifted an entire slab house onto a set of railway cars and moved it down the street—everything his hands could do when they weren't holding a weapon.

Mick Joseph had lived an entire life before Vietnam and another unspeakable life while he was there. Elise also wrote of things she understood—corn growing high in her father's summer fields, planting wheat in fall. Her favorite Black Krim tomato seeds. She didn't write that she'd packed her white chemise in tissue paper and a Dillard's box for safekeeping, or that every once in a while she put it on in the privacy of her room and wondered what Mick had so disliked when he saw her that it caused such restraint.

It was noble, and right, and fair what he did. And yet, Elise felt cheated.

His letters grew sparse as he neared the end of his deployment. She received a typewritten letter from the war office in Washington, DC, that there had been an explosion of some kind and Mick had been the only one who survived. How strange and stricken she felt to suddenly hold this leafy sheet of paper in her hands as his next of kin. His last name now hers. After that, she heard nothing at all, only the date on which he was scheduled to return. She found comfort in other things—her work, her church, her sisters. When he appeared as a thundercloud from the sky, blessedly spared, alive, and declaring that they were moving to western Pennsylvania, she said what any woman who had been on her own for a year would.

She said no.

"This isn't even a real marriage," she said to him and his empty eyes as he stood before her in just the same manner as their wedding night.

He'd been scared then. Now he was gutted.

"You're free to do what you want," she said. "As am I."

Thing was, though, she wasn't. Her father still held that soft spot for a fellow soldier and understood things Elise could not.

"You'll go with him," her father said, plain as that. "He's earned your loyalty."

And maybe that was true, though Elise so desperately wanted her own loyalty to earn. Her father had taken away her chance to make her own choice. To remain with her sisters, who, in time, would find husbands of their own. What else could she do? She packed up her white chemise, her blue and white dress, her apron, her tomato seeds, and she hoped for the best.

Mick wasn't himself. Elise could tell, even though he'd been a stranger when they married. His hands shook when he wrote, and he didn't want to play the piano sitting in the sanctuary of the Presbyterian church they'd started to attend. They'd moved into an old train caboose, and Mick spent the day chopping wood, and painting houses and porches for pocket money. He could have found an office job, or worked as a janitor, or gotten a shift at a steel mill, but he didn't. Mick needed to be outside. He had family nearby, but after they offered two hundred dollars for the rent on the train, they stayed away.

For the first time, Elise's heart broke for her husband. He had a government who hadn't come to his aid, and a family who thought money could take the place of love. She remembered that smile on his face when he'd tapped her on the shoulder, how he'd spun her around a gymnasium as if gravity did not exist. To her surprise, Elise found she knew what he needed. She was his family now.

That was the moment she became Mick's wife.

One evening, after a month had passed and the day's crossword was done, Elise slipped on her chemise and went to where he sat in a wing-back chair. Mick had a ring of dirt beneath his fingernails, a crowd of tiny screws in each pocket. She leaned over him, ran her fingers through his hair, and touched him with a tenderness she didn't feel. They hadn't spoken much since he came back—or much at all—but his body began to say what his mouth couldn't.

She heard him sigh as he gathered the hem of her gown in his fists and pulled it over her head. Then he took her into his arms and rested his head between her collarbones.

"Do you remember," he whispered, "the tablecloth you wore to that stupid dance?"

She nodded, her hands still in his hair. He looked up at her.

"I swear to you, I have never seen anything or anyone as beautiful as you were in that dress." He ran a thumb against her lip. "I thought of it every night."

Elise leaned in to kiss him, and Mick began to tremble.

"I don't want to hurt you," he said.

You already have, she thought.

"You won't," she said.

He took her to bed, and they found a kind of happiness together. It was all they had in those days, and it was real. Elise required so little of him. Mick's ability to focus came and went as well as his desire to hold down a job. He'd had enough of taking orders against his will.

Elise got pregnant and brought home a son. Named him in a way to make her husband proud—and he was. But his joy took residence in smaller and smaller parts of him, leaving the rest to drift like deadwood. She saw it—his vacant eyes while Baylor wailed, the long stretches of time that passed where he said nothing to her at all. *You cannot count on me*, his face seemed to say. Elise worried when she got pregnant again that Mick wouldn't be able to lift himself out of the valleys he fell in, for longer and longer stints at a time.

There were doctors, a mandatory hospital stay. Elise was left alone with Baylor on her hip. Whether being by herself was easier or harder, she couldn't say. When she went to fetch Mick from the hospital, after the drugs, after the electric shock, it reminded her of how battered he'd been on the day he came home in his uniform and somehow had to transform from a soldier back into a human. Like he'd been forced to bet on himself and lost.

Mick climbed into the car and didn't bother to insist on driving, even though with her belly Elise barely fit behind the wheel.

"I want a house," he declared as they pulled onto the main road and the mental hospital stayed in the rearview mirror.

"All right," Elise said.

"And I want my own business, in my own name, with a legacy to out-last me. I'll build it for my sons, so they won't be forced to enlist because they have no other choice. They'll never have to answer to anyone other than me."

It took such great force to make this shift, to fill this immortal cavity, that it would be the heft of all Mick Joseph's life would become.

Elise nodded, unsure whether this was a flight of fancy, of which he had many. Yet within the month, Mick found and purchased the great house, though it was a skeleton then. When he brought Elise to see it, all their belongings tucked in the trunk of their Ford, she paled at the sight of horse shit on the floor, the craters in the roof, the stench of rank rainwater festering under a film of dust.

Mick jaunted around the wreckage, undeterred, prophesying what the house could be.

"Here will be the music room for my piano," he said. "And here will be your kitchen, decorated in blue and white—just like your beautiful dress. Here will be our family dining room with the biggest table you've ever seen."

He held a glimmer of the boy he'd once been, tap-dancing on a vinyl floor and laughing at her sour jokes. Here was a man she could love and work alongside. She only had to find a way to make this version of him stay. If she was to survive, and her boys with her, she needed Mick to thrive.

Elise rolled up her sleeves and found the cleaning supplies she'd packed behind the driver's seat. In a pair of Mick's old work pants, she got down on her hands and knees and began to scrub the kitchen floor with a brush. Baylor squealed in the playpen beside her.

This is going to be good, Elise thought to herself. *This will be good.*

And it was good—everything she had built, even after she was angry and tired and spent. Even though she'd never been given what she needed to be a good wife, or mother, or friend.

And though she didn't live to witness it, what Elise saw for herself that day came true through the work of her children, tenfold.

The day moon was out on a sunny June morning when Baylor Joseph finally opened his eyes. He'd been in the hospital for two nights, and the doctors had little else to say of his head injury but "wait and see." He was lucky, they said. Bay had known to fall feetfirst because Mick had taught him. In time, his broken ribs and fractured bones would mend.

The rest of the Josephs—except for Mick, who was painting over the purple splotches on the ceiling of the church sanctuary—had been seated just down the hall from Baylor's room. When they heard a great growl rumble through the antiseptic air, there was no denying who it was.

"Hey," the voice called out. "Who's the fucking family hero now?"

Waylon shot out of his chair and ran to his older brother, as he always had and he always would.

The brothers stared at each other for a minute while Waylon openly wept.

Baylor curled his lip and said, "Who died?"

"You almost did, asshole." Waylon sat on the edge of the bed and touched Bay's leg. "You should have worn a harness."

"That phrase is gonna go on your tombstone," Bay said.

Way gently pressed his forehead against his brother's. He didn't need a business with his name on it, or a father to rescue, or a list of all the promises he'd kept. All he needed to be a Joseph was here before him, breathing in and out.

"Just wear the fucking harness," he said.

"All right," Baylor relented. "All right."

They talked as if Baylor would roof again, even as they both knew he might not. But Baylor—selfish and full-hearted and rough and ready to change—deserved to believe that he hadn't already missed his best moments. Waylon would do whatever he could to help Baylor hold on to that hope, the same way Baylor had made sure he held on to his wife.

Shay and Marley came into the room, and they were so overcome with relief that they forgot to call Mick and tell him his son had survived. The other absence among them was Elise, who would have wanted to stand guard in that hospital alongside her children, even as she'd been the one to drive them apart. All of them—Baylor, Waylon, Shay, and Marley—had risked a piece of themselves to protect her, and they'd failed.

And yet when Elise had nothing left to give, still she'd given them one another.

Two years later, the Josephs gathered again at the same hospital when Marley gave birth to a baby girl. Evangeline Ruth was born during a hurricane, and the sound of her voice sprinted through the empty hall as the overhead light flickered in the storm. When Waylon emerged with a tiny infant swaddled in pink, his brothers lurked at the mouth of the hallway, squinting to get a good look.

"She's just a newborn," Marley called from the delivery room. "Not an alien."

Shay crept forward to hold her first, followed by Baylor, and then the baby returned to her mother. And that was how Evangeline grew—passing from one pair of Joseph hands to the next. Baylor rocked her to sleep, Shay pushed her in the swing, and Waylon sang to her at night. As she grew, she became bold like Marley, tender like her father. Unpredictable like Mick, and a lover of books like Elise.

When she was older, she asked about what had happened to her grandmother.

In the Joseph family, there would always be three stories of Elise's death. The first was that it had been an accident. Plain, simple. The second was that Elise begged for it. Brutal, compassionate. The third was that her husband had done it of his own accord. Selfish, discreet. No one would know the true story except for Mick Joseph himself, and he'd take it to his grave, where he'd lie beside his wife.

Marley might have taken her daughter to see Elise's headstone at the cemetery where she and Waylon once watched old movies, might have let Evie trace her fingers over the words there chiseled in stone—

Loved by her daughter-in-law and sons

Instead Marley took Evangeline to that old church attic, hoisted her into its crawl space, and helped her climb to the peak of the bell tower. Then she clipped her to the safety lanyard installed when Waylon finally replaced the shingles. From there, as they looked out over their home, Marley pointed toward the swooping road that led to the highway beyond the cedars, and this was the story she told her daughter.

Two young women arrived in this town, twenty years apart. The first was named Elise, the second named Marley. They lived in the same house. They loved the same men. They raised their children. Elise had never loved Marley like a daughter, and yet together they built a family.

"There's more to this life than just trying to survive it," Marley told Evangeline. "Maybe your grandmother never had the chance, but you and I do."

With her mother's steady arm at her waist, Evie stood on the ledge of the bell tower and reached both hands out into the sky. A breeze curled through her fingers, and Evangeline Joseph let herself lean toward it. That soft wind took flight and called her higher, like the opiate of a piano's prelude, the hush of rainfall on a midnight roof, the way a heartbeat flutters like a wing.

Acknowledgments

Even though the characters and events in this novel came mostly from my imagination, I'm the daughter, granddaughter, niece, and sister of some phenomenal roofers. If you've traveled throughout the Rust Belt, you've probably seen or stood beneath one of their trusty roofs. I'm extremely grateful for their big hearts, their artistry, their ingenuity, and their senses of humor. I love you.

Deb Futter, my incredible editor, has made this book my best one yet. Deb, you are beyond a dream come true. As Waylon would say, I feel like I won the lottery with you. Thank you for making this process so much fun. Randi Kramer, thank you for your wonderful edits and expertise. I love getting to work with you and the entire Celadon team, who has ushered this novel into the world with an unbelievable amount of skill and heart. So many thanks to Jennifer Jackson, Anna Belle Hindenlang, Christine Mykityshyn, Anne Twomey, Jane Elias, and Frances Sayers, and to Howard Chen at Dreamlite Photography for such a beautiful author photo.

Meredith Kaffel Simonoff has been my advocate and fail-safe for more than ten years. Thank you for being my true north in some of my toughest moments, and in my best moments, too. I'm so lucky to share this writing life with you.

I have the best writer friends on the planet. Anica Mrose Rissi was the first to love the Joseph family as much as I do. Thank you so much for helping me believe in myself. Danya Kukafka has talked me off more ledges than I can count. Thank you for your steady friendship and listening ear.

My writing group has seen me through the tail end of one pandemic, two different books, and an infinite number of small daily crises. Julia Fine, Katie Gutierrez, and Sara Sligar are some of the smartest, kindest, and funniest writers in the game, and I love you all to the moon and back. You make me better in every single way.

Ellen O'Connell Whittet, work wife and true-blue friend, thank you for always being just a text away and for understanding exactly how I feel, even when I'm not able to express it.

I was lucky enough to study alongside some of the best memoirists during my MFA. Sherisse Alvarez, Rick Dixon, Cecilia Donohoe, Sangamithra Iyer, Jessie Male, Cynthia Polutanovich, Lia Ottaviano, Vanessa Schuh, Jill Shreve, Krystal Sital, Samantha K. Smith, and Sharon Dennis Wyeth—witnessing the way you all shared your lives on the page gave me such strength. To the DeSalvo family—thank you for the phone calls, the love, and for the best lunch dates anyone could hope for. I love you all so much.

Tracey Lange, I admire you more than words can say. Thank you for reading this book and offering your support and friendship. It means the world to me. Matthew Quick, getting to meet you was one of the highlights of my career. Thank you for your warmth, support, humor, and wisdom. Amy Meyerson read this book in a flash and offered extremely timely edits. Thank you for your enthusiasm, your friendship, and your keen eye.

To my friends from home—Amanda, Hannah, and Kathy—you inspire me in so many ways. Your huge hearts are found in every single page that I write. Also huge thanks to my Jersey crew: my PCC family, the Boyds, the Hahns, the Shiehs, and the Solemas.

Many thanks to everyone at the Gernert Company, especially Nora

Gonzalez, for always making everything so smooth, down to the tiniest detail. Michelle Weiner at CAA—I can't imagine a more talented and dedicated person to represent my books for film and television. Thank you so much for your faith in me.

It's no exaggeration to say that dancing every morning with Caleb Marshall, Haley Jordan, Allison Florea, and Cameron Moody was instrumental in finishing this novel. Thank you for being the best start to my workday.

Dad, I will treasure forever the map you drew for me of the church steeple. That story provided just the spark I needed. Mom, thank you for showing me what it means to flourish in a career and as a mother. Your spaghetti will always be my favorite meal.

My sister and brother continue to make my status as a middle child the best thing ever. I love you both so much. And to my husband and our two kids—I don't know how I got lucky enough to call the three of you mine, but I'm keeping you forever. You are the very best part of me.

About the Author

Amy Jo Burns is the author of the memoir *Cinderland* and the novel *Shiner*. Her writing has appeared in *Elle*, *Good Housekeeping*, *The Paris Review Daily*, and the anthology *Not That Bad*. A western Pennsylvania native, she now lives in New Jersey with her family.